# "STRUMPETS OF THE WORST KIND"

Surgeon Superintendent
James Hall, London, 1836

LYNNE HUME

Published by:
Boolarong Press
38/1631 Wynnum Road
Tingalpa Qld 4173
Australia.
www.boolarongpress.com.au

First published 2018

A catalogue record for this book is available from the National Library of Australia

ISBN: 9781925522990 (paperback)

Cover: *Penal Colony Tasmania*

Cover design by Boolarong Press

Typeset in Cormorant Garamond 12pt by Boolarong Press

Printed and bound by Watson Ferguson & Company, Tingalpa, Australia

*To all our resilient foremothers*

# *Acknowledgements*

I have drawn from many sources in researching this book, and would like to acknowledge the work of those who have gone before me in the quest to bring the past to life in the present. Cascades Female Factory was my first port of call, after witnessing a re-enactment on a rainy day in Hobart that captured my imagination and spurred me on to find out more, much more. I then discovered the work of historians whose painstaking work into convict women provided me with factual information around which to build a story. Long hours poring over primary and archival material in the Hobart State Library of Tasmania, the Female Convicts Research Centre, Hobart museums and trove.nla.gov.au allowed early colonial Australia to come to life for me personally.

Fellow writers and readers have generously given of their time to read early rough drafts to help me hone in on my first foray into the world of fiction: Deborah Norris who generously read my first awkward attempt when it was in the pre-novel stage; Catherine Hanrahan and Kelley Mether when it was in the next stage of development; Rosanne Debats and Jacinta Elks when it was in its final stages. The Queensland Writers Centre and the Hachette Australia Ms Development Program team deserve special mention as they made me realise that writing fiction is a very complex enterprise. To my other fellow writers on the latter program: Shelley Banks, Robin Doreian, Helen Burns, Denise Beckton, Craig Vaughan, I thank you all for your encouragement along the way. I am also grateful to fellow writers Sean Crawley and Pamela Mariko for their passionate discussions about writing fiction.

Lastly, I thank all the trees who provided the reams of paper to get to this point.

Lynne Hume

# *Contents*

# *Prologue*

*Take heed, Sir, and watch your step. The convicts are depraved thieves and vile dissemblers, refractory and insolent to the greatest degree.*

*Do you not think it might be their circumstances, Sir?*

*Nae, that is not the case. The poor are incorrigible. And the women are worse than the men.*

*They are strumpets of the worst kind, irredeemable thieves and prostitutes who have inherited criminal tendencies and carry the taint from birth. Artful, deceitful, drunken, dissipated and of a bad disposition. Indeed, many of them are worse than the male convicts and more troublesome.*

*Be on your guard, and don't waste your sympathy on any of them.*

Surgeon Superintendent James Hall
to newly recruited
Surgeon Superintendent Robert James
London, 1836

# PART I

Chapter 1

# *Newgate Gaol, London*

*15th April 1836*

Temporarily blinded, Maggie Burnett had to strain her eyes to make out shapes in the pale light cast by the turnkey's lantern. The stench that greeted her nostrils was foul, worse than anything she had experienced in the alleyways of Cheapside. She found herself in a small holding area facing a cell crowded with women. The gruff, phlegmatic turnkey unlocked the heavy barred doors and pushed her inside.

Dozens of women were crowded into the filthy cell. Shivering with cold, they had only the bare floor to sleep on with its thin covering of straw. The rags they wore weren't enough to keep them warm; she could see that, and she wondered how long they had been there. They smelt awful. The whole place reeked of piss, vomit and excrement. She could feel the bile rise in her throat as she edged her way round, side-stepping the muck seeping from the latrines, stopping next to a woman whose glazed eyes stared into nothingness.

As Maggie slunk down she felt an overwhelming ache to be with her family. She had never missed them so much as right at that moment. What would she do without them? And how would the little ones survive without her?

*They'll be eatin' their tea now*, she thought, *not far from 'ere, but they may as well be a hundred miles away*. Her eyes smarted when she remembered how everything had changed the night her mother died. Such a long night. The screams of childbirth pierced the air until the early morning light squeezed through the windows of their cramped lodgings. Then silence. Both her mother and her new-born baby sister were dead.

Maggie looked around. There were even more women in there than she first realised; even babies and toddlers, all sickly looking little mites by the look of it. Opposite her were two women in irons, their legs and arms shackled to a long, heavy chain set into the wall. Not much room to move like that. The one with the wooden yoke around her neck had an angry look on her face. Not to be messed with, that one. The other one seemed to be sleeping; a fitful sleep by the look of it as her body was twitching.

A clamour erupted as the women shoved each other to get to the food that was coming. She could hear someone ladling it out from a bucket into their wooden bowls as the women pushed past, desperate for their share. She got up to join the rowdy makeshift queue, and was handed a bowl full of something that looked like soup. Back at her spot, more memories of her brothers and sisters flooded back. The boys would be teasing their giggling sisters and their father would be two sheets to the wind; like that since her mother died. She brought the soup to her lips but could not drink it.

'Do you not want it?' said someone in an Irish brogue. Maggie looked up at the owner of the voice and shook her head. Before she could say anything the girl had grabbed the bowl and was slurping down its contents.

'You'll not be that fussy after a week in this place.'

Maggie took a closer look at the girl rapidly scraping the bottom of Maggie's bowl for the last bit. Even in this squalid place her long auburn hair stood out and prison life hadn't dimmed her deep green eyes.

'Yer from Ireland then are yer?'

''Tis true, that I am. From County Cork. You're probably missing your family. All of us feel that real bad when we first come here.'

Maggie nodded.

'What were you charged with?' asked the Irish girl, putting the empty bowl down next to her.

'Pickin' pockets. What about you?'

'Larceny. Like most everyone else.' She paused for a moment before looking up. Maggie could see the girl wanted to talk but an older Irish woman called out to her, 'Kathleen, come over here lass and hearken to this,' and Kathleen walked away.

After two weeks Maggie was so hungry she too waited anxiously for the daily ration of slop. Bored and frustrated, the coming of the food, such as it was, created a break in the dreary prison routine. The whiff of prison had seeped into her clothes and her unkempt hair was as lacklustre as the others'. The jingling of the turnkey's clutch of keys took her attention and she saw a newcomer being shoved in to join them before the cell door was slammed shut behind her. Maggie watched as the woman adjusted to the darkness, waiting for her to recoil at the squalor and their dishevelled appearance. Once inside, the tall slender woman untied the lavender ribbons of her bonnet, loosening a mass of fair curls. She could see clearly now, and the horror in her face caused some of the harder women to laugh out loud. Maggie felt sorry for her. When the woman started to weep, she went over to her.

'What's yer name?'

'Sarah,' she whispered with downcast eyes. Her whole body was shaking as she raised her hands to cover her face. Her clean clothes with a tiny sprig of lavender tucked into a buttonhole made Maggie aware of how much her own clothes had taken on the grime of prison life, even in the short time she had been there. She looked the newcomer up and down. Her dress, bonnet and shoes were not those of someone from Cheapside, and none of the other prisoners would have looked like her, even on their first day. She was refined. That's what Maggie's mother would have said about her: 'refined'. Maggie was curious.

'Where d'yer come from Sarah?'

'Oxford.' Sarah looked up then, her startling blue eyes darting around the crowded cell. Maggie moved closer, waiting for Sarah to pluck up the courage to say more. When she did speak, her voice was so low that Maggie could hardly hear her.

'I have never been in such a place in my life. Whatever will become of me?'

Sarah's posh voice made Maggie think Sarah might be a vicar's daughter, or something like that.

'You'll get used to it. What was yer charged with?'

'I was accused of stealing in a household I was sent to as a governess,' she said, fumbling for a handkerchief in the pocket of her blue dress. 'But it is untrue. I did no such thing.'

*That's what they all says*, thought Maggie, but looking at her closely, the fine features, the way she stood – straight and tall, it might be true. When Sarah started weeping again, Maggie thought she'd leave her be, not ask any more questions for now. *Plenty of time for that.* One thing they all had was time.

'The worst part is not knowin' how long we has to stay 'ere before the ship takes us to Van Diemen's Land,' Maggie said to Sarah, slumped next to her against a greasy wall caked with tallow fat. The candle-lit torches burned even in daytime, casting a faint glow and dark shadows over everything. The smell of fat and smoke quickly seeped into skin, clothes and matted hair in this place. Melancholy swirled through the place like heavy fog. Maggie felt the boredom and helplessness pulling her down.

'Even them angry ones is too worn out to care,' she added, looking around at the other women. 'Bein' poor don't matter so much when there's alleys full of folk bustling about and your family to keep you company.'

'Yer know Sarah,' Maggie said, turning back to Sarah who was lost in her own thoughts. 'Yer never did tell me how yer come to be accused of thievin'. I know yer didn't do it, but what did happen?'

Taken by surprise at a question that came out of the blue, Sarah jolted out of her thoughts of home, pausing for a moment while the memories came flooding back.

'I'll tell you then Maggie, how I ended up in this predicament.' Maggie waited, watching Sarah's face. 'But where should I start?' She stood up to stretch her legs, then got into a more comfortable position next to Maggie.

'You already know that my father was a teacher and we had lots of books, and I learned to play the piano and speak French. And that I was an only child.'

Maggie nodded.

'And that my parents were killed when the carriage they were in was upturned and they were both thrown from it.' A soft wistful look came over Sarah's face. Maggie took hold of her delicate hand.

'Well, the local vicar and his wife took me in and arranged for me to be employed in the large home of a well-to-do gentleman, Mr. Bloomsbury, who lived out in the country with his family, about twenty miles away. I was to be governess to their three children: twin boys nine years of age, and a girl, Jane, who was then twelve. I was very fortunate for I had my own small room and they were kind to me.'

Maggie was imagining what it must have been like living in such a grand place; having a room just to yourself and a bed you didn't have to share with your sisters and brothers. And on top of that, there were other rooms in the house.

'How I missed my parents,' Sarah swallowed, trying not to give way to tears. 'But I got used to my situation, and after two years I believed I would be with the Bloomsburys for many more to come. The two young boys were well disposed toward me, and I enjoyed being their governess.

'But it was not to last. When Jane turned fourteen, she took a dislike to me. I knew not the reason, except that perhaps she was well disposed towards the new gardener, a good-looking young man of twenty-two.' She looked around at some of the younger convicts, not quite women, and compared them in her mind to the privileged Jane.

'She became obsessed with him, and when he turned his attention toward me, she became extremely jealous. She began by telling tales about me that weren't true, then one day she accused me of having stolen her fine lilac woollen shawl. Everyone was shocked at this accusation, but upon inspection of my room, there it was, the shawl, in a dresser drawer underneath other items of my clothing.' Sarah slid her hand away from Maggie's to reach into the pocket of her apron for a hanky.

'I knew Jane must have put it there, but Mrs. Bloomsbury felt I could no longer be trusted. I was charged with having stolen property to the value of three shillings. And you know the rest.'

*Might be Sarah's the only one of us done nothin' wrong*, thought Maggie, looking around at all the other women. *And here she is with the likes of us*. The two of them sat thinking about this sad state of affairs.

Suddenly their attention was taken by loud swearing coming from the two women in irons. The Scottish woman, Agnes — the one with smallpox craters and a thick scar that spread from her eye to her chin — was shouting at the top of her voice. With their legs chained against the wall, neither woman could get comfortable and they almost came to blows.

'She's got a temper on her has that one,' said Maggie standing up to get a better look at them. 'I knows other women like her. No family ter fight for 'em. So alone in the world they gets so they don't give a tinker's cuss.'

Slinking back next to Sarah, she whispered, 'I wonder what she did to get transported for fourteen years.'

'Yes, I wonder,' Sarah whispered back. 'Perhaps she killed someone. Most of us got seven. That's bad enough.'

One morning, when she saw Agnes was in a quieter mood, Maggie went over to her, curious to find out what her crime was. She slid down next to her and waited.

'Them chains must hurt somethin' awful.' No response.

'What do yer think it'll be like on the ship?' she ventured.

'I dinnae ken,' Agnes said with a sullen look. At least she said something. Encouraged, Maggie changed tactics.

'I'm in for pickin' pockets.' At that, Agnes looked at Maggie, her small brown eyes taking in Maggie from head to toe, but she said nothing. Maggie persisted. 'Where're you from Agnes?'

'Perth. Where the lucky ones work at the mill chokin' on the dust floatin' in the air from the cotton.' She was silent for so long Maggie could see she wouldn't find out anything else about Agnes until she prodded her. So she told Agnes more about herself and how she'd ended up in Newgate Gaol, all the while watching Agnes' face.

Agnes' chains scraped as she shuffled to turn around to take a good look at Maggie. This girl didn't seemed frightened of her, not like that tall fair one who scuttled away every time she glanced her way. This one was smart and nimble and had that innocent look that fooled the bastards.

'So, how did ye get caught?' she muttered.

Pleased with having got Agnes' attention, Maggie went on with her story.

'One night I spied a young gentlemen a bit worse for wear. By himself he were. I thought, he's right for the pickin', this one. So I went up to him and said, innocent as I could, "It's a very wet night sir," and he agreed. "It is indeed, my dear," he said. "You look wet through sir," I said to him. "I know a nice warm room in lodgin's not far from here where you could dry off, if yer'd like to follow me." He said later in court I'd looked like "a nice, sweet-faced young lass, though poorly clad, so I followed her." I took him along a couple of dark alleys until we reached the lodgin's I told him about. He were even more lost by the time we got there, and when we stopped outside the place I'd taken him to he said to me, "This is a dark hole of a place, my lass." And I agreed. "It's always dark here, I'm always scared to come this way all alone at night," I told him.'

Agnes took a long look at Maggie's face, flushed from remembering. By this time, a couple of other women were listening.

'I felt sorry for him really, as he were bein' nice to me, but I kept thinkin' of me poor brothers and sisters waitin' for me to get back with somethin' for them to eat. So I put me hand into his coat pocket. Luck is with me tonight, I thought, for his pocket were heavy with coins. When he felt me hand in his pocket he knew he'd been had, so I grabbed the coins and run as fast as me legs'd carry me.

'But me luck didn't last. He started shoutin' out for help. "Help!" he bellowed, "Police!" At that, a constable come runnin' in our direction. He could see I were tryin' to get away. Quick as a wink, he realised what'd happened and grabbed me as I tried to run past him. I ended up in court. "Guilty!" said the Judge. I was that afraid. Transportation! Seven years in a place so far away! I never thought this would happen. This will kill me, I thought. Either I'll die in Newgate Prison, or I'll die at sea, and never see England again.'

'Van Diemen's Land can be nae worse than ma life in Scotland,' Agnes said glumly, then withdrew into herself again, moving away as far as the chains permitted.

Maggie approached Agnes again one restless evening. Clutching her daily ration of slop and bread, she edged closer to Agnes, and sat beside her until they'd both finished their meal. She was itching to find out about that long scar.

*I'll 'ave to be careful askin'. She won't like me pryin'. Best to come straight out with it, I reckon.*

'Agnes, if you'll pardon me for askin', how did you get that scar on yer face?'

Taken aback at such direct prying, Agnes stared, looking Maggie up and down. But to Maggie's surprise she answered. ''Twas a slasher that done it tae me.'

Maggie knew about slashers, they were the horror of all the whores in Cheapside. She should have guessed as she'd seen scars made by them before.

'I be walkin' down an alley one night, past some whores pressed agin a wall. All of a sudden I be set upon. I didnae see it comin'. Up behind me, out of a doorway, like he was waitin' specially for me. He was that quick, I didnae have time tae defend maself. He said tae me, "This is for gettin' in the way of Molly". I dinnae ken no-one called Molly, I said tae him. But he paid nae attention. Instead, he said he'd been paid tae do a job, and that's what he was goin' tae do. He had a sharp, foldin' razor, the sort with a white handle that flicks out real quick. With nae another word, he cut intae ma face, then poured a bit of acid over it, sayin', "A wee bit of this should mark ye proper".

'Then, quick as a flash, he was away. I was bleedin' like a pig, I can tell ye, and the pain was somethin' terrible. I still dinnae ken what I did wrong, but when I had time tae think about it, I figured he'd got me mixed up with a whore what had cheated on a brothel-keeper.'

'That's what slashers do in London too,' said Maggie, remembering a scar on the face of one of the whores she knew.

'Oh aye. I was a whore 'til that happened, then I couldnae find too many customers that fancied ma looks, so I had tae turn tae somethin' else tae make a crust.' Then she was silent. She had a brooding look on her face that warned Maggie not to ask any more questions for now. Shifting the chains around her legs, she turned her back on Maggie.

Rumours were floating about that there might be a murderer in their cell. Maggie had learned that only troublemakers or those under a sentence of death were put in irons in Newgate's women's prison and in the final days leading up to a hanging, the condemned were sent to another cell to await the noose. Just as Maggie was wondering if Agnes had murdered someone, another convict sidled over to her.

'See young Sally over there what lets the red-haired guard take favours with her?' Looking over at the big-breasted Sally, Maggie wondered what Sally got from the guard in return. Being a whore, she wouldn't give out favours for nothing. 'She told me that tomorrow there's goin' to be three people hanged: two men and one woman.'

'What did they do, do yer know?' Maggie whispered.

'The men is highway robbers and the woman stabbed a man to death with a kitchen knife. The hangman's noose will be round their necks soon after dawn.'

Maggie's eyes widened. She'd heard about executions but never seen one. 'I heard there's lots of people goes to hangin's.'

'You're right there. Some rich toffs pay as much as ten pounds for a seat in a window overlookin' the gallows, especially if they be well-known.'

'I wonder if the guard knows their names?'

'No matter; at the crack of dawn tomorrow there'll be the clink and rattle of chains as they shuffle their way along Deadman's Walk to the gallows.'

Talk of the hangings surged through the cell. There hadn't been this much excitement in months. Maggie took a sidelong glance at Agnes to see if she was listening to any of it. She seemed not to care what the women were talking about, and appeared deep in her own thoughts.

'They's always done on a Monday,' said one woman, chest puffed out and keen to look as if she knew a thing or two, 'and on the

Sunday night afore, the gallows outside the Debtors Door be draped with black cloth.'

'My husband Charlie told me that when a prisoner gets his head chopped off,' said another woman, 'they have to sprinkle a lot of sawdust on the scaffold there's so much blood spurts out.'

Maggie looked over at Sarah. She was sitting with her eyes closed and her hands to her ears. As more women joined in, the talk got louder and more animated, difficult not to be party to it all, and impossible not to hear. One old woman began to cackle, showing her gums and a few blackened teeth, and with great relish told everyone about a hanging she'd witnessed.

'It were a man what was hanged,' the woman went on, 'and such a crowd there to watch! Thousands there was. Some of the folk in the crowd was shoutin' at others standin' in front of them, tellin' them to take their hats off. I wondered at that. Was it a sign of respect, thought I, for a prisoner about to meet his Maker? But no, it was so they could see better. They wanted to watch him squirmin'. There were a lot of pushin' and shovin' with people strainin' their necks to get a good look at the poor bastard as he walked up the steps to the scaffold. Folks had waited all day for this and they didn't want no-one blockin' their view. When the noose were placed about his neck and the final prayers finished, the Under Sheriff give the signal for the hangman to do the job. When the drawbar fell with a loud clap, I could see him strugglin'. His legs swingin' wild for a bit, then his whole body were still.'

Filled with self-importance at having everyone's attention, she embellished her tale. 'I were close enough to see his eyes pop out of his head and bloody froth ooze from his mouth and nose. And he'd shit himself too. He were that scared. It were right entertainin', it were.' And she guffawed.

'My cousin were hanged,' another woman said, 'but it turned out badly. The poor lad was in a terrible state, jerkin' about for so long the hangman had to jump down through the trapdoor and pull on his legs hard until his neck broke.'

'I went to a hangin' with me family for a day's outin',' said another woman. 'Folk would try to get there early to get a good view. And there was plenty to look at, even before the hangin's. People would be tellin' stories, young rascals would be runnin' about amongst the crowds, scuffles'd break out, and there were plenty of food and drink for them with the coin to buy it. Them rich folk paid plenty for tickets in ring-side seats set up close to the gallows.'

'That's right. And there was pie-sellers wanderin' the crowds, and tankards of ale for sale. A good day out.'

'Aye,' agreed another woman, nodding.

'And plenty of trade for us whores!' laughed a buxom woman.

Stories exhausted, the talk petered out and they went back to tending to their own needs. Maggie wondered again about Agnes. Was she the woman who'd stabbed a man with a kitchen knife? She didn't look as if she cared tuppence about anything, but in spite of Agnes's surliness Maggie had started to have a soft spot for her. She was taken out of her thoughts about it all when she heard someone screeching and shouting gibberish not far from her. It was one of the mothers. She was getting worse, wailing and throwing her arms about. Maggie pitied the small child clinging to its mother's skirts, and went over to see what she could do for the poor little thing. She crouched down and held his hand until his terrified eyes began to look calmer. There was nothing else she could do.

That night, guards came in to fetch the woman wearing the wooden yoke; the one chained next to Agnes; the one who was to feel the hangman's noose around her neck the next day.

Weeks stretched into months. Then finally, one of the guards had some news. They were to be taken to the docks the very next day, he said, to board the ship that would take them to Van Diemen's Land.

Maggie and Sarah tried to stay together, but in the melee of departure the next morning they were separated and Maggie was pushed into the same open cart as Agnes, to follow a string of other open wagons and carts carrying the women to Woolwich docks. Rattling along the cobbled streets in the drizzling rain, they looked out at crowds of jeering onlookers. A couple of bold young men — cheeky lads not old enough to have hair on their chests — shouted out, 'Hey tarts. Give us a look at yer tits!' Others threw things at them, yelling and swearing abuse. Some of the convict women in the carts in front shouted back, but most of them were too tired for that. Amidst the hubbub of horses, carriages and drays, their vehicles rumbled on, through the London city streets, passing row after row of blackened timber houses, narrow alleyways with half-starved dogs, and people calling out to each other from one rickety tenement house to another. The smoke and fumes from millions of chimneys and factories made it hard to see clearly in the early morning fog.

Passing Cheapside, Maggie looked around at the familiar streets and the people staring at them. Hanging on to the side of the cart she strained her neck to see if she could see anyone she knew, maybe she would get a glimpse of one of her brothers or sisters. Was that her young brother Fred down there, carrying his little sister on his back? But they soon turned a corner and rattled into an area she was less familiar with.

The carts slid over horse manure, human waste and rotting debris. Maggie watched the horses from the carriage in front leave their muck on the clay-grit roads, and small lice-haired sweeps clean the way for pedestrians to cross from one side to the other, hoping to pick up a few pennies for their trouble. That's what Fred did sometimes to make a miserable few pennies. But he wasn't there that morning. A few miles on, the carts turned another corner and there it was: noisy bustling Woolwich docks on the River Thames.

The women's eyes darted about, trying to take in everything at once. Crates were being loaded onto wheeled trollies and large boxes filled with merchandise from far-flung foreign parts were arriving on the dock. Men were shouting out orders and others were running about to obey them; whores with large breasts bursting over their bodices were bending over sailors worn out from a night of drinking. One old whore was almost bare-breasted, her bosoms two pendulous flaps of skin, but she didn't seem to care. Men on horseback were making their ways in both directions along the dock, passing scallywag children with cheeky faces and merchants shouting out to passers-by in the hope of enticing them to buy their wares.

'Aye, it's good to be in the thick of it all agin,' Agnes exclaimed to Maggie, her usual morose and disgruntled manner aroused by the sights and sounds, her dull eyes now alive, and her scarred face showing elation.

In the water, several large ocean-going British vessels with sails furled were anchored next to foreign ships, and small rowboats were ferrying sailors to land from one of the French ships harboured not far from the prison hulks. Smartly-dressed women, weary from standing, sat on their trunks not far from fishmongers unloading large baskets of fresh fish from a nearby vessel. Agnes guffawed when she saw them turn their faces away from the oily smell of the men and the fish, and reach for their lace handkerchiefs.

'Plenty of business here for a crafty pick-pocket,' Maggie said under her breath.

Their procession of carts and wagons eventually stopped. The arrival of so many women caused heads to turn in their direction and added to the dockside chaos. Some of the timid women looked terrified. Apart from the Irish women, most of them had never seen the sea and had never ventured further than the square mile they knew well.

'Get down now,' ordered a guard. 'Stay quiet and do as you're told.'

A nearby fisherman, joking with his mates, shouted in Agnes' direction, 'Hello luv, d'yer want a quick fuck afore yer gets on the transport ship?'

'Not if ye be the one tae do the fuckin'!' Agnes shouted back.

'Keep quiet, whore!' a surly guard shouted at Agnes striking her with the butt end of his rifle. It was bedlam and the guards were in a bad mood. Even the men in charge seemed at a loss about what was to happen next. After much bustle and confusion the women were herded nearer to the docks then ordered to line up to board their transportation ship. Live pigs and sheep, squealing and bleating alongside caged fowls, had been boarded earlier. Barrels of biscuits, sacks of flour, oats, and malt had been stored below, stacked against the bulkhead, as well as scores of wooden boxes containing bottles of liquor and gunpowder. Now it was the women's turn.

Picking their way over the uneven gangplank, Maggie looked up at Sarah, two women ahead of her, wondering how she was reacting to the insults coming from the dock, and the eager lustful faces of the sailors on board eyeing them over from head to toe as each woman stepped on board.

The odour from the one hundred and forty-eight females and five children wafted past the tall uniformed Surgeon Superintendent, Dr. Robert James, standing at the top of the gangplank. *They're a dirty, bedraggled lot*, he thought, *pale and weak from hunger and in a lamentable condition.* He remembered the dire warnings of Surgeon Superintendent James Hall, but then he noticed the tall fragile one with the fair hair and the demeanour and carriage of a woman of good breeding. He wondered why she was with this rough-looking lot. When Sarah walked towards him, her head bowed in shame, he could not see her eyes. It was only when she happened to look straight at him for just a second that he could see they were of the clearest blue, the colour of ice. He was taken aback.

Stepping on to the main deck, Sarah noticed the sly glances coming her way. A few of the bolder crew members were nudging and winking at each other. The younger women were revelling in the attention, flashing coquettish looks at the best-looking crew members.

*I shall never forget this day as long as I live*, Sarah thought.

'Form rows of fifteen. Be sharp about it,' ordered a guard, once all the women had embarked. 'And be quiet!'

Dr. James walked along the lines of women, briefly inspecting them to ensure that they would be fit enough for the voyage. He ordered three women to be removed and returned to Newgate: two with incurable debilitating illness and one with obvious signs of madness. The rest of the women were issued with bedding, cooking and eating utensils, and the grey regulation clothing they were required to wear. Maggie's eyes searched for the children. Each of their faces was filled with awe, their eyes wide and shining with fearful excitement. She looked up at the rigging and the great sails that would soon be unfurled, the officers and crew, and the sea itself. While she felt the children's excitement, her whole body trembled with fear.

But something else was happening. Coming aboard were the two Quaker women who had paid regular visits to Newgate as representatives of the Ladies' British Society: Mrs. Elizabeth Fry and her companion. Chattering stopped as all eyes focused on these two plainly dressed women in their dark bonnets. They carefully stepped off the gangplank with the help of an officer who led them to a spot where they might address the women.

Mrs. Fry looked at the sad, bedraggled women facing her, greeted them, then slowly opened her Bible.

'From Matthew 6:14-15' she read out aloud, '*For if you forgive other people when they sin against you, your heavenly Father will also forgive you. But if you do not forgive others their sins, your Father will not forgive your sins.*' She knelt down then, her companion Anna by her side. The convict women felt obliged to follow suit. It was a strange sight: a woman preacher, the mass of convict women on their knees, the noise from the docks, the silence on the ship. Some of the sailors had never been on a transport ship carrying women convicts and were confused as to what they should do: stop work to show respect, or continue with their tasks? With a 'hoy' from an officer, they went on with their tasks, but more quietly, their eyes on the women.

'May the Lord be your guide and protector on the journey you are about to take,' Mrs. Fry prayed slowly. 'May He save you from danger and keep you free from harm to body and soul. Dear ladies, I wish you well on this perilous journey to Van Diemen's Land. May you once again be reunited with your loved ones back in England after serving your sentences. Amen.'

'Amen,' repeated the women. As they rose from their knees the two Quakers walked among them distributing calico packages. 'This will help you to pass your long voyage in a fruitful manner,' Mrs. Fry told them. 'I urge you to pray and trust in the Lord. May God bless you and keep you safe.' Mission accomplished, they were helped down the gangplank; their small gloved hands carefully holding on to the railings.

Almost time for the women to be herded below, prior to the ship's departure.

'Well,' said Maggie, staring at the scene around her. Those lucky enough to have loved ones on the dock to say goodbye to them called out piteous farewells, crying and wailing at this final moment of departure. 'Take a good look Sarah. This might be the last time we'll ever see England.'

One of the Irish women began to sing in Gaelic, a mournful song of loss, and others sang along with her. Even hardened sailors stopped to listen.

'Oh Maggie,' said Sarah, clutching Maggie's hand and sobbing, 'it is more than I can bear. Whatever will become of us so far away from home?'

Chapter 2

# At Sea

*19th August 1836*

'Stop shovin' you, and let Sarah through,' Maggie said as she pushed her way through the crowd to vie for the best of the sleeping bunks. 'Railed in like sheep in a pen, we are, one on top of the other. We'll have to get used to these bleedin' rails. Hard enough ter get down here on all them ladders. And I didn't like the sound of that hatch slammin' shut behind us.'

'Me husband said once I'd served me time, he'd come out to the colony and we'd be together again,' said one woman once the frantic jostling and arguing over bunks had settled down.

'I reckon we could send for our children to come out after us as well,' said another hopeful.

The only light piercing the gloom squeezed its way through a thin crack in the now tightly locked hatch. Buoyant chatter was soon replaced by the grim reality of their quarters in the orlop deck, the ship's lowest level, as different women realised their predicament.

'It ain't half dark down here.'

'Gawd, there ain't no windows.'

'Might be better if them lanterns was lit. I can't hardly see.'

'If there's trouble at sea,' Sarah whispered to Maggie, 'how will we get out – all these women through that small opening?'

One of the Irish women started to panic, 'I can hear the water above us, there's water all around us! Jesus, Mary and Joseph!' Her panic was infectious. Some of the women near her began to howl and shriek. Even anchored at the dock the ship was moving beneath their feet and several were already looking green around the gills. Trapped below, they could hear the great sails unfurling, thrashing about with thunderous cracking noises. The crew was running from one end of the ship to the other, obeying the officers' loud and urgent commands. It was frantic and the women were terrified. Then, with a groan, the ninety-two foot, three-masted vessel with its precious cargo weighed anchor to begin a 13,000 mile perilous journey that would take them across two mighty oceans from the northern to the southern hemisphere, until it reached the port of Van Diemen's Land at the other end of the earth.

'Them Quaker women said these'll keep us busy. I wonder what's in them,' said Maggie, pulling open the drawstring of her calico bag. 'Look, it's got sewin' tools and little patchwork pieces. I wonder how many of us knows sewin'. Me mother showed me how to mend socks and the like but I ain't never done any of that quiltin'.' After looking at the fabric pieces, the needle and thread, and the tiny pair of scissors, she sighed, gathered it all together again and stuffed it back in the bag before sliding it under her thin pillow. Stretching out on her narrow bunk she reflected on all they had experienced in just one day – leaving Newgate, seeing the crowds of people on the docks, being herded up the gangplank, the men on the ship. And that Surgeon Superintendent. Tall and good-looking, he were. What were his name? Dr. James. Yes, that's what it was. She sat up and looked over at Sarah.

'That Dr. James is real handsome.'

Sarah's eyes widened a little at the mention of Dr. James and her cheeks became pink. 'Let's hope he is kind as well as handsome.'

'I reckon we're goin' ter need a lot of that Sarah! I don't think none of us is safe on this ship with all them sailors. Unless the doctor does his job proper. But I'm sure his room is far away, and them sailors is sleepin' just above us —.'

Seasickness was rife on board. Women who did not suffer themselves tended to others, some of whom were retching uncontrollably. With not enough buckets to cope with the quantity of vomit, the acrid stench permeated every inch of the women's quarters. Agnes was having a worse time of it than most. Maggie took the last bucket she could find and went over to help the now very sick Agnes. Holding the bucket and the back of her neck, she called out to Sarah to come and pull back Agnes' long hair and provide support for Agnes' back. Sarah brought a damp rag and wiped Agnes' face. They stayed with her until Agnes was spent and lay back on her bunk falling into an exhausted sleep, then went up on deck.

'Thank goodness we've been allowed up for some air.' Sarah pointed to another two women hanging over the side, retching, their faces chalk white, their clothing sprayed with vomit and salty water.

'They're the lucky ones. I wish they'd all made it up here. Poor Agnes. It stinks of vomit down below.' Maggie took a gulp of fresh air. 'See that stout woman bein' sick on the other side, she's the one what slipped down the ladder and landed on her back. She were too heavy for me ter lift so I had ter get one of the sailors ter fetch the doctor.' Dr. James appeared on deck to see if any of the seasick women required his assistance. 'Speak of the devil!' she said as he walked over to them. At first his eyes lingered on Sarah's face with its milky-white skin, then slowly down her slender body causing her to blush and lower her eyes. But it was the practical Maggie he turned to.

'I would like to see you in my quarters. I am looking for someone to help me in my surgery and I have noticed that you are very good with the children and can think quickly. I shall arrange for someone to bring you to the surgery so I can discuss this more with you.'

'Why yes, sir, I'd be happy to. When does yer want me to come?'

'After lunch today would be convenient. I shall send someone to fetch you.' And he took his leave, but not without another glance at the now nervous Sarah.

Maggie hesitated outside the door after the sailor had left, trying to make her hands stop shaking. She stood there for a few minutes before daring to knock.

'Enter,' said the deep male voice.

He was sitting behind his desk, head down, writing. She peered around the cabin. Light was coming in through windows, not dark like the orlop deck. Shelves with all sorts of bottles, rows of books, medical equipment, and two narrow beds for patients. Still intent on his writing, she took a good look at him. Handsome, sure enough, with his black hair, long thin nose, and hands that look like they had never done a day's hard work. He put his pen down and looked up at her. Not able to hold his gaze, her head dropped. He got straight to the point.

'I see from the charges list that you come from London and are the eldest of many siblings.'

'Yes sir. I got lots of brothers and sisters.' She looked up then, forgetting her discomfort in her eagerness to please. 'And I looked after them all meself after me mum died.'

'Mmm ... that should have given you much practice at caring for children. I have also noticed that you are willing to assist anyone who is sick. You were right in calling for me when the older woman fell down the ladder. I think you are just the person to help me during the voyage. You could learn much by doing this, young woman, and leave the ship with new skills. What do you say to this?'

'Oh yes, sir, I'd like that very much, sir.'

'I have notes here in your record that you can read your letters. Is that so?'

'Yes sir.'

'Very well, we can start today as there is much to do.'

Back in the women's quarters she went straight to Sarah, bubbling over in her excitement. 'He showed me where everythin' was – bandages, ointments, scissors, and told me not ter touch anythin' unless he said so. The main thing, he said, were that I could take orders and do what I were told. He's very pertricklar about us all keepin' clean, and wants me ter help at the daily musters with the inspections – makin' sure everyone's heads and clothin' is proper clean. I know the women won't like that. I already heard a couple of them sayin' I were a lucky girl ter be picked out by the doctor. From the way they was lookin' at me I could see they didn't like it one bit.'

'Never mind about them Maggie.'

'He asked me if I knew me letters, and it's true I do, but I ain't too good at it. Do yer think yer could teach me to read and write proper?'

'Of course. We can get started right away. I brought two books in my bundle of belongings, so we can start with them.'

'*Ca-tarr-hal aff-ek-shuns.*' Maggie had made a mental note to remember new words each day so that Sarah could show her how to write them down. Sarah's careful, elegant script spidered with ease across the paper as Maggie leaned close to see how her sounds matched the letters. 'That's what eight people on the sick list has got,' she said once she'd copied the words herself. She straightened up to look at how her writing compared to Sarah's, then looked at her.

'Dr. James says it's the cold and wet what's the trouble. Others is sick in the stomach. He says it's because of the *bac-ter-ia* in the water we've been drinkin'. Some has got *ul-cer-ated* tongues and fevers.' Maggie took the pen from Sarah who had written the extra two new words down for her to copy.

'He's treatin' a lot what is seasick. Lucky you and me has got our sea legs.'

Over the next few days the ship cleared the channel and they were on their way to the Atlantic Ocean. They fell into the pattern of ship life: daily musters followed by breakfast at 8 o'clock, dinner at 1 o'clock, tea at 4 o'clock. The food was a lot better than Newgate Gaol. None of that filthy slop, and they were even given a glass of wine with a sherbet of lime juice and sugar after dinner. One of the sailors said it was to stop scurvy. No matter what it was for, all the women looked forward to it. Wine after dinner — like toffs.

On fine days they were allowed up on deck for fresh air.

'I'm gettin' the hang of movin' up and down the ladders, but it ain't easy,' Maggie said to Sarah. 'The trick is ter wait a bit once yer puts one foot down, then move with the roll of the ship before yer puts the other foot on the next rung.'

'Yes. It's too bad that old woman didn't learn that as well,' Sarah replied, looking around to see if she could see her. 'But since she fell flat on her back, she's been more careful.'

Each day, well before sunset, women up on deck were herded down below again and the hatches firmly slammed shut after them.

It was at night when the fun and games began.

'They's openin' the hatches!' shouted a startled woman whose bunk was nearest to the locked hatches. That first night, the sailors were hesitant as they descended the ladder into the women's quarters. They had no inkling what sort of reception they would get. If there were a fracas, the Captain might get to hear of it, and they would be in trouble. But it was worth a try. The first sailor gingerly stepped on the first rung of the ladder, whispering to others waiting their turn, 'It's bloody dark down here.' Suppressed laughs and words of encouragement from the others filtered down past him to the women who, by this time, were all looking his way, trying to make out what he was up to and if others behind him were getting ready to follow. As the sailor stepped off the last rung, one excited woman greeted him with eager anticipation, 'Over here luv, I'm over here. Come and see what I can do for ye. Ye'll not be sorry.'

Hearing these words of encouragement, three more sailors made their way down the ladder, groping around in the gloom. There was muffled laughter, cursing, petticoats and skirts being ruffled, and grunts of pleasure as the sailors found their mark. The terrified Sarah sat bolt upright, reaching across her bunk to find Maggie's hand, 'Please God, don't let them come near me.' Maggie held on tight to Sarah, trying to think quickly about what she could do if they were approached.

'Don't worry Sarah, they won't come this far. Our bunks is a long way from the hatch.' She was right. There were enough willing women for these few sailors not to be bothered with those too far away. They did not stay long that first night, scarping it back up the ladder to their own quarters after a few quick thrusts, leaving the women to giggle and whisper. When the last of the men left and the hatch was locked down tight with a bang, Sarah stopped gripping Maggie's hand and both of them let out sighs of relief.

'I am so afraid after last night,' Sarah said to Maggie the next morning after a fitful night's sleep.

'It'll happen again yer can be sure of that.'

They were up on deck along with other women for their daily stretch in the fresh air. A brilliant morning, crisp and clear with a soft breeze, the early glow spreading slowly over water striped from the sun's rays. A good day to be alive. The bold sailors from the night before eyed the women over, wondering which ones they'd had. A quick fumble in the dark and an even quicker scramble up their skirts had left them ignorant of the women's faces. And the women were none the wiser. There was a lot of nudging and head nodding from the sailors, and whispering between some of the women, their flirtatious eyes pausing on the most handsome of the sailors. If only they could see better at night down there.

'There's going to be more trouble tonight,' Sarah whispered to Maggie, her eyes darting back and forth from the sailors to the women.

Sure enough, two hours after sunset the hutch creaked open and sailors crept down the ladder. A few more this time, some bearing bottles of gin and whisky. One approached a fuming Agnes, waiting to give them a clip over the ear if they tried anything.

'None o' that ye nasty bastard,' she said to one unfortunate who made the mistake of touching her breast, grabbing his testicles and squeezing hard with her left hand and landing a punch to his jaw with her right hand. 'Ye'll get none o' that from me for nought.' Wincing in pain he let out a howl before pushing further down the rows of bunks towards Maggie. Quivering next to her, Sarah was shrinking into the back of her bunk, trying to make herself invisible.

'Lemme go. Get your soddin' hands off me,' Maggie shouted, struggling to fight him off. Fortunately for Maggie, Agnes had followed him. When she saw him try it on with Maggie, Agnes was furious. She grabbed both his arms, twisted them behind his back, then kneeded him in the groin with such force that his body buckled and he shouted out in pain.

'Off back up where ye came from,' she threatened, 'or ye'll nae hae any balls tae use agin!'

Set free from Agnes' vice-like grip the sailor skedaddled as fast as he could. He couldn't get up the ladder and through the hatch fast enough. With such a commotion going on the other sailors made a run for it as well, thinking the Captain might hear of it.

The next morning when things had settled back to normal in the women's quarters, Maggie went over to Agnes, grateful that she'd come to their rescue.

'Ahh, them sailors didnae ken who they be messin' with. Times I get so angry I dinnae ken what I be doin'. I could hae throttled the bastard. I can see how ye be with the wee ones and it got me tae thinkin' about ma only friend in this harsh world, ma poor Peggy, back in Scotland.'

Intrigued, Maggie urged her on.

'When I was cut on ma face by that slasher, ma friend Peggy found me bleedin' like a pig. She looked after me as best she could but not long after, she found herself up the duff and starvin'. By the time her wee babe was born she said tae me, "I can't bear tae watch it starvin' Agnes, it be more than I can bear." When I see ye with the wee bairns I remember Peggy.'

'What happened to Peggy?'

'Two weeks after the babe was born I spied her standin' on a bridge over the river, the bairn in her arms.' She paused. 'Next night she was standin' in that same place. No wee babe in her arms.' Her eyes glanced to one side as she remembered. Maggie was so surprised to hear Agnes talk so much that she dared not interrupt.

'The day after that, they dragged her dead body from the river. A nobody that no-one cared about. Well, I went intae a terrible rage.' Agnes' fists were clenched, her face red and twisted in anger. Maggie could see how, when her ire was up, there could be no stopping Agnes. 'Ma only friend dead. And I thought tae maself, all those rich bastards dinnae care a spittle about all of us. When I saw ye in trouble with that sailor lad, ma anger was up, and I thought back tae Peggy.'

She went silent at that and moved away to be by herself. Knowing Agnes, Maggie knew that was all she was going to get from her for now.

Nearing the Bay of Biscay the breeze was perfect, filling the sails and enabling a sleek, rapid crossing. Most of the women were up on the main deck in the balmy weather, soaking up the fresh air and busy with the daily airing-out of their bedding, spreading it out wherever they could find a space. Sarah and Maggie were waiting in the line-up for the weekly wash in the salt-water tubs before the eight o'clock breakfast.

'Dr. James don't need me as much now the weather is good.'

'Two more women to bathe, and then it's our turn,' said Sarah, seeing a woman come out from behind the screen around the tubs.

'That salt water is so itchy.'

'Yes, and it makes everyone bad-tempered, but at least we'll be clean for a while.'

'Best not to wear any knickers – just makes it worse. With no knickers we can just hitch up our petticoats when we needs to go.' Sarah nodded, more interested in watching the screen for another woman to finish bathing.

'Yer know, Dr. James asks about you a lot. "How is that tall fair girl going? Sarah, isn't it?" And I knows he don't have to ask that. He knows yer name. He's got a soft spot for you, he has.'

'Oh no, surely not,' Sarah blushed.

'I knows it's true. He can't take his eyes off yer whenever he sees yer,' Maggie insisted, looking at Sarah. But it was Sarah's turn at the tubs and she thankfully escaped any more talk of Dr. James.

After several days at sea, Maggie handed Sarah a note that Dr. James had given her to pass on. Sarah looked at it in disbelief and opened it with trembling fingers.

'He wants me to visit him, *to spend a few moments in conversation as it is some time since I have had the pleasure of the company of a genteel woman*, he writes. Whatever should I do?' she asked Maggie, the note shaking in her hands and a deep blush creeping up her neck. 'I cannot refuse.'

'Yer should write back to him, Sarah,' Maggie said with a pleased look on her face. 'Tell him you'd be happy to talk with him. It'll be like yer old life – genteel and respectable. Besides, it's a good chance to get away from the orlop deck for a bit.'

Hearing her timid knock at his door, Dr. James opened it and ushered her to a seat at a small table set with two glasses, a flask of wine and some refreshments.

'Do come in Sarah. May I call you Sarah?' he said.

She could barely look at him the first two nights, nor respond to his questions with more than a *yes* or a *no*. She kept asking herself, what would my mother say to all this? But what else could she have done but to agree to his request? Besides, in his cabin she felt safe. Each time Sarah returned to the convicts' quarters from Dr. James' cabin, she was reminded of the danger she was in. It was not only from the men who descended the ladder once the hatch was opened, but she was even more afraid of the women. There was no mistaking what they were doing. Even the innocent Sarah could not feign ignorance. The sighs, grunts and moans of men and women, and women and women together could be heard throughout the entire sleeping area, escalating until they were spent.

*It could happen to me any time on this terrible voyage*, she thought.

'In my village,' she said to Maggie, 'I never had more to do with men than a courteous greeting at church, and polite conversation in the homes of my parents' friends. While one young man used to look my way after church on Sundays, he had never called on me. Now I am alone with a man every night. Whatever would my poor parents say about this? They would never have imagined it to be possible. But then, they would never have thought I would end up in prison, accused of theft. Oh dear. I feel very confused to be singled out by Dr. James and to go to his cabin so often.'

Maggie could only think of the advantages of being singled out by Dr. James and how lucky her friend was, but she knew Sarah by now.

'Things is different now Sarah. We are far away from our families or anyone what can protect us. We have ter look after ourselves as best we can on this ship.'

A few days later, Sarah confided in a curious Maggie about what had happened the previous evening in Dr. James' cabin.

'When I spoke to him about my love for my parents, and how devastated I was when they were suddenly out of my life forever, I began weeping. I was so embarrassed, but I could not help myself.' Maggie could see she wanted to say more but was reluctant, so she lowered her chin and raised her eyebrows to encourage Sarah.

'Well, then, he gently touched my hand in such a manner of sympathy and compassion that I broke down and shook with grief. It was then that everything went so fast. He put his arms around my shoulders and drew me to him, murmuring, "My poor dear Sarah," over and over, stroking my hair and touching my cheek.' She became a mess of nervousness at that point. 'I don't know what came over me — I felt so protected in his arms — and out of control. I could not pull back from him.'

Maggie listened intently, watching the agony on Sarah's face.

'I soon found myself responding to his kisses — and then — and then — in his bed! Oh dear, whatever have I done? How alarmed my dear parents would be if they were to know.' She hung her head, ashamed and confused. 'I have not encountered such kindness since my parents died.' Again she hesitated, looking more embarrassed than Maggie had ever seen her. 'I have been so frightened at night with sailors coming and going.' She was trembling by this time and looking down, fidgeting with the folds of her skirt, then wringing her hands, 'I have never been in such close contact with a man, and he is so kind.'

'No need to worry Sarah. He's a doctor, so yer won't need to worry about nothin',' said the practical Maggie. 'You'll be right. You'll be safe with Dr. James.' Maggie hoped she was right, and thought, *I won't say no more about all this unless Sarah brings it up herself. I know Sarah and how hard it were for her to tell me this. And Dr. James'll know what to do. Them doctors knows a thing or two about not gettin' a woman in the family way. I seen them English overcoats in the infirmary, them what he gives to the officers on board to use with their women. It will be all right.*

By the time the ship had travelled further into the North Atlantic Ocean, the sailors' nightly visits were anticipated by the women, some eagerly, others with dread. But there were enough willing women to make the reluctant ones feel safer. Sarah visited Dr. James almost every night and the 'conversations' continued. The glasses of red wine helped. She felt safe, and loved by her gentle Robert, in spite of terrible feelings of guilt and not a little shame at what she was doing.

Maggie woke up one morning earlier than anyone else. She glanced over at Sarah sleeping in the bunk next to her, then at the bunk on her other side, where one of the young Irish women was sleeping.

*Such a quiet one, she is, never talkin' to anyone. Just pinin' away for Ireland, and not eatin' enough to keep a sparrow alive.*

Maggie looked a bit closer at her. *Siobhan's face is awful pale*, she thought. She got up to see if the young woman was unwell, but when she tried to awaken her, there was no response and one arm swung heavily over the side of the bunk.

Siobhan, Maggie realised to her dismay, was dead.

'Sarah!' she called out as quietly as she could, 'Sarah, wake up!' She went over to her friend's bunk to shake her awake.

'What's wrong?' said the sleepy Sarah.

'I think Siobhan is dead!'

On hearing this, Sarah was wide awake and out of her bunk, hurrying over to the Irish girl.

'Oh Maggie, she's not breathing and she's as white as a ghost.'

By this time, others were awake and curious to know what Maggie and Sarah were doing hovering over Siobhan's bunk. A crowd formed around the dead girl. Two of the Irish women became hysterical and began to wail.

'What happened?' they asked. 'How could she die?' Fear and panic spread like the plague through the orlop deck.

'We'll have to let Dr. James know,' Maggie said, hurrying over to the ladder, knocking loudly on the locked hatch. One of the sailors heard her urgent calls for help and opened the hatch to see what the fuss was about.

'There's a woman what's died down here. Can yer fetch Dr. James?'

Other Irish women had joined in the plaintiff wailing.

'She was always terrible sad, right from the beginnin', the poor girl,' said one of Siobhan's friends as they waited for the doctor. 'Us Irish people feel homesickness so bad, but I've never seen the like of it as this. She cried from mornin' 'til evenin' and not one of us could bring her out of her sadness.'

'I've been watching this Irish lass from the time she boarded,' Dr. James said to Maggie when he arrived to see what had happened. 'She was always sitting by herself in the same place, so forlorn and sick with grief and homesickness. Such a melancholy young woman. I've been concerned about her for quite a while now, especially as she refused any nourishment. She appears to have died from a broken heart, malnutrition, exhaustion, and the lack of a will to live.'

Two of the crew came to lift Siobhan's body from her bunk, making their way through the narrow opening of shocked women. It was no easy task to manoeuvre her body up the ladder and through the hatch. Maggie was told to accompany them to the infirmary. After placing the body on one of the patient beds the sailors left. 'Stay here and wait for me to report the death to Captain Hastings,' Dr. James told Maggie, 'then we will do the necessary.'

Alone with the dead girl lying stretched out beneath the rows of medicine bottles on the shelves, she wondered what 'the necessary' meant.

'I ain't never had to do nothin' like this before,' she said to herself. She had seen the body of her grandmother when she was young, but the grown-up women took care of it. All she knew was that it had to be bathed and dressed, but she was considered too young to help them. On the night her mother died, the midwife took care of the baby and the doctor made arrangements for their bodies to be taken away. Standing next to Siobhan and looking down at the blue-tinged face of death, fear prickled her entire body.

*I wonder what's goin' to happen to us all. We could all die at sea like poor Siobhan. In the middle of the great ocean far from anywhere. Yer family back home not knowin' yer were dead, and never bein' able to see any of yer brothers or sisters again.* Riveted beside the dead girl, she was too afraid to move.

Dr. James returned, bringing with him one of the older Irish women to help Maggie. She knew about dead bodies. Together they started preparing the corpse, washing it from head to toe, then wrapping it in a plain white sheet, carefully sewing it tight to hold Siobhan firmly inside. All the while the Irish woman was softly keening and making the sign of the Cross.

'The body will need to be weighted down with ballast in order for it to sink,' Dr. James told them matter-of-factly, to Maggie's horror. Finally, they covered it loosely with the Union Jack for the burial at sea.

When the Captain was ready, the ship hove to, and everyone on board was summoned up on deck by the macabre tolling of the ship's bell. The normally garrulous women were silent, pressed together in the small space around the corpse. Apart from the normal sounds of sailors going about their duties, the men were quiet as well. Siobhan's body was lifted onto a plank, the ship bobbing and rocking from side to side, a small speck in the vast ocean surrounding them and the Captain read out a simple prayer for burial at sea:

'We commit this body to the deep, to be turned into corruption, looking for the resurrection of the body when the sea shall give up her dead and the life of the world to come through Our Lord Jesus Christ; who at his coming shall change our vile body, that it may be like his glorious body, according to the mighty working, whereby he is able to subdue all things to himself. Amen.'

The plank was tipped at an angle so that her body could slide into the ocean from beneath the Union Jack. All the Irish women began to wail in the otherwise eerie silence. The sailors bowed their heads, the Catholics among them crossed themselves. Sarah and Maggie were as overcome with grief as the Irish women.

After a few moments of silence, the sailors went back to their tasks, the women went below, and the ship turned south-west to continue the journey.

'When I heard the loud splash as her body hit the water and all the Irish girls began to wail, I thought I would die with the sadness of it all,' Sarah said to Maggie when it was all over. 'Looking out at nothing but ocean and that poor girl forever at the bottom of the sea I wondered, how many more of us will die before we reach Van Diemen's Land?'

Dangers were ever present as the ship steered its course through good weather and bad. Sometimes force-five gales threatened to tear the ship to pieces. When the weather improved, a large white albatross followed in the ship's wake for two days. 'That's a good omen,' a sailor said to Sarah when he saw her looking up at the sleek bird.

'Is it now?' she said, and thought, *I hope it's a good omen for us women as well as the ship*. By the fourth week the ship crossed the Tropic of Cancer into the seas off the west coast of Africa.

Just after supper one night — too early for any sailors to appear through the hatch — the Irish girl Kathleen started singing as she often did in the women's quarters, softly at first, to idle away the time:

*Ye London maids attend to me,*
*While I relate my misery,*
*Thro' London Streets I oft have stray'd,*
*But now I am a Convict Maid.*

*In innocence I once did live,*
*In all the joy that peace could give,*
*But sin my youthful heart betrayed,*
*And now I am a Convict Maid.*

Her sweet voice and the words of the lament captured the attention of the women close to her and they took up the refrain, it was a song they'd heard in the streets and alleys of places they had come from, being sung often in the pubs and around the small street warming fires on a cold evening. '*And now I am a Convict Maid*' they sang, Kathleen leaving time for them to finish before moving on. Singing for all the women, her voice became stronger.

*To wed my lover I did try,*
*To take my master's property,*
*So all my guilt was soon displayed,*
*And I became a Convict Maid.*

*Then I was soon to prison sent,*
*To wait in fear my punishment,*
*When at the bar I stood dismayed*
*Since doomed to be a Convict Maid.*

By now, everyone in the women's quarters were listening to the words that mirrored their own lives and took up the chorus with great gusto, the sound of their voices wafting up through the hatch and into the sailors' quarters.

*For seven years oh, how I sighed,*
*While my poor mother loudly cried,*
*My lover wept, and thus he said,*
*May God be with my Convict Maid.*

*Far from my friends and home so dear,*
*My punishment is most severe,*
*My woe is great and I'm afraid,*
*That I shall die a Convict Maid.*

To their surprise, they heard the refrain taken up by the sailors, their deep voices adding to those of the women, '*That I shall die a Convict Maid*'. The sailors even sung along with Kathleen for the last two stanzas.

*I toil each day in grief and pain,*
*And sleepless through the night remain,*
*My constant toils are unrepaid,*
*And wretched is the Convict Maid.*

*Oh could I but once more be free*
*I'd ne'er again a captive be,*
*But I would seek some honest trade,*
*And ne'er become a Convict Maid.*

When it came to the last refrain all their voices could be heard throughout the ship, lifting their spirits no end.

Agnes loved to watch Kathleen singing. She'd taken a real fancy to the auburn-haired lass with the flashing green eyes.

*Aye, she's a beauty*, Agnes thought, a thin smile appearing on her face, *but not for the likes of me. She dinnae hae nought tae do with any o' the sailors, but I ken she be nae like me neither. She's a looker, all the same, and can she sing.* Lost in her thoughts about Kathleen, she failed to notice that the plump woman in a bunk along from hers was searching under her thin mattress for something. The woman looked over at Agnes, misreading the pleased expression on Agnes's face.

'Here you! You stole my bottle of gin you old bitch!'

'I did nae such thing!' said the irate Agnes.

'You hid it, I know you did.' She shoved Agnes off the narrow bunk sending her spread-eagled onto the floor, and began rummaging through Agnes' paltry belongings, certain she would come across the bottle of gin.

Furious, Agnes got up and went for her. Grabbing her shoulders from behind, she spun the woman around and landed a resounding smack across her face. The two women were a match for each other, punching and tearing at each other's clothes, sending each other sprawling into nearby onlookers. Soon the two battlers were surrounded.

'Fight, fight!' called a toothless older woman with glee, getting up off her bunk to make sure she could see it all at close hand. Everyone was yelling, egging them on. Nothing like a good fight.

'Give her one for me Agnes.'

'Good on yer Martha. Hit her harder.'

Then a couple of onlookers got involved in the melee, pushing, scratching, hair pulling and punching until some of the more sober women put a stop to it. But not before Agnes landed a punch on Martha that sent her reeling back. Knocking her head on the edge of the bunk as she went down, Martha let out a high-pitched screech of pain. The sound was so arresting it stopped the fight. Blood oozed from Martha's head and a frightening dark red puddle spread out around her now unconscious slumped body.

'Now you've done it! You've killed her!' one of the women shouted at Agnes.

'We got to get help,' said another woman hurrying over to the hatch. 'There's someone down here bleeding to death,' she called out, knocking on the hatch as hard as she could. 'Fetch Dr. James!'

'Look at this,' said one, 'here's her bottle of gin, at the bottom of her own bed! Agnes didn't steal it. Martha just didn't look proper.'

'I told her I didnae take her bottle o' gin,' Agnes said, her dress torn and her own battered face already beginning to show purple bruising.

Martha's head wound looked bad, the blood kept gushing out and there was a deep cut at the side of her forehead. Maggie went over to her to see what she could do, then took the sheet off Martha's bed, pressing the end of it on to the wound to try to stop it bleeding until Dr. James arrived. Twenty stitches had to be sewn to close the wound of the concussed Martha.

The next day Dr. James told Maggie that Agnes would have to be punished for such a serious offence.

'What's going to happen to Agnes then?' Sarah asked when Maggie reported this bit of news.

'Well, he said the Captain said it were up to him to decide what sort of punishment: head shavin' or solitary confinement in the ship's coal hole.'

'What is that?'

'Sounds like they put you in a black box and they leaves yer down where the coal is stored. I didn't like the sound of it meself.'

'Oh, poor Agnes.'

'Dr. James didn't like it neither. He said it sounded *too extreme*. So the Captain said he could order Agnes to have her head shaved in front of everyone instead, and he decided on that.'

They both touched their long hair. They'd seen women with shaved heads at Newgate.

'But it's better than being locked in a black box in the dark,' said Sarah, shuddering at the very thought.

Two sailors escorted Agnes up to the main deck, roping her wrists and ankles to a chair as she sat astride it. All the women had been ordered up on deck to witness the public humiliation of Agnes MacDonald, and sailors on duty were gawping at the proceedings. A sailor holding a pair of shears stood to one side of Dr. James, awaiting his orders.

'Proceed,' said Dr. James.

Feeling the first scrape of the shears Agnes watched the locks of her hair feather down onto the deck around her feet. Snip, chop, hack. The sailor moved slowly around her. The old feelings of anger and hate bounced off each other, fuelled by despair and anguish at the unfairness of life. She maintained an outward appearance of measured fury but wept inwardly at the shame of it all. The other women watched in silence as the shears sliced and hacked at her thick hair, removing great chunks at a time. Even those who did not like Agnes felt her humiliation. The sailor had never cut a woman's hair before and his incompetence resulted in trickles of blood falling on Agnes' shoulders as he nicked her ears. The watching women had seen head shaving before and a few knew first-hand the humiliation of it. They all hated this punishment and felt sorry for Agnes to be shamed in front of the ship's officers and crew.

When it was over, and Agnes was allowed to return to the women's quarters, the scar on her face was more noticeable, raised and angry without the softening effect that a frame of hair offers a plain woman's face.

'They can cut ma hair, but what do I care?' she said with bravado. 'It means nought tae me.' But they all noticed she was a lot quieter for a few days, and no-one spoke to Martha.

As the ship neared the Equator, the heat became oppressive, exacerbating everyone's discomfort and bad moods. Entering the well-known doldrums, the wind dropped completely and the ship became motionless for three days. Arguments started over nothing. At the end of the third day a light breeze turned into a good wind and the ship was on its way once more, entering the southern hemisphere and the waters of the South Atlantic ocean.

For a few days the mild weather and fresh sea breezes buoyed their spirits, but two days before reaching Cape Town the wine supply was almost depleted, causing another bout of discontent and quarrelling.

'Cape Town at last!' exclaimed Sarah as the ship slid into the South African harbour. 'My father used to tell me about stories that the missionaries brought back from Africa.' She and Maggie looked out towards the harbour before it was time for them to be herded below while the ship moored. 'I dreamed of what it might be like, and of being married to a missionary and visiting Africa.'

'What did you think you'd do there?' Maggie asked. She'd never heard any such stories.

'I imagined myself surrounded by little black children, and I would be teaching them to read and write. I would learn their ways and we would be so happy, my husband and I, helping them to understand the Bible.'

Maggie looked at her as Sarah's face fell, thinking how this would never happen now; another dream shattered.

The closer the ship moved to the port, the more excited they both became at getting so close to Africa. They were allowed up on board and even from where the ship was anchored, they could see the strangeness of Africa, the black people in their colourful clothes and the commotion and flurry of activity in the busy port. But it also reminded them just how far they were away from home.

Harboured in Cape Town for the next few days, supplies for the rest of the long journey were brought on board – enough of everything to last until they reached Van Diemen's Land and the long-awaited fresh water supplies replenished. Enough fresh water to be able to wash bodies, clothes, bedsheets, and the vast piles of sanitary rags. The women and children lined up for their turn in the washtubs. One by one, grateful bodies slipped behind the modesty curtain and into the waiting tub.

'Oh I never would of thought I'd be so happy ter have fresh water ter bathe in, and clean clothin' what ain't been washed in scratchy salt water.' Maggie squealed with delight as she immersed herself in the tub, wanting to stay there forever.

'Hurry up girl, there's lots of us waitin' our turn.'

'I can't wait to wash me hair.'

'Yer must be finished by now. Get a move on. We're all waitin'.'

Maggie wallowed in the tub until an impatient woman screamed out, 'Get the fuckin' hell outa there and let us have our turn, ya bitch!'

When Maggie got out, someone in the tub line-up had the bright idea they should all sing a song and each time they got to the end of it, the woman in the tub had to get out and let another one in. That seemed to make them less impatient to wait their turn, and ensured equal time for all. After every fifteen women, the water in the tub was changed.

They were aching to go ashore, but this was not permitted. Officers and some crew were rowed to Cape Town in the longboat. Some of the women plied their trade with crew from other ships in port, with sailors acting as go-betweens. Maggie saw foreign seamen sneak on board, escorted below by the go-betweens. She heard the women swearing at sailors wanting to pay with foreign money.

'English coin or a bottle of somethin' yer bastard! None of that foreign coin.' She stayed on deck for as long as she could.

On the twelfth of November the ship left Cape Town. 'Next stop Van Diemen's Land!' one of the sailors said. Cape Town was a welcome relief, but there were still weeks to go. They'd been at sea for such a long time. Nerves had worn thin and tempers were frayed. Some women had been handcuffed for violent and abusive language and Agnes had got into trouble again when she struck out at another woman, causing her injury. By this time Dr. James' patience had waned. It was the coal hole for Agnes.

When Agnes returned from the blackened confines of the coal hole, her face was pale green from sea-sickness. She was bent over and her legs were wobbly from being cramped up in a coffin-like box just five feet two inches in height. Maggie and Sarah went over to her and silently handed her a damp rag so she could clean herself up from the mess of her own bodily discharge. No-one dared speak to her and she could not be coaxed into any jollities. Maggie sat by her side silently the rest of that day, knowing that Agnes was suffering, but also that she needed to suffer in her own way.

Within a few days the winds whipped up and the rain pelted down. The scream of the wind in the southern ocean gale added to the groan of overstretched canvas and the thunderous sound of mountainous waves that lifted the ship up and sent it crashing down with a shudder. Listening to the howling noises from above, many of the women huddled together for comfort.

'I heard tell there were a ship wrecked just three year ago. A convict ship like ours.' Maggie whispered to Sarah, both of them bundled up in their thin blankets, their shawls held tight around their bodies.

'Yes, I heard about that too. The *Amphitrite*, wrecked off the coast of France. It didn't make it as far as we have,' Sarah whispered back, teeth chattering. 'Only three people survived. None of them convicts.'

On the second day the winds increased their intensity and the waves became gigantic, tossing the ship about like a child's toy, terrifying everyone on board. When the whole vessel shuddered and seemed to buckle under the sea's ferocity, shrill screams of panic came from all corners. Maggie was overcome with terror, 'Fuckin' hell, ain't nobody safe at sea. We might all drown!' she cried out, gripping the side of her bunk to avoid being catapulted out. Those not holding on for dear life were sent flying out of their bunks.

'We be doomed!' screeched one woman.

They could do nothing but cling to each other and hold on firmly to anything at hand. The pitching was unbearable. Anything not tied down shot out in all directions. Plates and cutlery rattled down the mess-tables, swooping up bottles in their way and sending them smashing onto the floor. Splintered crockery and glass were everywhere and water penetrated every level of the ship.

There was an ominous crack, like something splitting, and a tearing rip as one of the canvas sails failed to withstand the mighty storm. The eerie sound of the howling wind above them, and the horror of being trapped below should the ship go down, created ripples of panic and loud wailing.

'We're done for!' shrieked one woman as another mountainous wave slammed against the side of the ship. Others reacted in deadly silence, the terror in their eyes as loud as the screams. Some prayed. Some called on God offering all sorts of promises should they be saved. The children clung to their mother's skirts, whimpering.

Their ship was a tiny, insignificant speck in the vast, tremendous ocean.

The storm lasted for several more hours before the wind abated and they were out of immediate danger. But there was much to repair and frayed nerves to mollify. Many of the women had suffered bruises, two had broken bones and most were in shock. Maggie was fetched to help Dr. James and heard about all the repairs that would have to be done: water to be bailed out, broken glass and plates carefully swept up, and the big job of repairing the torn sail.

'I'll only feel safe from the sea when I'm off this ship and walkin' on the cobblestones of Hobart Town. Ain't nothin' as dangerous as a ship at sea,' murmured Maggie, lying in her bunk next to the sleeping Sarah at the end of it all, her eyes closing in weariness. 'I don't never want to go on a ship never again in me life.'

The ship made its way further south and the weather became kinder. The women had learnt that the ocean was a great beast to be respected, but it was also a mystery of astonishing beauty. They witnessed amazing sights: schools of flying fish, pods of dolphins, seabirds circling the ship from time to time, sharks, and occasionally whales of enormous size, all of which prompted shouts of delight mixed with fear.

Agnes was up on deck with other women, looking out to sea hoping to see another dolphin. Glancing up at the billowing sails she noticed a sailor up in the riggings. Watching him, wondering what it might be like to be up so high and looking out at the ocean, she saw him miss his footing and suddenly he was flying through the air right in front of her very eyes, plummeting into the ocean below.

'Man Overboard!' shouted a sailor. Agnes watched the young sailor flail about in the sea. To her dismay, she saw an ominous fin hovering nearby.

'Shark!' she yelled at anyone nearby, and others began shouting and screaming as loud as her. To Agnes' horror, she watched the sea around him rapidly turn scarlet. No-one could see which part of his body had received the creature's teeth, but the blood was profuse. He was panicking and more blood rose to the surface of the water as he thrashed about. Two of the crew threw him a rope with a lifebuoy, frantically calling out for him to grab it so they could pull him to safety.

'Catch the rope! Catch the rope!' everyone was shouting to him, feeling almost as much terror as the lad himself.

The ship leaned as everyone ran to the same side. There were shouts, cries of anguish and frantic efforts to save him. But to no avail. He remained in the ocean for quite some time surrounded by his own blood, and in spite of all the crew's efforts, he was swept away into the vastness of the sea where he quickly disappeared from view.

The mood was sombre that evening, from the officers' quarters to the women's quarters below. The young man's violent death had affected them all.

The next day the weather was perfect with a wind that filled the sails, enabling the ship to make good progress. After the shock of the sailor's death and the depressing effect it had on everyone on board, the Captain allowed the men to fish if they wished. Several of the men hauled in good catches, providing fresh food for the evening meal, and they laughingly encouraged the women to try their hand at fishing.

'I'll have a go,' said Maggie.

'Aye, and me too,' ventured Agnes.

Two sailors jumped at the chance to show them how it was done. Everyone watched, all laughing at the two women trying to prepare the fishing lines.

'Well,' said Maggie, 'I ain't never done no fishin' before, but there's a first time for everythin' I say,' and she threw in her line.

To Agnes' surprise the line she was gripping gave a tug, and with the help of one of the crew, she hauled in a good catch. 'I caught one! I caught one!' Agnes shouted in delight, the look on her face full of awe. No-one had ever seen her so happy. She could not stop talking about it.

'What a day. I ain't laughed like that for a long time,' said Maggie to Agnes later in the day. They were sharing a portion of the fish that Agnes had caught. Cook had sent it to her specially.

'This be the fish I caught.' Agnes said for the third time.

'And it's delicious Agnes.' Thinking about the day they'd had out on the ocean, clean air, sunshine, she added, 'them sailors must have excitin' lives. To live out at sea with all what happens. But I wouldn't like it meself.'

'It would be better than livin' in the places we come from, lass. Still, I wouldnae like tae be at sea all the time. I'll be glad when we get on tae dry land agin.'

'But to be out in all the fresh air, far from grey, damp London. I reckon it would be a good life. My young brother Fred was always talkin' about how he'd like to go to sea. He loved listenin' to sailors' stories.' She looked away, her eyes gazing into space. 'Yes, Fred would really love it. I wonder if I'll ever get to tell 'im about it all.'

Finally, on the twentieth of December, six weeks out from Cape Town, the southernmost point of Van Diemen's Land, Tasman's Head was sighted. They were all on the main deck when they heard the cry, 'Land Ahoy!' Everyone cheered and jostled each other for the best view from the ship's rail.

'We're nearly there!' shouted a couple of the women, turning to hug those around them, old grievances and resentments giving way to laughter and chatter. They had to strain their eyes to see the spot of land in the distance that would be their new home.

'That sick woman I told yer about what's been in the infirmary for over a week, passed away this mornin' poor thing,' Maggie told Sarah.

'Oh how sad. That makes two convict deaths on the voyage.'

'Dr. James told me her grave "would forever stay unmarked". That's what he said. Not even a simple wood cross is allowed on a convict's grave.'

They were both silent at that, to think of being buried so far from home, a nobody with no-one to care whether you were dead or alive.

Sarah broke the silence, 'Then her grave will be never be tended by relative or friend. What a terrible thing.'

Standing next to them at the rails on the deck listening, Agnes looked over at them.

'Aye, it be a sad thing. Tae come all this way, only tae die at the last minute.' As the ship glided into Sullivan's Cove, a square flag was hoisted – half red, half white to signal that women prisoners were its cargo.

'Four months on this ship. I didnae think we'd ever make it,' she added. The stark reality of an unknown future mixed with curiosity and the sheer relief of finally being able to step on dry land again showed on all their faces.

Moving through Storm Bay in the mouth of the River Derwent with the port of Hobart Town and its 14,000 souls, Sarah remembered something she'd heard Robert mention one evening, and said under her breath, '... a place where men outnumber women by seven to one. We are British women in a foreign land. May God help us.'

# PART II

Chapter 3

# *Sarah*

*20th December, 1836*

It seems to have a strange beauty of its own, this place, but it is so alien that I doubt any of us will ever feel at home here. When the ship moored in the harbour, all of us searched the shore for any sign of familiarity — something, anything — that we could identify with as home. The tall spindly trees that we had seen on the coastline as we glided into Sullivan Cove were a silver-blue colour that had little resemblance to English trees; high-flying bright coloured birds circled above, screeching like banshees, and a looming mountain appeared to wrap itself around the whole of Hobart Town. No English winter here. Even though it was December the weather was mild, the air crisp and clean. There was an eerie silence to the place.

Our arrival filled me with so much melancholy and homesickness for England that I could scarcely bear it. I found Maggie, and reached for her hand, sensing she was feeling as I was.

The excitement we had all felt as land was sighted gave way to some misgivings. We had no notion of what to expect.

There was a bustle of activity when the Lieutenant-Governor of Van Diemen's Land came on board with a few of his officers so that the Captain could hand over his cargo of women. There would be another set of rules for us to obey now.

'See what that man is carrying?' I said to Maggie as quietly as I could, pointing with my eyes to one of the officers. 'That must be the Conduct Register that Robert told me about. They call it the Black Book. They write down everything about us in there.' Robert had told me that it kept being added to during the seven years of our sentences – how we behaved inside the Factory and on assignment to the settlers, the reasons for us being dismissed and returned to the Factory should that happen. Everything. That book could let us out of the Factory for good, or keep us in. The officer carrying it had it tucked under his right arm, moving it to his left so that he could comfortably shake hands with the Captain.

Maggie was taking a good look at the register, and carefully whispered back to me. 'We was told if we behaved we might get an early ticket of leave.'

'That's true. If we don't get into any trouble at all, we might get two or more years off our sentence.' I'd been so happy to hear about that myself and thought if I am on assignment to a good household, I should not have any problems. But then I remembered that it was not always our own choice. Sometimes other people make trouble for us no matter how good we are.

After hours of waiting up on deck in silence with nowhere to rest, the day dragging on with all the paperwork to be finalised, I could feel everyone's weary impatience. If only it were over and we could get off the ship. The smell of cheap scent that some of the women had put on for this special occasion was making me quite ill and I was beginning to have a headache from its sweetness. By midday, it was done, and we were put into groups of twenty to be ferried ashore in longboats to Hunter Island.

It was not easy getting on and off these boats. I almost fell backwards into the water but managed to right myself in time. I felt the cold slap of my wet skirt around my ankles and saw that others were just as soaked. Our boots were filthy by the time we squelched our way across the muddy causeway. We could see a lot of men on the other side waving and calling out to us but I could not hear what they were saying until we got closer.

'Hey there me lovelies! Me name's Tom!' one called out, flailing his arms about wildly, pushing in front of others.

'Look over this way sweetie, I'm the man for you,' called another as loud as he could. We had no idea who he was shouting to. As we got closer I heard one very loud voice who must have spied Irish Kathleen. 'Hey luv, you with the red hair, what's yer name?'

There were hundreds of them looking us over, back-slapping, shoving, and joking amongst themselves. Some were shouting out their names and wanting to know ours. The coarser ones made lewd comments about what they might offer us. A few of the women shouted back at them, laughing and liking the attention. We were all having trouble walking. Having not touched land for four months we were walking with a sailor's gait. Beside me, Maggie mumbled.

'Blimey, I can't hardly walk straight on land no more. Feels like it's movin'.' The men laughed at us. No doubt they knew about that.

When all of us were on the mainland and standing in rows as we were commanded to do, we were handed over to the colony's straight-backed soldiers in their crisp, scarlet uniforms. We must have looked a sight next to them, our own worn clothes and weary bodies and them in their clean pressed uniforms. Once we started walking, I knew that was the end of anything more to do with anyone on the ship. I looked back, thinking of Robert, wondering if I would ever see him again. The last night we were together, he had said to me that he had gained great affection for me and was troubled and very sad to part from me. I felt the same, but then I thought, what is the use of that when you have a wife and children back in England? I must say I went through a mixture of feelings – resentment, sadness, fear. Had I changed so much on this voyage over?

After some confusion, and orders being passed down the line of soldiers accompanying us, we started our long march, struggling up a steep hill for about two miles before coming to a straight portion of road that was easier going. But it was hot and we were tired and thirsty. A little further on I heard running water and saw there was a rivulet running alongside a shady track we had turned into. The mere sound of running water made me feel a little cooler. It was a pretty place and my hopes were lifted. Until, that is, I saw the grey two-storey stone building ahead: Cascades Female Factory, shaded by that dark forbidding mountain that seemed to wrap itself around the whole of Hobart Town; its shadows spreading over the whole building.

The jaws of the great wooden entrance doors with their black iron locks opened wide to swallow us up. The children were whimpering, their tired mothers with shoulders drooping with fatigue, dragged them along. Once the last straggler had been herded into the open front yard to await processing, the heavy prison doors slammed shut behind us.

'It's so quiet here,' I said to Maggie when I spied her nearby in the shuffle to get us all sorted out as quickly as possible. Like me, she was flushed from the long walk, and perspiring, fanning her face with her hand.

'And so hot. That walk nearly killed me. I aren't half thirsty.'

A woman wearing a black dress buttoned tight to the neck with a white bonnet tied under her chin approached us all, jingling a large bunch of keys. She ushered us into a kind of holding room and announced she was the Matron.

'There are three hundred women and children here now counting you lot,' she said, 'so you'd better behave yourselves.'

Looking her up and down, Maggie said, 'She's young for a Matron, only a bit older than you Sarah, by the looks. I wonder how long she's lived here and what she's like. I'm sure we'll find out soon enough.'

Matron told us that our possessions were now in the Commissariat storage in Hobart Town and would be returned to us once we receive our tickets-of-leave. Her sharp eyes swept over us. By the look on her face I could see she was searching for any signs of troublemakers.

'If anyone disobeys orders, neglects their work, uses profane, obscene, or abusive language, is guilty of insubordination, or any other conduct deemed turbulent, disorderly, or disrespectful,' she said in a stern voice, her eyes spanning the room, 'they will be punished by the Superintendent.' Looking to see if we had taken this in, she added, 'It is very important to observe the utmost cleanliness, regularity of habits and entire submission to the rules, including the greatest quietness.'

We were each handed two prison dresses, two aprons, two caps, two pairs of stockings, two rags for the monthly bleeding, and two simple bonnets. I felt the cloth of the shapeless shifts between my fingers, thick and coarse – not encrusted with salt, but still prickly on the skin. The next order came – to undress and wash ourselves from the large buckets of water nearby. Fresh water again at last! It was cold on my hot body and such a relief. Off came the last of the salt and grime that had accumulated on my body and clothes from weeks at sea after Cape Town. Our heads were checked for lice, our old clothes were put to one side. I found out later that if the lice had taken too great a hold, the clothing was all burned. If no lice were found, clothes were washed and used again.

After bathing, and putting on the new clothes we had been given, I looked around at the other women. All our clothing was the same, except for additional letters on some of them. Some had a big yellow 'C' on their left sleeve; others had yellow 'C's sewn on both sleeves and one on the back. I didn't know what to make of all this. Mine and Maggie's had no yellow C's. I looked over at Agnes and saw that hers had the maximum number of yellow C's. *This must be a way of sorting us out*, I thought. We were then ushered into a holding area, where a warden was waiting for us.

He addressed us by our Police Number, looking us up and down to check us against his records in a thick ledger he had in one hand, a pencil in the other.

'Step forward when I call your name.'

'Prisoner 234,' he called, and Maggie stepped forward. 'Stand to be measured,' he ordered, indicating the measuring rod on the wall.

'Height, five feet two inches. Eighteen years of age. Oval face with ruddy cheeks, hazel eyes, long dark brown hair,' he went on, checking physical particulars against his ledger, writing down in a side column any extra comments that might have been omitted. 'Full component of teeth, no visible pockmarks, no distinguishing features. Yard One, First Class. Go over there.'

As I was standing next to Maggie, I thought I might be called straight after her; but I was not.

'Prisoner 378,' he called. It was Agnes' number. 'Stand to be measured.'

Agnes threw him a tetchy look and stepped forward with bad grace.

'Five feet two inches. Twenty-three years of age. Round face, low forehead, dark complexion, brown eyes, shorn dark brown hair ...' He made a special note of that and gave her a more intense look, 'badly stained teeth, rough-looking, deep scar on left side of face running from below eye to chin. Through there to Yard Three. That's Crime Class,' he said with a snigger, 'over there.'

'Prisoner 323,' and it was my turn to step forward. 'Five feet four inches. You're a tall one. Age nineteen. Oval face, no marks, long curly fair hair, eyes blue. Yard One.'

It was one of the Irish women's turn. Kathleen. The one Agnes had had her eye on. 'Prisoner 425. Five feet one inch. Age eighteen, round face, freckles, long auburn hair, green eyes. An Irish I'll be bound. Over there, Yard Three.'

'Look at that,' Maggie pointed out the women who had been sent to Yard Two, Second Class. 'Yard Two women all have Yellow C's on the left sleeve, and Yard Three women have them on both sleeves and on the back.

'And ours have none. So, that's why they're sorting us out,' I said.

When the new intake of over a hundred women were all cleaned and sorted, we were directed to an area where meals were taken and told to sit down at the mess-tables. Bowls of watery ox-head soup with a chunk of brown bread were slapped in front of us. After eating, Matron's husband, the Factory's Superintendent came in and told us he was going to read out all the rules that we would be following for the whole time of our imprisonment in the Factory.

'Rule Number 1,' he began, pausing to straighten his corpulent, short body up to its full height before reading from a few thick pages he held in his hand. 'No talking, no laughing, no whistling, no singing.'

Ah, that was why it was so quiet in this place. Why is it that we cannot talk or laugh? Is it so terrible to laugh and sing?'

He read out a list of rules so long that many of the physically and emotionally weary women dozed off before he had finished. I saw Agnes had fallen asleep, and my eyes rested on her for a while, thinking what a sad person she was. No longer afraid of her as I was in the beginning, my heart went out to her, especially after what she had suffered. From my own experience in Newgate and on the ship, it came to me that in order to survive each one of us had to do whatever we could. That must have been Agnes' life since she was born. Always fighting to stay alive. Poor Agnes.

Suddenly the Superintendent's voice changed from the low monotone of list-reading to a louder one with an air of authority and Agnes jolted awake. The Superintendent was telling us about compulsory church attendance inside the Factory. Hearing that, a woman near me muttered, 'That means we never get outside, even to attend church.'

'Bells are rung at half past five in the morning for morning muster in the yard after which you will clean the rooms and bring in the wood before breakfast at a quarter to eight.' he went on.

'Gawd, he's still not finished,' Maggie whispered to me, her head lowered so as not to be seen talking.

'After breakfast there will be prayers, followed by work assignments until one o'clock. Bells will be rung for dinner at one o'clock until half past two, at which time the bells will be rung for you to return to work until five o'clock in the afternoon. Supper bell is at half past seven, followed by evening prayers. On Sundays there is full Chapel service.'

Maggie screwed up her face in disgust not bothering to whisper this time, 'Gawd, there are bells for every bleedin' thing. I'll be dreamin' of bells.'

'No talking!' Matron warned, glaring at Maggie.

When the Superintendent was finished, we were told to stand, form into groups according to which yard we'd been assigned to. When that was done we were shuffled into groups of twelve, then marched to our sleeping quarters. Maggie and I made sure we had hammocks alongside one another in our dormitory above the open yard of First Class. By this time we were so exhausted we fell asleep almost at once. I just heard Maggie murmur, 'I'll have to watch out for Matron. She must have eyes and ears all over 'er head. No talkin'! Bleedin' hell!'

Our first night was filled with the sound of thunder, and lightning flashes that lit up the sky, keeping us awake for hours in spite of our exhaustion. Unlike the gentle misty rain of England, the rain came pouring down, as if to warn us that we had better watch out for ourselves. I dreamt that I was still on the ship and when I awoke I didn't know where I was at first. I looked around. It was cramped, but not as bad as the ship. We could see daylight, and there was an end to sea-sickness at least. The one chamber pot in the far corner of our dormitory was overflowing.

We had arrived in Hobart Town just before Christmas. I'd thought of all the Christmases I'd had with my family and how special this day was for us. But here, what a soulless time it was in the Factory. Christmas Day passed like any other, except that the daily church service in the small Factory chapel was longer than usual and filled with dismal sermons rather than hymns of joy. Reverend Broadwater had no imagination when it came to sermons.

Our meals were regular, mostly bread and gruel made with oatmeal and water, or watery soup made of vegetables or barley. If we were lucky there might be scraps of meat from ox or sheep heads added to the soup to give it a bit of flavour. At least we never starved, and we were not bothered by the fear of sailors. Every day passed the same as the one before, the daily routine punctuated by the ringing of bells.

'Them bleedin' bells!' said Maggie one morning, 'I dream about them. Last night I woke up in the middle of the night thinkin' it were time to get up but when I looked round, everyone were sleepin' like babes.'

Matron had assigned me to work in the hospital and Maggie to the kitchen the first week. The thought of warm bread baking in the kitchen put a smile on her face.

'That'll be the best place in winter bein' warm and all, and with them nice smells of bakin' bread,' she'd said. But after a few days of scouring pots and pans Matron told her she was to work in the nursery as they were short-handed.

I was happy to be in the hospital where I could help people. Two other women from First Class were working alongside me, caring for the sick convict women in the narrow beds. They were only in hospital if they were seriously ill, or had broken bones, or to deliver babies. In and out as quickly as possible, and no fussing over any of them. We were permitted to talk to each other about the patients and our work. We had strict orders there was to be no idle gossip. No matter if this were the rule, women will always gossip. I found out that Agnes had thrown her lot in with some women in Crime Class who were always causing trouble.

'I wonder what she did to get fourteen years,' said Maggie when we'd finished our day's tasks and were eating our evening meal. 'I never did find out what she were in for. I'm that glad I weren't put in Crime Class. It sounds bad from all accounts. The poor women what's there has got the worst jobs. They has to wash dirty linen at them horrible washtubs all day, liftin' heavy wet sheets and other stuff. It's a back-breakin' job that one, the washtubs. And they get soaked through themselves. Must be awful in winter when it's cold. No, I def-in-itely wouldn't like that job.'

'One of the women in the hospital told me that the washtub women had hands that were spongy and continually blue with cold, even in summer,' I told Maggie. 'We can't do anything to help them with their aches and pains from hard work.'

'Poor things,' Maggie said, looking down at her own hands and thinking about the aching joints and back problems of the women who'd been doing this work for a long time. We'd seen them leaning over the tubs, wringing linen with their bare hands and heaving it all up onto the washing lines that ran the length of the yard.

'Another horrible job what I do-not-want-to-do is pickin' oakum,' said Maggie as we sat looking down at our empty plates. I could see her looking around to see if we'd all been given the same amount of food. Even though we never starved, it would have been nice to have larger portions. And no chance of anyone leaving any scraps on their plates. Then she looked at her hands, by no means those of a lady, but still not riddled with rheumatism, or cracked and covered in sores.

'Pickin' oakum, yer have to untwist old rope and pick out bits of tar from it so the rope can be used again. They uses it for caulkin' ships. The salt and tar on the ropes rips yer hands somethin' awful. One of the women what had to do that for a time had hands that was red raw and real sore. That's what she said to me. Their hands bleed and the salt in the cuts is that painful.'

'And if they complain or act up they are sent to an isolation cell. That's what someone in the hospital told me,' I added. 'I don't think I could bear that. All alone in a cramped dark cell with little food and no-one to talk to.'

I thought again of the time Agnes was sent to the coal-hole on the ship. Poor Agnes. She'd never said a word about what it was like to anyone. I think I would die if I had to suffer that. Then I remembered what it was I had to tell Maggie.

'One of the women from Second Class came up to me this morning in the hospital. She had some ribbons hidden in her apron pocket and wanted to find someone to trade them with. She told me that if you've got money in here you can get extras, even more food.'

'Is that right? Those what's workin' in the kitchen would have a good chance to pass on food, all right. I could do with a bit of extra grub.'

'Yes, they could get scraps of meat, and some bread and tea from the kitchen if they were quick. They'd have to be careful. But sometimes money and food is brought in from outside when a woman comes back from assignment.'

'I heard that too, even extras like bottles of drink, fugs of tobacco and jewellery.'

'Did you know Maggie, that there's a turnkey here who can be bribed?'

Maggie's eyes widened on hearing this interesting bit of information.

'If I could get out on assignment, I wouldn't want to be comin' back here. No sir.' Her eyes went glazed like they usually did when she was thinking about something serious. 'But if I did, I'd make sure I had some money to bring back in. Or grub.'

By this time, everyone was getting up from the mess table and the empty plates were being collected by the kitchen women. Maggie got up to move away from the table.

'We mightn't have to stay here long.' Her face showed little hope though. 'At least I've got the babies in the Nursery to look after. Poor little mites.'

'We didn't have any black marks for bad behaviour on the ship, so it shouldn't be long,' though my confidence in an early assignment had begun to waiver. I thought it would have happened sooner than this.

We could see Mount Wellington from the Factory yard, with its thick forests of strange trees and ferns. In late afternoon its shadow spread over everything like a menacing beast, making the whole place dark and cold, even in summer.

'Most of the babies in the Nursery is sick,' Maggie said to me one evening as we were preparing for bed. 'Sad, thin little things

– so tiny they're two in a crib what's no more than a wooden box with rockers on the bottom.'

The first time I heard this I was horrified, imagining small, sick babies stuffed into a wooden box like a coffin. Each time Maggie returned from the Nursery her face showed her concern and she had some awful tale to tell about a baby or toddler.

'No loving mother to hold them. I want ter pick every one of them up and cradle them in me arms. But there's so much work and so many of them. Besides, Matron don't like the babies to be coddled.'

We were both in tears thinking about all those poor children.

'When a convict becomes pregnant she has to come back to the Factory as soon as it shows. Straight into Crime Class. The crime of bein' pregnant with no husband. It don't matter how she got in the family way,' she said. 'It's always the woman to blame.'

My face became hot with shame. What if that had happened to me? I started thinking then, how it had all begun — the note he'd sent, the 'conversation' evenings, the wine, the privilege of being in a comfortable cabin away from the sailors. Yes, the first few meetings were, just so, conversations such as I would have had with visitors my father and mother had known. But things changed. He had taken me in his arms, in kindness at first, and then — at first it was a kiss ...

I became aware that Maggie was still talking about the Nursery.

'Once the baby's born, it's put in the baby yard. The ma is only allowed to visit until it's weaned. "Once baby is weaned," Matron said, "the mother has no more to do with her child. And when the child is old enough, it's sent to the Queen's Orphanage". That's how it is.'

'Oh Maggie, how awful. The poor mite left without its mother.' We both shook our heads, thinking about the stricken mother only a few yards away from her baby and then of its being sent to an orphanage when its mother could easily have looked after it inside the Factory.

'She would only be able to visit her baby in the orphanage if she worked her way up to First Class and was lucky enough to be sent in service to a place what give her time off on Sunday.'

'But even then, how would the mother get to the orphanage?' I asked, thinking about it a bit more.

'By walkin'. So it would only happen if she was somewhere what was walkin' distance from the orphanage. She could be sent miles away. Then she'd never see him, not 'til she got her ticket of leave. Could take years.'

Before we drifted off to sleep, Maggie added, 'Matron told me lots of babies here die before they make it to the orphanage. "More babies die in the Factory than outside in Hobart Town, mainly from bronchitis or pneumonia and we can't do anything about it." That's what she said to me.' She was still mumbling about babies but her voice was so low by this time that I scarcely heard her, both of us overcome with weariness.

We made sure to keep our voices low at night, as we were not permitted to talk to each other. The convict in charge of our dormitory was a friend from the ship, so she let us get away with whispering. I had some fresh news to tell Maggie. We were always on the lookout for what it was like in service here, and swapped information whenever we heard something new.

'The cook told me about assignments outside. They're all different.' Maggie was taking her shoes off and getting into her nightdress. It had been a long day and we were both tired. 'A woman was sent to a household where the mistress was a convict herself, married to a free man. They didn't give her any clothes, and not much food. She had said that theirs was a poor household and that she should do whatever she had to, to get her own 'extras' as long as she didn't trouble them. They even let her go out drinking and stay out all night if she pleased!'

'Well I never!' Maggie shifted a little once she was in her hammock, leaning closer to me. 'Don't that take the cake!'

'But it didn't turn out too well in the end. After six months, she got into a bit of trouble in a public house and because the owner of the pub knew she was from the Factory he sent for a constable who brought her straight back here. Never mind about the mistress.'

Our hammocks swung as we both lay back, thinking about how strange it all was. A convict allowed to go out all night whenever she wanted to.

'I heard a different story meself,' said Maggie, turning on her side towards me again. We were getting used to the swinging hammocks and had learned how to master them without falling out — by holding onto the sides with both hands before making any movement.

'One of the women in the nursery told me that on her first assignment the mistress treated her so bad she complained and were sent straight back 'ere for bein' insolent. She said if yer don't like bein' in a household — but only if it were worse than here in the Factory — best refuse to work. We has to think about it real careful though, what's the worst of the two: assignment or prison?'

I pondered on these two choices, 'Let's hope there are places where the master and mistress are good, and it's a decent place to be.'

We leaned away from each other and said no more, both of us wondering what was going to happen to us on our first assignment — if it ever happened.

The trouble in Yard Three started with just a bit of singing and merriment. Everyone in the Factory could hear. It was the loud arguments that woke us up, and the sound of glass shattering. It sounded as if there were violent brawls going on. Then we heard footsteps running from Matron's quarters down to Crime Class and after a while things got quiet.

When I arrived in the hospital the next morning, there was Agnes, lying next to three others, all badly bruised and gashed. Agnes had dried blood all over her arms.

'What happened to you Agnes?' I asked her.

'I was havin' a bit of a lark with Cate and Ellen. After a while one o' the other lasses told us tae quiet down or Matron would bring the Superintendent and we'd be in real trouble.' In spite of the state she was in, I could see she was still excited, even proud in a way, and wanted to talk about it.

'Well, by that time, I was half mast tae the wind and I didnae like this lassie tellin' me what tae do. So I told her to shut her trap, and she answered me back sayin', "it's you what should shut your trap." Ma anger got the better of me by then and I went for her.' Agnes was bolder and more confident now she was with others like her. I waited for her to go on.

'Then Ellen came over tae help me, and it got out o' hand. One o' the lasses picked up a shard o' glass from a broken bottle on the floor and started lashin' out at me. I felt the glass stab intae ma body and there was blood all o'er me. Well, by that time the noise we be all makin' brought Matron and Superintendent down tae put a stop tae it all.'

'From what I could make out from Agnes,' I told Maggie later in the day, 'there's a group of women in Crime Class who call themselves the Flash Mob. If there's any trouble, someone in the Flash Mob is usually involved. The ringleaders of the Mob are two Irish women, Cate and Ellen. Matron finds them a terrible nuisance and hard to control.'

Maggie was wide-eyed listening to all this and did not interrupt, hanging on every word.

'After she told me what had happened, Agnes went quiet – you know the way she does, and I didn't learn any more.'

'I don't never want to end up in Crime Class,' was all Maggie could say. 'Someone else we have ter watch out for is that chaplain. One of the women in the nursery told me that when she sees Reverend Broadwater struttin' about the pews preachin' about the fires of hell for us sinners, she almost pukes. He gets so worked up about it, his beaky nose starts wobblin' and he puffs up like a rooster.' We both laughed at that, imagining the reverend as a rooster wearing a collar back-the-front. 'The bastard feels up girls all the time, she said. Pious old git.'

'We must be sure to stay out of his way then,' I said, horrified to hear such news about a man of the cloth.

Two and a half weeks after Christmas we Yard One women were told that a local settler wanted a convict for domestic service and that he would be coming the next morning. When she called for us to be ready, Matron had said, we would have to be quick about it and form orderly lines in the yard for the settler to make a selection.

Maggie and I looked at each other with excitement. 'That'll be you what's chosen first I reckon Sarah. Looks like Dr. James were true to his word.'

'Oh we don't know about that!' I said, flushed and excited, thinking the same thing but not daring to hold out too much hope. I had waited so long for this. 'Perhaps he just went back to England and didn't think anything more about me. Perhaps he didn't really mean what he'd said. Perhaps he thought I was just a loose woman with no morals.'

'Thems a lot of *p'raps,* Sarah. No, I reckon you'll be the first to go. But *p'raps* he'll want some of us others as well.'

Neither of us had much sleep that night. I was tossing and turning, dreaming of leaving the Factory and in my dreams Robert appeared, assuring me. But how much notice could I take of dreams?

I made sure I looked spick and span for the line-up, taking more care than usual with my appearance, running my fingers through my hair, putting my bonnet properly in place, and patting down any creases in my skirt. Matron walked down the rows of women lined up and six of us were ordered to step forward, including myself and Maggie. The other women were told to return to their duties. The six of us all looked at each other out of the corner of our eyes wondering if it were possible that the settler might select all of us. Matron left us, walking over to the Factory office. After a few minutes she opened the door and walked out towards us. We strained to see who was walking behind her. It was a gentleman and his wife, both of them dressed in plain clothes, nothing fancy like some of the other people we'd glimpsed on our long walk to the Factory that first day. The couple came over to the six of us, looked us over quickly then came back to take a closer look at me. Satisfied that they had found the right one, they walked back to the office with Matron.

When Matron returned to our line-up, she announced, 'Sarah Hamilton, step forward. The rest of you can go back to your tasks. Gather your things Sarah. You will be on assignment in a house of Quaker gentlefolk in Hobart Town.'

I was so relieved to be chosen, but turned to Maggie, desperately sad that I would be leaving her. I had only a brief moment to speak to her, as I knew she would be occupied in the Nursery when I left.

'I'll try to get word to you Maggie, about where I am. Take care of yourself dear friend. I wonder what Quakers are like.' We quickly embraced and I hurried away.

Chapter 4

# *Maggie*

*5th February, 1837*

For the first two weeks after Sarah left, I were that lonely. Would I ever see her again I wondered. Seven years without me friend in this gloomy place. When I weren't workin' in the Nursery, I moped about by meself in the yard, not wantin' to talk to anybody. But it got worse. Much worse.

At the next mornin' chapel, after Reverend Broadwater's usual rantin's to us women about sin and wickedness, eyein' us all over like we was she-devils, he come over to me. 'Would you please stay behind after the others have gone. I would like to discuss the children in the nursery,' he said to me. But he had a peculiar look on his face when he said it.

'What's he up to?' I thought. Somethin' fishy here. 'I can't say no, he's our Reverend. Can't just walk out.'

When all the other women went he sat himself down in one of the pews and pointed with his hand to the space next to him, lettin' me know he wanted me ter to sit down beside him, 'so that we might be more comfortable'. He put down the Bible he was carryin', and moved a bit closer to me. 'I was wondering how you are doing with the babies and children in the nursery. Maggie your name is, isn't it?'

'Yes Reverend,' I answered, startin' to feel real uncomfortable. He were lookin' at me through them spectacles what make yer eyes real big. First at me face, but then his eyes slid down to me breasts.

'You know you can always confide in me.'

*What's he on about?* I thought as his clammy hands lifted mine from me lap and his fat fingers began strokin' mine. His breath were so close to me face I could smell his breakfast. Still not sure of where this were leadin' but knowin' it weren't goin' to end well. I looked away from him, tryin' to pull me hand away. But he kept an iron grip on it. From the garbled rot he were talkin', I could see he weren't interested one little bit in the toddlers and babies in the nursery. No sir. I'd seen that look on men's faces before. Suddenly he grabbed at one of me tits with his free hand, forcin' me down on to the hard pew at the same time. *He's a bloody octopus, he is,* I thought as I tried to fend him off.

'Lemme go, stop that!'

But too late. He'd yanked at me chemise, his face sweatin' like a pig and dived into me breasts with his wet sloppy mouth, squeezin' them with one hand while the other one slithered up me legs.

'Get off me yer bastard. Yer no Christian, yer ugly fat lump!'

His heavin' body moved off me just long enough for him to fumble with his cossack to get out his fast-swellin' purple cock. But he took a bit too long. In that split second I pushed him with all the force I could muster, and the slim bench were too narrow for us both. We fell with a loud thump onto the floor between the pews, a pile of flesh and tangled limbs.

'Help!' I shouted at the top of me voice, 'Help, someone! Help!' I kept it up so long that he stood up, tidied himself up, and straightened his cossack to cover the lump between his legs. Just in time, for by now two of the other convict women, hearin' the noise and the shouts, come runnin' in.

'Stupid girl,' he said to me in front of them, makin' out like it were my fault. 'What are you up to, trying to seduce me?'

They wasn't stupid. They could see what he'd been up to, but it was the Reverend's word against mine and he told one of them to fetch Matron.

'What's going on?' she said when she arrived, out of breath and lookin' annoyed at bein' called.

'Why, this sinful girl tried to seduce me Matron, baring her breasts and enticing me — right here in the church. No respect whatsoever. When I tried to cover her up for decency's sake, she shouted out that I was attacking her. Disgraceful hussy.'

'That ain't true Matron. Reverend tried to force 'imself on me!' But even as I said them words I knew it weren't goin' to make one bit of difference.

'You are a wicked girl. Go back to your dormitory. I'll deal with you later,' Matron ordered. 'There's no place for trouble-makers in Yard One. You others, go back to your chores.'

After me trouble with Reverend Broadwater, Matron sent me to Crime Class. No more hopin' for a early assignment now, even if Dr. James had put in a good word for me like he said he would. Not fair me gettin' blamed. But then, who said life were fair, eh? I'll just have to make the best of it.

Still no word from Sarah. I didn't think I were ever goin' to get out of the dark place I were in when she left. Grey buildin' to live in and grey fog in me mind. Whatever were I to do with meself? At least with Sarah around we could natter to one another and have a chat about things. I wish she'd write. I were sittin' on the wooden bench in Yard Three thinkin' about all this when one of the Irish girls come up to me. It were that red-headed one, Kathleen.

'I heard what happened Maggie,' she said to me as she sat down beside me, 'I still haven't been out on assignment yet either.'

'It's a shock comin' here. Different to Yard One. The women here looks like they doesn't care what happens to 'em. In Yard One there's more — I dunno — hope. They might be picked for service and the chance to get out.'

The Irish girl give a nod, 'I know what you mean. You have to be more careful in here too. Some of the women have been here for a long time, and get up to all kinds of shenanigans. You don't know the half of it Maggie.'

'It's goin' to take a long time before we get outa Crime Class. Unless we scarp it,' I said to her. Funny me sayin' that. Scarpin' it didn't cross me mind before. We was both quiet then. She were prob'ly thinkin' the same as me, wonderin' what we'd do if we did escape from the Factory. Lost in our thoughts, the bell went, lettin' us know it were time to get back ter work.

Me job in Yard Three were pickin' oakum. That awful job I didn't never want to do — pullin' hard bits of tar outa old rope so they could use the rope again. It didn't half rip inta me hands. They was red-raw by the end of the day, and all blistered and cracked — the first day anyway, before they become hardened to it. I could see Kathleen liftin' heavy wet sheets outa the wash-tubs and hangin' them up on lines strung across the yard and Agnes next to her, bendin' over the washtubs with her arms up to the elbows in cold water, scrubbin' at sheets and soldiers' laundry what'd come in from outside to be laundered.

First oppertunity we got for a break, Kathleen joined me again.

'To pass the time away,' she said to me, 'after Matron and Superintendent retire for the evening, us women tell each other stories and if there's any grog to pass around a couple of us might start singing, then doing a bit of a jig. It keeps us entertained. You'll see Maggie. Sometimes we dress up a bit in anything we can find, bright scarves, flashy earrings, anything that jingles, and colourful ribbons and shawls. It makes us feel good, like we're free.'

Me eyes brightened at the prospect of havin' a sing-song and a laugh. 'I've heard yer all from Yard One. A coupla times I heard Matron scurryin' down at night when there were a loud din goin' on.'

''Tis true Maggie. We love to sing ditties that poke fun at people, especially the Matron and the Superintendent. Matron doesn't like this at all. It makes her so cranky!'

I saw Agnes makin' her way over to me then, just as I were thinkin' of goin' over to say hello to her. She took a good look at Kathleen, then turned to me.

'Hello, lass. I heard about that bastard Reverend and what he did tae ye. The dirty bastard, pretendin' tae be righteous, when all the time he's thinkin' but nae else than liftin' up young lasses' petticoats. And he calls himself a Christian. Me and some of the others hae got somethin' planned for him. Make no mistake about it!'

'What have yer got planned Agnes?'

'Never ye mind just yet, Maggie. But it won't be long. We'll get him. He'll be sorry he ever tried anythin' on ye lass,' she said with a sly grin and a wink and walked away.

I soon found out that Ellen had been transported in 1830 and were the ringleader of the Flash Mob what Agnes had joined up with. I looked around to see where Ellen were, and spied her standin' in a corner in a group, Agnes next to her. Such a tiny thing is Ellen — must be less than five foot tall. Yet a little ball of trouble. Looked like she were popular, though.

The woman standin' next to me could see where I were lookin'. 'That's Ellen,' she said, 'After just three weeks in the Factory when she first arrived, she'd been charged with forty-eight offences! Not hard to do though, you can get into trouble inside or outside the Factory for the least little thing. Ellen's been in and out of solitary a lot. It doesn't make a bit of difference to her. She doesn't seem to care.'

We both sneaked another peek at the wiry little Ellen. Such a cheeky air about her. Yer could see she weren't no-one to mess with, in spite of her bein' so tiny. I thought to meself I'd be sure to keep clear of that Flash Mob. I didn't want to get on the wrong side of anyone in here.

'One woman who's a bit afraid of Ellen,' the woman beside me went on, 'told me that one time Ellen was sent back to Crime Class from assignment outside and made to wear the spiked iron collar. They didn't say what she did. She's always gettin' into trouble for runnin' away and goin' off to a pub in Hobart Town. But that time, she got the collar and a month in solitary. It's a terrible long time. They say it's the longest in solitary that anyone's ever had in here.'

'Musta been serious. I wonder what she done. A month! I'd go mad,' and we both looked at her again. Couldn't help admirin' someone like that. That long in solitary and she didn't go insane. We'd all heard the mad mutterin's, screams, and nightmare sounds comin' from prisoners locked up in solitary too long. That's a sound yer'd never forget, I thought, the sound of a woman gone mad. But four weeks. Gawd!

A month went by. Then two. Then three. Children was dyin' in the Nursery and we heard their little dead bodies was taken out under the cover of darkness. (News travels like fire in 'ere, no matter which class yer in). Nobody knew where they was taken, or what happened to 'em. It were a mystery. The last death in the Factory were infant Thomas. Instead of bein' hushed up this time, the case of this dead baby reached the newspapers, causin' an outcry from the public what read about it, as well as anger from us convict women. Early one night when Crime Class were quiet, even the Flash Mob, I were sittin' with a couple of others, listenin' to the talk among the women.

'Did ya hear about that woman who come in with her baby Thomas?' one of them said.

'That I did. She's Irish, from the county next to mine,' said another one. 'I heard she came over as a free immigrant and 'twas arranged she would marry her emancipist husband as soon as she arrived. Because they didn't have much money, the two of them, she worked as a housemaid for a family in Hobart Town.'

'Aye, that's what I heard as well,' said Agnes, joinin' in.

'But she were charged with stealin',' I added to the talk, recollectin' the story. I tried to remember just what it was she'd been accused of nickin'. 'A silver plate I think, from the household. I don't know if it were true, but she ended up in trouble. And she already had baby Thomas as well by that time. Before she come here to the Factory some sort of arrangement were promised to her husband that his wife'd be able to look after Thomas and nurse him herself so's he weren't weaned too early.'

'That's the way it was,' said another Irish woman. 'But the promise wasn't kept, and when he was put into the nursery she wasn't allowed to see him.' We shook our heads thinkin' about it. 'Well she was that upset – she pleaded with Matron and Superintendent to be able to look after baby Thomas. But they said she could not, and she didn't get to see him for five days.'

I could see she were gettin' a lot out of tellin' the tale, like a true Irish, and she looked around at all our faces hangin' on, waitin' for the rest.

'She was frantic by that time, weepin' and callin' out for him, tryin' to get through to the nursery.' By this time she were makin' all the sounds along with the story and she were gettin' us all in. 'When she did finally see him, the poor little mite was so sick, and altered much for the worse. He just lay without movin' in his mother's arms.'

All of us women was real quiet then, sittin' around imaginin' the poor mother with her small baby limp in her arms. We'd seen some bad things, but when it come ter the babies, all of us women was close to tears, especially the ones what was mothers themselves.

'She begged Matron to give her a scrap of paper to write to her husband about poor Thomas,' said the same Irish woman. 'Matron told her if she didn't behave herself she'd be going into a cell, never mind about any piece of paper.'

'Aye, but the poor mither found another way tae send a message to her husband,' said Agnes, 'through the same turnkey I know.'

'As soon as he received his wife's note,' said the Irish woman, who seemed to know more of the details than Agnes, 'he demanded that Thomas be given to him to look after. Not wanting any more fuss about it all, the Superintendent allowed him to take Thomas. But it was too late. By the time Thomas was taken to his father's home, he was too far gone, and after only a couple of days, the poor little mite died. His mother never saw her child again.' And she sat back, crossin' her hands in her lap, lookin' like that were the end of the story.

'Poor wee laddie. Nobody cares about people like us.' But Agnes were wrong there. There was folk outside didn't like what they read about the goin's-on in here — babies dyin' and the like. It were in the newspapers.

'This place ain't called the Valley of the Shadow of Death for nothin',' I said to Agnes one day. 'In the last three months there's been twenty deaths, and no inquests about any of 'em. I heard it from someone in the nursery. It ain't just the babies. Them outside is lookin' into Barbara Hunter's death last week. None of us knows what happened to her neither.'

'Aye. Barbara Hunter,' Agnes said. 'Ma turnkey mate said he read about it in the newspaper. We didnae even hear about it 'til then. They wrote her death was *due to Di-a-ree-a and fever* because of *neg-li-gence of the medical officers.* That's what he read out loud tae me.' I thought, if Sarah was here I could ask her how to write them words down.

'Likely nothin' will come of it,' I said to Agnes. Still, I thought, there might be some good people in Hobart Town what want to make things better for all of us. Just like Mrs. Elizabeth Fry back in London. And now Sarah's outside, why she might be able ter do somethin'. But I doubt things'll ever change. I wonder why Sarah don't write?

One mornin' in October when Agnes and me was sittin' together in the yard, Agnes said she had a bit of information from her favourite turnkey.

'There's some do-gooders comin' tae visit us tomorrow. Not that they do much good! They think all we hae tae do is mend our ways and everythin' will be fixed — nae idea what the likes of some of us hae been through.'

'What have yer heard Agnes?'

'It be the Governor of Van Diemen's Land comin'!'

'I heard that too Agnes, and he'll be bringin' some good society ladies with him so they can see what conditions in here is like.'

'Aye. Well, we got somethin' planned for them they will nae be expectin'!' Agnes had a pleased look on her face like a cat what swallowed the cream. Like yer do when you know somethin' top secret. Her eyes was dancin' with mischief and her pasty skin had a bit of a flush to it. 'Reverend Broadwater will be on his best behaviour,' Agnes went on, 'tryin' tae impress the Governor and his party of fine ladies and gentlemen. They might be seein' more than was planned!'

At that, she walked away laughin', a sight nobody seen too often. She joined Ellen and some others huddled together, schemin' about somethin' and then burstin' into laughter. At different times in the afternoon they'd keep doin' that together, huddlin' and laughin'. The Flash Mob were quiet that night. Whatever they was plottin' looked like it were goin' to happen the next mornin'.

After breakfast we was told to tidy ourselves up and to march in a orderly line to the Chapel. A bit later when we was all there waitin', we saw the Governor's party enter and move to a platform behind a railin', raised up a bit where they could see out over the heads of all us women. The Governor were standin' there, and next ter him was his wife and two other ladies dressed up in their gloves and hats and lookin' important. There were a couple of soldiers in uniforms as well, with rifles. Standin' ter the side of all of them was the simperin' Reverend Broadwater, the bastard what got me sent to Crime Class.

We was all told ter stand, and sing the first hymn. The Governor's party joined us in liftin' our voices to the Lord, and when it were finished, Reverend Broadwater made his way to the pulpit, dressed in a cossack what had been specially laundered and ironed to impress the party of visitors. Pumped up old rooster. He turned to them and bowed, then opened his mouth to begin the sermon he must have spent many long hours preparin', first lookin' down at all of us women and rufflin' his feathers. Real pleased with himself he were. If only them ladies knew what he got up to, eh?

The Governor was lookin' a bit bored with it all, like he wanted to be somewhere else. But I saw the ladies in his party takin' a good look at us convict women. They was real curious about all of us, lookin' us over from head to toe, makin' notes in their heads about what they was goin' to tell their friends next time they had 'em over for a cuppa tea. Prob'ly never seen so many bad types so close up. That'd be it. Yer could see they thought we all smelt terrible, the way they kept pullin' their dainty lace hankies out of their purses to cover their noses, but tryin' to do it secret-like, so's not to appear rude.

It were dead quiet for a minute while Reverend Broadwater shuffled his sermon papers. When he were about to speak I happened ter glance over at Agnes outa the corner of me eye. She were lookin' at Ellen. Real intent. Like she were waitin' for some kind of signal. Looked like there were a plan afoot. Somethin' big were about ter happen. For a minute time seemed ter stand still. A lot of the women was fired up ready for whatever it were. It were like when we was on the ship in the doldrums, before the wind come up ter send the ship on its way. Everyone waitin'. The Governor and his party were like statues up there, likely thinkin' whenever were he goin' to start the sermon.

I looked at them, then back at Agnes and followed where her eyes was lookin'. To where Ellen were. Then I saw Ellen give Agnes a wink. Such a cheeky excited look she had on her face. Then it happened, what the Flash Mob and all of them in the know had planned. What's this, I thought. In the next second, the Flash Mob all turned their backs to the pulpit, hitched up their skirts, and bent over to flash their bare bums at the Reverend and the Governor's party!

Well! None of us others knew anythin' about this plan. But that didn't make no difference. Straightaway, the rest of us follered their lead. Hundreds of bare arses all pointed in the direction of the Governor and his party! Not content with that, we all smacked 'em with a almighty *whack*! Like a ship's sails crackin' in the wind. The Governor were dumbfounded, frozen in shock. It were plain he had no idea what to do. I took a peek up at them all. The ladies eyes was wide like they couldn't believe what was goin' on. Then they looked at one another and started laughin' in spite of tryin' not to. Their lace-gloved hands fluttered up to their faces tryin' to cover their laughter and compose theirselves. But ter no avail.

It were bedlam. Not from us prisoners. No sir. We kept bendin' over, holdin' on to our skirts above our waists while wardens, constables and anyone what could be mustered at short notice run about in a flap. But what could they do with so many women? We was already in prison, and we was quiet as lambs. I thought Reverend Broadwater's eyes'd pop outa his head! Meanwhile, the Governor and his party was ushered out quick-smart.

When we was back in our quarters, before Matron had decided on what punishment should be meted out for such shockin' behaviour, we laughed so hard, we couldn't stop. We laughed about it for weeks. In the end, the ringleaders, Ellen, Agnes, and two others was put into solitary, and all of us was given bread and water as punishment for three days. But was it worth it!

One time the next month, I found meself next to quiet, timid Josie Wilson. We come over on the same transport ship but we didn't have much to do with each other on the ship. One evenin' I were standin' behind her when we was movin' along the line to get our stew, and we sat next to each other at the mess table. I were lookin' down at me bowl of stew thinkin' it would be nice to eat somethin'

a bit different, and wonderin' what I could trade to get some better grub, when Josie surprised me outa me thoughts.

'How are you today Maggie?' she said.

'Not real good, I didn't sleep a wink last night.'

'Me neither.'

'Sometimes I think the night-times is the worst,' I said to her, 'I stay awake for hours, thinkin' of me family, me body achin' for the missin' of 'em, and listenin' to the groans and nightmares of everyone.'

'I know,' she said. 'It's quiet and dark except for the snorin' and moans of them lucky enough to sleep, and others callin' out names of their loved ones and children in their dreams.'

'I wonder if any of us will ever have anythin' but a life of hardship.' I looked around at the sad faces of most of the women. Even when they was playin' up they was still a sorry lookin' lot most of the time.

'I know what you mean.' After a bit she come closer to me, like she wanted to tell me somethin'. I could see she were lookin' at somethin' on the other side of the room, but I couldn't make out just who or what. Then she said, 'I don't sleep because I'm afeared. See that woman over there Maggie?' she said to me, pointin' with her eyes to Thelma what always had a scowl on her face. 'Don't let her see yer lookin' at her!' she said with panic in her voice, her eyes openin' wide when I looked where she were pointin'.

'Yer mean Thelma? The rough one with a bit of a limp?'

'Yes, that's the one.'

'What about her?'

'One night, she said I'd stole a fug of tobacco that belonged to her. She said to me: "I knows yer got it. Yer hid it inside yerself." I didn't know what she was talkin' about and I never had her bleedin' tobacco. Before I even had time to deny it, she sat on my hammock, and her friend, tough as her, pinned me down, holdin' me so I couldn't move. Thelma pushed up my skirts, rough-like, and her hand grabbed me. Then with such a force, she shoved her fingers up as far as she was able, keepin' her hand there for some time, movin' it about, convinced I'd hidden baccy in there!'

Well, I knew what she meant, all right. Poor shy little Josie havin' ter put up with that.

'When they did this to me, I was that frightened and in terrible pain. I was in agony for hours and finally had to get help. By mornin' I was white as a sheet and doubled up. There was big patches of blood over my skirt. Matron come to see what the fuss was about and soon as she saw me, she sent me to the hospital. When the doctor come, he said, "who did this to you?" But I was too scared to tell him in case Thelma got back at me again another time.'

We both turned back to our stew and didn't say no more. Bleedin' hell I thought, Crime Class is right scary. Knowin' what happened to Josie I said to meself, I'm goin' to keep quiet as a mouse. If that Thelma looks like comin' me way, I'll slip away as far as I can before she can get to me. But yer have to stay always on the look-out.

I'm that sick of bein' in here — I think I'll talk to Agnes about gettin' out. When she gets out of solitary, that is.

## Chapter 5

# *Agnes*

*20th October 1837*

Back in a solitary cell agin. Stuck in this unholy place with barely room tae move. No-one tae talk to. Not enough room tae lie straight out, gropin' in the dark for somewhere tae relieve maself. A filthy floor tae lie on, a small stool next tae me and a bucket tae piss in. Three days with nae light. Darkness and silence with nought tae do but fight against ma own wild thoughts.

Ma last time in solitary be on the ship. That Dr. James had it in for me from the start. He didnae like ma looks and had me pegged as a troublemaker. The bastard. Not content tae shame me on deck — orderin' a sailor to shave ma hair in front o' the whole ship, aye. "Troublemakers will not be tolerated on this ship," he said as a warnin' tae others. That be after the tassle I had with Martha. The next time I got intae a fight, he was set on sendin' me tae solitary. Not enough tae shame me on deck. In any case, I had nae hair to shave by then. Nae, it was a punishment I would ne'er forget.

The memory o' it comes floodin' back tae me now. Forced intae the gloomiest part o' the ship where they keep the coal for the galley fires. The coal hole. Hole be right. Black as pitch it was. Just thinkin' about it makes ma blood run cold. Them two sailors that took me down shuddered when they saw where they had tae put me. I was that close to them I could feel it, and hear them draw a breath. I dinnae think they'd seen it afore. Only heard about it. The Black Box they called it. They felt sorry for me when they opened up the door and pushed me inside. I heard one o' them say, "Poor bitch, I wouldn't wish this on anyone". Then I was left down there by maself after they'd gone.

I thought I'd suffocate, or drown just from the sound o' the water all around me. No air, and ma own vomit tae keep me company. What sort o' cruel mind would think o' punishment like that? A tight wooden box, rockin' and pitchin' with the rhythm o' the ocean. Water oozin' in through cracks in the wooden floor. Ma clothes stayed wet the whole time. Damp was everywhere. I had tae be standin' up for the whole time, or crouch. Nae room tae spread out and lie down. I had plenty o' time tae feel the walls — scratches on it that felt like the poor soul in there afore me had scratched her name on the wood. I tried tae feel over the letters tae make out what the lass's name was. I could nae work out how she could hae done it. She must hae taken in somethin' sharp.

Twenty-four hours I was locked into that torture of a place. By the end o' the twenty-four hours ma feet were like prunes and ma wet skirt clung tae ma body, blue with the cold. Not fit for any human bein'. When they came tae fetch me the next day, ma legs had cramped up and the sailors had tae drag me back tae the women's quarters. I could see they were almost sick with the smell o' ma vomit and what had leaked from ma body. Does nae bear thinkin' about. I'll go mad if I do.

Now here. In a solitary cell at the Factory. But this time nae rockin' and pitchin', and nae sound o' the sea or smell o' the bilge and salt air. I should be able tae stand it. But three days be a long time in the dark with just bread and water shoved in tae keep me from starvin'. Nightmare beasts be ma only companions, and vivid memories o' dark alleys full o' tall dark shapes forcin' me to do all manner o' things with ma scrawny child's body.

When I was about six years old, I found ma mither lyin' dead in an alley. The back o' her bloodied head was caved in and she was face-down in a cesspool. From the look o' her she must hae been there all night — she was covered in sewer rats chewin' at her ears and nose. Her fingertips was almost eat away. An old woman found me cryin' next tae her body and rockin' back and forth. She took pity on me and told me tae follow her tae her place. I stayed wi' her for a year or so. She was an old whore, too old tae get much work but she was kind tae me in her way. When she died o' the consumption I was back out on the streets agin with no-one tae look after me. Not yet eight years old, I had tae survive as best I could. I roamed around and met other bairns livin' on the street, dirty urchins like me. We had tae learn tae take care of ourselves real quick, or end up dead.

We were hungry all the time, scratchin' for crumbs o' bread, and tryin' tae keep out o' the way of both the law and the men roamin' around lookin' for young bairns tae satisfy their lust, or a virgin tae cure their syphilis. Stupid old buggers. They liked findin' young'uns. If they found one wanderin' around alone at night, they thought they were in. No family tae contend with there, and they could get away with anythin' at all.

I teamed up with a lad a couple o' years older than me. Then another girl came on the scene. And a bit later, another couple o' bairns. We kind o' looked out for each other. If someone was in trouble the others would help. If they were around that is.

One night when I was ferretin' through some rubbish for somethin' tae eat, a gentleman came up tae me. I knew from the familiar look in his eye that he was up tae no good. He was tall and dressed like a toff. Thin but strong. He grabbed me and dragged me intae a nearby alley and soon had me backed up against the wall. His hand started gropin' me all o'er, then moved quickly down to between ma legs. I shouted out, hopin' that some of the other bairns might hear me. Just as he was about tae do the deed, some o' the other bairns came runnin' and got his attention — just long enough for me tae push past him and run for ma life.

The winters were the worst. We had tae do anythin' we could tae keep from the cold and starvation. Sometimes we'd sneak intae houses if people accidentally left a window open or a door unlocked, beddin' down 'til the early hours o' the mornin'. Afore we left we'd ransack the kitchen for any food tae take with us. Might be lucky. If there was nowhere like this, we had tae find old newspapers, or scraps o' rags tae act as blankets and sleep on the streets. The only clothes we had tae wear through the bitter cold o' Scottish winters was rags and tatters, with nothin' tae cover our bare feet, purple with the cold.

Ma daily bread and water be comin'. I can hear. Next, there'll be a thin shaft o' light peekin' through afore they shove it in. When the light comes in I'm blinded by it at first, then I see the cockroaches runnin' about fast, tae get away from the shock o' the light. Then blackness agin. I have tae keep talkin' tae maself so I don't go balmy.

Ma name be Agnes. Agnes MacDonald. If I say it oft enough, I be still a person.

I was but thirteen years old when a man forced himself on me proper hard. Real rough he was. A couple o' months after that I was beat up by another bastard. That one was dressed up like a gentleman too. After that, I bled a lot. From what I saw come out o' me I must hae been in trouble. It made me so ill, I thought ma time had come.

When I recovered from ma illness, I met up with a lively group o' lads who taught me how tae survive through beggin', thievin', and entertainin' folks in the local markets. Because I was young and bonnie then, ma job was tae dance and sing in such a way as tae encourage passers-by tae throw pennies into an old hat we had. Safety in numbers. We could call out tae each other to run if we saw trouble comin'. I lived this way for over a year, movin' from one market tae another, and one street corner tae another, until one day I was nabbed. Other times I'd been able tae escape by guile and a fast run but that day I was nae match for the strong arm o' the law, and found maself locked up.

I was let out after a wee while, bein' just a young lass, so I went back tae ma old street friends, and survived by gettin' work as a whore. After a year or so ma body was showin' that I was nae longer a lass but a young woman and I had plenty o' men comin' after me — a different kind o' man then — them that like full-grown women instead o' bairns. More roughin' up. No end tae that. Some men seem tae get more excited when they bash up a whore. I learned tae look out for one gentleman who was a pertickly cruel and nasty piece o' work. When I spied him, I'd run as fast as ma legs would carry me.

Ye have to be on the lookout all the time.

Over a couple o' years I lost ma looks from all the bashin's, especially after the knifin' by the slasher. With a lot o' practice, I became skilled at thievery. Pickin' pockets mainly, an art taught tae me by some o' ma older mates. Much later, I turned tae the art o' child strippin'. When ye spy one o' them well-to-do bairns, it's easy. Ye start a bit of a conversation with them. 'How are ye goin' there ma bonnie sweet thing?' ye might say. 'All alone are ye?' Then ye promise to give them a doll, or some sweets, or even a pony — if they follow you.

Well, what else could I do? With ma looks after the slashin', I couldnae get too much money with the whorin'. There were plenty o' pretty young things for that. Anyways, it was good money — the child strippin'. Until I got caught, that is.

It was the night I saw a young lad. Must hae wandered away from his parents when they were nae payin' attention. He was one o' those lads that are doted on by his parents and spoilt. But full o' curiosity. When I spied the clothes he was wearin' I knew there would be a good market for them. Fine stockin's, leather shoes with buckles, tailored breeches and a jacket of the best wool out of the mills, as well as a silk shirt and a fancy woollen hat on his head. I looked around tae see where his mither was but she was nowhere tae be seen. *Here's an easy steal,* I thought tae maself. When I'd done the deed I hurried away from the place fast as I could. I heard him cryin', but paid nae heed. Two blocks away I ran intae the arms of a policeman, suspicious o' what I was carryin'.

I was charged with 'abductin' a young boy'. Bad enough, they said. But tae leave him 'stranded and near-naked in the cold evenin' air' was what got me ma long sentence. 'He could have died,' said the judge if a passer-by had nae heard him 'cryin' in distress.' I didnae ken what all the fuss was about. He got sick, but he didnae die. Anyways, because what I did was considered a 'heinous crime', I got double the usual seven year sentence o' transportation.

Fourteen years! How was I tae know the bairn would get that sick? It was nae like I murdered someone.

Mind ye, after years o' gettin' away with all kinds o' petty crimes like the time I stole a watch and chain from a rich toff on the street, and other crimes I'd rather keep quiet about, I suppose I was fortunate tae nae be taken a lot earlier. They could hae got me for robbery another time — like when I threatened a toff with a knife as he were comin' out of a brothel in a dark alley. I only meant tae put the fear intae him so he'd part with his money, but he fought back. So I let him have it. He was just a little man, not much bigger than me, and was he scared!

I hate solitary. Some o' the women put in solitary fall ill tae madness or terrible melancholy. Got tae keep maself occupied with other thoughts. There's rats in here too. I bide ma time by listenin' tae them runnin' around ma cell. Somethin' tae do tae pass the time away. Ma name is Agnes. Agnes MacDonald.

That transport ship. Vile it was. Except for the nights o' singin' and cavortin' with the women in our sleepin' quarters. The ones that hadnae thrown in their lot wi' the sailors. We had a rare old time, we did. I got used tae bein' punished, and came ashore in Van Diemen's Land with ma hair cut real close tae ma head. I didnae like that ship's doctor.

One night there was a terrible tae-do down below in the orlop deck. A lass called Tilly wanted tae mark herself with the memory o' her boyfriend back in London Town and decided tae prick a tattoo on herself. She managed tae get hold of a piece o' bone from the cook, and whittled it down tae a sharp point. She asked one o' the other women who knew her letters tae write down the letters of his name so she could copy them on her arm. Then she started prickin' herself with the sharpened bone, copyin' the letters this other woman hae showed her.

She used lamp soot tae rub into the skin tae make the ink. Did it when we were all down below deck so she wouldnae be found out. She would hae been in trouble if the Captain or the doctor got wind of it. She waited until the hatch was well fastened, and every night for a week, on her right arm above the elbow she added bits tae the tattoo: 'ILJC', the initials o' her boyfriend, James Cocker, after the letters for 'I Love' — and a heart as well. I watched how she did it.

Now when Mavis, another lass from the same place as Tilly back in London Town, found out that James Cocker was one and the same person as the man she thought was hers, it caused a terrible tae-do, with the two women screamin' at each other and punchin' and pullin' each other's hair. Another three women dragged them apart and told them tae be silent or we'd all be in trouble. That put an end tae it for the time bein', but durin' the whole voyage Tilly and Mavis would glare at one another. Ye could see they hated each other.

That's what jealousy does tae ye, eh?

I hae tae grope around for the bucket tae pee in. Cannae see a thing. I dinnae ken if it be day or night in here. Only when they bring the food — such as it is — then I know it's daylight. But when the cell door slams shut agin, it be night for me until the next lot o' bread and water. Ma name is Agnes. Agnes MacDonald.

I can feel this spiked collar somethin' terrible today. Heavy it is too. I have tae keep talkin' tae maself as I cannae sleep too good with that stickin' intae me. They keep the collar for the ones that play up a lot. Ellen told me she had the collar when she was in solitary.

What a lark is Ellen!

Ellen, Cate, and others in Crime Class made ma life in the Factory bearable. Ellen's the mainstay o' the Flash Mob. We get up tae all sorts o' mischief. A lot of our shenanigans is even reported in the newspapers. I heard they was comparin' us tae creatures in some play written by a man by the name of Goat, or somethin' like that. He wrote some play called *Faust*, and in this play there was somethin' they called '*abominable Saturnalia*'. I didnae ken about all this, but that's what one o' the turnkeys told us after he read the newspaper.

It makes ma time in solitary pass when I think o' what the Mob gets up tae.

When the Matron finishes her tasks for the day and retires tae her quarters with her husband, us Mob gets up tae some mischief. For I was in with them all right. As soon as I was put intae Crime Class. In the dark o' night, one or two of us might start tae sing and make merry, and the rest take up the song if they know it. We like tae dress up and sing dirty ditties once it gets dark, and smoke baccy in our pipes and drink the sly grog we sometimes get our hands on. That way we feel we be in charge of our lives and let the devil take the rest o' them.

These times the air is thick with baccy smoke and the smell o' warm bodies, cheap perfume and the noise from our dirty ditties and cursin', as well as the shrieks o' passion comin' from the darker corners. We really let our hair down and near forget we be the *stain on Van Diemen's Land society*. On nights like this, we take care tae post a guard at the place where Matron can enter our area and discover what we're up tae. Not that she can't hear it all from her bedroom. She can. But by the time she gets from her own quarters back there on the second floor, tae ours, all she sees is us women back in our places, innocent as wee bairns.

We all have tae attend divine service with that pudgy-faced fuckin' dog's breath of a minister. He stands up there spoutin' righteous rubbish about sin and how we will all go tae hell if we dinnae mend our ways. His bulbous nose wobblin', all his chins quiverin', and his wet mouth sendin' out sprays o' spittle into the air as he delivers his sermon.

What a fuckin' hypocrite! Standin' up there in the pulpit preachin' tae us on the sabbath about our wicked and immoral ways when on week days, every chance he gets he makes different women lift up their skirts for his pleasure, or even in the pews themselves when no one be watchin', forcin' his short, fat, sweaty body on the young weak women without their consent. If any of us make the mistake o' reportin' him tae Matron, it be the woman faces the consequences. If he ever tries that on wi' me I'll tell him tae skedaddle, and twist his privates until he screams in agony. Poxy old fart.

The most wicked of all, he said, is those of us what 'engages in unnatural connexions'. This was whispered about by them outside as somethin' vile and obscene, but we didnae give a damn about them. We be considered tae be 'daughters of the devil'. Though I suspect many o' those old gossips and narks outside the Factory might want tae act as we do if they had the chance.

We thought up a system inside that allows us tae slip outside some nights. The turnkeys can be bribed tae let us out, and then back in, as long as we make it worth their while. There's a track just behind the Factory. It's only a couple o' miles walk tae Hobart Town.

On the way in there be spots where folk pass out after a night o' drinkin' a wee too much whisky. Kicked out o' the pub by the owner, they head for the riverbank. Those with nae home set up camp next tae the stream. Right at the end o' the track when it starts tae be town there be cheap houses where whores can entertain the Redcoats and whalers.

We pay the turnkeys with cash or grog the times we scarp it, and smuggle in extras for ourselves — snuff, cigars, pipe baccy, grog. Anythin' we can get our hands on. Some o' the women like ribbons and perfume as well. It's easy enough tae get coin tae buy grog — with slippery hands in a sailor's pocket, or a bit o' extras on the side.

Sometimes we get caught, especially if we play up and they can see we're from the Factory. Our favourite places tae frequent for an evenin' o' jollification, are the public houses in Hobart Town. I've been caught and sent back for singin' ma lungs out and 'carryin' on in a public house'. Ye have tae be a bit sly if ye dinnae want tae end up back here afore the night is out.

Hobart is full o' drinkin' dens and sly-grog shops that sell all kinds o' home-made liquor. Them Temperance Society ladies don't know the half of it. I had tae keep out o' sight o' them soldiers in their uniforms because they like tae keep their eyes on what goes on around the wharves. That *Commercial Hotel* on the Old Wharf is always good for a bit o' fun. It's real noisy, the pipe smoke so thick you could cut it, and always awash with rough seafarin' men — real big drinkers. But I can drink some of 'em under the table. In for a penny, in for a pound. I've stayed up all night drinkin' with 'em, on nights when the local whores are too busy tae spend time talkin' tae me. The publicans dinnae seem tae take too much notice o' keepin' tae closin' times. The whale lamps burn all night.

Times outside the Factory I could hae run away into the bush — but it be nae place for the likes o' me. At least, in the Factory, it be the devil ye know. In any case, I'd rather be with ma special friends here inside than outside and havin' tae fend for maself agin.

I feel sorry for the poor little mites born in the Factory here. They dinnae stand a chance. When these wee babes come into this sad world, who knows what will become o' them? The mournful wailin' of their mithers when they're separated from them is a terrible sound, not easy tae forget. The mither might be sent back tae the same household agin and agin, tae suffer the same fate. Hobart Town is full of orphans. The ones that manage tae live that is.

Only one day tae go before I get out o' solitary and off comes the spike collar. Ma name is Agnes. Agnes MacDonald.

Chapter 6

# *Sarah*

15th January, 1837

When Matron told me I had been selected for assignment, and to prepare myself to leave, she gave me no indication as to where I would be going. I could only think that Robert had kept his word, and that I would be going to a safe household.

I was sure I would be under close inspection by my new master and mistress, so I tidied myself up as best I could, attending to my hair and making sure the folds on my dress were draped as elegantly as they could be. I bundled up the extra set of Factory clothing we had been given when we first arrived, put on my fresh bonnet, and said a quick goodbye to my dear friend Maggie. How I shall miss her! Filled with silent questions, I became very nervous and quite agitated about it all. In my short time at Cascades, I had heard stories from the women about all sorts of unpleasant things that had happened to them in service.

I was handed over to a tall man with good bearing. The woman standing next to him, I thought, must be his wife. She had a gentle face under her bonnet, and was plainly dressed, her clothes lacking the frills and trinkets of the women I'd glimpsed in Hobart Town when we'd walked from Sullivan's Cove to Cascades Female Factory after leaving the ship.

The couple said they were Mr. and Mrs. Bridges, and that they were Quakers.

Along the road into Hobart Town from the Factory we passed houses, tall buildings, and the Barracks — where soldiers in red uniforms, brass buttons glinting, were standing about talking to each other. At one point we came to the crest of a hill and I could see through to Sullivan's Cove. Travelling closer to town, the spire of St. David's Church came into view, in what seemed to be the centre of town, near the harbour. Quite a few people were walking about, some stopping to chat, others busy with commerce. I could see gentlemen riding horses, and others moving about in gigs, drays or carts. It didn't take long before we arrived at our destination, the pleasant but modest house of Mr. and Mrs. Bridges.

I was to share an attic room at the back of the house with fifteen-year-old May, the kitchen help. When I met the shy young May, she told me she had lived all her life at the Queen's Orphanage in Hobart, and had been sent out as a domestic servant to the Bridges at the age of fourteen. How awful to have spent one's whole life in an orphanage. At least I had experienced the comfort of a warm loving family until I reached an age to take care of myself. I was so sorry for poor May. I wonder if she ever met her mother, no doubt a woman from the Female Factory who was probably pining for her child all those years.

Our small windowless room contained two narrow beds pushed hard against a wall on either side. A hook on each wall allowed one item of clothing per person. Placed between the two beds was a tiny side-table with a candle-holder and a bible on top. Beneath each bed there was space for our meagre possessions, and a chamber pot to share. Plain, but adequate, I thought to myself, though it would have been nice to have a window for fresh air.

Once I had deposited my small bundle of belongings on the bed May pointed to as mine, I was informed that the mistress wanted to see me straight away. I hurried down to meet with her, anxious for her to think well of me.

'Your duties,' said Mrs. Bridges, 'are to mend and sew clothing for the household, and you may be asked to help out sewing small items for the stock we have at our drapery shop in Liverpool Street. You will also be called upon to help look after our two children and to help Samuel with his reading and writing.' The children were already in the room as they had been sent for so that I might meet them. 'This is Samuel, he is seven years old, and that is Lilian, she is five.' The little girl was very sweet, and the boy seemed well-behaved, standing straight and looking respectfully at his mother.

It all sounded reasonable, and I thought I would get along very well with the two children. When the brief introduction was done, Samuel and Lilian were told to go to their rooms to play and Mrs. Bridges turned back to face me.

'You are not to go out of the house without obtaining permission,' she said. 'No alcoholic beverages of any sort are allowed on the premises, and you are never to have any in your possession. That would be instant dismissal. Nor are you at any time to visit with people who drink alcohol. We Quakers have very high moral standards which you will learn about, and we adhere to the principle that prosperity must not come at the expense of piety.'

Well, I thought, that does sound strict, but I can abide by all this. I must be careful she never finds out how things were on the ship. Now that I am once again with a pious, moral Christian family, should they discover my relationship with Robert, I would no doubt be sent back to the Factory post-haste. I determined they would never know. I was in a safe place here, and wanted to stay. Though I must say, my conscience was troubled by this secret. For an unmarried woman to have known a man in that way. Whatever had come over me? I could feel the heat rising up my neck just thinking about it.

I was brought back from my musings about Robert, by Mrs. Bridges telling me about their family's drapery business. Fortunately she had not noticed my embarrassment, or took it for something else.

'Everything we sell in our shop must conform to the Quaker code of dress: simplicity, and without guile or vanity. One's dress needs to reflect the wearer's moral condition. Gaudy, flash dress is only worn by gaudy, flash women, not pious and genteel folk.'

With this in mind, everyone in the household was expected to dress with sobriety and decency — not difficult to do in our shapeless prison clothes. I haven't seen their drapery shop yet, but I think it must be very fashionable to cater for the ladies and gentlemen of Hobart Town. That is, fashionable, but plain. I could see I was going to learn a lot about Quakers. I had only heard about them when we were visited by Mrs. Fry in Newgate Gaol, so I thought that although they were very stern, they must also be kind, as Mrs. Fry was a good and kind person. Having informed me of the Quaker requirements, Mrs. Bridges then looked kindly at me and said softly, 'I do hope you will be comfortable with us Sarah. I am pleased to have you with us.'

After the initial stern warning, she said that with such warmth I felt assured that my stay here would be pleasant. And safe. No men are employed in this household. My stiff body relaxed. I'd been so on edge.

The staff consists of the cook Mrs. Smith, a jovial, free woman as wide is she is high, who seems to be well in charge of her kitchen and young May, and there is a domestic who lives outside coming in to do household chores three times a week. I am the only convict on assignment here.

It was on my first night in the small room I shared with May that I felt a loneliness so profound I was overcome with sadness. Up until that moment I had been surrounded by women, children and my close friend Maggie. Even the evils of prison life, the dangers of being on board the ship, and the short time I had spent at the Female Factory, did not prepare me for this night. I thought of the care bestowed upon me by Robert. My thoughts drifted back to Robert's cabin. I closed my eyes and imagined myself safe in his arms. It was Robert who gave me the confidence and strength to keep going in spite of all that was happening. I thought of his tender embraces, the warmth of his body against mine. When I had become one with him, I felt that I had changed from being a girl to being a woman, and that I would never be the timid young person that I had been when I stepped on board the ship. I would cope.

But now his absence. This would test my resolve. I was living in an unfamiliar home, in a strange country at the end of the world, with a family I did not know, and I was a convict. It would take all my courage to adapt to this new situation. The enormity of my parents' loss once again overwhelmed me. I thought I might die of loneliness. I could barely speak to May when she suggested we pray together beside our beds. I knelt down quietly beside her and then pulled back the covers of my narrow bed, slipped in between the sheets, and shook with quiet weeping until I fell asleep.

The next day I asked Mrs. Bridges for some writing materials so that I could write a letter to Maggie. That evening, I put pen to paper.

*15th January, 1837*

*Dear Maggie,*

*This is my first week on assignment in Hobart Town. The household is small and all the people are Quakers, as you know, I think. Mr. and Mrs. Bridges are kind people and I think I shall be well here. I share a room with a young girl called May. I am occupied with the two children and with sewing.*

*Oh Maggie, I do so miss your company and friendship. I feel so alone, and the death of my poor loving parents is now more on my mind than ever. I do not know how I shall get this letter to you, but I shall try my best. I hope you are well and safe.*

*Affectionately,*

*Your loving friend, Sarah*

I would ask the cook if she knew a way I could get this letter to Cascades Factory and into Maggie's hands. When I got to know her better, that is. But at least it is written.

With each day that passed I became more acquainted with the pattern of daily life in the Bridges' house. The children were very polite, little Lilian enjoyed playing with her dolls and chattering, and young Samuel tried his best to emulate his father's serious nature. I gradually got used to my situation, and in time I became a little less melancholy.

In the kitchen one morning, when I walked in to join our cook for a cup of tea, I saw she was engrossed in reading a newspaper. She looked up when I entered, bidding me to sit down on one of the wooden chairs next to her.

'Look here,' she said, pointing out a particular section of the newspaper, 'there's plenty of work. Once you get your ticket of leave you shouldn't have any trouble at all. There's no lack of employment for free women. Experienced milliners, dress-makers, straw-hat makers and good needlewomen are highly sought after,' she said, pouring me a cup of tea.

'See this, you could even work as a governess like you did back in England.' She pointed to an advertisement in *The Hobart Town Courier* to show me what she meant. We both leaned over the newspaper to peer more closely as she spread it out over the table, then she proceeded to read out aloud:

'*Governess required in a respectable Protestant family, a lady competent to educate five children in English and French (divested of provincial accent)* ...' She read carefully and slowly, and had a bit of trouble pronouncing some of these words, but then went on, '*writing, common arithmetic, drawing, music, history, geography, plain and ornamental needle work — will be treated as one of the family; salary not an object to a moral, accomplished person who will devote her best energies to her pupils.* And it gives all the details about how to apply. You could do all of that Sarah.'

I nodded my head to agree with her. It was true, I was able to do all they were asking and could see that it would not be difficult to find work once I was free.

'If you stay here and don't get into any trouble, Mrs. Bridges will give you a good testimonial. Too bad you haven't got your ticket of leave right now!' she said, then looked at me, triumphant to be the bearer of such good news.

'Yes, it's a pity I cannot apply now. It sounds very promising, but I've only just arrived in Van Diemen's Land.'

*If I have no marks in the Black Book*, I thought, *I could get off much earlier than my seven years*. And then we went to talk about other interesting items in the newspaper.

When Mrs. Bridges wanted me to sew with her we sat in her parlour, the heavy curtains opened to let some light into an otherwise dark room. I was curious to see what a Quaker parlour room would be like. All very neat, I noted, with crotcheted antimacassars on an armchair (no doubt made by Mrs. Bridges herself), a silver tea-set placed atop a small round table covered with an embroidered tablecloth, and two high-backed chairs. The fireplace against the wall looked as if it would be very inviting during the long winters, but at present the weather did not call for it. A parlour like any other, in fact, but with less bric-a-brac.

One afternoon when we were sitting together sewing she said, 'I'm so pleased Dr. James recommended you to us Sarah. He told us you were a very honest and trustworthy person from a good family. We went to Cascades Female Factory especially to look for you, on his suggestion.'

That's how I found out that it was my Robert I have to thank for my fortunate position. I know he would not have said anything about what passed between us on the ship. Again, I felt a tug of separation, but tried not to dwell on it. And it was taking me a while to get used to being treated in a civil manner once more, and to being in the presence of upright people who made me feel part of their family. But I was ever cautious, for my earlier experience in a good household had led me to convict life and Van Diemen's Land.

After a few moments of quiet sewing, with both of us engrossed in our work, she went on to tell me about Quaker beliefs, looking up at me over her *pince-nez* spectacles.

'I have to wear garments that reflect female modesty, but I can still add some ribbons of a subdued colour, one or two pearl buttons, and make a few alterations to spruce up my old dresses. This is perfectly in line with our view of not wasting anything, and of being frugal.'

I was helping her re-work her old blue muslin dress. She was changing the sleeves and I was lifting the hem an inch, cutting off the edges that were frayed from wear.

'Two of our Quaker friends Mr. Backhouse and Mr. Walker,' she went on, 'have come out to Van Diemen's Land as missionaries and are taking an interest in the plight of the Aboriginal people. Like all Quakers, they are intent on improving conditions for those less fortunate. They have both dined with us here and have some very interesting stories to recount about their travels.'

I looked up at her, such a kind woman herself, so I was interested to hear about these Quaker missionaries.

'These two gentlemen also want to improve the conditions of convicts,' she said. 'Over the course of one of our dinners, Mr. Backhouse talked a great deal about a penal colony that he had visited: Port Arthur. It's well known to be a terribly cruel and fearful place, and almost impossible to escape from. It seems that the most disorderly and irreclaimable convicts are sent there, and the punishments for transgressions are severe.'

I'd heard about Port Arthur. Well, I thought, it sounds as if someone is trying to help us convicts then. I wonder if they will succeed? She spoke a bit more about missionaries, then became more engrossed in her sewing and lapsed back into silence. The Quakers spend a lot of time in silence.

'Sarah,' said Mrs. Bridges the next day, 'I want you to pick up two pale-blue ribbons and two tiny pearl buttons which I ordered last week. Our shop is still awaiting a shipment of these things from England. I have written a note which you will give to the shop-owner once you arrive there.'

'Yes, Mrs. Bridges,' I replied, remaining with my eyes down so as not to show my excitement at the prospect of leaving the house.

'I'm entrusting you with this task as I am too busy with the children today to go myself.'

I was thrilled at the possibility of seeing shops and buildings, and glimpsing what life might be like in town if I were free. Mrs. Bridges knew that I would not try to run away. Where would I go? I knew no-one here except other convicts, and I could not be better treated elsewhere. She gave me directions so I would not get lost. While apprehensive about going out on my own, I was looking forward to seeing what it is like in Hobart Town, and to be taken for an ordinary person, not a convict. For by now I was dressed in garments that Mrs. Bridges had provided me. Plain hand-me-downs, but not those of a convict. So no-one would be any the wiser.

With Mrs. Bridge's note for the shop-keeper in my hand, and detailed instructions on how to get to the shop, I took my first step outside the door of the house, turned right, and walked into town. How good it felt. For the first time in many months I could feel again what it was like to be a free woman.

Hobart Town is built on the water's edge, in a most beautiful harbour and the view from the town toward the sea is exceedingly lovely. I could appreciate the beauty of it all now without the outward shame of my convict status. As I looked along the Derwent River I saw two whaling ships, a sealing ship, many smaller vessels, and a transportation ship that was bringing in more convicts. Men this time, as the flag signalling women aboard was not displayed. The smell of the sea gave a freshness to the air that was most agreeable.

There was a hubbub of activity, as you would see in a seaport back home. It reminded me of my first sight of the seaport at Woolwich before we boarded the transport ship. Traders with stalls were selling their wares, barber shops too, and butcher stalls with flies buzzing about the carcasses of meat. Men and women traders shouted to passers-by to come buy their wares, and there was a boy carrying a cage of bright-coloured birds.

I looked again at the directions on the piece of paper Mrs. Bridges had given me. The Mather Drapery shop was on Murray Street, so I would have to turn into Liverpool Street. There were rows of shops, a few with big windows that you could look through from the street to see the wares for sale inside. I dawdled past them, not stopping, but allowing my eyes to linger on the mannequins to see what they were dressed in. Not for long, just enough time to hear the sound of a horse and carriage jingle past. I walked past some two-storey buildings and then spied Murray Street. There were several drapery shops, but I finally came across Mathers.

When I entered the shop, there were all manner of items that caught my eye. I hadn't seen the like of such lovely things in one shop in such a long time. Soft, sumptuous kid gloves, just waiting to be touched and appreciated, sat atop a wooden display case; there was a bounty of silks, plain and figured satins, and an assortment of ribbons of the newest and most vibrant colours to tempt any tastes, as well as more subdued colours for the less audacious ladies. Mrs. Bridges had said that the ladies from the really rich households in Hobart ordered only clothes that came from Paris and London and would not be seen in anything made locally. But this shop had very fine clothing, ladies' and gentlemen's apparel. There were leather shoes, and fancy boots, and so many fancy hats that I could but stand and stare at it all!

I walked slowly past velveteen coatees, sleeved waistcoats, black and fancy silk handkerchiefs, and up to the counter. When the gentleman behind the counter asked me what it was that I required, I passed him the note that Mrs. Bridges had given me, requesting the ribbon and pearl buttons. As he was fetching the merchandise, I glanced around at the other customers. An elegant lady with her two daughters, both dressed in the extreme of fashion and finery, were looking at hats. The woman glanced in my direction, dismissing me as someone of no importance. I could almost read her mind — *obviously a domestic servant from the clothes* — she would have been thinking. A young man with costly-looking rings on his fingers, and chains and shirt-pins encrusted with gems, was perusing the watches on display. When I'd entered the shop he looked at me, taking me in from head to toe with a quizzical look on his face. I could see he was wondering who I was and my station in life. I was so glad that I was not wearing convict clothes as I would have died with shame to be seen in them.

My eyes went from him to a simply dressed young woman who, I ventured to think, was also on a fetching mission for her mistress. She glanced at me with a look of some familiarity. I dared not speak to anyone however, as this was my first time out. When the gentleman behind the counter handed me the parcel for Mrs. Bridges that he had wrapped in brown paper, I thanked him and hastened out of the shop.

On the way back I took a wrong turn in one of the streets. I must have turned right instead of left. I opened my purse to get out the directions, ready to retrace my steps. It was then I realised to my dismay that the directions Mrs. Bridges had given me had been written on the back of the note I had handed to the store-keeper. Instead of returning to fetch the note I thought I would try to remember how to get back. But when I tried to retrace my steps I found myself in the waterfront district of Wapping and in a street that I had not been on before. It was full of terrace houses just like the ones in England, as well as public houses and hotels. So many hotels, taverns and inns! Why, everywhere I looked I saw them. I started counting them: the Scotch Thistle, the White Horse, the Red Lion, the Lord Nelson, the Hare and Hounds. Must be more than a dozen, I'm sure. I realised that I had not seen these buildings on the way to the shop, and by this time was getting very anxious. Outside the hotels a few drunken men and women sprawled about, some still clutching bottles even now, in broad daylight. This was not the place for a young lady to be. I started to become frightened and hurried along, in and out of a maze of alleys, more and more confused as to the direction I should take. Wherever was I? And how on earth was I to get back to the Bridges' house? By this time, there were more people of dubious character about and I began to panic. I was in Wapping, and lost.

Then I heard footsteps behind me and turned to see a large man with a full dark beard, quite a way back from me, but coming in my direction. He was alone and seemed intent on catching up to me. I became terrified as from my quick glimpse he looked extremely rough and wore the clothes of a seafaring man, possibly a sealer or whaler, and I had heard stories of their treatment of women. I quickened my pace. But so did he. By this time I was almost running but still he kept up with me. I turned a corner, thinking to enter a tea-house if there were one to be seen. Alas, only sly-grog shops and pubs in this area. Nowhere to escape to and ask for help. He was getting closer, hurrying along as fast as I was myself. I was almost fainting with fear.

Then he called out, 'Miss! Miss! Stop!'. I was frantic by then, fearing the worst as he caught up to me and spun me around. His grip on my elbow was strong as he took hold of me. I looked into his well-worn seafaring face, his black beard, his straggly hair protruding from beneath his hat and could smell the sweat from his body. His piercing dark eyes looked directly into mine registering the terror in my eyes, at which time he let go of my arm.

'Miss, you dropped your handkerchief. I have been trying to catch you up to return it to you,' he said.

I could not believe what I was hearing and was so relieved I burst into tears.

'Why, whatever ails you Miss?' he said to me.

'Oh ... it's just that ... I am lost,' I said, not wanting him to know that I had been running away from him. When I told him the name of the street where the Bridges' lived, he obliged me by giving me directions, and handed my handkerchief over to me, after which he returned from whence he had come.

I still felt flustered, and so foolish. With his directions I arrived back at the Bridges' house, flushed and out of breath, but relieved that nothing untoward had happened to me.

Mrs. Bridges was pleased with the ribbons and beads, considering them in accordance with the spirit of Christian simplicity, and not too fancy.

'We'll add them to the blue muslin dress immediately after lunch this afternoon,' she said. I did not tell her that I had got lost, nor anything of the bearded gentleman. Sitting together once again to work on the dress, Mrs. Bridges began to tell me about the wife of Sir John Franklin, the new Governor.

'Lady Franklin supports the work of Mrs. Elizabeth Fry back in England,' she said, picking up some fresh blue thread and putting it through the eye of the needle she was holding. 'The Quaker lady you said you had met, Sarah.'

I looked up at this, feeling flustered to hear she thought I had actually met Mrs. Fry. But I said nothing and she was so intent on her task she did not see the blush that came over my face.

'The Franklins have only just arrived in Hobart. Everyone expects they will be a welcome change to Governor and Lady Arthur.'

I wondered why, but did not ask as I did not want to appear rude or forward.

'When Mrs. Fry discovered that Lady Jane Franklin was coming out to Van Diemen's Land, she asked Lady Jane if she would be so kind as to look into the plight of convict women and perhaps see if she herself could do anything to help them.' Taking her eyes away from her needle for a moment, Mrs. Bridges now looked over the top of her spectacles at me, 'Lady Jane has a lot of influence over her husband I hear.'

I hoped Lady Jane would visit the Female Factory and keep Mrs. Fry informed. But I had my doubts. From what our cook had said, Lady Jane believed convict women were *ever tainted with their crimes,* which did not sound too promising. After a few moments of silence Mrs. Bridge's thoughts had drifted to another topic.

'One of the drapery shops employs a convict tailor. He's paid nine pounds per year to make clothing!' she said, clearly amazed at the convict's fortunate position. 'If any dressmaking work is carried out by convicts however, it has to be kept quiet. If it becomes known, patrons would not buy the clothing. They would say it had been touched by the convict stain.'

From all this talk of stain, it seems they think that they might catch something from us that is degrading.

I'm learning a lot about drapery and clothing from Mrs. Bridges. Some people prefer lambswool stockings, but unbleached cotton socks seem to last longer. Hard-working people look for garments and materials that are coarse and strong and that endure being washed many times. Good riding habits are also sold in the shops. Riding hats and black veils with ribbons to tie them, along with riding boots, are all necessary items for the ladies riding side-saddle. The ladies look most dashing sitting upright on their horses. I wondered what it must feel like to be dressed like that, on a horse, and to be sitting so high from the ground, alongside one's husband on his horse — If my parents had not died, this is what my life might have been like. But I must not think about that. I am very fortunate to be here.

I kept hearing about currency lads and lasses, and when I was with our cook again having one of our cups of teas in the kitchen in the brief respite between the mid-day and evening meals, I asked her what this meant.

'It means people who were born here in the colonies,' she explained. 'The first-generation Australians. Englishmen born in the old country are Sterlings — like the Sterling pound they use over there. People born out here are like Currency pounds, the money we use out here. The Sterlings feel they are superior to them but the currency lads and lasses don't care tuppence about what people think. They're proud of being born in Australia and very independent.'

I could see young May look up at this, her eyes sparkled at the mention of currency lads. She was hanging out to hear more.

'Some of them go swimming in the sea during really hot days in summer. They frolic around and enjoy themselves no end. The strong sun here makes their skin a dark tan colour, not white like the skin of the ladies and gentlemen. They don't care about that either. In fact, they like being tanned even though brown skin is considered low class and coarse, like natives or labourers who have to work outside in the hot sun. White skin is much admired by the gentry,' Mrs. Smith said.

I looked from Mrs. Smith to May who by this time was staring ahead of her with a tea-towel in her hand.

'Very few of the ladies in society will even go horse-riding here, in spite of having done so back in England, because they fear losing their pale complexions,' Mrs. Smith added.

May, who was listening to all this with her mind still fixed on the currency lads swimming in the sea, asked glassy-eyed, 'I wonder what it would be like to venture into the sea, like the currency lads and lasses?'

'Don't you be thinking about such nonsense, young May,' admonished cook. 'Just concentrate on your work. Superior people do not swim in the sea or even go to the beach. For a woman to have skin touched by the sun is to plummet from gentility to coarseness.'

That seemed to put an end to the conversation.

In my small bedroom that night, I began another letter to Maggie even though I had not heard back from her. I wondered if she had ever received it.

*25th February, 1837*

*Dear Maggie,*

*I miss you my dear friend, and wonder how you are doing. I am so lonely here without you to talk to.*

*I am learning about the Quakers. As well as simplicity of dress, they believe in the 'inward light', that we can experience God inside ourselves, and that human disobedience to God's will is what causes problems. I must say I do not understand this well myself as it is so very different to what I was used to back in England. I have not yet been to one of their meetings but I am told that they sit together in silence, listening to the still small voice within. They address each other as 'thou' and 'thee' and refuse to doff their hats or bow to anyone, believing that we are all equal in God's eyes.*

*I have been out of the house on errands. There are shops in Hobart Town that you would like very much, I'm sure. I am finding out all sorts of things about the latest fashions. Mrs. Bridges showed me a picture of the new style corsets, which the ladies are wearing underneath their outer garments. It seems the high waistline has fallen out of fashion and now corsets are longer, reaching from the armpits to the hips, giving a most attractive hourglass figure to the woman wearing it. If you lace the corset extremely tightly, the waistline is very much reduced, and sometimes it is so tight that women become almost faint with the agony of it all.*

*The bones used in these corsets come from whales, probably whales that have been caught in the seas off Van Diemen's Land! Imagine that. A lady in England or France might be wearing bones from the very whaling ships that are now berthed at Sullivan's Cove!*

*I wonder how you are faring and whether you have been sent out on your first assignment yet. I do hope you receive this letter. I shall try to post it to you next time I go on an errand for Mrs. Bridges.*

*Affectionately yours,*

*Sarah*

Mrs. Bridges relaxed her rule about servants leaving the house for just one day of the week: Sunday, so that we could attend church. On one of those Sundays at church I met a convict girl called Nancy who was working for another merchant family in Hobart Town. She told me that she had a little boy called Charlie, who had been placed in the Queen's Orphanage — where young May grew up. She said that the following Sunday she would be allowed enough time to visit him and asked me if I would I be able to go with her.

By this time Mrs. Bridges knew she could trust me and when I asked her for permission to visit the orphanage with Nancy, she said yes.

It took us a long time to get there as we were obliged to walk some miles from Hobart Town. It was Nancy's third visit to little Charlie since he'd been taken away from her in Cascades Factory Nursery and she was so excited to be seeing him again. It was my first visit to Queen's Orphanage and I was very curious to see what it was like. I'd heard that seven hundred children lived within its walls.

On the walk there, Nancy told me about her little boy's father, the spoilt son of the household she had been sent to on her first assignment.

'He was a cocky young man,' she said, 'he thought he could get away with anything, and usually did. When he took me aside, he was spiteful and nasty. He forced himself on me, and then twisted my arms behind my back and pinched me hard when he was finished with me. Each time he had his way with me, my body was covered in bruises.'

'What a horrid person! Did you tell anyone in the household what he had done to you?'

'It would be his word against mine and his mother thought he could do no wrong. Who do you think she would believe? Once I became pregnant it was back to Cascades Factory. Straight to Crime Class. But I was glad to get away from him.'

We were almost there now, and as we quickened our pace, she added, 'I gave birth to Charlie and when he was old enough to be weaned, he was sent away. I didn't see him again. He's three years old now.'

There it was ahead of us, a large gloomy building where so many poor little mites were housed. When we entered my heart sank and I felt such sadness. Such hollow, unhappy little faces looking up at us piteously. I could see that Charlie didn't even recognise his mother, but when she showed him affection and hugged him, he responded to her. She wept when she saw his crestfallen little face at our departure. It was so hard for us to tear ourselves away from him and from other little ones clinging around our skirts. We did not speak on the long walk back to Hobart Town, so upset were we.

I shall never visit that place again, but I am sure it will be on my mind forever. If only I could do something to help the children.

Mrs. Bridges and I have become quite close. She told me that she has had women from Cascades Factory who were far from satisfactory. She has no idea what life is like for us convicts. Once I was ignorant of such things too. How long ago that seems now.

'My first convict nurse-girl was dirty beyond all imagining.' she went on. 'She drank rum, smoked tobacco, swore awfully, and was in all respects the lowest specimen of woman-kind I had ever had the sorrow to behold. It is most inconvenient to be without a proper person to look after the children. I thought about employing a free woman in that capacity as the convict women had not turned out well, but I thought I would try another convict one more time. And then you were highly recommended to me.'

*26th March, 1837*

*Dear Maggie,*

*Although I have not heard from you, I shall keep writing.*

*I often get an opportunity to read the newspapers here. Many times there is some report to do with convicts, or the Female Factory. I think about you and wonder if you are still there. We saw a piece that talked about the Flash Mob at the Factory as being an 'unholy sisterhood'. I hope you are out of any danger.*

*Our cook told me some very disturbing news and I do hope it is not true. She said that some motherless babies are sent out to baby farms. When I asked her what this meant, thinking they would be places of fresh air and good conditions, she said that they were not at all such places. Rather, it refers to people who take in an infant or child for payment, and while they are supposed to care for them, there are some unspeakable practices which are too awful for me to write down on paper. I do hope this is mere idle gossip.*

*I miss you and would dearly love to hear from you. Perhaps you are already in a good household, as I am.*

*Yours affectionately,*

*Sarah*

Chapter 7

# *Maggie*

*15th January, 1838*

Still no word from Sarah. I wonder why she don't write?

After a dreary hot Christmas Day it were a Friday when Agnes were able to talk the turnkey inta lettin' us out. She promised him a bottle of rum when he let us back in. 'Don't worry lass,' Agnes said with a wink, 'I've done this afore. I ken exactly where tae go. Once we get goin' it be only two miles intae town. We'll go tae ma favourite waterin'-hole, *The Commercial Hotel*. Ye'll be right. We'll hae ourselves a good time then make it back tae the Factory afore anyone is up.'

It were dark, hardly enough light to see where we was goin'. Agnes knew how to get to the start of the track what runs along the rivulet — where we gets our water from. We had to stay real quiet until we was far enough away for anyone inside to hear us, especially Matron, who would 'ave called guards quick-smart. I wondered — but only for a minute — if it really would be all that easy to get back inta the Factory again. But by then, I didn't care much.

It were excitin' to be outside. The air were crisp and clean, and the rivulet kept us on track, it were pratickly a straight line into town, like Agnes said. I were shiverin' a bit, and couldn't tell if it were from the cold or fear. We had to push through bush and low tree branches, the leaves and twigs catchin' on our clothes and hair. We run alongside each other when the track were wide enough, stoppin' ter take a breath every now and then. It took us about a hour — the dark, the scrub, and our long skirts stopped us from movin' any faster'n that. We could hear the noisy pub even from the end of the track. Agnes led us through some back alleys. *Just as well Agnes knows where she's goin'*, I thought, *because I bleedin' well don't.* Before too long we saw a whale oil lantern swingin' from a rusty sign over the doorway: *The Commercial Hotel.*

As soon as we opened the door, the smoke and the smell — salt air, grog, men's bodies, and baccy pipes — smacked us in the face. The pub were crowded, full of noisy men shoutin' and laughin', some arguin', and all of them swillin' their drinks like it were their last one in this world. Lots of sealers and whalers there were, a rough lot what would pick a fight in the blink of an eye. The men looked us up and down as soon as we walked in. Not too drunk for that, I thought. Their eyes moved away from Agnes and I could see them lookin' at me hair, a bit of a mess from brushin' against branches and the like, and then down from me sweaty face to me breasts. From our clothes the men knew we was from the Factory, and Agnes' shorn hair were a dead giveaway.

'This be more like it, lass. We'll hae a good night of it, ye can be sure!'

'But how are we goin' to pay for our drinks?' I said, tryin' not to shout it out to be heard in all the noise.

'Don't ye be worryin' about that. We'll soon hae a drink and plenty more!' said Agnes as she nudged her way through the crowd towards the bar. It weren't too long before a couple of men sidled up and started talkin'. One of 'em were a strong, good-lookin' young man with black hair, a cheeky face and a twinkle in his eyes.

'What'll it be?' he said to me. I could hear he were Irish.

'I'll have the same as you.' I had to shout back at him so he could hear me over the noise. He looked around for somewhere to sit away from the noisy bar, with men shoutin' orders at the barmaids and elbowin' each other ter get their drinks from the counter. Spyin' a couple leavin' a small table with two chairs, he nodded at me to follow him.

'My name's Benjamin Doyle, from County Kerry,' he said once we'd sat down. And I told him mine. He plonked me glass of ale down in front of me. It were so full, some of it splashed over the top and spilled onto the small table. Bold as brass he added, 'I reckon you're a convict Maggie Burnett, from the way you're dressed.'

'You're not wrong there,' I said. 'I'm from the Female Factory. Scarped it for a night out. We'll be sneakin' back in before they're any the wiser.'

'I'm a convict as well, Maggie. Transported to Port Arthur. Fourteen years, I got. I was lucky not to see the hangman's noose. I got into a fight in a pub in Ireland, and in all the hullabaloo I stabbed a man. He didn't die, but he was badly wounded. My ma always said I'd get into trouble with my boldness and temper. And she was right,' he laughed, 'I was just seventeen.'

I took a closer look at 'im, he wouldn't be much older'n that now — a bit battle-worn but with that twinkle in his warm brown eyes he'd always look younger.

'Port Arthur's a hard place. A man can get up to three hundred lashes with the cat o' nine tails 'til his spine's opened to the air and blowflies. They tie you to a post and pull your arms up by a rope so hard your chest is squeezed. First time I was flogged, I felt the flesh coming off my back and heard the flogger curse as he was sprayed with blood. I got fifty lashes that time. But there was another time I got a hundred.'

I wondered what his back looked like with all that floggin'. He was a handsome one, was Benjamin Doyle, I were takin' to him. He had a way, all right. A lot of them Irishmen is like that.

'One felon got two hundred lashes. One hundred across his backbone, between his shoulder blades. The other one hundred he got across his haunches. They were jelly in the end. Poor bastard.'

I didn't want to hear much more about all that floggin'. I were curious to know how he'd got out of Port Arthur prison. I heard tell it weren't easy to escape from there. 'How did yer scarp it from Port Arthur then?'

'I'll tell you that Maggie. It's a long story, but being as I'm Irish, you probably expected that,' and we both laughed.

'At Port Arthur, I spent weeks working on the chain gang. If a man just looked the wrong way at a guard he could be ironed and made to do hard labour on the roads. Two of the men on it with me were Michael Dooley, another Irishman, and an Englishman by the name of William Smith. Michael was transported for political rebellion, and William, an educated man as he was, for forgery. I tell you Maggie, it's that painful having to do heavy work in irons. The short chains are the worst, there's no room to move your legs properly and you have to shuffle along taking really short steps. You feel ashamed, a grown man shuffling along, bent over like an old man. And they chafe your skin something terrible. Some men say they'd rather be hanged than forced to work in short chains.'

He leaned back on his chair and took a long pull on his baccy pipe, watchin' me as he let out a thick curly ring of smoke what floated up into the air. 'Well, the three of us got to talkin' whenever we could. All of us had put up with days in solitary as well, but eventually we got off the chain gang and put to other work without heavy irons around our ankles. Michael and me had been flogged more than once with the cat — 'twas one of them cat o' nine tails made of the hardest whipcord. To make it worse, it'd been soaked in salt water then baked in the sun to dry, makin' it like wire. The nine tails had eighty-one knots that cut into your flesh like lard.'

Sittin' in this dark little corner of the pub watchin' him tell his story, I could see he were rememberin' it all. I couldn't help the tears that flowed from me eyes just thinkin' of the pain this wild young Irish lad must've gone through. At least us women weren't flogged. A spiked collar's better than floggin'. I leaned across the table to hold his hand, lettin' him know I were sorry for his sufferin'. He looked up at me then, with a smile before he went on with his tale.

'William was a more careful type than Michael and me. He went along quietly obeying orders, not looking sideways at any of the guards so he wouldn't be picked on. He was desperate to escape though. He thought if he could manage to get to New South Wales, he'd be able to start a new life for himself under another name.' He took a long pull on his baccy pipe then let out another thick curly cloud of smoke, watchin' it float up inta the air before he went on with his story.

'As I said, the three of us got to talking, and after a while we went on to the subject of escape and how we might go about it. We decided that the best way was to swim the narrow channel separating Port Arthur from the mainland, taking our chances with the sharks the guards kept saying were in the water, and the long distance we'd have to swim. We made up our minds to do it.'

He paused to re-light his pipe. I shifted in me chair a bit, takin' a quick look round the pub. It were crowded all right. I could see Agnes were still at the bar, drinkin' and havin' a grand old time. She were talkin' to a couple of whores dressed for business with rouged cheeks. She were holdin' a glass, prob'ly picked the coin for it from the pocket of the sailor next to her. He looked like he were three sheets to the wind, so it wouldn't be too hard to slip a hand into his pocket and come up trumps.

I looked back at Benjamin all the while tellin' his story. While I were listenin' I took a good look at him. He were wearin' a dark red shirt with a white kerchief round his neck, knotted at the front, and black knee-length boots with a black leather belt over loose trousers. Dashin' he were, but I could see yer wouldn't want to get on the wrong side of him, even with them nice brown eyes.

'We kept an eye on the moon for a few days, figuring our best chance would be on a dark moon. On the night we agreed upon for the escape there was no moonlight. It was black as pitch, making it good for bolting without being seen. That day was without any problems for the guards, so no attention was directed to any of us. We managed to meet up at the water's edge, as arranged. Not speaking a word to each other, we kept as quiet as we could, even when we slipped into the cold water. We swam for our lives, all the time thinking of the guards' warnings about the shark-infested water.

'William struggled to stay the distance and Michael and me took turns to help him swim the last two hundred yards. It was touch and go, but we made it to the other side. We managed to drag ourselves on to the shore, but we were that knackered, and freezing. That water was like ice. Our clothes were dripping wet and we were real hungry. But even if we'd had food we wouldn't of dared to light a fire.

'So we walked into the thick bush, clambering over rotten logs, tearing our clothes and skin on creepers and prickly brush. There was no track so we had to fight our way through the bush with just our bare hands. After what seemed like hours, and our hands and arms scratched to pieces, we thought we were far enough out of sight to camp overnight, still afeared that at any time we might be discovered once the alarm was raised that there were three escaped criminals.

'With no fire to dry out and get warm, we huddled close to each other, covering ourselves with branches, ferns, and foliage, hoping this might hide us as well as keep the chill off. If someone happened by while we were sleeping, we thought, they wouldn't easily see us. And sleep we did. We were exhausted.'

He could see me strainin' to look through the pub window to see how late it were gettin'. It were hard to see outside, but there weren't a ray of light from outside, so I guessed there was still a long time to go before Agnes and me had ter be on our way. He could see what I were doin' and said, 'We've still got plenty of time. It'll be a few hours before the sun comes up.'

We took another swill of our ale, lookin' at each other real close and I could feel that somethin' special were happenin' between us. The way he were lookin' at me face and me long hair and then back inta me eyes, I could see he wanted to get to know me *much* better. Then he started up with the next part of his story.

'We woke up the next morning terrible weak from hunger and our efforts the previous day. With the sun just about to rise we were anxious to move on, our first thought being food. We knew we had to look for clothes as well. Our prison slops would give us away as bolters. If our luck held, we might find horses too.

'Around the middle of the afternoon — we'd been walking since sunrise — we spied a run-down old slab hut, a make-shift kind of house. Making sure we were well hidden from view, we watched for a long time for any comings and goings from those who might live there. After about half an hour I went first — to see if there was anyone inside. It was empty, so I signalled to the others and we walked in. There wasn't much there, but we took the lot — clothes, blankets, and all the food we could carry. I felt sorry for the bastards, but we were starving and we had to get out of our prison clothes.'

'That's quite a story Benjamin Doyle,' I said when he paused and looked down at his empty glass. Must've been all this talk of hunger made him thirsty. Both our glasses was empty by this time.

'Another one Maggie?'

As he walked over to the bar, I took a good long look at his broad shoulders and the swagger in his walk, and pictured what his back must be like with all them scars from floggin's. Then me eyes spied Agnes with a pleased look on her face, comin' in from outside the pub with a drunken sailor. He were so drunk he wouldn't have seen Agnes' scarred face in the dark. He would've just been thinkin' of the promise of her fanny and a quick romp. And knowin' Agnes, if there was any loose change in his pockets, she would've had that as well. By the time Benjamin got to the bar, he were almost standin' next to Agnes. She were gettin' into the grog with the extra coins she had now, and enjoyin' herself no end, havin' a bit of a sing-song.

Benjamin come back with our drinks and sat down.

'So what did yer do next?' I asked him.

'Well, here 'tis then Maggie. With warm clothes and some food in our bellies, we set off once again. We were headed for the Huon Valley, a bushy forest region where we knew other ex-convicts and bolters were hiding out. The plan was to hide out for a couple of months and then try to get to New South Wales somehow.

'It took us almost two weeks to get to the Huon Valley. On the way, we kept ourselves alive by keeping our wits about us and stealing food from any settler's hut we passed. We were lucky not to get caught as the word would have been out about escapees and they would be looking in earnest for us. But luck was with us. Anyways, to cut a long story short, that's where I've been, in the Huon valley, and where I live now. It's rough but I'm free, and every now and then I come into Hobart Town for a drink. But I have to take care not to get caught, or it'll be back to Port Arthur for me."

I started wonderin' what it might be like to be that free, out of the Female Factory, and livin' like that meself. Sittin' there with him through the long hours of the night, talkin' and findin' out about each other, I were feelin' more and more taken with him.

'You're a lovely lass. I do like you Maggie.' He looked at me real hard, thinkin' about somethin', but not sayin' what were on his mind.

'It's a good life in this country if you're not stuck in a prison. I live mostly off the land. There are plenty of small animals to catch. And those kangaroos make good eating as well. We had to have rifles for hunting, but that wasn't too much trouble neither. When I needed money, I joined up with a bushranger who showed me the ropes.'

'So yer one of them bushrangers are yer. I heard about them all right. Never thought I'd ever meet one.'

'I tell you what Maggie. Why don't you forget about going back to the Factory and come back with me to my camp. You'll like it in the Huon, and I'll look after you.'

Typical Irishman, I thought, easy promises. Still, I did wonder...

Another few rounds of drinks and the whale oil lamps was dimmin'. A low pink light outside warned us the sun were almost up. By this time, I'd made up me mind. 'I'll do it! I'll come with yer Ben.'

Agnes caught me eye by that time and made her way over to me, pushin' and shovin' the drunken sailors aside to reach me. She'd have to get out of here quick to make it back in time. She were full of the grog, but not so drunk she didn't know the trouble she'd be in if she didn't get back in time for the turnkey to let her in.

'We got tae get back fast lass, the sun's almost up. We'll hae tae run the track.'

'I ain't goin' back.'

'What do ye mean, ye'll nae be goin' back?'

'Ben wants me to go away with him, and I'm goin'!'

'Do ye know what ye be doin' lass?'

'I can't take it no more in that place, and he says he'll look after me.'

'Well, I can't argue with ye, I don't hae the time. Good luck tae ye lassie, I'm off.'

'Thanks Agnes!' I shouted to her as she scurried away holdin' a bottle of rum; and there I were — by meself with a bushranger, a man I just met in a pub.

Chapter 8

# *Maggie*

*16th January, 1838*

After Agnes left, Ben bought us another drink then we left too. His horse were tethered at the back of the pub and once he helped me get up on it, he mounted as well and we was off. It took hours to get to the camp and I were that tired. After me escape from the Factory, drinkin' all night, and then ridin' for hours, I could hardly keep me eyes open. The sun were well up before we was even half-way there, and while I were excited to be sittin' behind Ben on his horse, and a bit fearful of what to expect, I were glad when he finally said, 'Another hour Maggie, then we'll be there.'

By the time the hour were up I'd fallen asleep leanin' against his back. I were jolted awake when he said, 'Wake up, we're here,' and took a sleepy look round. We was in a dense forest of them tall gum trees, and there was two make-shift tents, set up in a clearin' with two men already startin' to do some cookin' over a open fire. A billy were on and when I got off the horse, a cup of tea in a tin mug were handed to me. It were that good — strong and hot and it smelt like burnt leaves. Ben showed me where I could sleep next to him under a tent a bit further away from them other two. He opened the flap and I could see there was just a couple of blankets on the ground. But I were that tired I lay down next to him and both of us fell asleep straightaway. We slept for hours.

The next mornin' I were stiff and sore and when I scrambled up I had a proper look at where we was. I could see the other two tents was Michael's and William's. Our camp were next to a fast-flowin' river, much bigger and wider than that rivulet Agnes and me run along when we scarped it from the Factory. It felt a bit chilly, the air were fresh and smelt different — a sharp smell it were, comin' off them tall eucalyptus trees; sharp but comfortin', and mixed with the musky smell of damp rottin' leaves on the ground. I ain't never been anywhere like this before in me life. Whatever have I done? I thought to meself, and what would I do if this didn't work out with Ben? I started to get real scared then. I had no idea where I were.

After a cup of that billy tea, Ben said he'd have to go off huntin' to get some meat for us to eat. So he left me there with them two men with their long bushy beards from livin' in the bush for so long. They weren't big talkers neither of 'em, and I were pleased enough at that. I didn't know what to say to them anyway, and it all felt so strange. I were scared of them too, seein' how I didn't known 'em from Adam. I kept close to our tent, just lookin' around at the trees, walkin' down to the river, havin' a bit of a splash on me face with the cold water, and hangin' around. There was strange sounds as well. A big eagle was flyin' high above us, and there was rustlin' noises in the bush. I didn't dare walk too far away that first mornin'. After a few hours Ben come back with a small animal he'd shot. He said it were a possum.

Ben stripped the skin off the possum while it were still warm, scrapin' the raw meat off and then drapin' the skin across the low branches of a nearby tree. Then he cut the meat into strips. Once the evenin' campfire were lit and it'd burned down to hot embers, he put the strips of meat on top and we waited for it to cook. Michael and William joined us to share the kill and sat around the camp hearth without sayin' much. Once they'd had their fill they moved off back to their tents. The sun had already gone down by then and the stars was bright in the sky. The only light were from a half-moon and the campfire. All them trees around us and above us sent scary shadows across everythin', even in the dark. I were lookin' out past the trees, hopin' there weren't no Blacks out there waitin' to spear us.

I looked over at Ben and could see that he was eyein' me. While the night before we'd both fell asleep we was that tired, I knew that weren't goin' to happen the second night. He stood up, threw water on the fire, and motioned for me to follow him into our tent. I'd never lain with a man before. I'd managed to escape the sailors on the ship, but I could see all their goin's on when they come down into the women's quarters, and could hear all the grunts and groans. But I didn't have no idea what it'd be like.

Lyin' down on the hard ground with only two blankets underneath me back, I felt every pebble and mound diggin' into me as he lay on top of me. Me hands felt the raised welts of the scars on his back when I put me arms around him, and I got a whiff of the musky smell of his body — from sweat, the possum he'd killed, and the bush. It were over quick, and I wondered what all the fuss were about. I didn't realise then that Ben hadn't had much to do with women himself. But we was to get used to one another quick in the next few months.

William left a few days after I got there. He were off to take his chances in New South Wales. Nobody never heard of him again. P'raps he made it there, p'raps he didn't.

The bush become home to me. I got used to livin' rough, cookin' on a open fire and eatin' whatever food Ben could lay his hands on, mostly wild meat. Everyone hunted the local animals — kangaroo, wallabies, possums. They was tasty and their skins was good to wrap around us when we got cold. Smelly though, puttin' their skins around yer body even after they'd dried out. Them possum skins was real soft and warm to wear. Plenty of fresh-water streams was full of fish too. We never went hungry.

And there was bags of flour to make that damper they all like, and black tea. Whenever anyone went into Hobart Town they'd bring back sacks of flour. We even got good at findin' food growin' in the bush. Sometimes there were a trade between the locals livin' in the area what were friendly towards us — meat for goods like flour, tea, sugar, or other things. Some of the settlers made deals with bushrangers, promisin' to keep their hidin' places secret in return for bein' left alone and gettin' meat and a share of the goods and money from holdups. Them what had stolen dogs from the settlers found it easier to hunt with the help of the dogs.

One time Michael and Ben forced open the door of a settler's hut, even though they knew the owner were inside. But they found more'n they bargained for: two men inside, not one. They didn't reckon on the owner's brother bein' there. Bold as anythin', they threatened to blow the men's brains out if they didn't do what they was told! They tied up the settler and his brother, takin' their time — real cheeky they was — and started to ransack their home.

In no hurry to leave, they took their time eatin' whatever food the settlers had in the house, and hung around firin' their pistols at targets and any passin' rabbits. After a coupla hours they left, leavin' the two unfortunates tied up inside, but not before they loaded up the horses with most of the settler's provisions. Leavin' the property, they met up with two constables what recognised them for what they was: bushrangers. But Ben and his mate was too fast for the constables. They drove their horses as hard as they could, then doubled back on them constables from behind to give them a surprise. They wouldn't have been expectin' that!

All the bushrangers take to the same ways. When they attack a man they make him throw his arms above his head, and then they stick the muzzle of a pistol, or a musket, if they have one (but they don't like muskets too much, they're too heavy to carry about) in his face, close to his ear. Well, they grabbed them two constables, took away their fire-arms and made them take all their clothes off. Then they handcuffed 'em and forced 'em at gunpoint to walk inta a nearby stream up to their middle. With no clothes on! Not a skerrick! They even hid the constables' clothes away from the house so when they was found bare-arsed it would cause a laugh.

They rode away from the scene as fast as they could for about thirteen miles before settin' up camp for the night, laughin' every time they thought of them two constables in the stream with not a stitch on their bodies. Cheeky rascals! The next mornin' they made off back home to our camp. But when Ben told me about all their goin's-on, I started to worry, thinkin', what if he gets caught? Wouldn't be funny then. But I didn't let meself dwell on that thought.

When I was lyin' with Ben at night, I'd softly touch the raised welts on his back and couldn't help the tears wellin' up in me eyes. To think he was treated in such a way broke me heart. He were good to me this wild Irish larrikin and we was gettin' on famously. On hot days we'd sometimes walk to a part of the river where there weren't nobody around. We'd strip off and jump in, splashin' around, havin' a real lark. He taught me how to swim and float on top of the water, then we'd stretch out on the riverbank lookin' up at the sun high in the sky, close our eyes, and dry ourselves in the sun.

'We're free as the wild gumtrees above us,' he'd say to me.

We loved to watch the birds, especially them black cockatoos flyin' way up high, screechin' and tearin' at the bark of dead trees to get at the grubs with their sharp beaks. I'd sit up sometimes to watch the quiet dragonflies hoverin' over the water's edge. Like fairies them dragonflies. It were magical. We'd watch them little dark lizards too, well hid between rocks and crevices 'til they moved and darted about.

'You have to be always on the lookout for snakes Maggie,' Ben said. 'And small scorpions. Their sting is worse than a wasp.'

Them hot days brought the flies too. They was always around, settlin' on any meat around the place. And at night it'd be the mosquitoes. Did they love me English blood! Made a feast of me they did.

Ben taught me how to fish as well. Different to fishin' in the sea. Not that I could do that too well neither bein' as the only chance I got were that one time on the ship. And he'd managed to get his hands on fowlin' pieces, pistols and shot, and he made sure I could handle a rifle and shoot someone if need be. When he said that it give me a bit of a fright. I don't think I could ever shoot nobody. But might be I'd have to some time, out here. Times like these I'd remember how dangerous it all was.

I shot mainly pigeons and other small animals, and learned how to cure the beef and gut the kangaroos the men got from huntin'. Wild pig were tasty but there weren't too many of them around. Why, we even planted a few vegetables. We got to know other bolters, ex-convicts turned farmers, timber-cutters, sawyers, as well as currency lads what was there because they liked the life. All of 'em said they was 'Emancipists'.

Ben and me made a frame for a hut from the sprouts of young, tall trees what grew around us. We covered the frame with some thick, shady boughs, leavin' an openin' at one end for a door. When we got better at this, we started usin' large pieces of tree bark for a roof, pilin' them all on top of each other real thick. Huts of folk what'd been in the bush for a long time was built from split gumtree logs, with mud to seal the gaps between, protectin' 'em from bad weather and snakes. Some men was good at buildin' things. Others what didn't know much about buildin' made their huts any old way — from whatever materials was around.

It were rough all right but we was free! Many a night we slept out in the open in them thick forests and valleys slopin' down to the Huon River. I never seen nights like this in Cheapside — a sky black as a inkpot, and all them twinklin' stars up there so close you could almost reach out and touch 'em. We used to try to guess what they was called, makin' up stories about 'em. Every night under the cover of our tent when Ben was asleep I could hear strange noises comin' from animals — snarls, screeches, snorts and growls. Ben knew what they all was, but I were afraid.

It were cold in the mornin' before the sun come up and a damp mist hung low, especially in winter. Real cold. But not grey like London. Here, the cold went to yer bones and frost bit yer fingers and ears, but in the middle of the day it might get warm. Sun might come out and the leaves and bushes be sparklin' with the wetness of drippin' frost. The rest of the year were nice, even hot 'til yer walked in the shade of the trees. The forests weren't like nothin' I ever seen back home. That black wattle in bloom is real pretty, and there was gum trees so high yer'd think they might touch the sky. Some of the trees had bark what come away in strips, peelin' off and floatin' in the wind. And so many birds and wildflowers about. Them green parakeets fly about in flocks and feast off blossoms from the wildflowers. I never in me wildest dreams thought it might be like this.

Life weren't easy by no means, but I were happy. As well as convicts and bolters there was men what had their tickets of leave but didn't want to live in town, or some just wanted to be free of polite society. At first I were afraid of bein' caught and sent back, but I were even more afraid of the Aborigines — and the snakes. One time a black snake come near us. A bite from a black snake is an ugly affair, I can tell yer. I saw a man bit by one of them, and in a few hours his body were as black as an undertaker's hat and he were soon dead. They're nasty creatures them black snakes! You have to be on the lookout all the time in the bush. I heard stories about Aborigines too, and how they might take to spearin' any white people they met up with.

Sittin' around the campfire one night, the dark woods all around us, the men was all quiet at first, listenin' to the cracklin' sounds of the fire and smokin' their baccy pipes. I liked these times when everyone were together, sittin' on logs lookin' into the flames, and we'd just had a fill of fresh meat. Then one of the men visitin' us from another camp started talkin' about how he'd met an old Black in 1831 what had seen the first ships come to Van Diemen's Land. He said the white men was "carrying wood" — that were the only way he knew to explain what guns was. And with them "pieces of wood" the white men killed two of his people. They all took fright and run away. No wonder they try to get back at us. The Blacks have real good eyesight and a keen sense of smell, he said. They can hide themselves so well a white man can't see 'em, and they know the country back-to-front. Another man we met what had lived in the bush for years made friends with Aborigines and learned their ways. They taught him a lot about bush foods. When I seen Aborigines for the first time I were terrified, but they just looked us over, watched us for a while, and then went on their way.

There was other women in the area at different camps, livin' with their men. A couple of them had littl'uns. We'd visit each other to have a bit of a yarn when the men was away from camp but we was all quite far away from each other. There'd always be a welcomin' mug of hot brewed tea and sometimes a bush dainty like the 'fat cake'. They taught me how to make it with flour and drippin'. When it's hot and brown, it's real tasty. We all loved the freedom and life without prison walls and floggin's. But some of the women got real homesick for England. Sometimes they'd talk about it, but that didn't help none; we was here and that was that. Better to be out here in the bush than in prison anyway, no matter it's hard sometimes and we get frightened, especially when we're left alone at night. The men stay away from camp sometimes for a coupla nights. They sleep out in the open, or in caves if they find any, or hollowed-out trunks of big trees.

As the months went by it were gettin' colder. Ben and Michael started raidin' much further away — settlements and homesteads for horses, guns and ammunition. My Ben was becomin' more darin' in his bushrangin'. His face would get excited at the prospect of holdin' someone up, stealin' from them, then ridin' away from the scene as hard as he could. I knew when he were itchin' to get out again. I could see the signs. He'd get a bit hostile and impatient, start talkin' about bushrangin' and what a thrill it were, and talk about nothin' but his adventures. I didn't like them moods of his. And he left me alone too much — talkin' and plottin' with Michael, for they was very close by then, the two of 'em. I were left alone a lot and I didn't like it.

When they started the sheep-rustlin' raids, and robbin' inns for cash, and more homesteads for arms and ammunition I become real worried. He's gettin' too bold by far, I thought. This ain't goin' to end well. The police will be out lookin' for them all right, and they won't stop 'til they're found. I didn't like this turn of events one little bit, and hated to see him go out on these missions, especially as he could be gone for many days at a time. Besides, I got lonely out there and yer never knew what might happen to a woman walkin' about on her own. We started arguin' about it all, but there were no way he were goin' to stop.

Ben and Michael kept to areas what was far enough away from Hobart Town as to make their capture hard for the Redcoats. Still,

I began to think about me own situation more and more, and how dangerous it'd all become. Though I were gettin' on with Ben, except for his moods, we argued more and I were afraid for meself when he went away for several days at a time, wonderin' if he were out there somewhere lyin' shot and wounded. Then what were I to do? Some of the other convicts was none too trustworthy, especially the ones what didn't have a woman in tow. I'd seen them eyein' me up and down quite a bit. I wouldn't be none too safe with them around.

I'd heard of one woman, like me, what'd come to live with an escapee out here in the Huon. She'd dress up in her husband's clothin' when she were alone, thinkin' the Aborigines wouldn't know the difference. The womenfolk of the Blacks 'ave been snatched from many of them and treated very poor, and sometimes they get back at white people. That's what I heard. I felt nervous on all counts, not only from Aborigines but from some of the wild white men roamin' the mountains, ready to murder anyone who looks at 'em, they say. And it's true. Some of 'em lived in caves and kept to themselves mostly, but if they become mad they could do anythin'. It frightened me to hear stories of what they'd done to women and young children if they wasn't protected by their menfolk. There's places even the troopers don't dare to venture. A trooper'd have to travel on horseback if he did go in, and be ready to get away from any surprise attack. That's why it's pretty safe from the law here.

At night in the bush by meself I could hardly sleep from fear. I could hear all sorts of noises — scrapin' and scratchin' and sometimes what sounded like footsteps outside. A few times I got up, picked up the pistol beside the bed and tremblin' with fear I'd open the door, expectin' to see the face of a wild man or a coupla Blacks out to get me. But there weren't nothin'. Most likely possums, they can sometimes make sounds like someone walkin' around, or maybe the thuddin' of a kangaroo or two movin' past.

There was many a night I'd be sittin' up in bed, holdin' on to the pistol and end up fallin' asleep like that. I'd often wonder what me friends in the Factory was doin'. I wondered about Sarah and if she were still with them Quakers. And I thought about Agnes and wondered if she were still scarpin' it for a night at *The Commercial Hotel*. I did miss 'em.

More months went by and I were by meself far too much. Ben would come back and it'd be all right when he were with me, but it got less and less. It were when Ben and Michael made the move to holdin' up coaches, that things turned nasty. And he weren't all that nice to me no more. Gettin' real edgy he were. Yes, the coach robberies was our undoin'. Our life took a change for the worse.

When they did the last stagecoach hold-up, Michael shot dead the driver. Michael and Ben both managed to get away, but the man and his wife inside the stagecoach had took a good look at their faces. Michael become a marked man and both men was declared outlaws, even though Ben hadn't shot anyone. They had to find somewhere else to hide out. Our camp weren't safe no more, so Michael left, but Ben stayed with me.

The law was lookin' in earnest for both of 'em after that, but specially Michael. Someone said they'd read in a Hobart Town newspaper that the coach driver was *barbarously murdered by runaway convicts*, and their likeness were on posters all over the town. People was callin' them *cruel ruffians* and *outlaws*. I was gettin' more nervous with every day that passed. It felt like we was just waitin' for the time a Redcoat would find us, even hidden out where we was, or someone would dob us in. Ben decided it were time for him to move away from our camp. 'I've got to hide out somewhere else Maggie,' he said to me, 'it'll only be for a short while, then I'll be back.'

But he didn't come back. There in the bush all alone I were then, for God knows how long. I began to wonder why I stayed there. I wanted to leave, but where would I go? I got word that they was caught. Michael were charged with murder and robbery; Ben for robbery and holdin' up a stagecoach. I were so lonely and scared. A couple of the women I'd met come to see me but only durin' the day as they wanted to get back to their menfolk and littl'uns. The nights become unbearable. What am I doin' here? I kept thinkin'.

But that weren't the last of it. When Ben were taken out of the cell to be moved elsewhere, he managed to escape! Now he were really on the run and he sent word to me to meet him. I were to go to *The Commercial Hotel*, the very place I'd met him. That sounded a dangerous idea to my mind. He give me a day and time to be there. Another week away. But while he'd been away I'd been thinkin', I don't want to be in the Huon no more without Ben, and though I were real fond of him I didn't want to live a life of always bein' on the run with someone the law were out to catch. It were different before, but now I were desperate to figure out a way I could change me life around. I knew Sarah would help me if she could. I were sure she'd still be livin' in Hobart Town, and still with them Quakers. It probably wouldn't be hard to find her. She'd probably stay with 'em 'til she got her ticket of leave. Somebody'd know where the Quakers lived. I could trust Sarah. I felt she would help me, or at least we could talk about what I might do.

But how to get Sarah on her own? I'd have to figure that one out later. So, with this in mind, I made me way to Hobart Town, gettin' a ride in a dray with a couple what was goin' to town for provisions. They had enough room for me in the dray, and I wouldn't need to be comin' back when it were full. So this is what I did.

By the time I'd managed a ride and we'd made it to town, it were the day I was to meet Ben. I decided to contact Sarah after meetin' up with him. First I'd see what Ben had in mind for the two of us. I waited until the pub were full of noisy drinkers and smoke before I went inside to look for him. When I opened the pub door I were hit by the old familiar smells of men's bodies and baccy smoke so thick yer could cut it with a knife. At first I didn't see him it were so crowded.

I looked around, and there he was. He were even sittin' at the same small table we'd sat at all night the first time I met him. Me heart skipped a beat — it brought back the memories of that night when I decided to run away with him, and all the things we'd gone through together in the bush. Ben thought he wouldn't be recognised 'cos he'd shaved off his beard and changed his name to Joe Ryan. And he did look different, I scarcely recognised him without his beard!

He saw me and beckoned me over, but just at that moment, before I'd taken a step towards him, three constables come into the pub to check on things. Sometimes they do that, random like. In spite of his havin' no beard, the constables wasn't fooled. After all, his poster was all over town. Still, somebody in the pub must've dobbed him in. There were a good reward for any bounty hunter.

Quick as a flash, they moved in on him. He weren't expectin' it, and they nabbed him easy. I saw him look at me as they shoved him out the door, a look of someone just about to eat a piece of cake only to have it taken away. When he nodded at me and winked, me heart sank. So close we was to gettin' together again, though how life would be better I didn't know. We was outwitted and there weren't nothin' neither of us could do. They'd took us completely by surprise all right, and Ben didn't have time to reach for his pistol.

So once again Ben were arrested and taken away. This time he couldn't escape. Later on I heard he were found guilty, given a extra seven years on his original fourteen, and sent to Norfolk Island. I remembered hearin' how that place were said to be even worse than Port Arthur. Oh my poor Ben, to suffer all that again and no doubt more floggin's! Me heart was fit to burst. I never saw him again.

In the meantime, there were I, standin' still with the shock of it all, still in *The Commercial Hotel* wonderin' what the heck to do. I looked around to see if Agnes might be there, havin' a night on the town. But no Agnes. I couldn't go back to the Huon, and I couldn't go lookin' for Sarah at that time of night. She'd be in bed and the house would be locked up, all quiet. What to do?

I made me way down to the start of the rivulet Agnes had took me along. At the town end I found a spot where there weren't nobody else, and slept the night by the side of the water. Afraid and cold, covered only by a blanket and shawl I'd brought with me from the Huon, I had a fitful night's sleep. Durin' the night I heard different people pass by, worse for wear and lookin' for a spot to pass out. But I were well hid. When I woke up at sunrise the next mornin' chilled to the bone, I dusted meself down and walked to the address I thought were Sarah's.

I waited for a couple of hours for her to show herself. Around nine o'clock in the mornin' there she were! My luck were in, I thought. She were carryin' a basket and must've been on her way to pick up somethin' for her mistress. I followed her down the street and around the corner, so we wouldn't be seen by anyone happenin' to look out the front window of the house.

'Sarah!' I called, and she turned around straightaway.

'Why Maggie! What are you doing here? Where have you been? Why are you in such disarray? I heard you'd escaped from Cascades, and nobody heard what had happened to you.'

We moved to a spot on the walk to town where we could talk more easy, so I could give her a rundown of what'd happened to me since I'd escaped, and me present situation. She listened, with a kind, concerned face at all I told her, then she said, 'I'm so sorry to hear all this Maggie. But there's very little I can do, except try to get some food for you. The Quaker family I am with would never condone my helping an escaped convict.'

Then we was quiet, both of us tryin' to think of a way out of me situation. I took a good look at Sarah while I was thinkin'. Then I realised what I must've looked like. In the bush for months, dressed in worn-out clothes too big for me what Ben had stolen for me from the washin' lines of settlers, with a dirty shawl round me shoulders and carryin' a tattered blanket. What a sight I musta been. She looks so lovely, I thought, and look at me, what've I become after ten months in the bush. Me clothes is filthy and me hair dirty. Next to Sarah, I looked like a poor ragamuffin. But I could see Sarah weren't thinkin' of how bedraggled I looked. She were tryin' to think of some way she could help me.

She opened her mouth to say somethin', thought better of it, but then decided to say it anyway, 'Perhaps the best thing you could do would be to return to Cascades and take the consequences. At least you would have somewhere to live, and food. And after some time in Crime Class — for they will surely put you there — in time you will be sent out on assignment.'

While I was thinkin' about that possibility meself, she said, 'Why didn't you answer any of my letters Maggie?'

'Letters? I didn't get no letters Sarah,' I said. 'Not one. I was hopin' against hope that you would write to me, but nothin'.'

'Oh, that's so sad. I wrote several letters. So that's why I didn't hear from you.'

Musta bin that bloody Matron, I thought. The letters would've come, but she wouldn't have passed them on to me when I were still at the Factory. Then when I scarped it, she would've thrown away any others. I said me goodbyes to me friend Sarah and we both give each other a big hug. Though I did see her face screw up a bit. I musta smelt terrible. We wanted to spend more time together but she had to hurry away on the task her mistress had sent her on. No dilly-dallyin'. I walked with her for a bit, then let her go on by herself. I had to think what I were goin' to do.

I spent hours tossin' things around in me mind. What to do? What to do? Not too many choices. I knew Sarah were right about goin' back to Cascades and turnin' meself in. I didn't have no money, I didn't know no-one except a few women livin' in the bush with their men, I didn't know no-one but Sarah in Hobart Town and she were a domestic in a religious household. I didn't want to go on the town and become a whore, and if I went back to pickin' pockets I'd be likely to get caught and end up back at Cascades anyways. No, I would have to give meself up. That way, I'd do me time and eventually be free.

And that's what I did. All them months after I'd escaped. I followed the same track back to Cascades Female Factory, and knocked on them big wooden doors, wantin' to be let in!

Chapter 9

# *Maggie*

*10th December, 1838*

When them big doors opened the guard were that shocked to see me he nearly passed out! He pulled me in, slammed shut the doors, locked 'em and went to fetch Matron. She couldn't believe her eyes neither!

Then looking very smug, she said, 'It's Crime Class for you my girl, and you'll be getting a hefty extension on your sentence as well. Mark my words.' But I could see she was wondering why I'd come back to the Factory.

So, there I were, back in Crime Class, with another year tacked on to me sentence. After all them months of freedom, fresh country air and plenty of food I had to face gloomy Yard Three with its grey despair. I met up with Agnes straightaway and found out that when she'd come back to the Factory without me that night all them months ago she'd kept mum about what'd happened — she didn't say nothin' about Benjamin. Just told people I'd decided to run away. All the other women thought it were a excitin' thing to do and said they wished they'd done it. But I could see they didn't really mean it. They'd be too afraid, not knowin' where to go and how to survive. No, assignment was better, that way they'd have somewhere to live.

Agnes could've told everyone about where I were headin' and made a lot of trouble for me and Ben. But she didn't. She were a pretty good sort really, and we had a sort of bond between us after that. When she saw me she hurried over, I could see she were wonderin' what'd brought me back to the Factory when I were so keen to scarp it. 'What are ye doin' back here lass?' she said to me.

Well, I told her some of what'd happened after I'd left *The Commercial* that night with Ben, and about his bushrangin' exploits, and the unhappy endin' for us both when he were arrested.

'And ye willingly come back here?' she said, starin' at me in surprise.

'I didn't have no other choice, Agnes. At least here I'm safe, and when I serves me time, I can go out as a free woman, instead of bein' on the run forever.'

'Aye, I ken what ye mean. I'd rather be here than takin' ma chances out there.'

Both of us fell silent, lookin' around at the goin's-on in Yard Three, shiftin' a little on the hard wooden bench. I looked at the women walkin' about with shorn hair, some of them tryin' to cover up the fact by stickin' bits of cut hair into the edges of their bonnets to make it look as if their hair was still long. Bonnets was useful like that. It worked until yer got up close.

'I went out on assignment once,' Agnes said. When she saw me eyes widenin' and me mouth open upon this amazin' piece of news, she went on, 'Aye, they were so hard-up for labour outside, they even sent some of us from Crime Class.'

'Where did yer go Agnes?'

'I was sent tae be a domestic servant. But when I talked one of the others, a wee lass in service, intae comin' out with me tae have a bit of a drap with a bottle o' whisky from the master's stash, I got caught and sent straight back here. I didnae last more than a couple o' days.'

I took a good look at Agnes then. She hadn't changed a bit in all the time I'd been away. I could see why she might be content with her life in here. Even though she hated them solitary cells, life weren't too bad for Agnes considerin' where she'd come from. Them villages in Scotland in the winter'd be more cold and gloomy than here where she were fed and had friends. With the help of the turnkey she could go outside for a drink and a night on the town every now and then, and in here she could play up with the Flash Mob. Only trouble was them solitary cells and the washtubs.

'So we've both had a bit of a taste of what it's like outside these walls, eh Agnes!'

'Aye, that we have lass. But inside or outside, nae matters tae me. I can still scarp it intae town on the odd night and get back in time.'

Yes, life for Agnes weren't all that bad here. When I looked away from her I started comparin' meself with Agnes, and reflectin' on me life outside the Factory walls. Until Ben got into trouble, I thought to meself, it were real nice to be outside. I ain't never been that free before. I don't want to spend the rest of me life inside here.

Back to the daily grind, and them bleedin' bells. I'd almost forgot about the bells. Hard work, eatin' and sleepin', chapel. And the boredom of it all. I kept out of the way of that bleedin' reverend. Not too hard to do. He was wary of me as well. And there were young ones easier to deal with. I'd forgot about all the squabbles between women when they ain't got nothin' to do. Most of the women was achin' to get out of Yard Three. It's goin' to take a long time before I'm out again with the extra year on me sentence. Unless I scarp it another time. But no, I ain't about to be doin' that. Still, I'm glad I went out with Agnes that night. I wouldn't have missed me time with Ben for the world.

To pass the time away at night in Crime Class, we'd tell each other stories. Some nights that were all there was to it. Or there might be a bit of a sing-song or two, often startin' with a favourite:

*Oh! my charming Nellie Ray,*
*They have taken you away,*
*You have gone to Van Dieman's cruel shore*
*For you've skinned so many tailors,*
*And you've robbed so many sailors,*
*That we'll look for you in Peter Street no more.*

The songs'd start off quiet, but if there was grog, like there often was one way or the other, the singin' would get louder and the ditties bawdier.

*When I came to my true love's door*
*I gently tirled the pin*
*My true love she arose and she*
*slipped on her clothes*
*And so softly she let me in*

*All the forepart of the night*
*We did both sport and play*
*And all the last part of the night*
*She slept in my arms till day*

*Fly up fly up my bonnie grey cock*
*And crow when it is day*

*Your breast shall be like the bonnie*
*beaten gold*
*And your wings of the silver grey*

All of us'd join in on the chorus. Times like these we felt we was a part of somethin', forgettin' our sorry lives for a bit. Some of the women'd look around for somethin' to top up their dreary grey prison clothes, and deck themselves out for a dance or two. There was all sorts of bits and pieces — stuff brought back from times we'd scarped it or come back to the Factory from domestic service. Silk scarves, flashy earrin's and trinkets, and bright-coloured ribbons and shawls. Nobody minded sharin' for the sing-songs. Baccy pipes would be lit and the air would be filled tobacco fumes so thick it felt like *The Commercial Hotel.*

Some nights there was quite a bit more grog. If a woman'd snuck back in with some hidden booty, or met a coupla sailors willin' to pass grog and food over the wall there'd be a lot more to drink. Yes, that happened quite often — women what'd scarped it for a night, like Agnes and me had. They might've had a good time with some sailors what was taken with 'em and knowin' they was from the Factory, the sailors might come by the next night. They'd call out or whistle from outside, wantin' to have a bit of a lark with 'em. Or they'd tie a basket full of food and a bottle or two to a rope and tell the women to haul it up and over the wall. Sometimes though, the poor bastards got caught for their trouble and ended up in prison for four months, with hard labour to boot.

Well, when there was extras like this, and the women got real drunk, things could get a bit outa hand. The grog'd make them merrier and more darin', and the songs and dancin' would get them worked up. These times I made meself scarce. Didn't want none of that. Not me. I was glad Sarah weren't here, glad she were tucked away in her bed in the Quaker house, safe and out of harm's way. Away from the gruff laughter; from the cursin', and women gone wild. At times they'd put someone on lookout to watch for Matron. When they was alerted by the lookout that Matron were on her way, they'd all get back into their bunks and be quiet. But soon as she went back to her quarters and they figured she'd be back there, they'd start up again. They liked to tease her like that.

Agnes told me that before she got friendly with the turnkey, she tried to get outside usin' other means.

'Aye. One time I pinched a spoon from the kitchen and started scratchin' away at a hole already there in a wall that faced the street. At first, I just wanted tae talk tae someone outside. I kept at it for a long time — nought else tae do anyway, then the hole got bigger and bigger and I thought, I could make it big enough tae squeeze through!'

'That must've taken yer a long time,' I said to her, imaginin' Agnes scratchin' away for hours on end.

'Aye. So when I thought it was big enough, I pushed ma head through, then tried tae get ma shoulders through. But it was a tight squeeze and I got stuck! I saw an old man passin' by and thought at least I could hae a bit of a chat with him. But the look on his face told me he were not interested in that — a woman half out of a wall o' the Female Factory! Neither in nor out. He started shoutin' out tae someone and before I knew it there was a constable on the scene.'

I tried to stifle me laughter picturin' Agnes stuck in the wall and the look on the old man's face! If Agnes had been a little bit thinner, and the hole a little bit bigger, she might've got away with it.

'Oh Agnes, what happened then?'

'What do ye think lass? Matron was called for. And I ended up in solitary.'

After that, Agnes found it were less trouble to be friends with a turnkey, and scarpin' it become less of a problem as long as she were careful. I were gettin' to be more friends with Agnes as the time went on. And I were pleased no-one ever found out it were her arrangement with the turnkey what made it possible for me to scarp it to *The Commercial* that night. So she didn't have to go to solitary because of me.

Thinkin' things couldn't get much worse here — I were that sick of bein' in Crime Class — when who should I see limpin' her way towards me but Thelma, the one what attacked Josie. Makin' a bee-line for me she was, a murderous look in her eye. Behind her, eggin' her on, were one of her cronies, a simperin' black-toothed hag of a woman ready for a bit of a tickle at someone else's expense.

'You've got it, I know yer 'ave.'

Me heart skipped a beat. I got a flash back to the ship and that terrible fight Agnes had with Martha.

'Got what Thelma?' I said. This could turn real bad.

'Don't try to play all innocent with me. Me love token. That's what yer got.'

'No. No, I ain't. I swear it.' I didn't have one of me own, but I knew how precious these copper pennies was with love messages scratched on 'em from back in the old country. I were terrified, rememberin' what Josie'd told me.

'Yer bitch, give it back.'

At that, she started swearin' at me and pushin' me around, slappin' me across me face. Then the scrawny old hag behind her come over and the two of 'em started inta me. They was the roughest women I ever met in me life. Weren't none as bad as them, even in Cheapside.

Thelma grabbed me clothes and ripped the top of me thin cotton dress to get at me, all the time lookin' for the token. Findin' nothin' there, she punched me, movin' down me body, tearin' at me skirts, finally givin' me such a kick in the belly that I reeled, doubled over in pain. Another drunken woman stumbled over, thinkin' she'd join in the fun, but lucky for me, she were too drunk to stand up, let alone bash me.

Thelma and her mate both worked themselves up into a frenzy and seemed to be enjoyin' it. Before they'd finished I were in terrible pain. I lay crumpled on the floor and I musta fainted. Nobody come over. Bein' night time, everyone were used to hearin' people yellin' and some punch-ups goin' on. Nobody knew it were me. Agnes musta been asleep or she woulda come over to help me. Yer can sleep through somethin' like that — bein' as everyone is used to it.

The next mornin' me eyes was puffed up so bad I could scarcely see, me ribs was sore, and me body were racked with pain. I felt the top of me head and found me hair were caked with sticky dried blood. When Agnes seen me, she called for Matron. Not like her to do that. But she could see the state I were in and that it were real bad. I lost a lotta blood and become real sick, so sick I were put in the Factory hospital.

After three days in the hospital I were covered in bruises and still real pale and weak, but Matron decided I should be put back to work in the Nursery, like when I first come here. Matron knew I were good with the babies, so she put me to good use. I just had to go back to Crime Class to sleep. I made sure I kept out of Thelma's way, and Agnes watched out for me too after that.

'Best tae keep out o' Thelma's way lass. She's gone a bit insane. Been that way since she arrived in Van Diemen's Land. She went mad after her stint in the ship's coal hole. Twenty-four hours in that dark hole of a place. I ken what it's like. Seems it was too much for Thelma and she went over the edge, intae madness. If ye be thinkin' of scarpin' it agin, I'll let ye know next time I'm plannin' another night on the town.'

The thought had crossed me mind. But no, I decided to wait out me time and try to get an early ticket of leave. Better to behave and try to get sent out on assignment.

When I had a bit of time on me hands, I started a letter to Sarah. I wanted to let her know what'd happened. I spent over a week addin' bits to it, not knowin' if she'd ever get the letter. It were the first letter I ever wrote.

*3rd February 1839*

*Dear Sarah,*

*How are you? I am well. back in the faktree. I have not heard from you but I am always hoping you will rite to me.*

*Things is not good in Crime Class. I got bashed. but I do the best I can.*

*Your loving frend,*

*Maggie*

It took me a few days to finish the letter. I told Agnes I had a letter for Sarah and she said she'd take it out the next time she planned to scarp it. She said she'd find some way of gettin' it to Sarah.

Goin' to the Nursery every day, I saw quite a bit of Matron. She told me a few things about herself. Not much. She's given birth to a lot of babies, not all what lived. Some of them died in here, in the Factory. Maybe that's why she's used to the death of babies and littl'uns. I think Matron has tried to make things better for all of us women. But there's so many of us and there don't seem to be enough money or food to go round. I reckon she don't feel it's goin' to get any better so she just overlooks things as they get worse.

Nothin''s changed much since I were in the Nursery before. Seventy children under three years of age is cramped into two small rooms. In the weanin' room there's even more tiny babies to take care of than when I were here before.

The children is so pale and sickly and they don't have nowhere to play in the fresh air, only the yard what's nearly always wet and don't see the sun for more'n four months of the year. Twenty infants dead already this year! Even sucklin' babies a few weeks old is deprived of their ma's breast, and the poor mothers is so weak from it all. Every day there's another poor ailin', tiny body. I'm afraid to look in the cribs for findin' a dead baby there. Only the strongest ones live. I wonder any of 'em do. When a baby's found dead in the Factory, it's taken outa here quick-smart. I don't know where they take 'em. I heard some outside in Hobart Town call convict children the *illegitimate spawn of the island's scum*. How can they ever have any luck in life bein' called names like that?

I do everythin' I can to help these babes, but it don't make too much difference. Good food and clean beddin' would help. But what they really needs is a mother's love — the mothers what are only a short distance away, but aren't allowed to take care of 'em. There ain't nothin' so sad as the sound of mothers softly moanin' for their lost children.

*2nd April 1839*

*Dear Maggie,*

*Finally, I have received a letter from you dear friend.*

*I was so saddened to hear you were indeed put into Crime Class and what had happened. I do hope you are fully recovered now, and will soon be going out on assignment to a good place.*

*Maggie, I have been to the Queen's Orphanage again! What a sad place. The children are clothed in coarse fabric to mark them as offspring of convicts, and their hair is cut very short. Chores and work training are expected from all but the very youngest of them and if they do anything that is considered bad, even the slightest thing, they are harshly punished.*

*Will this ever change? If only I could do something to help them. One of them clung to my skirts for most of the time I was there. It broke my heart to look into their dear sweet faces and see the longing there. Such little helpless things with no-one to give them a proper home and love.*

*Take care of yourself dear friend. I hope it will not be too long before you find a decent place with a kind family. Keep writing to me. If only we both had our tickets of leave.*

*Your loving,*

*Sarah*

Now that Sarah and me has found a way of gettin' letters to each other, we can find out more about what is goin' on in each other's lives. Baby farmers. I never heard any more about them, but I still wonder what happens to the dead babies that are sneaked out at night from here.

*5th June 1839*

*Dear Maggie,*

*I am so pleased to have received another letter from you. I continue to be more acquainted with the ways of the Quakers. They do not bear arms and refuse to go to war as they are a peaceful people. I am so grateful to be living in this house and I am getting used to their views on simplicity and their way of speaking. They have a rule about not marrying out of their religion so if one were to marry a Quaker they would have to become one.*

*Now there has been more in the newspapers with regard to Cascades Factory Nursery where you are, and people in Hobart Town, including all the Quakers, are ordering that something be done about removing the children from there, never mind about expense or inconvenience.*

*Let us hope dear Maggie, that something will be done now! I do hope you are well.*

*Yours affectionately,*

*Sarah*

*7th July 1839*

*Dear Sarah,*

*It is good to hear from you. I am still working in the Factory Nursery.*

*Agnes were put in solitary again last week. That red head Irish girl Kathleen were sent out on service and I might be sent out on service soon. I have been behavin meself and Matron said there were more people wantin help and she might send me out.*

*I am well, as I trust you are too dear frend.*

*Maggie*

Must be all them people up in arms about conditions in Cascades Factory Nursery has caused it to be closed down now. The babies is bein' sent to a new house near to town until they is weaned and old enough to be sent to Queen's Orphanage. About time I say. They reckon the new place ain't as damp and is better fit out, but it's crowded all the same, with up to one hundred children, and forty-five women still breast-feedin' babes. Sometimes a doctor visits, but the convict women has to take care of the babies best they can. It's a easy to walk into town from there and convicts sneak out a lot. With no matron and not even a constable in charge of 'em they can slip out to the sly-grog shops and pubs whenever it takes their fancy. They likes to look in shop windows as well — imaginin' theirselves in fancy dresses. That's what I heard.

Another letter from Sarah. I'm gettin' them when they come now. Matron has changed her mind about me and knows I won't be scarpin' it again. She knows all I wants is to get out of here.

*1st September, 1839*

*My Dear Maggie,*

*I do hope you are well. For myself, I am still safe and well. I have been treated so well here, Maggie, and have learnt so much. I must tell you that I have become a member of the Society of Friends (this is what the Quakers are called), and have met so many kind people.*

*One person in particular, dearest, who makes my heart beat faster each time I am in his company, is Mr. William Cotton, whom I met after only a short time into my service with the Bridges. I believe that he feels the same about me but is a little shy, as am I, in expressing his feelings. He does not seem to mind that I have been sent to Van Diemen's Land as a convict. I relayed to him that I was entirely innocent of the crime for which I was transported, and he believes that this is so.*

*Oh Maggie, I wish I could see you so that we could talk further on this subject. I have not told him about Robert and the transport ship. I dare not.*

*My fondest regards to you, dear Maggie. God be with you and keep you safe.*

*Affectionately,*

*Sarah*

Well, Sarah has met someone. I'm happy for her. Somethin' good has happened for me beautiful friend.

Matron come and told me that because there's a shortage of women servants, I'd be goin' out on assignment tomorrow. At last! A chance to have a bit of freedom again. That's if it's a good place. But who knows? I wonder where I'll be sent.

Chapter 10

# *Maggie*

*10th September, 1839*

Clutchin' me small bundle of belongin's, I walked out of them big wooden gates into the world outside for the second time. Outside the bleedin' Female Factory at last! I felt free, even if it were only to be a servant. No more of them damn bells. No more of the smell of hopelessness. I didn't know then it'd be the last time I'd ever see the inside of that place and how much me life'd change from that day on.

Matron told me I'd be workin' on a sheep property and it were a long way to go. 'You better be ready to leave as soon as they come,' she said to me, 'no dilly-dallying. Your master will not wait.'

'Yes Matron,' I said to her. *Whatever you say Matron. I can't wait to get outa here.* But them was only me thoughts. If I'd said them out loud she would've put me straight back into Crime Class for insolence.

Mr. Richardson, me new master, were standin' next to a light one-horse vehicle what had a seat behind for a servant such as meself. On the other side of the road were a two-horse dray loaded up with goods and a driver, a surly-lookin' character what just nodded at me. Them two big workin'-horses looked as if they'd done this before and they was used to haulin' heavy loads.

'You can sit in the back there Maggie,' he said, pointin' to the gig. 'It's a long way to the property, so make yourself comfortable. Could take a few hours and the roads in the Interior aren't up to much.' I could hear his Midlands accent. From the look of him I reckoned he were a serious man what brooked no nonsense, but prob'ly a decent one.

'Our farm produces most of the food we eat,' he said to me once I'd settled in the back with me bag next to me, 'but we still need to buy things like flour, tea and sugar. We'd almost run out of these. Takes a long time for things to get over here and orders come in dribs and drabs. I had a big order this time, but some of them didn't come in this shipment. My wife will be disappointed that some furniture did not arrive. But she'll be pleased to see you. She really needs some help.'

Once we got started, it were a bit too noisy to talk much. Them convict roads in town was pretty good and we drove along at a fair pace, but as soon as we come to the edge of town and into the country the roads was full of holes and in a bad state. They wasn't built for none of them fancy four-wheeled carriages town folk liked to ride round in, and sure as eggs not built for a gig.

We bumped and rattled our way outa Hobart Town 'til we reached the crest of a hill what opened out to hills leadin' to the Derwent River valley. So much land! It spread out in front of us like it went on forever. Real nice it were with some small farms and houses scattered here and there. Then a bit further along the countryside become thick with clumps of tall trees. It felt good to be out of that gloomy Factory. I were surprised to see so much land without hardly any people anywhere. It smelt different too, and there was strange bird sounds I ain't never heard before, even in the Huon. Birds here is different to England, that's certain, not that yer see too many birds in Cheapside, only them pigeons really.

Out of the corner of me eye I spied one of them large lizards. Its fat eyes stared back at me like it were just as curious about me. Mr. Richardson were used to this part of the country but it were strange to me.

*Whenever will we get there?* I thought. *Must be soon.* As we kept goin' I saw a dead kangaroo at the side of the road, its body were all bloated up and its legs was stickin' straight up in the air like a whore waitin' for a customer. And swarmin' with them sticky black flies yer see everywhere out here. They was a nuisance them flies.

In spite of them potholes our horses was movin' at a fair pace in the mornin', but as the sun started gettin' up and the day got hotter, the heat were too much for them. By mid-day the sun were beatin' down on us all somethin' terrible. I could feel it on me back, piercin' through me clothes, and I started to wonder if we'd ever get to where we was goin'. Already we was all sweaty and covered in dust and the hair under me bonnet was stickin' to me neck.

Poor old nags, I thought to meself. Them provisions on the dray must weigh a ton. They slowed right down as the day wore on, the sweat runnin' off their backs as they dragged theirselves up and down steep hills and through forests of straggly gumtrees. Too hot for anyone to talk; too hot to do anythin' but just sit and be bumped along for hours. The only sounds besides the horses snortin', the rattle of the wheels and the squeakin' of the leather bridles come from a few birds flyin' high in the sky makin' a *caw-caw* sound. There weren't a whisper of wind.

We stopped a few times to water the horses and let them rest a bit, but Mr. Richardson were keen to get home so the stops was short. I dozed off a few times, wakin' up sharp each time we hit a large stone or a hole.

Just when I thought we mightn't arrive 'til after sundown — for by this time it were well into the late afternoon and the sun was startin' to go down — the horses turned a curve in the road and there it were before us: more than a thousand sheep grazin' in the distance and a large ramblin' house off the road at the end of a driveway.

'There it is. That's our property,' said Mr. Richardson, full of pride. Blimey, I thought, this is a bit grand! And I started to get excited again, to think I'd be livin' in such a place! Course I wouldn't be livin' in that large stone house. That'd be for the family, but there was gardens in front, full of flowers and in spite of the heat, everythin' was green. Looked like there were a windin' creek to one side of the house with flowerin' plants that must be special to Van Diemen's Land. I never seen them in England. And them huge old gum trees stood tall and straight, not a breath of air movin' their leaves.

I could see he were real glad to be back home and with his family again.

'It's a grand house,' I said to him, then thought, *but I'll be in the middle of nowhere, out here.*

As if readin' me thoughts he said, 'It's quite isolated, but our neighbours live not too far away, about fifteen miles, and my wife has a lot to keep her occupied, what with the children and the garden. And we have several other workers here.'

Fifteen bleedin' miles, and he thinks that's not far away! No chance of poppin' in for a quick cuppa with the neighbour's maid then. Still, it's pretty with all them colourful flowers, and the house is real nice it is. When the gig finally stopped in front of the house I stepped down, holdin' on to me bundle of clothes. Mrs. Richardson come out to greet her husband, bringin' the three children with her. They was all excited to see their father again and not too interested in me. When they got around to me, Mr. Richardson said to his wife, 'This is Maggie'.

And without any pretence she said, 'Hello Maggie, I'm very pleased to have you here.'

'Good afternoon Madam,' said I. She looked like a nice person but by this time I felt that tired and it were all that perculiar, I almost felt like weepin'. I knew I couldn't. Just that I really did feel strange and so alone, knowin' no-one at all out here. I didn't know what sort of a place I'd come to or what any of the other workers'd be like, and with all the stories I'd heard from the other convicts what'd been sent out on assignment, it could be a terrible place. I started tremblin', thinkin' of all the things that could happen to me, but I couldn't let any of 'em see how I felt.

'When you have settled in to your quarters, please come to see me in the house and you can meet the children properly. Pearl will show you the way,' said Mrs. Richardson to me.

With that, another girl around me own age come to show me where I'd be sleepin'. She looked me up and down.

'I'm Pearl,' she said. 'You'll be sharin' a room with me. I'll show you where it is.'

She took me around the back of the house, to a small room with two beds and a coupla push-out windows, in a buildin' separate from the main house.

'That's your bed. The other one's mine,' said Pearl. I put my small bundle on the bed she showed me, wishin' I could crawl into it and get some shut-eye, but she added, 'Mistress is waiting for you.'

'I'm here on assignment from the Factory as well,' Pearl said as we walked back towards the house. 'But I've been here almost a year now.' Then it must be all right, I thought, givin' meself a quick tidy-up as we walked. 'I don't have long to go before I get my ticket of leave,' she added, 'but in the meantime, I have to sweep, mop, scrub floors and doorsteps, make all the beds, empty the bedpans, get up the linen, and anythin' extra if needs be. You're the lucky one, you are. You get to look after the Mistress's children.'

I wondered then, if Matron had felt sorry for me, bein' bashed up like I was. But prob'ly not. She knew I were good with children, and it looks like that's what I'll be doin' here. Now to see what the littl'uns is like.

'We get visitors here sometimes,' Pearl went on, not worryin' whether I was listenin' to her or not. 'When that happens everybody has to lend a hand, even a lucky one like you.' By that time, we was at the house. Pearl took me in to the room where Mrs. Richardson was waitin' with the children. She knocked on the door first before enterin' and then she left.

'I'm so glad to have more help with the children,' Mrs Richardson said to me. While she were lookin' me up and down I took a quick look around the room. Real nice it were. Big blue curtains, pulled back to let the light in, and chairs covered in blue cloth with roses on it. A vase of flowers was on the round table next to her. She looked over at the boy. 'This is Harry, who is seven years old,' then she pulled the girls in close, her arms round their shoulders, 'and these are my two girls, Alice, who is four, and the little one Jane, who is just two.'

'Well, I'm very pleased to make yer acquaintance children.' What sweet little girls, and Harry don't look too difficult. Yes, I think I'll like it here all right.

'All the children were born here on our property. In the fourteen years we've been here we've had very few problems with our workers. Mr. Richardson is of the opinion that if an employer treats his workers generously and fairly, there should be no reason for them to be anything but honest and fair in their dealings with us as well.'

I noticed she said 'employer' not 'master'. That were a good sign I thought. I should be treated fair then.

'Thank you madam, I'm sure I'll like it here very much, and will do me best.'

'Our workers have stayed for long periods of time, some for many years — before and after their tickets of leave. They like it here. One man and his family have been with us for eight years, and are living in a small dwelling a short distance from our house. You can read and write I believe?'

'Yes, madam. And I loves children. I were lookin' after the little ones at the Factory nursery, and I took care of me brothers and sisters back in England, especially after me ma passed away.'

'I'm sorry to hear that Maggie.' When she said that she sounded like she meant it. 'I'm sure you and the children will get on well.'

'Thank you madam.' Then she looked at the door, givin' me the hint it were time for me to leave.

'Pearl will show you to the kitchen where the cook will give you some supper, and I shall see you in the morning. Report back to me here.'

Pearl took me to the kitchen and the cook sat me down at a big wooden table where staff ate, put a plate of sandwiches in front of me, then went back to her work. She had to get on with preparin' food for the family and didn't have no time to waste talkin' to me. I'd have to get to know her later. I ate me sandwiches in silence and quick, bein' that hungry from the long journey, but lookin' forward to gettin' into me bed.

When Pearl and me was back in our bedroom and I were puttin' on me nightgown, she told me she'd been in Van Diemen's Land five years already and just had two more years to go before her ticket of leave.

'I'm being careful not to get into any trouble. That way I can ask the Richardsons for a letter of reference for an early ticket of leave, before my seven years is up.' I wondered where she was plannin' to go when she were free, but she went on before I had a chance to ask her. 'This is my fourth assignment. It's not as bad here as some of the other places. One day I found two young striped bandicoots, pretty little soft creatures like great mice, and brought them to show the children. They were real happy about that and fussed over them, so Mrs. Richardson said they could keep them as pets.'

I knew what a bandicoot were because I used to shoot 'em in the Huon, but I didn't let on about that.

'There are four men working on the property,' Pearl said, telling me everything she could about who did what. 'The two shearers are currency lads: Thomas and Arthur. They're paid wages. Then there's Henry, a convict on assignment like us, and John, a ticket of leave man. He keeps to himself, does John. All the men sleep in a big tin shed near the house close to where the horses are. You have to be careful of the men in the shed. They're all looking for a woman, and the two currency lads are very free with their smiles and enticements for adventure, so just watch out.'

After I'd been there for a week or so, I'd met them all, and I made sure they knew I weren't interested in 'em except for a chat. We'd all have a chance every now and then for a few moments of what Matron would call 'idle chit-chat'. The men liked to have a bit of a yarn at the back of the shed, lookin' out at the property where the sheep was grazin'. I enjoyed them times, it felt good to be out in the open air, and lookin' out on a big stretch of country. The older man reminded me of me father before he'd taken to the drink.

Before too long it were Christmas again, and not anythin' like the dismal one at the Factory. The weather were hot and dry, and we was at the other end of the world, somethin' I still couldn't get used to. Instead of a English Christmas with mistletoe and fir trees — for them lucky enough back in England — there was bouquets of summer flowers decoratin' the house, and the young girls was dressed in white muslin frocks to stay cool. But the heat didn't stop no-one from eatin' a hot Christmas dinner with roast beef and lamb and hot Christmas puddin' with thick custard poured all over it. That's what the family had anyways.

Except for the cook and the kitchen staff, us workers had our own Christmas dinner Australian style, out in the open under the shade of a tin roof near the men's sheds. Everyone walked around wishin' each other 'Merry Christmas' with smiles on their faces, excited about Christmas Day. It were hot when the day started, but by the middle of the day it were scorchin', and our clothes was stickin' to us. By the time we was ready to eat we wasn't that hungry. But that didn't stop nobody.

'Come over here Maggie, and I'll show yer the art of sticker-up-cookery,' one of the men said to me. I followed him over to a bench what had a dead kangaroo on top. Looked like it'd been shot not long ago. Its glassy eyes was thick with black flies and its underbelly were sliced open, the gizzards spilled on the shed floor. The dogs was makin' a meal of that. Some bloodied chunks of meat was already sittin' on the bench.

'What's that then?' I asked him, wonderin' what on earth he meant. 'Sticker-up-cookery? Well, I never.'

He cut up some of the meat into chunks with a sharp knife then broke a stick from a nearby tree branch, whittled it down and sharpened it at both ends. Then he cut up the chunks into smaller pieces and pushed 'em up the sharp ends of the stick, leavin' a bit of space in between each one. Then he wound a nice fat bit of fresh bacon around the top end of the stick.

'See, now yer sticks it in the ground, close by the fire, to leeward; yer have to be careful it don't burn.'

He looked proud of himself showin' me how to do this, his leathery face sweatin' under his broad-brimmed hat. I watched as the bacon sizzled and spat its fatty liquid, drippin' down the stick on to the lean kangaroo meat.

'Smells like beef grillin' in a London chop-house,' I said to him, 'the smell's so good it makes me mouth water.' He looked real pleased at me sayin' that. I didn't let on that I'd eaten kangaroo meat many times before. But it weren't cooked like that. What a funny name to call it, *stuck-up kangaroo.*

When it looked like it were done he handed me one of the skewers full of juicy meat. It smelt delicious. I put a small piece in me mouth, blowin' on it first to cool it down a bit, wonderin' what it would taste like.

'That's real tasty,' I told him, 'a bit like hare, don't yer think?'

'Ain't nothin' as good as kangaroo meat cooked over an open fire,' he said with a big grin on his face as he tucked into it.

Feelin' full from our hearty Christmas meal and a little bit sleepy from the afternoon heat, we all went down to paddle our feet in the cool stream, and lie on the grassy bank under the shade of some gum trees. Some of the men jumped inta the water, callin' out to us all to jump in. They splashed around and laughed and looked like they was enjoyin' themselves no end.

'Come in!' they called to the rest of us, 'it's so cool.'

Pearl said, 'let's come down one day and have a swim by ourselves.'

'That'd be lovely.' I thought of the times I'd spent in the river with Ben after he'd taught me to swim, but tried not to stay long on them thoughts, pleasant though they was. Me thoughts drifted to Christmases I'd spent under dismal, grey London skies, cold and hungry, wishin' there were more food on the table. Now, here I am.

I ain't never goin' back to that Factory. Life could be real good in this country if yer had yer freedom and weren't hidin' out from the law.

With the real hot weather and no rain for the past week, Mr. Richardson were worried about bush fires. He said bush fires destroyed everythin': sheep, fences, crops, stacks, houses. Everythin' could be swept away by a bushfire and no-one were safe. They had to control 'em before they got too wild and spread. One were reported only a few miles from our property, and we was frightened their flames would creep up close. All the men on our property went off to help the neighbours save their home and animals from the ragin' flames. When they come home they was dead weary and smellin' of bush smoke after hours of fightin' fierce flames. The trunks of the trees stayed smoulderin' for days, leavin' a blackened countryside with a thick haze and a burnt smell hangin' about for a long time.

We was given time off to go to Sunday service every week in the little church a few miles away. On the way, Pearl liked to drop in on Colleen, an older woman workin' for the local vicar.

'We just have time to have a cuppa before the church bells ring for the service,' Pearl said to me the first time I went. On the way home we'd stop at a deserted part of the river, and if there weren't no-one else around, we'd strip down to our under-garments and jump inta the water. I loved it when we could do this. It were so cool on them hot days. Pearl stayed in the shallow water and were that surprised I knew how to swim. But I didn't tell her nothin' about how I learned.

Night time the mozzies, daytime the flies. Our cook hung switches of gum leaves at doorways and windows to keep the flies from gettin' inside the house but they got in anyway. And trails of ants in the kitchen. Cook put bowls of sugar in dishes of water so them ants couldn't get at the sugar.

Weeks went by, then months and it were soon the middle of the year and a cold, crispy winter again. Snow fell this time, but it didn't stay long on the ground. It were hard to keep warm in the early mornin' and me fingers was blue with the cold. There was fires lit in some rooms of the house but it were drafty, and on windy days the cold air would seep in through the cracks, makin' a whistlin' sound. We had knitted gloves up to the elbows. Gloves without fingers so we could still do our work. Cook knew how to knit and she showed us how to make our own gloves and a warm scarf with scraps of left-over wool from the house. I weren't too good at the gloves, but the scarf were easy. Once yer got the hang of the knittin' that is. Some nights we'd sit around the fire in the kitchen with cook after all our chores was done, knittin' before goin' out in the cold and then jumpin' quick-smart inta our beds. Took a while for them sheets to warm up.

We never wanted for food. Plenty for everyone and a lot of meat. The inside staff ate meals at the kitchen table. The men workin' outside, ate together around their campfire and did their own cookin' in the tin shed. Pearl and me could hear them sometimes at night when the wind were blowin' our way.

I heard about the Emancipists when I were in the Huon, so when people talked about 'em here, I knew what they meant. Convicts and ex-convicts was callin' themselves Emancipists. What they all wanted was to have the rights free settlers was entitled to, specially once they'd served their time and wasn't convicts no more. Even a lot of the free settlers leaned to this way of thinkin'. The Irish was all for it.

'Emancipists can live like toffs in Van Diemen's Land,' said Pearl. 'If you're wealthy you can do all right, even become respectable, especially if you hide the fact of your convict past.'

I wondered how anyone could hide bein' sent over as a convict.

'People get to like it here and can make a go of it once they're free. They don't hanker after going back to the old country once they make some money. Some of them manage to get their own land. Why, some women manage to have their own businesses without a man in tow! I heard of one who had a hat shop, and one who even owned a pub,' said Pearl.

Pearl's words made me think — well — it might be possible to do all right in the end.

It were soon nearly summer again. Me days in service was spent in risin' early to look after the Richardson children and helpin' Mrs. Richardson in the gardens. Sometimes Pearl and me went out on a hot summer's night to lie on the grass under all them bright stars in the inky-blue sky, talkin' and laughin'. It reminded me again of me months with Ben and I'd wonder what he was doin' right at that minute. The night air durin' the warm weeks of summer were filled with the smell of eucalyptus and flowerin' wattle, the sound of croakin' frogs, and the scurryin' movements of small animals. Ben would've loved it here. He's prob'ly still in some awful prison. Poor feller.

Horse race meetin's was all the thing. All the men was keen to go to the race-track twenty miles away. Why even us women was in on the excitement. Mr. Richardson give us a Race Day Leave Pass in January so we could all go together in one of the drays. Cook give us some lunch baskets to take, and the lads had saved up a bit of money so they could place a bet.

Well, what a day! There was that many people there — from near and far. Right crowded it were. A nice day too. Sunny. We was all in our best clothes for the occasion and did we have fun! Us girls wandered around lookin' at everyone and how they was dressed and takin' in the admirin' glances from some of the young men. But we didn't want them followin' us around, so if a couple looked too keen, we'd walk over to join our own men, talkin' mostly about what horses they was goin' to bet on, and how much they would win if they was lucky. They was goin' to blow all the coin they'd saved up and the devil take the hindmost!

At lunchtime we found a nice spot under a tree to set up our picnic basket. No grass around, but the shade helped to keep off the hot sun. Cook had done us proud with her bread, meat, cheese, and a cake. And there were some soft drinks in the basket as well. A good spread it was. Then after lunch, another horse race. We all went to the fence and watched this one. The main race of the day. When the startin' gun went off we was all cheerin' on the horses, jumpin' up and down and callin' out our favourites even if we hadn't bet on none of them. Two of the men won and went home with extra money in their pockets!

It were a grand day. Under strict orders to return by sunset, the older worker John were put in charge of us and he made sure everyone were rounded up so we didn't let Mr. Richardson down. There were plenty of beer and spirits if yer had the coins, and a couple of 'em got a bit drunk. But after a night's sleep everyone were up and ready to begin work the next mornin', a bit bleary-eyed and worse for wear.

They couldn't stop talkin' about their day at the races for weeks!

The Richardsons had a vegetable and herb garden as well as an orchard. When both of the gardens was progressin' well, Mrs. Richardson left the tendin' of them to us workers. She didn't have long to go before her new baby was ready to be born. Durin' her lyin' in, she were sick a lot and I had me hands full lookin' after the other children by meself.

We was all worried about Mrs. Richardson. When it were time, the midwife come and we could all hear what a bad time Mrs. Richardson were havin'. Mr. Richardson asked me to wait and see if I could help the midwife. She'd come out of the bedroom every now and then, and I were at the ready if she needed help. She looked worried, did the midwife, and that didn't give me no confidence in how it was all goin'. Sadly, things didn't go well. She give birth to a tiny baby boy on the eighteenth of December 1841, but it were born sickly, and everyone in the household were upset and nervous about the way things was turnin' out. For a week we was all walkin' around with long faces, and bein' as quiet as we could goin' about our work. We didn't have no thought of Christmas that year.

Alas, the poor little boy died just three weeks after bein' born, the first soul to be buried in the family plot on the property. It were a very quiet day when they put him in his tiny grave on the eighth of January 1842. All of us took the loss real bad. The Richardsons was good to all of us and it was like we lost one of our own.

But life goes on, and there was work to do. So only one month after that sweet little boy was laid to rest Mrs. Richardson took solace in her much-loved gardens.

What she were most passionate about was her large gardens of flowers and shrubs. She liked to look after them herself, and she asked me if I could help her when I wasn't busy with the children. Sometimes I'd take the two littlest ones with us and we'd all spend the mornin' tendin' the gardens, the littlies doin' what they could, and laughin' and playin' amongst the flowers. It were that lovely, what with the smells from the different flowers, them what grew natural out here, and them what grew from the seeds sent over from England. People over here like to grow flowers what reminds them of the old country.

There was poppies and bright-eyed marigolds, as well as geraniums and hollyhocks. Mrs. Richardson taught me how to write these words down after I asked her. I were tryin' hard to improve me readin' and writin' all the time. She were real nice to me were Mrs. Richardson. She even lent me a book to read sometimes. I never would've thought, in me wildest dreams, that I'd be lucky enough to be in such a good place.

I was learnin' so much about plants, herbs, and flowers from Mrs. Richardson, and from watchin' what was happenin' in different seasons — whether they liked sun or shade, and all them sorts of things. Me favourite bit of the garden were the small lavender field. When they was all pale purple, I loved to walk along the rows of 'em. It were like I were waftin' on a cloud of pale purple perfume.

Chapter 11

# *Maggie*

*5th October, 1842*

Life went on and the seasons come and went: short summers and long winters. Them winter nights was bitter cold. Sometimes there were a light coverin' of snow over everythin' but it didn't rest long on the ground. Pearl were waitin' for her ticket of leave. Wouldn't be long now. That's all she could talk about. She were goin' to live in Launceston, in the north, when she was free. She had a friend there what said she could stay with her. There were plenty of work up there her friend said.

When Mr. Richardson come back from trips to Hobart Town, he'd bring us all some small gift. Real thoughtful he were. Us women got give somethin' to deck ourselves out in, might be a piece of ribbon, or a simple bonnet. One girl kept hopin' she might get white stockin's or fancy material for a dress. One was hangin' out for them modern stays. But I reckon she had high hopes, that one!

The men got a extra ration of baccy or a handkerchief, never anythin' yellow. It reminded them of when they was convicts, them ugly black and yellow uniforms what they was forced to wear on the chain gangs. They called 'em *magpie suits* because they was half black and half white to begin with, then they changed to black and yellow. The trousers was fastened with buttons all the way down the leg so they could get dressed without havin' their leg irons removed. That's why all the men didn't like the colour yellow.

Lots of times people got sick. The 'flu went the rounds a few times, and the children got colic and dysentery, even whoopin' cough. The littlest one were so sick we thought she was goin' to die. But she survived. Another time one of the horses pullin' the dray become frightened in a fierce thunder-storm and got out of control, resultin' in Mr. Richardson sufferin' a broken leg and gashes on his face and body when the dray rolled over. The driver broke a collar-bone and was black and blue all over his body. The poor horse broke its leg and had to be put down.

We started hearin' about conflicts between settlers and Aborigines, though we didn't see none of it, bein' in an area where there was few Blacks. Or so everyone thought. We heard some had been killed by the settlers and them what was left was bein' moved to Flinders Island. I were still fearful of Aborigines because of stories I heard. Me time in the bush never cured me of that. But I felt sorry for 'em as well. They was prob'ly livin' a good life before all of us arrived.

One night I dreamed I were swimmin' in the river at the Huon bush camp. Nobody around. Ben were off somewhere for a few days so it were just me and the fish down below. It were early mornin', time when the mist were still swirlin' over the river. Cold, bracin'. One of them real nice days. I let meself float like Ben taught me to do. When I woke up, I felt a pang of longin' — to be that free again, to feel the fresh silky water huggin' me body and not a soul around for miles. Free.

With the dream still on me mind, I saw that Pearl were up gettin' ready for Church like always, chatterin' away. I were still half in the river.

'Come on lazy-bones, better get ready or you'll be late for Church,' she said, bringin' me down to earth. Still a mite fuzzy from sleep, I thought, I don't want to go to Church today.

'I'm feelin' a bit poorly,' I said to her. 'I might skip Church this Sunday.'

Well, she weren't expectin' to hear this. She looked at me, her hands stopped pullin' on her bonnet for a minute. I could see she were wonderin' if I were really sick, but she musta thought it were true because she stopped lookin' at me suspicious like, and finished dressin'. Besides, she knew we both liked our Sundays off together.

'Please yourself,' she said, 'but there won't be anybody here. Everyone's going.'

When she'd left, I got up and went for a wander, checkin' first to see if anyone else were around who might dob me in. It were only a white lie I told. Not like it were goin' to upset or hurt anyone. It weren't that far to the spot on the river I knew nobody went to. There weren't a soul in sight. Real quiet and the river were sparklin'. I slipped off me clothes and walked in. The cold took me breath away, but then I got used to it and stretched out to float on me back like Ben had taught me to do, gazin' up at the sky, takin' in the silky feelin' of cool water over every inch of me body. I were lookin' at how many shapes there was in the clouds and havin' a relaxin' time when I had the peculiar feelin' I were bein' watched.

I let me legs sink down to the bottom. I weren't in that deep I couldn't stand up, and I looked to the riverbank. At first I thought I were imaginin' what I saw. But no. There he were. Black as night, standin' half hidden behind the trunk of a tree, starin'. At me. I froze on the spot. And for what seemed like ages, we was both rooted to our spots starin', both of us, and not movin' a muscle. He were as naked as I were. His black eyes held mine, but I weren't frightened of him. Funny that. It were like we was in another time and place. He were holdin' two long thin spears and he had some thick scars over his chest. Must've been a good five minutes we was like that. There was a rustle in the bushes, probably a small wallaby, and it broke our gaze. He walked off then, calm as yer like.

I stayed in the river 'til I were sure he'd really gone, got dressed, and hightailed it back to the house. Real odd it were. I didn't tell nobody, bein' as how I couldn't explain why I were down at the river. Funny I weren't scared though.

We had a visit from the Quaker missionaries, Mr. Backhouse and Mr. Walker. There was just the two of 'em, ridin' up on their horses, with a extra packhorse in tow for their goods and chattels. All of us scurried about gettin' clean linen and bedsheets, and the cook set about preparin' a hearty meal for 'em after their dusty trip. Farms like ours give hospitality to travellers and these two gentlemen was known. They'd earned a good reputation for themselves, bein' kind Quaker folk what come to Van Diemen's Land to help people. Of course I knew about them from Sarah, but most folks here had read somethin' about 'em in the newspapers. They was grateful to find respite for their horses, a comfy bed and hot food before goin' on the next part of their journey.

They brought with them a letter. For me! It were from Sarah! Well you could've knocked me down with a feather! I put it in me apron pocket to read later. I were that excited to get that letter!

They said they was travellin' around preachin' the gospel to scattered settlers, investigatin' the penal system, promotin' Temperance, and lookin' into how Aborigines was bein' treated by white settlers. They asked us all if there'd been any troubles with Aborigines where we was and Mr. Richardson said 'there had not'.

Mr. Backhouse told us that in some places the conflicts between settlers and Aborigines was gettin' much worse. They'd met Blacks what had been *per-se-cu-ted* and *dis-poss-essed* of their lands. I thought if Sarah was here I could ask her how to write down them two words. No matter. I were listenin' real close to what they had to say about Blacks.

Attacks on settlers was common, they was sayin', bein' as how whites got at them. The settlers wanted more land for their sheep and cattle, and the Aborigines wanted to keep their huntin' grounds and sacred places. They realised we whites was here to stay and there'd be nowhere for them to go in the end, and their food supplies would be finished. It was no wonder they was fightin' back. Mr. Walker said land were very important in their culture. They had ceremonies involvin' their religion, he said.

Mr. Backhouse said they was goin' to visit Flinders Island, where most of the Aborigines was livin' now, after *the Black Line*. When Mrs. Richardson asked him what the Black Line was, the two men was silent for a bit, then they told her it was the Government's *attempt to rid the colony of the conflict between Blacks and white settlers*. From the look on his face though, I wondered if there weren't more to it than that.

I finally had a chance to open Sarah's letter.

*16th August, 1842*

*Dear Maggie,*

*I was so pleased to receive your letter. So when I heard that Mr. Backhouse and Mr. Walker would be going your way, I determined I would write to you and they could deliver it.*

*We have been having to tighten our belts in Hobart Town as the drapery business is going through hard times. Women still require outfitting, but most of them are not spending the amount of money on clothes they have done in the past. I hear that the sale of wool is not fetching as much in the London market as it did.*

*The price of fat is high now and whale oil and candles are costing more. Some of the merchants have been supplying people with bad fat and we have had fat that becomes quickly riddled with maggots, making the lit candles smell terrible. Everyone retires at an early hour, not only for early rising, but to limit the amount of candles needed.*

*But I have some good news as well, dear friend. I have received my ticket of leave! Not only that, but Mr. William Cotton, the kind man I met some time ago, has asked me to marry him! Arrangements for the marriage are being made, and we shall be married this year.*

Well, fancy that. The Quakers don't go along with the notion that convicts are a stain on society then. He must be a good man. What good news that is.

*Some more news Maggie. There's a Catholic lady back in London called Caroline Chisholm who helps women find a place to live, and employment when they first arrive here. I'm sure this will help them. How different to the way all of us women on the transport ship were received when we came out.*

*I so look forward to hearing your news Maggie, dear, and still miss you very much.*

*Affectionately,*

*Your dear friend, Sarah*

When I read that, I had such a ache in me heart. Whenever would I see Sarah again?

The next day the two Quaker men was gone and just three months later they went back to England. After they left us I dreamed of a tall, thin, black man watchin' over us all. His body were painted and his eyes was piercin'. He was standin' with his left foot on his right knee, and his right hand was holdin' on to a long thin spear. From time to time, if I were out of the house around sunset, I thought I spied him in the distance, just for a minute. Then he'd disappear.

Not long after the Quaker men left us, two of the convict men workin' on the boundaries of the property, clearin' the ground and puttin' up a fence, was attacked by natives throwin' spears at 'em. Our two men managed to run back home, but not before one of 'em was speared in the leg. His mate helped him back. But he lost a lot of blood and when the wound healed there were a nasty deep scar on his leg, and he walked with a limp.

They was lean times after that, but while we had our fair share of sickness and heartache, there were joy as well. Mr. Richardson bought a piano for the family and the children learned how to read music and play simple tunes. Mrs. Richardson could play the piano, and we was all that happy to hear the sounds of music throughout the place. When any visitor come, the children was shy but pleased to be asked to entertain 'em with a tune.

I come to know as much as Mrs. Richardson about the plants and flowers in the garden, and I learned about the native ones as well. I learned about me favourite, Lavender, as I was pertickly taken with this plant. Its proper name is *Lav-an-du-la an-gus-ti-fo-lia.* Mrs Richardson showed me how to write this down. She were pleased I wanted to know all about the plants. There's all types of lavender, and different colours, from a kind of pink to dark purple. Lavender likes full sun and not much water — luckily — in this country. If yer harvest the flowers just as they open and hang 'em to dry in a dark room they keep their nice smell. They can be used for everythin' from cookin' to healin'. They like plenty of room and their bushes can get quite large.

Lavender can be put into soaps and hair washes too. Mrs. Richardson and me started makin' small muslin bags to put the dried herbs in. We put some in wardrobe drawers to make the clothes smell nice and keep away them silverfish that makes holes in our clothes. Mrs. Richardson said that you can get oil out of the flowers, and that it's good for fixin' up burns and wounds. And if you put it on insect bites or stings it feels real good and yer smell nice too. Keeps away them pesky mosquitos too.

We started makin' tiny lavender pillows of *potpourri* as well and put 'em under the children's pillows to help them sleep. They're nice added to the outside wrappin' on presents too. Mrs. Richardson did this one Christmas day. There seems to be no end to what lavender can be used for.

We got newspapers from time to time so we found out what was goin' on outside the property; just a bit later than them what read 'em in Hobart Town.

'There are many new emigrants coming into the country and the flow of new people necessitates some way of dealing with them when they arrive,' said Mrs. Richardson one day, reading the newspaper and looking over her new spectacles. 'Now the country has more labourers than they have jobs to give them.'

I liked it when she read out things to me from the newspaper.

'I heard of a lady in England,' she said, 'who every year sends out a whole family from the poor but hard-working classes to the colonies. She encourages people who seem to be of an active and adventurous turn of mind, and willing to work hard.'

She turned a page of the newspaper, careful not to get the black ink on her dress. 'The fresh air and superior climate in Van

Diemen's Land are an incentive for those who do not mind leaving civilization behind them to make their way in a new world,' she read out.

'That's interestin',' said I, wonderin' if I would ever have come out here if I weren't a convict. Don't think so. And from what she went on to read in the newspaper, it costs a lot of money to set yerself up if yer not in service. I'm glad I don't have to spend money on food. Sounds like it might cost a pretty penny. It's good to know these things. Even when I gets me ticket of leave, I'm stayin' here. I don't fancy havin' to fend for meself. It mightn't be a bed of roses bein' entirely on me own.

Another letter from Sarah!

*15th February, 1843*

*Dear Maggie,*

*I do hope you are well, my dear friend. Mr. Cotton and I are married and we are so happy! We had a quiet Quaker wedding in Hobart Town. Who would have thought my life would turn out so well?*

*Mr. Cotton is very encouraging of my wish to help out at the Queen's Orphanage. I am so concerned about the children, as you know, so I have volunteered my services and will do whatever I can to be of assistance.*

*I hear about Cascades Female Factory from time to time. It now holds five hundred women, and the lack of discipline inside is often referred to in the newspapers. More solitary cells have been introduced — avenues of them. Visitors remark on the extreme silence inside the Factory. Remember how we noticed the silence ourselves when we first arrived?*

*Apparently the silence now is due to the fact that their food rations are reduced to half, and visiting surgeons have introduced drugs like* ipecacuanha, *effective for women with fiery temperaments, but it causes nausea.*

*How glad I am that we are no longer there, Maggie. It seems to be getting worse instead of better. As well, there are more free settlers coming over and it's getting hard to find work. I heard that crowds line up at the hiring depots each day looking for work, but most are turned away. Without a job, they are forced to survive as best they can.*

*I do hope you are well and happy. I'm glad you are still with the Richardsons.*

*By the way, I think I saw Agnes in Hobart Town one day but I am not sure.*

*Affectionately,*

*Sarah*

Well, I wrote back straight away, congratulatin' her and her husband. I was that happy for Sarah.

I were granted an early ticket of leave, in spite of me extra year after I scarped it that time. I didn't have no more black marks against me after that. And Mr. Richardson's letter of recommendation were good. He's real nice, is Mr. Richardson. With me ticket of leave I could have left the Richardsons and gone out on me own. But I chose to stay, for I were sure I'd find no better place, especially with all them free emigrants lookin' for a situation. As a ticket of leave holder I were entitled to be paid for me work, and Mr. and Mrs. Richardson was only too happy to have me stay on.

Sarah and me kept writin' to each other so we both knew how our lives was goin', but we didn't get to see each other in person.

Just the letters. They took weeks to get here, bein' as how we live such a long way from Hobart Town. But every now and then, post would come through on horseback or Mr Richardson would take letters to be posted when he went into town for supplies.

Another year went by. It was 1844. Mr. Richardson said he wanted to employ a carpenter to build an extension to the house what would include verandahs, and do carpentry work about the property. The wool prices had started to rise again, so there were talk about a schoolroom bein' added for the Richardsons' growin' family. By this time, Mrs. Richardson had another baby: a fine healthy boy this time.

An advertisement was put in one of the Hobart newspapers, and Mr. Richardson went to Hobart Town to interview some of the men what had applied. In due course, he brought back with him a newly arrived free emigrant. His name was Patrick Sullivan. From Ireland.

Chapter 12

# *Agnes*

*20th March, 1844*

So this be the pattern of ma life: in and out o' Crime Class (but mostly in), on assignment, returned tae the Factory. Aye, I've been out on assignment. Twice. If there were nae such a want for convict servants in Hobart Town, I wouldnae hae been sent out at all, bein' in Crime Class that is. Within a couple o' days o' arrivin' at one household I was charged with bein' out o' bed in the wee hours o' the Sabbath and bein' drunk. It was after the night I spent with one o' the other servants — Jane, her name was — a convict like me. She'd already served six of her seven years in the Factory, in and out on different assignments. She said she'd been transported for stealin' a hanky. For a lousy hanky! Seven years!

She was nae goin' tae come out drinkin' with me, but I talked her intae it. Poor lassie. She'd got in the family way the first time she was out on service. Only sixteen years old, and there she was thinkin' she was goin' tae be all right in the household because the mistress was nice tae her. But the master had other ideas for this one. Too pretty she was. When she was alone in the wash-house one time he came down from the house and spied her there all by herself. He mustae thought it was too good a chance tae pass up. She was pressed tae do what the master wanted for the next six months. When she couldnae hide her condition nae more she was sent back tae the Factory, straight into Crime Class. Before that, she'd never been in anythin' but First Class. Her first assignment was tae that bastard.

Jane didnae want tae do anythin' wrong, but after I persuaded her it'd be all right and nobody would find out, we stole whisky from the master's hidey-hole, and snuck out — at midnight from the servants' quarters — into the bushes at the back of the house where we wouldnae be seen. We got caught sneakin' back intae the house, and reported tae the mistress. Well, there was a right tae-do. The master's wife was angry when she found out what we'd done, and when I talked back tae her she said, "Give me none of your cant girl," gettin' more angry than ever at me, her face red as blood.

But the mistress liked Jane, and when Jane told her she was really sorry for bein' disobedient, the mistress just give her a stern warnin' and told her never tae do anythin' o' the sort agin. I was pleased for Jane as I liked the lassie and she told me she felt safe in this house. I was thought tae be the troublemaker and sent right back tae the Factory.

What did I care? We were made tae work from dawn tae dusk in that house, told tae do this, and told tae do that. No time at all tae ourselves. It was hard work and never endin'. The master was an old misery, and the mistress demanded her pound o' flesh from me, treatin' me like scum. So here I be, back at the Female Factory. They said I stole money as well. No matter if it was true or nae. Three days in solitary on bread and water, then it's back tae Crime Class and the washtubs.

One time I was accused o' puttin' a master's child in danger because I walked away when I was supposed tae be lookin' after the bairn. Why, when I was the age o' that bairn I was oft out on the streets havin' tae care for maself, ma mither lyin' drunk on the floor o' the dingy room we lived in. With no food tae eat, I'd gae away from home in search o' food, pickin' up scraps — whatever I could put ma hands on — and keepin' out o' the way o' fuckin' men lookin' for a nice piece o' young pussy. So I saw no reason tae stay with this bairn from a snooty upbringin'.

Ma not takin' proper care o' the bairn was called a 'serious offence' and taegither with accusations of insolence, I was back in Crime Class agin, after a week in solitary with a heavy spiked iron collar round ma neck. No-one ever thought ma own experience as a child be criminal. I wondered why what I did was so bad that I had tae be treated in such a way. I've heard tell o' much worse things done tae children by servants than just leavin' them. I never struck or ill-treated the bairns. Nor did I pass them grog, or take one out all night with me, like some. One convict even taught her master's eleven-year-old daughter tae sing bawdy songs and told her what sex was all about.

Some o' the women put in solitary fall ill. Others, like me, just get more defiant and find solace in the grog. But when the iron collar was taken off ma neck the last time and I was out o' solitary, I thought tae maself, how can I change ma life tae get out o' Crime Class? I was gettin' a wee bit tired of it all. Besides, with all the scarpin' I'd done from the Factory I started tae like being outside and thought tae maself, maybe I could have a better life out there. Most o' ma mates were all gone — put in other prisons, got their tickets of leave, or gone who knows where. Life were nae as much fun without the lasses from the Flash Mob. Besides, I'd made a few mates outside in the pubs, mostly with barmaids and the like.

Only one answer tae all of this: behave maself! Let Matron see I were nae goin' tae be a thorn in her side nae more. I wouldnae hae to completely change ma behaviour but I'd be more careful about bein' caught and nae hae tae go back into that dark lonely cell wi' the smell of damp sinkin' intae my skin.

And that's what I did. Aye, me, Agnes MacDonald. It were nae easy thing, I can tell ye, but after a wee while, Matron could see that I was nae more gettin' intae trouble, and after a few months I was allowed intae Second Class, Yard Two. Intae the silence with all those lasses so desperate tae get out they stayed quiet and did what they were told. They didnae dare play up. No singin', no dancin', no merriment — almost like bein' in solitary. And no chance of me scarpin' intae town for a wee drap of the good stuff. I wondered, could a body die of boredom?

But I promised maself. I'd have tae make the best of it. I'd just think of it as bein' in solitary but more comfortable and with other lasses tae talk tae. I'd use ma old technique o' talkin' tae maself and rememberin' things. That stopped me from goin' balmy in solitary — all those memories.

Now I remember one lass I talked tae when I was in Crime Class. A condemned woman she was. 'Well,' I said tae her afore I knew that, 'ye look like a bonnie wee lassie so what ye be doin' in Crime Class?'

'I killed my husband,' she said. Just like that! 'I killed my husband.' I was nae expectin' her tae say that, and no-one else in here had heard about it. She was pretty quiet and didnae mix much with anyone. Over the next couple o' weeks she started tellin' me how it came tae be, how she ended up in this trouble.

'I was transported for theft,' she said tae me, 'and got seven years like nearly everyone else. I got an early ticket of leave for good behaviour after being here for five years. After a bit as a paid domestic, I met a young milkman when he was delivering milk to the house I was in. Quite the lad he was, and I did fancy him. He was looking for a wife, he told me, and before too long we were married and settled into a small cottage in Hobart Town. I thought my life would be changed for the good from then on, and my old life was behind me. But this sweet life didn't last long. We both started drinking, just a couple of drinks at night to begin with, then more and more. Beer and rum mainly. Then sometimes we'd drink long into the night. With the drinking binges, we'd quarrel, and he'd get angrier and louder, then he used fisticuffs, bashing me around.'

I took a closer look at her then and could see she'd been roughed up. I've seen many a lass that's been badly treated and I ken the signs. Her nose had been broken and there were scars on her cheeks and around one eye. Not as deep as mine, but still there.

'Well,' she said, 'one night, it was much worse than all the others. The quarrelling and fighting turned more brutal. I thought he was going to kill me this time. I took it as long as I could, then started to shout out for help. Just kept it up: help! help! The neighbours were used to hearing our fights, but when they heard me calling out for help they thought it had got out of hand. But then it quietened down a bit — he'd got the wind up see, so he stopped after I shouted out for help.'

She waited a bit, then went on tae tell me the rest.

'But after more of the rum he started up again. This time he picked up a piece of thick wood from an old broken chair lying in the corner, and he started bashing me with it — across my legs, then my arms and my stomach — before he fell down in a drunken swoon. I was in a bad way, but not so's I couldn't drag myself up off the floor. I couldn't take any more of his bashings.'

Well, by this time I was caught up in this lassie's story and I was sittin' on the edge of ma seat, waitin' for what was comin' next. I could see it all in ma mind's eye, and felt I was in the house with her, seein' him out tae it on the floor, the piece of wood lyin' next tae him with her blood on it. And I waited tae hear what happened next. She paused for a bit, then looked like she was back in their house and seein' him lyin' there.

'I picked it up,' she said, and as she told me this she made as if she was pickin' up a real block of wood, liftin' it high o'er her head, 'and I hit him with it as hard as I could, on his head. I just kept it up to make sure. Blood all over the place there was — on the floor, the walls, all over me — then everything went quiet.'

And she went quiet as well, I didnae say nae more and we both sat there taegither, her starin' ahead. After a while she told me that when the constable found her husband dead and her sittin' there dazed and starin' ahead with blood all over her, he arrested her on the spot.

In spite of all the bashin's she'd put up with from him, they wouldnae entertain her pleas for clemency.

'No, it's murder,' they said, and she was condemned tae a public hangin'. So she ended up back in Cascades for the last three weeks o' her life, awaitin' the hangman's noose. Her bein' Catholic she was visited by a Catholic priest, along with some nuns. On her last night on this earth they come and took her tae the condemned cell in Campbell Street Gaol, and the next day she was hanged.

Poor thing. Life is hard, and that's the truth o' it.

I started thinkin' about what I might do once I was outside for good. I could catch up with Maggie. See what she'd been up tae these past years. I heard she was out on a property a long way from Hobart Town. I started thinkin' how I could earn a crust once I'd left the Factory, but I put that thought aside. Too hard. Best not tae worry about it and wait 'til it happens. From there I went driftin' off tae the far corners of ma mind tae pull out some memory. One tale that come tae mind were that woolly-haired young black lass (aye, it were nae only white folk transported tae Van Diemen's Land). Her left eye were blind, covered in a kind of grey coatin'. Another face marked with scars. Real deep ones too, like the welts on a man who's been flogged wi' the cat. She never talked tae no-one, just sat in a corner all by herself most o' the time. We all thought she was strange, bein' black and different tae rest of us. And her not talkin'. But everyone let her be.

One day, ma curiosity got the better o' me and I went o'er and sat alongside her, friendly-like so she wouldnae be afraid o' me. After a while of passin' the time o' day, she began tae respond tae some o' ma questions and told me her story — how she ended up here in the Factory, a year before I got here maself.

It was hard tae understand her, on account o' she had a foreign way o' talkin', but what I made out from her story was like this. Her name was Celia. Her folks, both dead now, were African slaves sent tae Mauritius tae work in the cane fields. That was where she was born. Born intae slavery, she was. Growin' up alongside her mither she was forced tae do slave work as well.

From the age o' ten years, her master started tae force himself on her. He raped her nigh on two years. The master's wife knew about this and instead o' bein' angry with her bastard of a husband, she vented her feelin's on the girl, pickin' on her for the smallest things, and even makin' up wrongdoin's in order tae have an excuse for beatin' her. The beatin's were mild tae begin with, but as the lass showed signs of turnin' intae a young woman o' great beauty the mistress got more spiteful. Celia's mither had also suffered from the mistress's temper and the master's lust 'til he turned his attention tae wee Celia.

The last straw for both mither and daughter was when Celia was that badly beaten by the Mistress flailin' her with a piece o' cane slit razor-sharp for the purpose that Celia fainted, fallin' down unconscious intae her own pool o' blood. Her face was cut about so bad she become disfigured and couldnae see out o' one eye.

After this act o' vicious cruelty, Celia's mither decided tae use an old folk poison, made up o' special ingredients and ground into a powder that could be put intae a drink. When Celia recovered from her beatin', she got the girl tae slip the poison intae the mistress's tea when she took up her breakfast tray. Each day the poison in the tea was made stronger. By the fourth day the mistress become real sick and after a week o' retchin', she succumbed tae the poison. The English doctor attendin' tae the mistress had seen other cases o' poisonin' in Mauritius and knew the signs. So he called in the local police to report his suspicions.

Both Celia and her mither was arrested. Her mither was accused o' murder and hanged but because o' Celia's young age, just gone thirteen years, the Court decided on transportation. Fourteen years.

So there she was, a young African lass sittin' quiet in a corner o' Cascades Female Factory havin' come all this way across the seas tae this land, nobody o' her own kind in sight, a poor lonely soul, even worse off than the rest o' us.

A year later she was taken tae the insane asylum, and no-one heard nought about her ever agin.

Ma nightmare beasts would come tae me in the black o' night. I've seen them so many times ye'd think they wouldnae scare me nae more. Sometimes I wake up at the sound of ma own voice screamin' out, and find ma bed soaked with sweat from ma thrashin' about wrestlin' with the demons.

At times I'd think back tae the transport ship. Some days were good. I wonder what Peggy would hae thought if she were alive and I were to tell her about how I caught a fish. Aye, that was a good day. Not too many o' them though. Best not tae remember too much. I still hae nightmares about the coal hole. But I dinnae dwell on that when I be awake. That suffocatin' box, the smell o' the black wood seeped in grimy oil, and the never-endin' swayin' o' the ship, the water high above me bangin' hard against the sides of it in the high seas, and me covered in ma own vomit.

With nought tae do agin I got tae thinkin' o' different times I'd slipped out o' here for a night at one o' the taverns. On the way intae Hobart Town one time, I passed a poor laddie stuck in the public stocks, his head and hands pokin' through the holes o' the heavy wooden frame, his ankles chained tae the post. I've been chained up like that maself a couple o' times back in Scotland in the stocks like that laddie. Ye body be in pain from stayin' in the same position all night, and ye feel such shame. Any bastard walkin' past ye might throw somethin' at ye and there be nought ye can do about it. Ye cannae even wipe ye face and by the time ye be taken out, there be dried food and muck stuck on it, and ye eyes might be stuck taegither. Ma neck would ache that bad after a night like that.

Wi' all the drinkin' places in Hobart Town, sly grog shops, taverns, and the like, I had ma pick o' where tae go the times I'd scarp it. I decided tae go tae one o' the grog shops in the dockside area o' Wappin' one time, one with gamblin' at the back. Gamblin' folk be more interested in bettin' than takin' notice of a convict woman out on the town. I could mix easily with the loud, drunken sealers and whalers, the whores and pimps, and them on a mix o' grog and laudanum. Nobody tae pay attention tae nobody else, unless there was a brawl.

Aye, ma thoughts took me tae how good it was to be out agin and part of a crowd o' boisterous drinkers in a dark smoky tavern filled with the smell o' whisky, pipes and cigars, and the reek o' sweat and fetid bodies. Just rememberin', I could almost smell it all. The daily sprinklin' o' sawdust on the filthy floor barely covered the vomit and the spilt drinks. But nae matter. I didnae care. Men stood everywhere drinkin' or sittin' at card tables gamblin', and I could hear a cock-fight goin' on in the room out the back. I felt right at home and got tore intae havin' a good time.

No payin' on the slate, so I had tae practice ma craft agin. I looked around at the clientele. Besides the usual rough lot ye would expect in a establishment like this, there was a few toffs mixed in, as out o' place as a fart in a kirk. Lookin' for a bit o' excitement away from their uppity wives at home, I bet. I looked around for the most distracted o' the drunks so I could slip ma hand into his pocket for a few shillin's. No problem there, and I soon had enough tae order ma first drink, a wee drap o' whisky.

After several more whiskys, a couple o' gins, and a lacin' o' laudanum, I was in a right bonnie mood and started singin' with the rest o' them. Suddenly it started gettin' a bit nasty. A sailor from a whalin' ship got tae quarrellin' with a sailor from a sealin' ship, and it got louder and rougher. Everyone could see there was goin' tae be trouble. The sealer pulled a knife and people scattered in all directions. He made a beeline for the whaler and all hell broke loose as he plunged the knife in the whaler's stomach. Blood everywhere. Bloody hell! I did nae reckon on this happenin'.

Everyone was shoutin', women were screamin', and a free-for-all started with more people gettin' in on the act. I decided it was time tae take ma leave, as I didnae want tae be found in the river, bloated and putrid, or end up a nameless female dumped on the outskirts o' Hobart Town. I got away and made ma way back tae the Factory, but not empty-handed. In all the excitement, no-one noticed a small woman o' no account swipin' a bottle or two o' rum. Aye, they were good times all right.

In 1839, they changed our food rations in the Factory. Bad enough what they gave us already, but instead o' real bread made o' wheat, they shoved bread made from peas and barley at us. Well, that caused a stir, I can tell ye. Us women in Crime Class created a racket. We broke up the spinnin' wheels, armed ourselves with iron spindles, and large stones, and hurled them everywhere, wantin' tae break as much as we could. We even threatened tae burn the buildin' down. Ma Scottish mate, Anna just plain refused tae obey the Superintendent, and when it quietened down, he threw her in solitary, in the cells with just water. Some of us others was charged with violent behaviour and makin' use o' *obscene language*.

After that time, seventeen of us was charged with causin' another riot. There was about one hundred and fifty of us in Crime Class at the time. We had nae access tae the yard as some men be workin' inside the buildin' and the authorities wished tae prevent communication between them and us. As if we could give a tinker's arse about the men. We were havin' a good time with nae need for any men. Some time in the afternoon, a few of us started dancin' and singin'. When the turnkey told us tae stop, we refused and just kept on goin' even louder than before.

Aye, we had ourselves plenty o' good times, but ended up payin' the price for it always.

# PART III

Chapter 13

# *Maggie*

*20th March, 1844*

When I first laid me eyes on Patrick Sullivan I thought, he's the tallest Irishman I ever seen. Big too, and strong. Must be about thirty years old, I reckon. But me heart started racin' same as it did when I first met up with Benjamin. So I thought to meself, blimey another Irishman, watch out for this one. When he looked at me, his big brown eyes with them thick dark eyebrows seemed to look right into me very soul. Stayed a bit too long on me, I thought. Rememberin' Ben and how it all turned out in the end even though it started good, I promised meself to be real careful with a man what made me feel like that. He were too good-lookin' by half and he made me feel that uncomfortable.

Patrick landed in Van Diemen's Land fresh off a ship from England, just three weeks before he come to the Richardsons, leavin' Ireland with its terrible poverty what looked like it was goin' to get a lot worse. He were all set to make a good life for himself and make as much money as he could, far away from what was goin' on in Ireland. No thoughts about settlin' down with a wife for quite some time, I bet. All the more reason to keep me distance, I thought. But he were very good-lookin' all the same.

In spite of me fears though, I started seein' a lot of Patrick. I tried to keep away from him, and for a coupla weeks, I did. But he'd keep comin' up to me to talk whenever he got the chance. He'd tell me about his life in Ireland, and his hopes for what he might be able to do in this new land. But though Patrick come over as a free settler and a carpenter, he were Irish and Catholic so he'd always be on the outer, not bein' a Englishman. The English didn't like the Irish one little bit. And in any case, he were on the side of the Emancipists.

''Tis a new country this one, and should be a free one with a new start,' he would say in his Irish way. 'We can all work towards bettering ourselves and making things the same for everyone.' I liked it when he talked like this. It made me feel we could all have a better life. I'd watch his face when he talked, thinkin' maybe this one's different. Maybe.

By this time, a lot of convicts had got their tickets of leave, includin' me, and was livin' free enough, but people still knew who they was. The Exclusives wanted to keep themselves separate from the rest of us convicts, even ones that weren't no longer convicts and had served their time. Didn't make no difference to them, they thought they was a cut above all of us. There was no way they wanted everyone to be equal. Patrick and me talked a lot together in our free time, but I were always careful to be on me guard, not to let meself get too close to him. I'd never forget the pickle I was in before and how I had to go back to the Factory with me tail between me legs and ask to be let back in.

When he were in Ireland, Patrick said, he'd dreamed about emigratin' to America, so he moved to England and found work as a carpenter while waitin' for an oppertunity to get on a ship to America. Then he began hearin' more and more about Australia with the promise that land were bein' give out freely to them willin' to work hard and make a go of it. So he changed his mind about America and decided to come over to Van Diemen's Land instead.

He was real interested in the bushrangers. I didn't tell him about Benjamin. Weren't nought to do with him, I thought. Every time there were an account in a newspaper about bushrangers, he'd read it out aloud to me. He followed any story he could get his hands on about Martin Cash, another Irishman, from County Wexford. I often wondered if I should tell Patrick about me life with a bushranger, but for some reason thought better of it. So I kept me mouth shut about all that.

'Listen to this Maggie,' Patrick said one time he'd got hold of a newspaper. 'It says here that Cash is *a man with a very ruddy complexion, a small round head, carrot-coloured curly hair, red eyebrows and whiskers, a low forehead and small blue eyes.*' When Patrick read this out to me, especially when it mentioned that Martin *had come from a good family*, he become even more excited.

'I know this man! He's the Martin Cash who came from the same place in Ireland as me! I heard about him in Enniscorthy when he got into trouble and was arrested by the police. It was in all the newspapers over there. He'd fancied a pretty young lass from our village who earned a living by making straw hats and bonnets. She returned his affections, but when he discovered a man called Jessop makin' advances to his sweetheart, he became enraged, and in a fit of jealousy shot Jessop.'

I watched Patrick gettin' more excited about all of this, and I got real interested meself, wantin' to know more.

'There'd been a lot of gossip about what happened,' said Patrick, 'because Martin Cash wasn't a ruffian. He was an educated man, so this affair got a lot of newspaper coverage.'

Then he read out some more from the newspaper:

*'The shooting occurred in 1827. Six months later, Cash was transported to Botany Bay, New South Wales, for seven years, in the Marquis of Huntley with one hundred and seventy other convicts, arriving in Sydney Town on 10 February, 1828.*

'If Cash hadn't been so well connected he would have hanged,' said Patrick lookin' up at me. Still I kept quiet about Benjamin. The longer I didn't say nothin' the harder it got to tell Patrick what'd happened in the Huon; how I'd lived with a Irish bushranger, about me life in the wild bush, and all the things we'd got up to. I wondered to meself what Patrick'd think about it all, and about me, if I ever spoke up about it. But for some reason, I decided to stay mum about it. I dunno if I did the right thing, but it become a big secret between us for the rest of me life. Me knowin' and him in the dark about it all.

He talked a bit more about what Cash had done, and what it was like in Ireland then. But then we was called to go back to our tasks. Patrick didn't talk no more about Martin Cash until he got his hands on the next newspaper.

It turned out that after servin' his time in New South Wales, Cash were given his ticket of leave. He stayed in New South Wales, workin' as a stockrider in the Hunter River valley for a few years without gettin' into trouble, but his wild nature come to the fore again and he eventually got mixed up in cattle duffin'. Not wantin' to be caught in New South Wales, he decided to hightail it outa there and take his chances further away. By that time he had a new girlfriend, a lass called Bessie. The both of 'em arrived in Van Diemen's Land in February 1837, on the *Francis Freeling*.

A few years later he were in trouble again! He discovered Bessie had been with another man in Hobart Town while he were away. Cash were real angry about it and swore to kill them both. On 29th August, he were spotted in Brisbane Street, near the old Commodore Inn, and there were a gunfight between Cash and Bessie's new paramour. That's what Patrick were readin' about — how the police got involved, with Constable Peter Winstanley right in the thick of it! In all the hullabaloo, Winstanley were shot by Cash and died two days later. He were in real trouble then, shootin' a constable. Cash were trialled for his murder, found guilty and sentenced to death by hangin'. In another round of luck though, he were granted a last-minute reprieve, and instead of swingin', he got transportation for life to Norfolk Island.

I wondered if Benjamin ever met up with Cash. Could be they had long talks about their bushrangin' days and what they'd both got away with, laughin' together. Why, maybe me own name come up in their conversations, with Cash talkin' about his girlfriends and Benjamin talkin' about me. What might he be tellin' Cash, I wondered. With all this ponderin' I hadn't been listenin' to what Patrick was sayin' to me, then when I come back from me thinkin', I realised he were still talkin'.

Patrick were against capital punishment, he were sayin', so he were pleased that Cash didn't have to end up on the gallows. He were impressed by what Cash were reported as sayin' after he'd been found guilty of the murder of Constable Peter Winstanley.

'Listen to what he said, Maggie:

*'May it please your honour. I am the man that has stopped murder myself in the bush; we never acted cowardly to anyone. I hope you will not think or consider that I am a man to do any cowardly or deliberate murder. Let me get into ever such close quarters, if I should have to fire I would not try to kill a man, but to cripple him so that I could get away. If I had been a man to do violence, there would have been a deal of murders committed since I have been in the bush. I do not beg for my life; I do not value it one straw.'*

After this, Martin Cash were a hero to all the Irish lads, includin' Patrick. He didn't say it in so many words, but I could see by the look on his face each time Cash's name come up. I wonder what he would've thought of my Benjamin, and of me stealin' out of the Factory to go live with him in the Huon for months on end. But still I said nothin'. There were many a time I almost told him.

By the end of 1844, I couldn't keep me amorous Patrick at bay any longer, and in December he asked me to marry him. Patrick bein' a free man, and meself with a ticket of leave, it didn't take long gettin' his *Letter of Intention to Marry* accepted by the authorities. Early in 1845 we was married in a small Catholic church near the Richardson's property. I were so happy!

To our joy, I become pregnant. Patrick were over the moon. We'd both yearned for a baby and Patrick never stopped talkin' about how he were goin' to grow into a big strong lad and they could do this and that together. He had such plans for his son and were so excited by the prospect of watchin' him grow into a man. When he were born we called him Ailill, after Patrick's father.

But soon after our little boy were born he become very sick, struck down with scarlet fever. Although we took such care of him, our poor darlin' child passed away. We was stricken with grief the two of us. We buried our little boy in his tiny coffin, not even three months old, on a grey day with not a ray of sunshine. Our dear sweet babe who we loved so very much we laid to rest in the cold, dismal ground. Standin' together at the cemetery on that bleak, sad day I started to wonder if I'd ever have any children.

That were a sad year and one full of death. As well as our own loss, an emigrant ship were wrecked off King Island, and four hundred and six lives was lost. Souls eager to make new lives for themselves in a new land, was all drowned at sea, so close to their destination. It made me think about how lucky Sarah and me was to have come through it all and to have things work out so well for us. Me thoughts turned to Agnes too, and I wondered what had become of her.

Patrick and me stayed on with the Richardsons for another eighteen months then in late 1847, when all the carpentry work for the Richardsons were done, we moved to Hobart Town so Patrick could look for more work. I were that sad to leave Amy Richardson, the children, and the place what had been me home for so long. A lot had happened to me in the years since I left England. I would never have imagined — growin' up in Cheapside — that me life and circumstances could've changed so much for the better. But I thought, I can see Sarah now. It made me so excited, the thought of seein' her in person after all this time. I wondered what'd happened to Agnes as well.

Hobart Town had changed since I'd been away. Comin' here after all me time in the country I were surprised at all the changes. There was more terrace houses, pubs, taverns, brothels and gamblin' houses, an more entertainment for visitin' sailors. The bustlin' waterfront district of Wapping were rowdier than ever. In Liverpool Street there was chop-houses, bakehouses, tanneries, booksellers and dancin'-halls. Everyone was sayin' our shops was as good as them back in England.

At night, the main streets was lit by whale oil lamps, givin' a soft glow here and there, mainly outside the pubs and hotels, like the old smoke-filled *Commercial Hotel* on the Wharf, still awash with seafarin' men. I walked past it a few times when I were out shoppin' for food at the markets but never went in. I knew Agnes would still have a few years to go on her sentence. But I thought of her a lot and wondered how she were doin' at the Factory. I felt our lives was goin' to be different now, but I didn't know how. Once we was well settled, I found out where Sarah lived with her husband, and went round there.

When she opened the door, she were that surprised to see me! She were as beautiful as ever, lookin' happy and contented.

'Maggie Burnett! Or should I say Maggie Sullivan! Oh, it is so lovely to see you dear friend. Do come in,' she said, puttin' her arms around me. We both had tears in our eyes. She ushered me in to her front parlour, a neat cosy room, real simple, her now bein' a Quaker and all. She made us some tea, and then we caught up with all our news. What a lot we had to talk about, the two of us, it were so long since the last time we seen each other. There's only so much yer can write in a letter. She said that Hobart Town were overrun by drapery and clothin' stores but they were doin' well, and life was kind to her. Then her children come into the parlour to meet me.

'Maggie, these are the twins, James and Rebecca, almost four years old, and that one is Ruth, the same age as the twins, and the youngest is little Eva, two years of age.' Once I'd met all the children, they was give a biscuit each and told to go and play.

When they was gone, she said, 'We adopted Ruth and Eva from the Orphanage. Oh Maggie, when I first went to the Orphanage it broke my heart to see the children. I have been trying to help out there as best I can. I have visited there many times, and on one occasion little Ruth came over to me, put her arms around my legs, and wouldn't let go. Then when I saw little Eva my heart went out to her. Such a sweet little baby and I could not bear for her to be left there. When I came back and told William about them, we both talked about our taking them in to be part of our family. And this has only recently come about. So now our family has expanded and our lives are so full.' As soon as she said it, she pursed her lips when she saw me face turn sad.

'Oh Maggie, I was so grieved to hear about your little son. I'm sure you will have another baby soon.'

'Now we're back and settled in Hobart Town, and Patrick has found work ...' I had to wait a minute to make sure I didn't start cryin', rememberin' all what had happened. 'We've settled inta a small cottage on Battery Point and I'm makin' it as cosy as I can. Some good news is that I'm goin' to open up a shop, sellin' flowers.' Patrick and me had talked about this with Amy Richardson before we left and we'd all decided it were a good idea for all of us.

Sarah's eyes opened in surprise at that bit of news. 'Where will you get the flowers from Maggie?'

'From the Richardson's property. Patrick will fix up the shop to make it nice, I'll manage the shop business, and Amy will make arrangements for the flowers to be picked from her gardens, bundled up, and delivered to the shop. The Richardsons will help with the finances 'til we gets on our feet, then we'll go halves.'

'Oh Maggie, that sounds like a lovely idea. And I could come and buy flowers from your shop. You were always the one for thinking of clever things to do. I'll get us some more tea and scones and you can tell me all about it. I would love to hear more.'

A few weeks after I left Sarah, it were 1848. By this time we'd found an empty shop in one of the main streets and set about buildin' up our flower business, fillin' it with all the colourful fragrant plants and flowers that I'd loved in Amy Richardson's gardens. As soon as folk got to know about the new florist shop, it become very popular. Over the next few months, with Patrick workin' hard and our shop thrivin', we was startin' to make a real go of it.

I kept askin' around to find out if anyone had any news of me old friend Agnes. I even went in to *The Commercial Hotel* a coupla times to find out if any of the barmaids knew anythin', thinkin' she'd be bound to have scarped it quite a few times since the last time I'd seen her. But they said they hadn't seen Agnes for ages. I s'pose she were still in the Factory doin' her time but I didn't never want to go back to that place even to ask about Agnes. I did think about her a lot though, and hoped she were all right. P'raps she'd started behavin' herself and were out on assignment somewhere.

One day Sarah come to our shop lookin' flustered and upset. I ain't seen her like that since them early days in Newgate.

'Why Sarah, what's wrong?' There weren't nobody else in the shop so I took her behind the curtain to the more private room at the back and told her to sit down. She opened her purse and took out a envelope what had been tore open. Her hands was shakin'.

'This letter. It's from England, addressed to me as Sarah Hamilton, not Mrs. William Cotton. It was sent care of Mrs. Bridges, to the address of my first assignment from the Factory in 1837.'

'Why whoever is it from, and why are you so upset Sarah?'

Sarah couldn't imagine who'd be writin' to her from England. When she left, she didn't have no family and she hadn't heard from no-one in all them long years. She passed me the letter. 'My dear Sarah' it said. As I read on, I couldn't believe what were written. It turned out the letter were from Dr. Robert James, from the transport ship!

*5th June 1847*

*My Dear Sarah,*

*I am wondering how you have fared over the years since last I saw you, the day I had to take my leave from your lovely presence to return to England in the transport ship that had taken you to Van Diemen's Land.*

*I have never forgotten you Sarah, and over these many years you have stayed in my mind. My two daughters are now married comfortably and my poor wife passed away just a year ago.*

*Now that I am a free man once again, with no obligations, I would dearly love to know your circumstances, and to make your acquaintance again. If I were to come over to Australia would you be in a position to accept me as a suitor, with a view to marriage?*

*I realise this must be a shock to you, but dear Sarah, I would be most grateful for your response, and eagerly look forward to meeting you once again.*

*Yours most sincerely and with great affection,*

*Robert James*

Well I never! Yer could have knocked me down with a feather. I had to read it again to make sure I understood what he were sayin'. So Robert really did love Sarah and never forgot her. After all this time. When I give her letter back she used it to fan her flushed face.

'Here, sit yerself down and I'll make yer a cuppa tea,' I said to her. I hurried over to the kettle, already with the steam comin' out, and poured us both a cup.

'Imagine if he were to come over.' She was beside herself with worry, her brows were wrinkled and her mouth tight, her hands workin' nervously. When she took hold of the cup it rattled in her tremblin' hands.

'You might have to tell your William about what happened between you and Robert James on the transport ship.'

Sarah paled at the very idea, and I thought she were goin' to faint.

'I could not do that. I'd rather die than have my William find out about all that. And it was such a very long time ago. Oh Maggie, what shall I do?'

'Then you'll have to write back,' I said, 'and tell him not to come.'

'Yes. I must write back straight away, tell him I am a well-contented married woman with children of my own now and plead with him not to come.'

'You could say you was grateful to him as well, makin' sure you was placed in a good household.'

'Oh yes, of course. Oh I do hope he doesn't even think of coming before he receives my letter. Oh dear, what a predicament!'

For some months after sendin' her reply to Robert, Sarah were afraid he would come anyway, and his comin' would put her in a very awkward position. She were that guilty and nervous about it all. We all had our secrets about the past, like most folk in Hobart Town. No-one except meself knew about her and Dr. James. Even two years later she were still worried he might come in spite of her advisin' him not to. But he never did. And that were the end of it.

By the end of 1848 I were with child again and we had another boy, a strong healthy one this time. We called him William. And in 1849, we was blessed again with a child. This time a girl, also healthy and well, and we named her Lydia. Our little home were filled with our lovely children and we was so happy. Our flower business was doin' so well by then that me, a ex-convict, were able to employ another convict woman to help look after the children, and a free settler to help out in the flower shop. I never would've believed when I was arrested in England, that me life could be so full.

Just after Lydia were born, Patrick received a letter from Ireland sayin' that his father had died. A new soul had come into our world, and an old soul had left. His mother died several years before the father's death. Patrick's youngest brother, Finian, sent the letter, gettin' the local priest to write it as he didn't know his letters, not like Patrick. At the end of the letter, Finian asked

Patrick would he send him the money for a fare to Van Diemen's Land, as Ireland were in a sorry state. There were a potato famine and everyone were starvin'.

When he finished readin' Finian's letter, his face looked that sad.

'I heard the famine was getting worse,' he said lookin' up at me with them eyes I knew so well. 'And people have nothing to eat and nowhere to turn. They're still trying to scratch a living from the land, but there's nothing there. They are slowly dying of starvation. Others go wandering the countryside to look for food and work.' He put the letter down on the table and stood up, pacin' up and down, real upset.

'Sometimes whole families are on the move. I heard tell they look like walking skeletons, their clothes hanging from their skinny bodies.' I could see tears wellin' up in his eyes, and felt it bad meself. 'Here, we're fortunate,' he said, 'we can go off shooting kangaroos and other game if we're hungry, but there, all the land is owned by the squires, and if you shoot anything, it's poaching.'

We was doin' well by this time, so Patrick sent Finian the money, and told him he could stay with us in Hobart Town 'til he got on his feet.

Six months later, we met Finian at Sullivan's Cove when his ship arrived. He was a good-lookin' young man of twenty, with a shock of dark brown hair and a winnin' smile. Charmin', like his brother. Little did I know that he was to become the bane of our lives.

By now, half the population of Van Diemen's Land was convicts or ex-convicts, and the workin' and middle classes was now mainly ex-convicts and their families. Most folk wanted to forget about their convict past and get on with their lives.

I thought I'd never forget me past and all what had happened, but I did want to forget about all the bad things, and I didn't want to flaunt our hard-earned new wealth neither. Not like some of them, tryin' to imitate the Exclusives. They thought they could get amongst them and be accepted. Some of 'em did, the clever ones what learned to quench their love of gaudy dressin', and quiet their behaviour so they fitted in. Some of them was sendin' their children to schools the elite went to, and buyin' big houses and properties in the areas favoured by the snobs. They thought that by doin' all this, they was in with 'em. But they wasn't; not really. The more genteel folk whispered behind their backs that 'they' would never really become 'one of us'. Maids talk, yer know.

The economy were better than ever, so everyone said. The price of wool were back on top again and they was sendin' a lot of it to distant ports. There was more whalin' ships than ever, and the Hobart Savings Bank had opened. Many people was tryin' their luck on the mainland — Victoria, and even New South Wales. Patrick and me decided to stay put, as we was happy and comfortable as we was and we had enough money comin' in. Our lives was goin' smoothly, without any setbacks.

Until, that is, we started havin' problems with Finian. He stayed with us for his first year in Van Diemen's Land and Patrick were pleased to have him in our house. But a few months after he come, Finian started causin' trouble. Only small things in the beginnin', like always cadgin' money off us, which we later found out he were spendin' on gamblin' and alcohol. Patrick found him a job, but Finian failed to turn up on time, then another job, but he didn't turn up at all for that one. This happened several times, in spite of Patrick havin' gone out of his way to persuade employers to take Finian on. No, he was full of the blarney, that one, and always had a reason for not turnin' up or not pullin' his weight.

Then he began payin' too much attention to me and makin' overtures. Gettin' real cheeky he was. I told him to stop, threatenin' to tell Patrick, but he knew I didn't want to cause a rift between two brothers. Eventually he give up on me and turned his unwelcome attentions towards Grace, a young girl of fourteen, come straight out of the Orphanage to help out in our house. It was Sarah what told me about Grace.

'She would be perfect for you Maggie. She's so good with small children, just like you, and she deserves a chance in a good household.'

So I took her on. A sweet girl. Poor young lass had been in the Orphanage from the age of two — took away from her mother at the Factory when she were just a toddler. Her mother'd never gone to claim her. Might be she'd died. We're not to know. She arrived at our home wearin' the Orphanage uniform: a blue-and-white patterned dress and a clean white pinafore, ready to work and wide-eyed, this bein' her very first time outside the Orphanage.

When she first come to take up service, I drew her a hot bath, and as she were undressin' I noticed scars on her body and asked her how she come by them. I'd heard stories from the convict women about their children in the Orphanage, and spent many a night at the Factory hearin' them weep for their little ones.

Grace told me that for the slightest offence a boy or girl could be beaten. One of the women superintendents in the Girl's Wing what had been there when Grace were between seven and twelve years old, was in the habit of takin' girls into her own bedroom, strippin' them naked, and with a ridin' whip or a heavy leather strap, she'd punish 'em for their wicked ways. The girls didn't have no idea what they'd done wrong.

Grace had never met anyone like Finian before and had no idea what he were up to. She were frightened of him, but didn't want to be sent back to the Orphanage — or worse, the Factory — so she tried to keep out of his way.

Knowin' what he was like I made sure I were in the house with the girl whenever Finian were there. But one day I were obliged to go out, and when I returned, I found Finian forcin' himself on her, the girl's skirts bunched up around her body and him pinnin' her down against a table. I immediately shouted at him to get out of the house at once, and helped the frightened girl. She were near hysterical. Still not wantin' to cause trouble between the two brothers, I took him to one side and told him that if ever he did anythin' like that again, Patrick'd be told.

Finian didn't pay no more attention to Grace, seein' he'd pushed me too far by then. Instead, he took his amorous attentions outside our home. But he kept on manipulatin' things to get his own way, appealin' to Patrick's sense of family whenever he looked like gettin' found out.

For the whole year he were with us he'd come home smellin' of alcohol, spendin' his time and Patrick's money gamblin' at the cock-fights around Wapping, mixin' with some bad types in sly grog shops.

Finally things come to a head, when even Patrick could take no more of him. One night there were a terrible fight in a bar at *The Black Swan* in Argyle Street. Two men was shot, several was wounded with knives, and Finian seemed to be at the centre of it all. Scarpin' it so as not to get thrown into prison, he didn't come home at all that night, nor any other nights, and disappeared from our lives. Although Patrick was worried about him, we was all relieved he was gone from our house.

Chapter 14

# *Agnes*

*16th May, 1850*

I couldnae believe it when I found out they'd issued a ticket of leave tae me! Aye, Agnes MacDonald now free! After all these years, a free woman! About time ye might say, me now bein' thirty-seven years of age.

They gave me the small package o' ma belongin's from off the transport ship. The clothes were so old by this time they were nae much good. And they didnae fit me nae more. I'd put on a bit o' weight — hard tae imagine with the food they give ye but there it is. There were a few shillin's as well. Money I'd kept from the old country and earnin's from whorin' on the ship when we stopped at Cape Town all those years ago. The government men wrote down how much money all of us convict women on the ship had on us when we arrived in Van Diemen's Land, and put it into separate convict bank accounts for us in Hobart Town.

I didnae get any money from assignments like some did because I didnae stay any place long enough. Ma behaviour kept gettin' me sent back tae the Factory all the time. I managed tae pick up a bit o' money each time I scarped from the Factory for a bit of a lark outside, but I spent it as fast as I got ma hands on it.

When I was finally granted ma ticket of leave and I heard the big gates o' the Female Factory close tight behind me, I realised I was really on ma own now. I got intae a bit of a panic. What was I tae do? After so long in prison, I didnae know how tae take care o' maself. I got so used to bein' a rebel, how was I to cope with freedom? How would I handle life on ma own? Where would I go? I didnae hae friends — apart from a few people I'd met in pubs. I didnae hae much money, and I didnae hae a place tae sleep. I'd been dreamin' o' freedom for years but now it was here...

But I did what I'd always done — headed towards Hobart Town. I followed the same track along the rivulet tae get there. I knew that track like the back o' ma hand. I passed the same spots thinkin' I don't want tae live like some o' them do, out in the open in the bush along the river. While I was walkin' I remembered Maggie and the time we scarped it, and her livin' in the Huon valley. I wouldnae want that kind o' life neither. I like tae be around pubs, taverns and people with lots o' lively noise. So I kept goin' and once in town I began lookin' for a place tae stay.

Not much around, that's plain, leastways anythin' I can afford. Finally, after knockin' on a few doors and gettin' *nae* for an answer, I found maself in Wapping, ma favourite place, and the next door I knocked on let me in.

'We got a small room up the top o' the stairs,' said the landlady.

'Right, then I'll take it,' said I.

Aye, small is right enough, up a fuckin' lot o' stairs tae a tiny attic room. The little bit o' money in ma possession won't last more than a couple o' weeks. But I'm free at last and now I got somewhere tae rest ma weary head.

Now what?

As I'd made up ma mind never tae go tae prison again, I couldnae go back tae thievin' on account o' I might get nabbed. I was nearly cleaned out after payin' for ma room so I'd hae tae think o' somethin' real quick.

I looked around ma little room. Poky, and none too clean, but I s'pose I was lucky tae find anythin'. At least I was near the sounds and sights o' civilization so tae speak, not stuck out in the Interior somewhere where there was nought tae do. If I was careful not tae get too drunk and intae trouble, I might get some work and save up some money for better times ahead.

The many times I'd been intae Hobart Town I'd met a couple o' people I thought I could look up. One of them was a barmaid at *The Red Lion*. Molly her name was. On previous occasions, I'd only been there for a good time, but with ma new promise tae maself not tae be sent back tae prison I thought I might ask around. See if there was any work tae be had. So I toddled off tae see if she was still a barmaid at *The Red Lion*. Sure enough, she was.

'Well Agnes, it's been a long time since I've seen you. What'll it be?' she said tae me.

'I'll have a wee whisky,' I said. Then I told her I was now a free woman. 'Do ye know of any work I could do tae earn a honest livin'?'

'Well, there's one for the books!' she said, 'Agnes MacDonald wants a job! I'll ask around and let you know.'

A couple o' days later, when I went into *The Red Lion* again tae see Molly, she told me the owner o' the pub needed someone tae do some kitchen work.

Quick as a flash I said, 'I'd be the girl for him.'

'It's a woman,' she said. 'The owner is a woman.'

'Well, that's even better,' said I.

That's how I came tae be workin' at *The Red Lion*, and keepin' maself out o' trouble. I started the next day. Ma job was more than just kitchen work. I was put tae liftin' anythin' that needed tae be lifted, nae too hard because they had a couple o' convict men on assignment doin' most o' the heavy liftin'. Ma other tasks were cleanin' the kitchen and the mess o' vomit and spilled drinks off the floor in the bar after a boisterous night o' liquor-filled customers. Ma days were pretty full with all o' this, but I didnae care. I was free, and I was gettin' a wage.

Now when I wasnae workin', ma time was ma own. Fancy that: no-one tae threaten me with punishment if I went out. I could go out and have a drink any time. I could even stay out all night if I was so inclined. Sometimes I picked up a bit o' whorin' on the side, but I wasnae too popular with the sober men. The sober ones wanted pretty young things, not a middle-age whore like me.

Bein' as how I was workin' there, I got tae know Sally, the owner of *The Red Lion*. Sal and her husband were both ex-convicts, served their time and got on the straight and narrow. Because both o' them had worked in pubs back in the old country, they didnae hae any trouble gettin' this one up and runnin'. They become licensees of *The Red Lion* not long after startin' work there, and stayed there together for five years. Doin' real well they were. I let on tae Sal that it was ma dream tae have ma own pub, so Sal showed me the licence and read it out tae me, seein' as how ma readin' skills aren't up tae much.

> *Licence to keep an Inn or Public House and to sell and retain therein Ale, Beer, and other Malt Liquors, and Wine Cider, Ginger Beer, Spruce Beer, Brandy, Gin, Rum, Whisky, Cordials and other Spirituous or fermented Liquors...to sell no other than good and wholesome liquors without fraudulently diluting or adulterating the same...And not to introduce or permit bull-baiting, dog or cock-fighting, or any other disorder or disturbance on any part of his house or premises, or get drunk in his said house, or knowingly permit any other person to get drunk therein...Nor suffer any riot, fighting, affray, tumult, nuisance, annoyance or disturbance to take place, or continue in, or on, the said house or premises...to run*

*peaceably and quietly, and maintain and preserve good order and rule...*

Well, no cock-fightin' on these premises then. If ye wants that, ye have tae go tae some other place not fussy about breakin' the rules.

Sal was expert at the innkeeper business, knowin' it inside out. They was also in with the constables, and even friends with some o' the Redcoats. There's a turn-up for ye.

'But then about six months ago,' she said, 'my husband was killed. He was working with another couple of men, moving some heavy barrels around. There was a mishap and one of the heavy crates full of whisky fell down on him and crushed his head in, and the top half of his body. The other two men ran out to fetch a doctor but by the time he arrived, my husband was lying dead in his own pool of blood. It was a terrible sight. Blood everywhere and his face was badly crushed. He didn't stand a chance.'

So after buryin' her husband, Sal kept up *The Red Lion* on her own, bein' the enterprisin' woman that she is. Out o' necessity, she got tae know even more than before about runnin' a pub. Under her management things got even better. She ordered in a whole new stock o' spirits, wine, malts and liqueurs, as well as all the usual, tae attract all kinds o' customers, gentlemen as well as the hoi-polloi. She's a clever one that Sal, and doesnae let anyone get the better o' her. I kept ma eyes and ears open, wantin' tae learn about wheelin' and dealin' in spirits and alcohol. Sal give me lots o' hints about it and we become firm friends as the months went by.

'You know Agnes, most of the women I know who've done well in business, were off the grog, if they were ever on it. If your husband isn't drunk all the time, you can make a real go of it if you work together. But a woman can do well if she's smart. Easier if you're married, but you can still do well if you're not. It's just a bit harder.'

I decided that was goin' tae be me, except I had no intention o' tyin' the knot with any bastard. I saved up as much as I could, put it in the new Bank of Hobart, and was careful not tae get so drunk I didnae know what I was doin', or get into any trouble with the police. I made a few extra shillin's from whorin' on the side if the oppertunity come ma way, but I got roughed up quite a bit. It was nae ma intention tae keep whorin'. I was doin' all right as far as the money were concerned. Enough tae pay for ma room, buy provisions, hae the odd drap, and add a bit tae ma savin's, tucked away in one o' them banks.

But I was lonely in ma poky little attic room. No-one tae talk tae. Reminded me o' bein' in solitary, the loneliness. I started feelin' a bit sorry for maself with none o' ma old mates tae play up with. I wondered where Maggie was by this time. But there were nae way o' findin' out. Last I heard about her someone said she was on assignment in the Interior. Besides, she's probably not wantin' to meet up with the likes o' me now.

Then I reminded maself I was free and could go out any time I liked tae hae a bit o' fun. No need to scarp it, just open the door and walk out. No need tae bribe the turnkey. No need to sneak about. I could stay out all night and not worry about havin' tae leave before first light tae get back tae the Factory. It was that simple.

So I thought, I'll drop in at *The Commercial*, just for old times sake.

It didnae look any different. Still the same clients, still filled with baccy smoke and the same old smells. Except there was a piano at one end o' the bar. Aye, that was new. Well, then, there must be someone tae play it. This might turn out tae be a jolly night, I thought tae maself. I fronted up tae the bar and ordered maself a wee drap o' whisky and looked around.

The usual whalers, sealers, scarpers and ex-convicts shoutin' and arguin' with each other, and a few tarts lookin' for a bit o' business. I watched as a couple o' whores come through the pub door for the first time that night, dressed up and lookin' around at the clientele tae see who'd be an easy target for their first drink, then tae business. They were mostly young ones. If I wanted to make a bit o' money doin' that tonight I'd hae tae wait for much later in the night for the men tae get blind drunk, almost passed out. But nae, I was nae in the mood for that.

I looked around a bit more. At a small table talkin' tae someone I recognised as the hotel manager from years back, there was a good-lookin' woman. Thick auburn hair cascadin' down her almost-bare back, curls fallin' over a low-cut bodice that topped layers o' petticoats and a red skirt. She was wearin' black lace-up high-heel boots as well, and her face had lots o' red rouge, real fancy, like a vaudeville act. Then I recognised her. Those green eyes gave her away. Blow me down! It was that Irish girl Kathleen from the transport ship, sittin' talkin' tae the manager!

While I was still takin' her in and how different she looked in those clothes, she got up and walked over tae the piano. There was someone sittin' at it by now, ready tae play, and without any further ado, she started singin'! There was still a lot o' noise and the usual carryin' on from the drinkers tae start with, but when she started tae sing, they stopped tae listen. It were one o' them popular ditties.

*I've got a coat and a nobby, nobby coat*
*I've got a coat a-seen a lot of rough weather*
*For the sides are near wore out and the back is flying about*
*And the lining's looking out for better weather*

When she urged them all tae sing along with her, every man there started the chorus:

*Here's to the grog, boys, the jolly, jolly grog*
*Here's to the rum and tobacco*
*I've a-spent all my tin with the lassies drinking gin*
*And to cross the briny ocean I must wander*

Then she sang the rest o' the verses, and each time the chorus came up, she'd egg them on tae join in agin. Well, she was a big hit. They asked her tae sing another one. So she did. They loved it. All o' the men wanted tae buy her a drink. When they left her alone, I went over tae her.

'That was a good song lass, reminded me o' when we were all in Crime Class makin' merry with the songs and dances! Ye've done well for yourself.'

'Oh Agnes! I haven't seen you for years. I've got my ticket of leave now.'

'Aye, and I've even got mine.' I saw the look o' surprise on her face at that. She must o' thought I'd scarped it agin. 'But tell me lass, what happened tae ye when ye left the Factory? Nobody heard anythin' about ye.'

'Well, the day when Matron suddenly told me I'd be going out on service, the master had sent his driver to pick me up. A surly character he was, with not much to say, so I still didn't know where I was going, except it was somewhere in the Interior. We were in the dray for hours, or that's how it seemed. Anyway, to cut a long story short, I was on assignment to the Crawfords, they had some sheep and a few cows, and there were other workers there besides me. But what about you Agnes?'

I told her about ma move tae Yard Two in the Factory and all that, and where I was livin' now. But I was keen tae hear more about what had happened tae her, so was eggin' her on tae tell me more. I was real curious to hear how she come tae be singin' in *The Commercial.*

'Like you, I didn't want to get into any more trouble,' she said. 'The Crawfords' place was a long way away from anything — no bars, no town, a simple life. Nothing exciting to do except sometimes race meetings and picnics. The Crawfords were good people and it was a decent place, so there I stayed until I got my ticket of leave in 1843.'

'Would ye like a drink lass?' I said tae her, and when she nodded, I ordered both of us another round, all the while watchin' her eyes, sparklin' away by this time after all that thirsty work o' singin' and carryin' on with the clients.

'A few months before that,' she went on, after takin' a swallow of her drink, 'a young currency lad from Sydney Town came to work for the Crawfords. Jeremy his name was. He was a musician and could play the accordion really well. On our free evenings I started singing along with his music. He was surprised I could sing so well. He kept saying what a good voice I had and how I could make money in the entertainment business anywhere in Sydney Town if I put my mind to it. Well I kept that idea in the back of my mind. When I was free, I thought, I just might try to earn my living by singing and maybe a bit of dancing as well.'

'What did ye do when ye first got out and into the wide world outside lass?'

She leaned one hand on the bar, took another swig from her glass, and thought back a wee bit on the time she was free from servitude and not afeared o' bein' sent back tae the Factory.

'Well, it didn't feel real to know you didn't have to go back as long as you didn't get into any trouble with the law. At first I didn't know what to do. And I felt so alone. I thought, where will I go?'

'Aye, it was the same for me.'

'I didn't know anyone in Hobart Town. First thing to do was find somewhere to stay. I looked around and found a room in a cheap lodgings house behind the Theatre Royal, just around the corner from the Black Swan Hotel. At least I had somewhere to sleep. And I didn't have to walk far to have a drink either. But I was set on not getting into trouble. So I made sure I never had too much to drink.'

'Ma sentiments exactly,' I told her. 'There's many a lassie raped and beaten, even killed, in the blink of an eye. Ye hae tae keep your wits about ye.'

She nodded. We both agreed that was nae going tae happen tae us.

'I looked around to see what I could do to earn some money. Not wanting to go on the town I asked around in a few taverns and the like, and was offered a job as a barmaid.'

I reckon her good looks did the trick. The men liked tae be served by a pretty lass. She'd be flirtin' and flashin' her big green eyes at 'em all the time.

'At first I'd just start singing a bit when I was bar-maiding. Then some of the whores in the bar would sing along with me, and the pub got louder and merrier than usual. Sometimes the sailors would join in if they knew the song. They'd stay longer and drink faster when this happened, and the owner could see he was getting more business.'

'Aye, it's thirsty work is singin'!' said I, and we both laughed, rememberin' some o' the nights in Crime Class.

'Well,' she said, 'the publican started to see it might be better if I had a spot set aside every night, take a break from the barmaiding. He got someone else to look after the bar while I did my act.'

I could see she would hae been a great hit, and when she added the flashy clothes and painted her face up special she would hae looked like a real entertainer. I took another long look at her.

'When the owner got a piano in and someone to play it,' she said, 'I added a bit of a dance to my show, and they all loved it!'

She was in her element I could see. The entertainment life suited her down tae the ground. After nae too long, some o' the customers went specially tae see her. O' course they bought drinks, but they could hae done that anywhere. Nae, it was her that brought the business. She was a hit all right.

She got so well known that other hotels and waterin' holes searched her out, offerin' her jobs. She got tae pick and choose after a while, and didnae hae tae act as nae barmaid agin. Instead, she moved around from one place tae another. Lucky I just happened tae walk in tae *The Commercial* that night.

I stayed workin' at *The Red Lion* for another year, and then was given ma Free by Servitude Certificate. This meant I was really free, and could go anywhere in the colony, even on tae Victoria and New South Wales if I were so inclined. But I stayed where I was, in ma wee room in Wapping and kept on workin' at *The Red Lion*, goin' tae ma favourite pubs in ma time off.

I managed tae stay out o' trouble. Almost respectable ye could say! I had a few mates by now — barmaids, ex-convicts like me, and pub-regulars. I even went off tae the horse race meetin's once or twice and bet on a winner one time. Made quite the stash, aye. But I was too cagey tae get caught up in the bettin'. I'd seen too many punters lose everythin' and I wasnae about tae do that.

I liked tae listen tae some o' the conversations in the pubs and what different folk were gabbin' about. Eaves-droppin', I s'pose ye'd call it. Some of the things I heard ye wouldnae believe. It were a way o' entertainin' maself once I'd had enough o' the singin'. Like when I was in solitary I'd search back in ma memory for stories tae think about tae keep maself sane. This was better, bein' in a noisy pub amongst a lot of boisterous drinkers, a whisky in ma hand and listenin' tae others talkin'. Ye can learn all sorts o' things that way. I'd sit maself down near a group o' men and just hae a bit of a listen.

Now one night at an inn I didnae go tae too often, up the road a bit but still in Wapping, I was sittin' down havin' ma last wee drap afore takin' maself home (I said I behaved maself, but I be nae Temperance Lady), listenin' tae the talk around me. Some gentlemen to ma right were sittin' at a small table and I leaned in towards them so I could hear what they were sayin'. One o' them was an educated man, a right toff by the sound of his voice, and well dressed in the sort o' clothes the Exclusives like to wear. There's always a few toffs who want tae slum it a bit. I saw this when I was in the big towns back in Scotland. They like tae see how the other half lives, and enjoy mixin' with the whores and the pimps, while all the while goin' back tae their posh houses and their prim wives after they've had a bit o' pussy with the lower classes. But this one seemed different.

He was doin' most o' the talkin' and the others' ears were glued tae what he was tellin' them. I didnae wonder for I heard him say he'd been addicted tae opium for many years. Comin' from such a gentleman I was surprised, so ma attention was really taken, and I had a good listen tae what else he had tae say. He went on about the opium for quite some time, then their conversation turned tae other matters. The perfect murder.

Murder! Now, I really pricked up ma ears, tae hear him talkin' about such a topic. Well I never! In all ma time drinkin' in pubs I never heard anyone talk about it out loud like that. He said the perfect murder is *one where the murderer has absolutely no motive for killing the victim.* I'd met a couple o' murderers in ma years in prison but it were always for a reason, like that woman who got bashed up by her husband and that black girl who tried to poison her cruel mistress. But murder for no reason. That takes the cake.

But all of his mates laughed out loud, called for another round o' drinks, and the conversation went on tae other matters. *Well, I never*, I thought, then ordered another whisky for maself before goin' back tae ma lodgin's.

Ye certainly hear some interestin' things in a hotel bar-room.

One night I thought I'd pop in to *The Commercial* tae see what Irish Kathleen was up tae and if she was singin' the same songs. Have a bit of a gab with her, I thought. But she were nae there.

The owner said she'd gone up in the world. She had toffs takin' her out for dinner and buyin' her all kinds o' jewellery and fine things. She'd become such a big draw that other hotels were out tae get her for their pubs, the posh hotels where the rich people frequent, he said. He told me the name of a couple, but they were hotels I didnae feel comfortable in, so I wouldnae go there. But I thought tae maself, while some of us convicts on the transport ship were still dirt poor, wanderin' the streets o' Hobart for handouts, or havin' tae take tae whorin' tae survive, there were some of us made it tae make a better life.

That was goin' tae be me, I thought. I wouldnae be singin' and dancin', but I was startin' tae ken a lot about lookin' after a pub and all that goes with it. I'd learned a lot from Sal, and others I'd been workin' with since I were a free woman.

# PART IV

Chapter 15

# *Maggie*

*17th May, 1852*

By the time we first heard the news of gold bein' discovered in Victoria, we was still livin' in Hobart Town. Doin' well for ourselves we was, Patrick with his carpentry work and me with me flower shop.

Me and Sarah saw a bit of each other and our children was growin' up knowin' one another real well — our very own currency lads and lasses, runnin' around in the fresh air, sure of themselves and of belongin' to a country us parents hadn't been born in. We would've liked to see more of each other, but there weren't a lot of time for neither of us. Both of us was busy with our families, and on top of that, me with the shop and Sarah and her Quaker friends helpin' out at the orphanage, tryin' to make conditions better for the children. I'd even see Agnes from time to time, usually at the market buyin' fresh food — me for me family and Agnes for herself. She seemed to be content, always havin' a bit of a chin-wag with people. A lot happier than when she were cooped up in that Factory. And she were gettin' a lot of tips about the hotel business, she told me. Her dream, she said, were to have a pub of her own. But she were still on her own, and I wondered how she would ever get the means to do somethin' like that.

Everyone were that excited about gold discoveries, first in New South Wales, then in Victoria. We was all abuzz with talk of gold that could be had for the takin'. Anyone could be rich beyond their wildest dreams, they was all sayin'. It were all anyone could talk about. By December 1851, the Mt. Alexander field at Castlemaine had attracted 20,000 diggers and talk was some of them gold diggin's was pullin' 23,000 oz. of gold a week! Men was leavin' good jobs to rush off to try their luck, thinkin' they'd all be makin' their fortunes and livin' in the lap of luxury for the rest of their lives.

Before all that talk of gold there was plenty of folk ready to work in Hobart Town but then the number of workers started thinnin' out all of a sudden. Folk was leavin' Hobart Town in droves. Streets what used to be crowded with drays, carriages, horses and people, was now almost deserted. Even the Superintendent of the Prison said he didn't have enough wardens, and the Colonial Surgeon was findin' it hard to get people to work in the Lunatic Asylum. Not enough men to do the shearin' and harvestin' neither. It were gettin' so bad that a lot of businesses had to shut down. Newspapers was tryin' to warn us all not to be hasty to get up and leave, remindin' us all of the gold panics in California. One newspaper even hinted that if people just waited, gold would come to Van Diemen's Land.

When Patrick and me read about incredible finds around Bendigo in 1852, with claims at Peg Leg Gully yieldin' 324 pounds of gold, and Eagle Hawk Gully become a magnet to diggers, we started thinkin' about goin' ourselves. Other ordinary people like us what knew nothin' about minin' was all joinin' the rush to the goldfields. It didn't seem to make no difference whether you'd ever done minin' before. By June, the papers said Bendigo had 40,000 people there!

*Gold* were the feverish word on everyone's lips. Every day we'd hear all sorts of stories about how people had made their fortunes. We didn't hear much about the ones what didn't, or the terrible hard conditions they had to labour under, or how hot it could get, or how cold in winter, and the sickness what come on people. Nobody wanted to hear about men returnin' in a wretched plight, gaunt and half starved, with empty pockets, droopin' heads and heavy hearts after they lost everythin' they had. No, nobody wanted to know about that.

'I wonder if we shouldn't try our luck along with all the others,' Patrick said to me one day with a sidelong glance, testin' me to see what I thought about it. I could see he had that familiar glint in his eye when he was thinkin' about somethin' he really wanted to do. 'We've done well for ourselves in the last few years with my carpentry skills being sought after, and your flower shop doing well. But we might do even better on the goldfields.' He looked straight at me then, and I looked back, seein' the excited look in his face. It were that moment we both knew we'd be headin' off for our own search for gold. 'I read in the newspaper that men are making hundreds of dollars every day, just like that!' he said.

'Well, why not us then?' I said to him. 'We can all go. We'll take the littl'uns with us.' And the more we thought about it, the more excited we got.

'We might make our fortune once and for all Maggie.'

So we decided to throw in our lot, sell everythin' we had, and take off to the goldfields. We found out other men was takin' their wives and children, and we didn't want to be separated from each other. I told Sarah our plans and she wished us luck, but I could see she were concerned in case we lost everythin', or somethin' terrible happened to us.

We left Hobart Town on the 1st of September, 1852, and found a ship that'd take us to Victoria. Another voyage on a ship. Somethin' I thought I'd never do again in me life. I hated the thought of it and when I walked up the gangplank I was took right back to England and the transport ship. All them memories flashed real quick before me eyes: the orlop deck, the sailors, Agnes gettin' her hair shorn off, me workin' in the hospital, the terrible storms out at sea, findin' the Irish girl dead in her bunk, seein' the sharks. But this time it weren't the long, terrible voyage across oceans in a crowded transport ship with other convict women. It were just to Victoria. And this time, I were a free woman with me husband and me two children.

The shops in Melbourne Town was flash, and popular with the lucky diggers just back from the goldfields laden with gold and cash. Some of the men was wearin' half a dozen thick gold rings on their fingers over their big, rough workin' hands. The women hangin' on their arms was buyin' the latest fashions from Paris and London, the newest style in boots and shoes, and the best and finest white kid gloves money could buy! None of the likes of them would've ever been able to buy things like before they struck it rich at the diggin's.

There was people in the streets from different countries. All them foreign ways of speakin' I couldn't understand none of what they was sayin', and wearin' all types of clothes I never seen before. Chinamen with pigtails and loose trousers was rubbin' shoulders with Aborigines wearin' barely anythin', just a blanket flung over their shoulders! Fashionably attired gents, just off the ship from London, was lookin' eager for adventure. The real established

Melbourne gentry held their noses even further up in the air in disgust and amazement at all these goin's-on.

Just as I were lookin' around me at the crowds and the hustle and bustle of life, I heard some angry shoutin' from a crowd gathered in a nearby street, near the Roman Catholic Cathedral. A man were about to be arrested by two policemen and someone were shoutin' accusations of horse-stealin' at him. His friends was shoutin' abuse at the policemen and the crowd was takin' sides, yellin', swearin' and pushin' with some force. It were lookin' ugly.

I thought I spied Finian among the crowd, but I hurried away as I didn't want to get involved and spoil our chances of leavin' Melbourne the next day. I decided not to tell Patrick that I thought I'd seen Finian because — well — it might not have been him anyway.

The streets was in an awful state. Dusty when the sun come out, and as soon as there were a heavy shower of rain — which could be any time — you couldn't cross the street without gettin' wet up to the knees. We bought everythin' we needed. Someone give a list of tools what they said was essential for anyone goin' minin' for gold: 1 cradle, 6 picks, a water lifter, 2 shovels, 2 zinc buckets, a crowbar, an axe, 2 pans and some nails, tacks, cords and a tomahawk, as well as a tarpaulin and a tent, a camp oven, iron pot, kettle, pots and plates and so on. We made sure we was takin' enough food to keep us goin' for a while: 250 pounds of flour, 60 pounds of sugar, 7 pounds of tea, and meat enough to start with. Patrick bought a horse and a dray to carry us and our provisions as well as a rifle to shoot animals for us to eat on the way.

Once we'd bought everythin' we left Melbourne Town at 6 o'clock in the mornin', prepared to camp on the side of the road at night if we had to. We was told it might take eleven days, but this didn't worry us none, we was that excited to be on our way. We didn't stay at none of them inns scattered along the road, not just to save our money, but because inns was places thieves and bushrangers lurked.

Hundreds of men was movin' in the same direction as us, like a trail of ants. Mostly single men but there was some families too. We all made our way accordin' to our means: in drays, buggies, on horseback, or walkin' pullin' carts and wheelbarrows behind. Some of the men went with nothin' but hope and what they could carry on their backs, pillagin' from locals along the way. But all of us had the same thought in mind: to make our fortune.

We was destined for Eagle Hawk Gully not far from Bendigo, all of us walkin' beside the cart for as long as we could. When the littl'uns got tired we put them on top of the cart. The further we went from Melbourne, the worse the roads got. The poor horse had a hard time pullin' all our belongin's up hills. We walked and walked, passin' the odd farm-house here and there, and public-houses where folk was sittin' on verandahs slakin' their thirst. Why, there was coffee-tents too in some places. All they needed was a tarpaulin tent, a stock of tea, sugar, and coffee, and a little bit of milk. Even them people was makin' a decent livin' with so many people passin' by.

When it rained, the road were deep in mud. When it were fine and hot, the flies nearly drove us mad. The dust stirred up by all the drays, wagons, horses and people, covered us from head to toe with a gritty, sandy dust. By the middle of the day the sun were high over our heads, hot for this time of year. We took to wearin' hats with veils to avoid the sticky flies. From time to time we met up with men comin' back to Melbourne from the goldfields havin' struck it rich. That give us hope, it did. Why, that might be us before too long, we thought.

If it rained at night and we was in a place what made it hard to set up our tent, we slept under the dray, after first tetherin' our horse to a nearby tree and tendin' to its needs. A couple campin' near us one night told us of diggin's on the borders of the Black

Forest, where they'd mined twenty-three pounds out of their claim, and two days after that, two hundred and six ounces more, makin' in all, gold worth eighteen hundred Pounds! Not content with this, they was goin' to splash out and spend their money in Melbourne, then go back again to dig some more!

Over the next coupla days we passed through some beautiful country, crossed over a coupla creeks, and moved across some stony plains. On the way, Patrick shot a wild turkey for us to cook on our camp stove, providin' somethin' different to our usual fare. Still we pressed on, over marshy flats, across fast-flowin' creeks, and on through thick woods on the edge of the Black Forest. Although we was told this area were dangerous, we was so worn out we stopped there, pitched our tent and rested our poor horse.

After ten days from the day we left Melbourne we reached Eagle Hawk Gully. They said it used to be filled with eagle hawks, but by the time we got there all the trees'd been cut down, makin' it look like a sandy plain covered in endless gravel pits.

What a sight to behold!

We was on a bit of hill overlookin' the goldfields and could see hundreds and hundreds of tents stretchin' forever. It were a bustlin' noisy town of tents. Children was bawlin', men was swearin', store-keepers was callin' out their wares. Women's tongues was goin' nineteen to the dozen! Atop a lot of the tents there was flags hoisted atop skinny poles to let everyone know what country the digger come from. They was from all over the world by the look of it. Not a tree left standin' and there were a stream windin' its way through the dusty landscape.

Everywhere we looked, the earth were dug up and men's heads was poppin' up and down out of holes. Between the holes the hard sandy clay were piled up into ridges. What must've been a quiet place in the middle of nowhere were now a beehive of bodies. Men was diggin', carryin' earth, and workin' the cradles at the edge of the water. We could hear the rattle of the cradle as it swayed to and fro, shingle washin' in the iron boxes, the noise of pick and shovel, and the voices of thousands of people. The busy hum of daily life on the goldfields.

It were hard to believe we'd finally arrived. We found a spot to pitch our tent, had our supper, fed and watered our poor horse, and left the unpackin' to the next day. We was very tired, but it were hard to sleep for our excitement and all the different noises goin' on.

There was rumours that Eagle Hawk Gully were close to bein' mined out. Some was talkin' of leavin' to try their luck at another site, Iron Bark. But we decided to stay put as there was women about at this one, some with babes in their arms, so we thought it'd be a safe place for children. Patrick were set on learnin' as much as he could, as quick as possible. Up early, he set off, visitin' as many holes as he could find so he could see how the system worked and what he'd have to do. All first-timers was as ignorant about it as we was. But everyone soon learned the ropes.

The diggers was unkempt from top to toe, scarcely ever bathin'. All of them had long hair and beards and a lot wore moleskin trousers, belted in by a black leather belt, topped by a bright coloured shirt open at the neck or a striped jumper, and boots up to their knees. Their hair was a unruly knotty mass, their beards was speckled with clay, and their heads more often than not was topped with a cabbage-tree hat. Any skin showin' under all that was a sunburned brown. What the colour of their boots was when they was new you'd never know, they was so covered in layers of thick clay.

I went about puttin' our provisions in place, and gettin' more comfortably settled. We had no furniture to speak of, just packin' boxes to sit on and very little else apart from the beddin'. I cleaned the tin utensils as bright as I could, set up the few things we had, and put the small piece of carpet I brought with us on the ground inside the tent, to make it a bit cosy. After a while, I were able to get my hands on a sheepskin and that made it more comfy. We soon settled down to life at the diggin's.

The place were like a beehive, honeycombed with real deep holes, as much as forty feet down. I could see you'd have to watch them holes near the water. The earth tends to fall away and yer could find yerself disappearin' into a hole and buried alive. I'd have to keep a close eye on the littl'uns.

'I saw two men pulling up a bucket from a hole thirty feet deep,' Patrick said to me after his first day of lookin' and learnin'. 'I asked them if I could watch how they mined. They'd already worked through two feet of surface soil. 'Twas a rich black mould, and under it was a bed of gravel about nine feet thick. When they got through that, there was a bed of red mud. They said that was where gold was generally found. And under that, resting on slate, was a layer of blue clay. That's the best sign, the men said, you can get gold in large quantities from that part.'

'You've found out a lot in the first day Patrick,' I said to him. He looked tired and bedraggled. We had supper and put the children to bed, then sat around our small campfire for a cup of billy tea like everyone else does here.

'The men told me how to pick a good spot and that all diggers had to get a licence tax. This was real important, they said. I'll have to go the five miles to Bendigo, and wait in line in front of the Commissioner's tent. It has to be paid every month.'

We both sat lookin' into the embers of the fire. It were a starry night, dark except for the red glow of hundreds of small campfires. And quiet except for a few dogs barkin', people talkin' to each other and the odd song bein' sung. Not like the night before when there were a bit of shoutin' and loud laughter, and some of the men were lettin' off pistols. The littl'uns was a bit scared and put their hands over their ears. But they was so tired they dozed off. I found out the shots was to make sure the gunpowder is dry in case they need to use their pistols durin' the night.

'We'll have to sell the horse. It costs too much to keep a horse at the diggings, and it's not going to be much use to us here really.'

'How will you get back from Bendigo then Patrick?'

'I'll walk. It's only five miles. I can do without a horse.'

'And we won't have to worry about it bein' stolen neither,' said I. I felt at ease about it all. Seems like things is goin' all right, I thought.

Patrick rode to Bendigo the next mornin'. The licence cost thirty shillin's, to be paid every month. Or if payin' in gold, half an ounce. He showed me what it looked like when he got back.

***VICTORIA GOLD LICENCE. No. 1720**, Sept. 15, 1852.*

*The Bearer, **Patrick Sullivan**, having paid to me the Sum of One Pound, Ten Shillings, on account of the Territorial Revenue, I hereby Licence him to dig, search for, and remove Gold on and from any such Crown Land within the Upper Lodden District, as I shall assign to him for that purpose during the month of September, 1852, not within half-a-mile of any Head station.*

*This Licence is not transferable, and to be produced whenever demanded by me or any other person acting under the Authority of the Government, and to be returned when another Licence is issued.*

*(SIGNED) B. BAXTER, Commissioner.*

On the back were a list of rules:

***REGULATIONS TO BE OBSERVED BY THE PERSONS DIGGING FOR GOLD, OR OTHERWISE EMPLOYED AT THE GOLD FIELDS.***

1. *Every Licensed Person must always have his Licence with him, ready to be produced whenever demanded by a Commissioner,*

*or Person acting under his instructions, otherwise he is liable to be proceeded against as an Unlicensed person.*

2. *Every Person digging for Gold, or occupying Land, without a Licence, is liable by Law to be fined, for the first offence, not exceeding 5 pounds; for a second offence, not exceeding 15 pounds; and for a subsequent offence, not exceeding 30 pounds.*
3. *Digging for Gold is not allowed within Ten feet of any Public Road, nor are the Roads to be undermined.*
4. *Tents or buildings are not to be erected within Twenty feet of each other, or within Twenty feet of any Creek.*
5. *It is enjoined that all Persons at the Gold Fields maintain and assist in maintaining a due and proper observance of Sundays.*

'The line-up every month is very long and it's a day wasted,' Patrick said, 'but if you don't pay the monthly tax right on the day, you can get fined three pounds, and you still have to pay for the licence on top of that. If it's not paid by the twentieth of the month, the fine can be between five to ten pounds!'

I thought about our savin's whittlin' down to nothin' if this happened.

'We better make sure it's paid on time then, Patrick. I hope to goodness we finds gold!'

'Police inspectors go round regularly checking people have paid. I heard they dress like everyone else, not in a uniform, but instead of carrying a pick or shovel, they carry a gun.'

I didn't like the sound of that and looked at him worried, 'What happens if yer can't afford to pay?'

'Then you have to work it off by labouring on the roads.'

I thought again about the money we still had. Enough of it to do us for a while, so maybe I shouldn't worry too much.

'Well, we still got a bit of our savin's left before we have to worry about that yet. And we've got the money from the horse.'

Patrick and me slept in the canvas tent with the two children. If it looked like rain, we put the tarpaulin over the top, peggin' it out so there was space between the tarpaulin and the tent. People what 'ad been livin' like this for a long time had tents worn out from the rain and the heat of the sun. They ended up tattered strips of old canvas that didn't protect them from anythin'. Them swags a lot of the men sleep in is real handy. When they're rolled up a man can put his blankets, clothin', chamois-leather bag for gold and any other small items inside, tie it up with leather straps, and sling it over his shoulders. The littl'uns liked it at the camp. They run around barefoot and wild, playin' at bein' miners.

We ate mostly mutton, and damper what I learned ter make from flour, kneadin' it and cookin' it on the hot embers of our camp fire. Yer knows when it's cooked — it sounds holler when yer tap it. To give it more taste yer can add salt. We had a tin billy with a wire handle, and when the water boiled, we'd throw the tea leaves in. It were pretty strong but yer got used to it. We could buy other food from the tent shops if we wanted extras. But we was tryin' ter save our coin.

Cattle and sheep was brought to the goldfields to be slaughtered and sold, so we had plenty of fresh meat. But the stink from them tents what sold it were somethin' dreadful. I were glad our tent were well away from all that. Folk sellin' meat made quite a lot of money, and it was a lot surer than minin' for gold. Not as excitin' as the promise of findin' a fortune though. Men worked hard at the diggin's durin' daylight hours, and after the evenin' meal, they sat around tellin' yarns, drinkin' and smokin' their baccy pipes. The newcomers nursed their bloodied and blistered hands from swingin' a pick most of the day. It took a while for a man's hands to get proper calloused and hardened so they didn't bleed no more. Patrick knew all about that.

Night were the time we heard some bad things happenin'. A man might be heard groanin' because he'd broken his leg by fallin' into a hole on the way back to his hut from hours of drinkin' around a campfire. Less often, we might hear the cries of a woman reactin' to a beatin' from a man. Once everyone were asleep, there might be the sound of a dog howlin'. There was lots of dogs. Mongrels more like it. Sometimes a rifle would go off, startin' the dogs all over the camps barkin'. What a hullabaloo!

Some people were drinkin' heavily, arguin' and gamblin'. There was so many men all cramped together, and not many women or families. Men what found small pieces of gold, wasted it away on the gamblin'. There were theft and disease and arguments. But mostly people rubbed along together fine. Unless they was drunk, the men was mostly polite enough. We stayed in our tent and kept away from it all as much as possible. I made sure the littl'uns were in bed early every night, and watched out for them durin' the day. The days was the safest. The men was too busy diggin' to be any problem.

Some men become greedy and suspicious, especially those what had discovered rich pickin's of gold on their lot. They didn't trust nobody then. We didn't find out anyone's last names as they were all too wary to give anythin' but a first name. They called each other 'mate'. Tempers was easily lost, and arguments and fights broke out. Men gambled a lot. Why, one night I heard a man gamblin' his own wife for sexual favours, and another offerin' his wife up to the nearest man who could supply him with a bottle of rum! But that was only when they was really drunk. Like I said, most of the time it were fine.

Chapter 16

# *Agnes*

*15th February 1853*

Hobart Town was all in a frenzy about the gold rushes. A few o' the patrons o' *The Red Lion* were gettin' ready tae leave for California on the first ship they could find that would take them there. Those that were nae thinkin' about minin' gold still thought there be money tae be made by sellin' the stuff people on the goldfields would be wantin', like boots and shoes — that sort o' thing. Tae ma mind, the men would hae done better tae look for gold.

But when gold was found in Victoria there were nae need tae go all the way tae America. Everywhere ye went that's the only thing folk talked about — gold, and how rich they could get. They were more excited about that than cock-fightin'. After listenin' about it all for months I thought tae maself, maybe I could go to the goldfields. Me. Agnes MacDonald. I would nae be diggin' for gold but with what I know about buyin' and sellin' grog now, I could easily set up a sly grog shop. Diggers might nae want boots, but they sure as hell wouldnae be doin' without their grog.

Since I was granted ma ticket of leave I'd been careful with ma money and done all right. Saved up a nice little nest egg. When I counted how much I had it was enough tae make me feel I could take a chance. Aye I'd do it, I said to maself. So I asked around in *The Red Lion* if anyone knew of a ship bound for Melbourne that might hae a space for one person. I didnae fancy gettin' on a ship again ever in ma life but that was the only way tae get there, and by this time, ma sights were set on goin'. I said goodbye tae Sal and Kate, and in February 1853 I got maself decked out ready tae leave Van Diemen's Land.

The ship was packed full o' folks with the same idea. Another horrible trip on a ship, but at least this time I would nae have tae suffer head shavin' or chains around ma ankles. And no coal hole. I kept ma distance from others and stayed quiet this time. I was gettin' good at that. I learnt that if ye don't look anyone in the eye, they usually take nae notice of ye. Ye could look around tae see what was goin' on, ye ken, but nae be noticed. And that made it easy tae listen tae what folks were sayin'.

There were dozens of vessels anchored at the port o' Melbourne when ours arrived. Large clipper sailin' ships, big steam ships, and small boats as well. Must hae been over one hundred vessels all sittin' there in the water. The wharves were packed with people bustlin' about, some of them didnae seem tae know where they were goin'. Drays and carts were rumblin' back and forth. A bit away from the crowds there were fenced yards and wooden pens holdin' live animals waitin' tae be slaughtered, pigs gruntin' and squealin', and entrails and bloody gore tossed intae the dusty grounds. It was bedlam. A lot o' sailors jumped ship when they arrived, thinkin' they'd be makin' their fortune the very next day or pickin' up nuggets off the streets o' Melbourne. Many a ship's captain had tae go searchin' for new crew tae make the trip back from wherever they came from. And it were nae just the seamen, some of the officers didnae go back tae their ships. I heard about a French ship where the whole crew jumped overboard. Swam tae shore they did. A couple o' small boats in the port spotted them and picked them up. It seemed the whole world was mad for gold.

As soon as we were allowed tae get off the ship, I took ma parcel of clothes, and ma money — well stashed away in ma bodice and a pocket I'd sewed in ma petticoat for safe-keepin' — and headed for the gangplank. Crowds, noise and hullabaloo like I've nae seen since I left the old country, and all kinds o' foreign voices jabberin'. Well-dressed gentlemen were elbowin' them that looked like they didnae have tuppence tae rub together. I noticed a lot o' single women too. I'd heard women were choosin' tae come out as emigrants, not convicts like all of us were. Most of them be lookin' for a husband. Plenty o' men tae pick from but whether there be any decent ones, that's another story. Might be tarts among them as well, thinkin' tae make a fortune. Gold fever was rife, and all of us were hungry tae get our bit.

I had tae push and shove with the rest of them tae get through the throngs on the wharf and join the long line o' folk walkin' tae Melbourne Town from the port. Ye didnae hae tae ken where tae go, just follow the man in front. When we were just south o' the town we come across a town o' tents on the banks o' the Yarra River, stretchin' as far as the eye could see. I hadnae seen so many canvas dwellin's in ma life. By that time I were tired, ma legs achin', and I wondered if I should stay there, in tent town, like a lot o' them from the docks were plannin' on doin'. I listened tae all the talk on the long march. But for ma purposes it was a better move tae set maself up in a small room right in Melbourne Town in the thick o' the pub area. So I kept goin', headin' tae the heart of town.

Ye knew ye was in the centre of town, aye. The streets were bustlin' with people, handcarts, men on horses, and all sorts o' horse-drawn vehicles, includin' wagonettes and horse-vans. One o' the streets had thrivin' businesses tae do with movin' people from one place tae another. And pubs aplenty!

Some wild-lookin' fellows around looked like they might hae come straight from the goldfields. Dressed in rough coats and dirty boots they were, their long beards and bushy hair pokin' out under them worn broad hats they all seemed tae be wearin'. They all carried bundles with their sleepin' sack and blanket rolled up, ready tae sleep anywhere in the open by the looks of it. Shovels and picks were slung across their backs and nearly all o' them had guns, or pistols in their belts. Some o' them even had big dogs on chains, half-hound, half-mastiff. If the men were on horseback the nags looked as tired as they did. I saw a man I'd say been lucky on the goldfields throwin' sovereigns up in the air like they were halfpennies, watchin' the bairns pounce on them.

'Plenty more where this come from,' he said. He must hae been half mad, or had so much money he didnae care what he did with it.

When I got over ma amazement at it all, I was pretty knackered. I looked around wonderin' how I'd find somewhere tae lie ma weary body. Somewhere like Wapping would be good. After a couple o' hours of askin' folk about somewhere tae stay I found a cheap room. Up another lot o' fuckin' stairs, but it was in the thick o' the drinkin' action. I was so tired after that long trip and the long walk tae get here, and all the lookin' around, that I put ma head down on the bed and did nae wake up 'til the next day.

I didnae know anyone here so had tae be more careful than ever. Hundreds of burly men, drunk nearly all the time, especially those just back from the goldfields. Lookin' for a good time. They didnae care much about the law, and as for women, a lot o' the men just raped them, willy-nilly.

It took some time and a bit of whorin' on the side for me tae get on ma feet agin, but I did it. I found another job in a pub, and kept ma eyes and ears open tae learn as much as I could about wheres and why-fors an' such. I asked around about how and where tae purchase grog at a good price, and I listened tae the gossip about the goldfields — the good and the bad things happenin' there, which were the best and closest goldfields, and how tae get tae them.

Then, blow me down, if I didnae bump into red-headed Kathleen again. In Melbourne Town. I wondered what she'd been up tae since the last time I set eyes on her.

There was a lot o' entertainment in Melbourne Town. As well as the half-respectable pubs where the toffs frequented there were the ones where I could go, wi' cock-fights and gamblin' at the back, the air blue with swearin' and smokin' — all the things Temperance folk call *vulgarity and offensive behaviour*. And there were plenty o' other ways tae be entertained for anyone wishin' tae divest themselves of their shillin's: vaudeville shows, music-halls, dramatic sketches, and what they call *theatre*. There was musicians aplenty, playin' all sorts o' instruments. And whores everywhere. Men comin' back loaded with money from the goldfields could spend it on anythin' they liked. Plenty o' ways tae relieve them o' the gold they'd spent months diggin' for. Fist-fights were regular in all the drinkin' places.

Now I like tae watch a good fight, like everyone else, but when they start bringin' out the knives and pickin' up glasses tae smash it gets very bloody and dangerous. I know the signs and I ken when tae scarp it.

I was in a hotel havin' a quiet drink when a brawl started up. At first I watched it. It's all pretty excitin' when ye be watchin', especially when there be a free-for-all. Tables upturned, glass smashin', punches flyin', folk screamin' out, women hidin' under tables, men tearin' intae each other. But then one o' the men grabbed a bottle and smashed it on the counter o' the bar, then in a rage he went towards another man, and with all his might he started stabbin' him in the neck. He was a big man and was really gettin' stuck into the poor bastard. Blood were spurtin' out of his neck and his chest and one eye got gouged. Fuck, I thought, I got tae get outa here real quick. So I scarped it fast and went out intae the street.

I wandered about a bit then, past a couple o' the dance halls. Plenty o' them here too. I ended up at *The Empire Hotel*, ready for a drap of whisky by that time, ma last for the evenin'. There were about fifty diggers standin' about smokin', chattin' and watchin' the dancin'. Diggers love tae dance. The floor was thick with dust, and wet in parts from spilt drinks. Men's muddy boots made parts slippery, and not a couple o' them landed on their backsides. Because there was only three dancin' girls, any man who didnae want tae miss out on the fun was obliged tae take another man as dance partner. I had tae laugh. It looked that funny tae see these huge long-bearded rough men dancin' together. But they didnae seem tae care.

I ordered ma drink at the bar and while I was waitin' for the barmaid to pour it I heard the man next tae me say they'd just added a new act, a pretty girl with a voice like honey. I looked across tae the other side o' the room and there was the new girl makin' her entry, dressed up in an eye-fetchin' outfit with shiny spangles that glittered in the lights when she moved. I took a closer look. Seemed like I might hae seen her before. Then I thought tae maself, why that's Kathleen, the Irish lass! Her dress was pretty skimpy and ye could see a lot o' her legs, not tae mention her tits. I could nae believe ma eyes.

When she finished her songs, I walked over to her, through the baccy smoke risin' in furls up tae the ceilin' and floatin' intae the crowds o' noisy drinkers. The punters were a bit quieter when her act was on, but soon as it finished they went back tae their loud talkin'. I jostled past them all and over to the bar where she was standin'.

'Well here we are agin, lass,' I said. 'I didnae expect tae see ye in Melbourne Town.'

She was surprised tae see me too. Och, she looked good, her tits lookin' like they was wantin' to burst forth from their tight corsets, her waist pinched it tae make it real tiny.

'Agnes! What are you doing in Melbourne?'

'I'm on ma way to the goldfields lass.'

'What then, are you going to be a digger?' she said, her eyes teasin'.

'Nae. I aim tae sell goods tae the diggers. Well, that's what I'm plannin' to tell the law. I'll be a seller o' grog. I know quite a lot about that now. But what hae ye been doin' wi' yourself lass?'

She pointed at a couple o' seats we could sit at while we talked and I followed her over. When we'd sat down and plonked our glasses on the wee table, she looked around as if she was decidin' how much time she could spend wi' me before she'd hae to get on with the job o' entertainin'. Then she turned tae me and I got them large green eyes full on ma face. She took ma breath away.

'After I saw you in Hobart Town that last time, I was doing real well, getting lots of offers to sing and dance.' She hadnae lost her Irish accent. 'Then I met a lad, a currency lad, a good looker the same age as me, a musician who'd come over from Melbourne for a bit of a look around.'

She moved her body and hands a lot while she was talkin'; after that dancin' she still seemed tae be pretty lively. I could smell her body up close next tae me. She'd turn this way and that tae look around, lean on the table, then look back at me.

'He said to me, "why don't we work together as a team act?" So that's what we did. We got lots of work. Sometimes we did four or five acts a night in as many hotels. The punters loved us, and we were a big hit.' She picked up her drink like it was thirsty work tellin' me all this.

'I bet ye were. Ye be lookin' good lass, I'll say that for ye,' said I, lookin' her over from top tae toe, just like everybody else was doin'.

Used to flatterin' comments, she just went on.

'Well, he said we could do even better in Melbourne. "It's much bigger, and more opportunities", he said to me.'

She was lookin' flushed and excited recountin' those early days, then her eyes closed a bit and her face looked sad. I waited for her tae go on with her story.

'It all went well for a while but then he started getting amorous. I didn't want any of that to happen again, so I kept him at bay. But I found out he had a bad temper. As time went on, when he saw I was getting too much attention he got jealous. He didn't like other men ogling me and giving me presents — flowers, jewellery, even fur coats — and wanting to take me out for suppers. His temper got the better of him.'

'What happened then lass. What did he do?'

'One night I accepted a gentleman's offer to dine in the best restaurant in Melbourne. Well, he hit the roof! I was in for it then. He started shouting and swearing, beside himself with jealousy. I took it for a while, but he got angrier and started getting rough, pushing me. Then he hit me hard and left.'

'What a fuckin' bastard! I would hae given him a right goin' over if I'd been there,' I said. I felt angry maself, but not at her. A bastard like that layin' intae a pretty young woman. Seein' her agin I felt smitten wi' her maself. But I knew she was nae that way. More's the pity.

'I had plenty of time to think about this turn of events,' she went on, 'and next time I saw him I told him I was going solo as an act and didn't want to have anything to do with him any more. So we split up. He went off to Sydney and I stayed here in Melbourne. But I missed him for a while.'

'Ye did the right thing lass. Don't need tae take that from anyone. We've been in too many bad places tae ever have tae put up with that agin.' I felt a bit protective of her, and was that sorry she'd had such a bad time from the bastard.

She went on to tell me how her life went then. It took a while before she got back on her feet again with that setback. With her looks and cheeky way though she was popular with the punters. It were nae just the looks though. She could sing and dance real good as well. It would nae be long afore she's back on her feet agin, with lots o' gentlemen toffs askin' her out. Nobody asked any questions about where she'd come from, and o' course she never let on that she'd come over as a convict.

She had nae bairns, or at least none anyone knew of.

After I left Kathleen I made ma way back tae ma pokey room a few streets away. It was late by then and I'd had a few more draps o' whisky than I'd planned on havin' so was a wee bit under the weather. There were still lots o' men wanderin' around, others dead-drunk and passed out in alleys, whores still lookin' to make a few coin, and me staggerin' past it all.

I was only a few yards from ma front door when I felt a rough hand on ma shoulder and the owner o' the hand spun me round and pushed me hard agin the brick wall. It happened so fast I was nae expectin' it. I had only a minute tae take in what he looked like. He was one o' them tall, black-bearded wild bastards with eyes like black pins under his broad hat and the square build of a sturdy sea-farin' man. I struggled, tryin' tae get him off me but he grabbed me by the neck and slammed me agin the wall again so hard I nearly passed out. With one hand around ma neck so tight I could scarcely breathe, he fumbled in his pants with the other, then pulled up ma skirt so fast he was inside me afore I knew it.

When he'd finished, he punched ma face for good measure, then took his leave. The bastard. When I got ma breath back, I scuttled intae ma buildin' and took maself up them stairs and intae ma wee room and passed out on ma bed. I woke up the next mornin' cursin' maself for havin' been stupid enough tae get maself intae such a pickle. Me. Agnes from the streets and alleys of Scotland, got by a black-bearded bastard in Melbourne Town.

I bought maself a handy small dagger then. And it stayed in the pocket of ma petticoat. If I ever see that bastard agin I'll make him pay. No mistake about it. I wouldnae let that happen a second time I can tell ye. But Melbourne Town be full o' men who looked like him and though I kept ma eye out for him, I didnae set eyes on him agin. But I kept that wee dagger on me. If another bugger come at me agin, no matter where, I'd let him have it.

Chapter 17

# *Agnes*

*2nd July, 1853*

After a few months in Melbourne Town, I worked out how tae get supplies o' grog at the best prices and heard all the gossip about different goldfields. Once all the grog was attended tae, all I needed tae buy tae set maself up on the goldfields was a canvas tent, a dray and a horse tae pull a heavy load. O' course, I had tae buy beddin' and food and the necessaries for cookin' — tin plates and pannikins and the like. Another lot o' purchases was items I was plannin' tae sell as a cover, so it were nae plain I was in the sly grog business. I had tae go tae all sorts o' stores tae find out what diggers needed, like shoes and shirts, and get a stock tae cover the hidden booty in the middle o' the dray.

By the time I got all that, I was nearly skin-flint. Poor agin, but determined tae make ma way.

It was a hard slog tae the goldfields. I were nae expectin' that. All ma thoughts were about bein' there and how I'd set maself up. Didnae think too much about the gettin' there. I followed the long trail o' people, mostly men, but some women with bairns. Only one way in and the same way out. No gettin' lost. We were like ants crawlin' towards a bowl o' sugar. Most folk had all the tools they needed for proper gold diggin': sluicin' rockers, picks and shovels, tents. And some sort o' firearm. They were nae goin' tae risk a hold-up by bushrangers without a fight. But they had them as well for huntin' wild animals for fresh meat.

Anyone with drays had them packed tae the hilt. Ye could see the ones with a bit more money. They were wearin' sturdy boots and movin' along at a good pace with two horses pullin' covered wagons. Some o' the men looked like bank clerks, only good for pickin' up a pen. I had a chuckle tae maself at that, thinkin' what their soft white hands would look like after a week.

Even the dismal sight o' weary diggers broken and starved, stumblin' back tae Melbourne Town, didnae put any of us off. All kinds o' people were on the march tae the goldfields. Even Chinamen. I hadnae seen a Chinaman before, but now there were hundreds o' them, all the same in their wide straw hats with a high point in the middle and their wide-sleeved tops and loose breeches. Chinamen shave their hair across the front o' the head but dinnae cut the hair at the back. They plait it in a pigtail that falls down their back, and tie it at the end with a ribbon. Some o' them go barefoot, or wear soft slippers or sandals, and they carry their belongin's in two big baskets hangin' from a long pole slung across their shoulders. And they shuffle, as if there be chains on their ankles. Convict men chained taegither on the road gangs walk like that. But these Chinamen didnae hae chains round their ankles. That be just the way they walk. People in Melbourne told me about them and how they keep tae themselves.

Some folk started off loaded up with more than they could carry. Ye see all sorts of things left at the sides of the dusty, worn track — spare clothes, blankets, axes, tablecloths, flannel drawers, kettles. I was glad I had a horse and dray. I followed the people in front o' me through streams and forests, across windy plains, past broken-down carts and dead animals, their carcasses buzzin' with flies and birds pickin' off the dead flesh. Every now and then I'd stop for a wee rest and somethin' tae eat.

After walkin' for hours I'd worked up a bit of a thirst and was pleased tae spy up ahead o' me a sign sayin' *The Flemington Hotel.* I was on the lookout for it as word had passed around about this pub. It was a grand buildin' with plenty o' stables for horses and lots o' good land around it. I stopped in front of it, brushed the dust off ma clothes and walked inside. It had the reputation o' bein' a posh refreshment stop for the well-heeled toffs on their way tae the goldfields. I was so thirsty I didnae pay nae mind to all that, but when I went up tae the bar tae order a drink they turned up their noses at me and I got elbowed out. No-one behind the bar took any notice o' me when I tried to order. Bloody snobs. Might be they'll be lookin' for a drink from me somewhere along the line.

Because I was nae welcome in that hotel I went tae the bar across the road, a more modest turn-out. Little did they ken what I had in ma own dray, well hid. I didnae dare uncover it for fear someone might see what I had. After a drink or two and a bit of a look around the place, I joined up with the other travellers and was on ma way agin.

Another place I stopped at for a drink I got intae a conversation with the inn-keeper. He told me that the day before, two bushrangers held up a canvas-covered wagon with two horses pullin' it. The driver made the mistake o' travellin' right up tae the time when it was almost dark and there was nae other soul on the road.

They be smart those bushrangers. They ken straightaway where the money might be and a large covered wagon with two strong horses pullin' it be bound tae hae more supplies than a simple dray like mine. It seems them bushrangers he was talkin' about were mainly after food and money. They didnae take the horses or clothes, or even gold-diggin' tools. They must hae been hungry. Might be they were prisoners on the run or hidin' out and new tae the game. The wagon owner said they sounded young — just lads — but they each had a rifle. They weren't too smart though, bein' as how they were holdin' up people on the way tae the goldfields afore they'd found their nuggets and made their fortunes. So I reckon they must hae been two young fellas out for a bit o' excitement.

Anyways, that made me think. And I made sure I kept with other travellers, and stopped before it got dark. Too dangerous on ma own.

The night afore I arrived at the goldfields it started rainin', a light fall but it came down all night and I didnae sleep until the wee hours. When I awoke the next mornin' a heavy grey mist greeted me. Ma body was chilled tae the bone and I got started even afore the sun came up, thinkin' I'd be a mite warmer when I started walkin'. Might be nae flies in the coolness but the road was covered in slippery mud, forcin' all of us tae move along at a slower pace. But like the rest I kept goin', walkin' alongside ma horse and when the sun came up the mud caked on tae ma boots and stuck there. Ma poor horse found it hard goin'. I never did get on that horse, just had him for pullin' ma cart o' goods. I wouldnae ken how tae ride a horse. Besides, I didnae want tae add tae the load.

It was the middle o' the day when the Eagle Hawk Gully goldfields suddenly loomed in front o' me from the top o' the hill.

What a rare sight! I got a shock tae see how big it was. Hundreds o' tents sprawled out as far as the eye could see — even more than the Melbourne Town tent site I almost stayed at. And atop the tents was all different flags flyin' on poles. Nae too many trees anywhere. Just tents and deep holes that must hae numbered in the thousands. Right next tae each o' the holes was a big mound o' dirt. The mornin' rain didnae stop the diggers. Nae, they worked on, sloshin' about in ankle-deep mud, not takin' a bit o' notice. Their clothes were all mud-splashed but they didnae give a tinker's cuss.

The trail took us past a tall gum tree at the edge o' the entrance tae the goldfields where a few people were havin' a bit of a gossip and lookin' at posters nailed tae the tree trunk. I stopped tae take a peek, but as I dinnae ken ma letters too well I listened tae other folk readin' them out aloud. They were about what was for sale, new shipments and the like — who had what — and government notices, by the sound of it.

*Just arrived! A new shipment of leather belts, and knee-high boots at the Alex MacGregor Tent. Buy quickly before they sell out!*

One of the notices offered a reward for the capture of a bushranger:

*REWARD: £250 for information leading to the apprehension of the parties who robbed the McIvor Escort, held up 14 miles out of Kyneton in central Victoria, wounding 3 troopers accompanying the escort and killing the driver.*

*By His Excellency's Command*

That got me tae thinkin' I could put up a notice of ma own. *New: Agnes' Coffee Tent. Tea, coffee, cool drinks and sundry items. The*

*MacDonald Tent.* O' course I'd hae tae get someone tae write it down for me, then I'd take it maself and nail it tae that very tree. I might hae tae get a Scottish flag of ma own tae put on a pole.

After askin' about a bit I found a place for maself and got tae work settin' maself up with ma tent and all ma paraphernalia. The Agnes MacDonald sly grog shop was nearly ready tae open for business. By the time the sun was ready tae set, I was done in, ready tae lie ma head down. First thing next day I'd see the lay o' the land and just start with goods like boots and such tae sell, keepin' the grog under wraps for a while.

It was a large goldfield right enough, and on ma walk around I could see I was nae the only one tae be sellin' grog in a Coffee Tent. A lot of the traders were women like me, once on the town but a bit old for that now. I had a bit of a chat with a few o' them. One told me that if the law find spirits anywhere ye be grabbed and taken tae the Commissioner's camp. If an officer comes by and says anythin', ye make out like ye be offerin' the customer a drink free o' charge. Last thing ye want is tae get nabbed and ye might even hae the tent burnt tae the ground. They do that sometimes.

When a sly-grog seller wants tae get more supplies, she lets one o' them merchants in town know and the grog's brought in, in 5-gallon kegs placed in the middle of a dray and covered over, like what I did, packed all round with sugar and tea and other goods so the troopers can nae see it. Grog comes in at night, in drays and fast spring carts, once the sellers hae made the arrangements.

After a while, when I started tae get low on ma stock o' spirits, I watered down some of it and mixed in a bit o' tobacco juice and blue sulphate and copper tae make it taste good and give it a kick. No-one seemed tae notice. Like I said, I'd learned a lot about the grog business and I learned even more on the goldfields.

The diggers were only interested in findin' gold. It was a rough life. From early mornin' 'til just before the sun went down the miners dug, cradled, and panned. At the end o' the day they were too knackered tae do more than cook a dinner o' mutton chops, hae a quiet smoke and a yarn around the fire, and roll into their sleepin' blankets.

Nae one o' them cared tuppence about their looks. Their faces were covered in thick bushy beards spattered all o'er with clay and their long matted hair hung around their shoulders under a dirty old cabbage-tree hat. Any part o' their face and body nae covered turned dark brown from the hot sun beatin' down. Ye couldnae see their boots, they were that covered in clay. They hardly ever washed and their clothes got dirtier and smellier as the months rolled on. There was one thing they liked tae wear — what they called a *Garibaldi* shirt with open neck and loose sleeves in a bright colour. Aye, that was a favourite o' the diggers. Lucky I brought some o' them with me. I heard about them back in Melbourne Town and had a supply ready tae sell.

There were nae as much trouble as what ye'd expect on a goldfield. Most o' the time the diggers were too tired tae make a fuss. Yarnin' around the fire at night, smokin' baccy and listenin' tae each other's stories was the main entertainment. That, and a bit o' music and some gamblin' — cards and two-up. They saved most o' their playin' up for when they went tae Melbourne tae spend any gold they found.

Once it seemed safe tae start sellin' ma grog, it were a roarin' trade. I kept gettin' lots o' punters comin' back all the time for more. It was a good life. There was always someone tae talk tae. Nae more solitary cell and I was pullin' in the coin. I could sleep in in the mornin's and be awake most o' the night. Aye. And like the diggers, I didnae care too much about what I looked like. There were nae interested in me but they liked ma trade. I was always on the look-out for the police. The men passed word along from tent tae tent if a constable were comin' so we could make sure they wouldnae see anythin'.

Fist fights become entertainment as well as a way o' settlin' arguments. Once a fight got started, them standin' by tae watch would form a ring around the two men, shoutin' and cheerin' as the two scrappers battered away at each other with bare knuckles. They'd make bets on who would win. A few o' them set up roped-off boxin' areas and made fortunes for themselves by goin' intae the fight entertainment business, leavin' gold diggin' tae others.

Folk made their money in all sorts o' ways. Women had tae be cleverer than men. Sometimes lassies from the towns come tae the goldfields tae fleece the diggers o' their money. Dressed up fancy in damask gowns, gloves and hats, and carryin' silk parasols (real out o' place here in this dust and mud) they'd parade around, and once they got what they came for, they'd drop the man o' their choice and return tae Melbourne, or Adelaide or wherever, with their own stash o' the gold. I'd be on the lookout all the time tae see if Irish Kathleen was one o' them. But nae. She didnae need to come tae the goldfields tae make her money.

Chinamen never came tae buy grog. They kept tae themselves, preferrin' tae stay taegither as one big family, livin' separate from everyone else. They sent most o' their earnin's back home tae their families in China. When they reckoned they made enough they'd go back there tae China and another lot'd come over. Chinamen are nae liked. They be too different and dinnae fit in. Many be bashed up. They be called 'Celestials' because China calls itself the Celestial Kingdom. Some Celestials make a bit o' money for themselves openin' up eatin' places and a lot of diggers develop a taste for Chinese tucker. And opium. They bring it from China in small tins. But the Chinamen dinnae make friends with outsiders. From the time they get off the ship from China they ken they nae be liked from the jeers and insultin' things shouted at them.

There be thousands of them on the goldfields. Hard workers and big gamblers too. There be lots o' Chinese gamblin' tents and opium dens. Word was that the opium in this goldfield was the best anywhere. I dinnae ken about that and didnae want tae try it maself. But ma curiosity got the better o' me, and one night I wandered through the rows of diggers' tents, past all the campfires and into the Celestial's camp well away from the rest of us. Coloured lanterns made it look like fairyland. The Chinamen were yabberin' tae each other, some eatin', some gamblin', and others sellin' food. They didnae pay me heed, and the diggers there were too interested in lookin' for opium tae be botherin' wi' the likes o' me. The sweet smell of opium was everywhere. Walkin' the narrow lantern-lit alleys between the tents I peeked in tae some o' them dens tae see folk lyin' down with long pipes heatin' up over oil lamps. Some were suckin' in the smoke, others were already out tae it in a deep sleep. I scurried away after that and went back tae ma own tent. Nae, I didnae want tae try opium. I'd stick tae ma baccy pipe and grog.

Methodist preachers were travellin' the countryside o' Victoria wantin' tae convert folk. I didnae want nought tae do wi' them, but some listened tae what they were preachin', bought bibles and went to their singalongs.

Folks here eat a lot o' *damper*, bush bread baked in the campfire embers when the flames are spent. Somethin' else they like is a cake called a *leather-jacket* made o' flour and water, raised with tartaric acid and carbonate o' soda instead o' yeast, and baked in the fryin'-pan. It comes up like the scones they make back in the old country. Ma favourite be the *fat-cake*. It be like a *leather jacket*, only it's fried in fat and is quick tae make. After tea, the diggers bake them in the campfire embers too. Somethin' else they like is a suet puddin', called a *dough-boy*. They eat a lot o' rice and potatoes, because they're fillin', and fried beef steaks or mutton chops, an' drink a lot o' billy tea in the bush, two or three pannikins, that's about three pints. After their tea and a yarn at night they be off tae bed early so as tae be up at the peep o' day.

The flies are fuckin' awful; they come out as soon as the sun rises, and tae stop them crawlin' intae your mouth and eyes, ye need tae wear somethin' o'er your hat, a veil o' net-lace if ye can lay hands on somethin' like that. When ye get a cut anywhere on your body there be an instant swarm o' flies feastin' on it. Nae relief at night. As soon as the sun goes down, the flies are nowhere tae be seen, but them pesky mosquitos come out.

All of us shop sellers be doin' good business. Rum and whisky are the favourites. Saturday nights a noisy set o' roisterers make a bee-line for the drinkin' tents. They drink all night, knowin' they cannae work on Sundays and can sleep it off. The police dinnae seem tae walk through the diggin's at night; they're better pleased tae take their money as bribes. Still, there be always the threat of a fine or worse if we be caught.

Many a night ye can hear revolvers crackin', rifles goin' off, dogs barkin', the din o' drunken squabbles and even cries of 'murder'. But it happens so often, nobody takes notice of it. There's nae been a murder committed here yet, not while I've been here.

One night there was a cry o' 'Boy in a hole! Boy in a hole!' We rushed out and there in a digger's deserted hole was nae a boy, but a young lass of eleven or twelve. The hole was at least fifteen feet deep and had water and mud enough in it tae drown her. 'I am sinking in the mud!' shouted the terrified girl tae everyone lookin' down at her. Her arms were flailin' about and she was diggin' herself deeper intae the mud in her panic. A crowd gathered around, pushin' and shovin' tae see what could be done. How tae get the lass out? Her mither arrived on the scene tae see it was her own daughter stuck down there. She shouted, 'Somebody fetch a rope to help my poor lass!' The girl was up tae her neck in the mud by that time, still cryin' and shoutin' out for help. One o' the men suddenly jumped intae the hole and grabbed her arms tae stop her from goin' under any more. She clung on tae his neck hard and the two o' them were stuck down there in that hole. Finally someone brought a rope but it were nae strong enough and broke with their weight. So a thicker rope had tae be brought. With this one, three men pulled them both out, the lass clingin' on tae her rescuer for dear life.

'She must 'ave been sleep-walkin',' her mither said.

Ye never knew who ye might meet on the goldfields. There were educated gentlemen diggin' alongside ruffians, and all sorts came tae buy grog at ma tent. The next couple o' days after the girl fell intae the hole I was doin' well and makin' a tidy sum o' coins, what with the grog and the other stuff I'd brought with me. Some o' the diggers paid with gold so I had ma very own stash o' gold.

*Life is pretty good here on the goldfields*, I thought tae maself.

Chapter 18

# *Maggie*

*30th July, 1853*

Our life at Eagle Hawk Gully were hard, winter and summer. A cramped tent with no proper furniture. Our beds was just rolled out blankets with a few possum skins to keep us warm through the harsh winter. We'd got soft after a good life in Hobart Town. But we was determined to stay at the diggin's until we'd made our fortune and could go back to a even better life in Van Diemen's Land.

Some couldn't take to this way of life and left. Them what stayed longer looked around to see how they could make shacks from trees, branches, bark, or bits of wood. Other huts was made of slabs, the roof covered with canvas or bullock-hides. Chimneys was made with sheets of tin or rocks and stones if they could find them. Everythin' and anythin' were scrounged and used in some way.

A few enterprisin' ones provided a tent boardin' house what they rented out to single men — a large tent fitted up with cot beds along each side, leavin' a narrow passage up the middle. I talked to Patrick about this.

'Yer know Patrick, if I 'ad one of them big tents I could start up a lodgin' tent for diggers,' I said. He looked at me, the way he does when he thinks I'm talkin' a lot of sense, with his head a bit to one side and a look in his eye.

'That's a good idea,' he said. 'What would you need for that Maggie, besides a tent?'

'Well I'd need some of them stringy bark couches about eighteen inches wide — that's all they needs to sleep on. And some blankets in case they don't have none of their own. I'd have to buy more food each week so I could feed them as well as give them somewhere to sleep. Mutton, damper, and tea, three times a day.'

'How much would you charge them for all that?' he said, considerin' it all.

'I reckon five shillin's for the bed and five shillin's for meals if they rented by the week. A casual guest'd have to pay twice that much.' I could see him calculatin' it all out in his head and when he'd done that, he broke out in a wide grin. As well as any gold we got, we'd have the money from me boardin' tent. It'd bring in a tidy little sum as extras while he was busy at the diggin's. So off he went to Bendigo a coupla days after I suggested it. It were easy enough to look after once I'd set it up. I just had to make sure I made plenty of extra food to take there each meal-time.

There was all kinds of make-shift shops: open sheds with bark roofs, humpies, tents and different kinds of things for sale from ankle jack-boots to ribbons, tallow candles to tea kettles, and tools for minin'. Saddles, frocks, flannels, wide-awake hats and blue serge shirts, green veils, shovels, and even baby linen, were all heaped up together in a variety of tent shops. Shoppers paid in cash or gold, or by swappin' one thing for another. Carts laden with more goods arrived regular. We was careful not to spend our money on extras, but if we wanted, all kinds of things was available. Everyone wanted tobacco, especially for the evenin' pipe-smoke around the campfire at the end of the day.

Some took to cheatin' in their dealin's, askin' to be paid in gold dust and when the weighin' were done there were a trick to it. The trick were to throw gold dust into a zinc pan with raised sides well rubbed with grease, so a lot of it stuck to the sides. Another trick was to let yer fingernails grow long, draw the fingers around the sides, gatherin' some of it up. The Chinamen was good at this. Many of them had real long fingernails. I think it was them what thought it up.

There was a fair share of shops sellin' sly grog by characters used to bein' on the wrong side of the law. And there's always enterprisin' whores wherever there's lots of men and money.

After a goldfield was goin' well for at least a year, like ours, more tradesmen arrived to set up their businesses. Iron-smiths, saddlers, coffin-makers, bootmakers, and candle-makers come in to ply their trades. And of course, there was more items to be bought and sold when diggers was leavin' and wantin' to get rid of things for good — like furniture, silver and glassware they didn't want to take with 'em. That's when I found things goin' for a good price. They pratickly give things away.

Success at the diggin's was a matter of hard work, luck, and not givin' up. Yer just had to be persistent. In the rainy season, a man might have to work up to his knees in water, sleep on wet ground in the pourin' rain, with his only shelter a blanket or a gum tree. In the summer he had to work under a burnin' sun, put up with mosquitos, pesky March flies, and hot dusty winds. Most of the time a digger struck it lucky and got rewards for his labour even though it might be small. Then all his hardships was forgotten in the excitement of the find.

To me surprise, after we'd been on the goldfield for a year, I met up with Agnes MacDonald. I were that glad to see her! Some of the times I'd spent with her come flashin' back inta me mind. It were a long time since I'd seen Agnes. The last coupla months in Hobart Town had been busy gettin' ready to leave, workin' out what to do with the business, and lookin' after the children. Agnes would've been just as busy as us anyway, savin' up coin from her job in the pub and determined to stay on the straight and narrow. I hadn't even bumped into her in the market like we did sometimes so she didn't know we'd planned to go lookin' for gold.

She were sittin' outside her tent, her elbows leanin' on her knees, smokin' a short clay baccy pipe and havin' a quiet drink by herself. A smoky haze leaked out through her nostrils and she were lookin' at passers-by. She seemed changed. Not as lively as she used to be. Yer could see her dress had seen better times. It musta been bright gaudy colours one time, but now it were faded from the sun, hangin' off her shoulders showin' two large saggin' breasts. She looked like she hadn't washed for weeks, but then nearly everybody else were like that here. Her straggly hair were dry and knotted, danglin' about her face — a face what had set into a — I dunno — a tired look. But for all that, she seemed happier somehow.

'Well if it ain't Agnes MacDonald!' I said. I were curious to find out what'd happened to her since the last time I'd seen her in the market down by the docks near Wapping. I could see she was doin' a good trade from her tent shop.

'Fuck me if it ain't Maggie Burnett! Ye be a sight for sore eyes, lass. What are ye doin' here?' Her swearin' were still equal to that of any drunken whaler in Hobart Town.

'We come to try our luck on the goldfields. I come here with me husband Patrick, and me two littl'uns.'

'So — ye brought your bairns along as well.'

'We're set up in a tent too but it's a fair way away from here. Patrick is workin' our diggin' right now and me bairns are playin' in the tent. I don't usually come this far. What are yer doin' here Agnes?' I paused, lookin' over her shoulder at the inside of the tent, the extra packin' cases for customers ter sit on and the supplies o' goods with bottles o' rum and whisky in plain sight. 'Now let me guess —'

We both laughed at that. It were bleedin' obvious what she were up to.

'Ye got it in one Maggie! Sit down here and we'll have a bit of a gab.'

She pointed to one of the packin' cases and I sat down. I were rememberin' some of the things what had happened on the ship and in the Factory, and especially that night we'd scarped it all them years ago. We had a good old gab about old times, then she started to tell me about how lonely she felt when she first got outside, free at last, but a bit lost and wonderin' whatever she were goin' to do. And about how she'd got to the goldfields. I already knew she'd met up with the Irish girl Kathleen a few times in Hobart Town, and she said she'd met her again in Melbourne Town. I knew how fond she were of Kathleen. Her eyes'd light up when she talked about her. Then I told her about my life since the last time I saw her in the market, and about Sarah as well. She listened, her eyes lookin' away from mine, but I could feel she was hangin' on every word I said. Every now and then she'd ask a question ter find out more. She had more scars on her face than the last time I seen her, and through the flimsy dress she were wearin' I could see that her poor body had been ravaged by more beatin's than she cared ter tell.

'Fancy us endin' up on the same goldfield!' I said. 'It's funny we haven't bumped inta each other before, but then I stay close to home with the littl'uns and it's mostly work and sleep.'

'Aye. I've been here for months and I don't venture too far from ma shop. I be doin' well. Diggers like their grog after a hard day's work, so I'm makin' good money.'

We was quiet for a bit and Agnes picked up her baccy pipe and lit it. She offered me a drink but I had to get back to William and Lydia before too long. Then she said, 'I learned a recipe for makin' a special drink the diggers call *Blow-my-skull-off*.'

'I never heard of that one Agnes. Why do they call it that?'

'Because it be so strong! Do ye want to know what I put in it?'

'I do!'

'It's a mixture o' *Cocculus indicus*, spirits o' wine, Turkey opium, Cayenne pepper, and rum. And ye add about five times the amount o' water. I sell it for two shillin's and sixpence a glass!'

Sellin' sly-grog were illegal, but this drink! I'd heard about that *Cocculus indicus* before. (It took me quite a while ter get me tongue around them words, and I know Agnes would've found it tricky as well, but a lot of people talk about it and when yer hear somethin' a lot yer remember.) It's a poison, forbidden by law. Some said it were used by witches! It weren't easy to get any supplies but it seemed Agnes managed to get hold of whatever she wanted. She'd become a real good businesswoman, our Agnes.

'That sounds deadly, Agnes.' And we both laughed. 'Might be you're a witch now, with that brew!'

Agnes thought that were real funny and laughed out loud again. It were good ter hear her enjoyin' a joke like that. I were struck by how much she'd learned since she'd left the Factory, and how she'd looked after herself with no-one in the world to help her. She were doin' well too, by the looks, even though she didn't seem to care too much about how she looked.

We talked some more about the past, and whether either of us had any news of what might've become of any of the other women we both knew. A couple of them had died, she said, another lot had married, and a couple had gone to other parts of Van Diemen's Land. But for the rest, neither of us was any the wiser.

Then we both went silent, and it were time for me to go back to see what me littl'uns was doin'.

When I fetched water from the river, I were careful to take it from upstream, or from the abandoned holes after a night of rain. I knew how easy it were to get typhoid and dysentery from bad water. That were somethin' Dr. James taught me on the transport ship. Them diseases was rife on the goldfields. Two men had already died and there weren't no real doctors about. Some pretended to be doctors but they was no more than quacks what knew next ter nothin'. This didn't stop them from chargin' high fees though — with so many accidents happenin' they got lots of practice. Men was often fallin' into open mineshafts, flagged only by a scarf or other bit of material. If they was lucky they'd only suffer a broken bone. Quite a lot of men was walkin' around with bad-set bones. Never mind about their bones though, when the real deep shafts collapsed on top of them they could suffocate before anyone could help 'em.

Sundays was the one day in the week when the diggers stopped work for the day. A minister come once a week to give religious services, and the air were filled with the sound of hymns. Not everyone went of course. Most preferred ter spend their precious Sundays enjoyin' themselves — playin' two-up, watchin' fights, goin' for walks, huntin' native animals for sport and a change of diet, or just restin'.

On our Sundays, Patrick took us for walks in the bush and we'd play games about what different animals we could see, and whether we knew any of the names of the trees and plants. We'd take our lunch down to the river not far away, and after eatin' we'd all jump inta the river, splashin' each other. Will and Lydia was old enough to learn how to swim, and they took to it like ducks. They loved the water. It were such a relief on hot summer days to swim in the cool river. Sundays turned out to be the best part of our time at the goldfields, and like everyone else we really looked forward to 'em.

Patrick and me loved this country. Each year everythin' become less strange to us. We felt at home, and the children was healthy and happy, not knowin' anythin' different — not any of the hardships we'd both had to face.

One night, Patrick and his mates was sittin' round the campfire, relaxin' and yarnin' as usual at the end of a hard day's work. Their talk turned to the Chinamen on our diggin's, how they kept to theirselves, not mixin' with anyone, and how they sold opium to anyone wanted to buy it. I were settlin' the littl'uns down in our tent but I could hear everythin' the men was talkin' about, and I could see out to the campfire if I pulled the flap back.

When I heard a man walk over to join them I peeked out through the flap. He were tall with dark-hair that were silver at the temples, and he had a long thin nose. You could tell he were educated just by the look of him, and that he come from a good family. He had a toff's voice. Patrick and all his friends called each other 'mate' and would hoot and poke fun at anyone puttin' on airs. But they didn't do that with this man. They looked at him when he come over but didn't say nothin', even when he sat down on one of the logs to join them.

Patrick and his mates was chattin' about the opium what the Celestials sell. None of them had ever took opium and they was all wonderin' what it were like. Listenin' to them, the gentleman piped up outa the blue, 'I can tell you what it's like,' he said, 'I am a regular opium-eater.'

Well, they was all a bit shocked at this sudden confession, and didn't know what to say. Patrick never had any desire to try opium, but he were curious why such an educated man might want to, and what it might be like. His mates was all ears too.

'I came here to purchase opium from the Chinese. I heard there were more Chinese on this goldfield than any other.'

They was all taken aback at him being so frank about it, and waited for him to go on. I pricked up me ears at this and began payin' closer attention to the conversation. The campfire was well and truly cracklin' by this time, and when the man paused, that's all we could hear. When he took up his story nobody interrupted him, but was they listenin' hard! I knew the men was followin' his story, but none of us understood some of the words he said.

'I was shown how to use, and how to take it from a street-walker who led me one night into an opium den. I was ignorant of the whole art and mystery of opium-taking, but once shown, I learned how to take the small clay bowl, fill it with the black paste, and heat it until it turned the consistency of treacle.'

As none of the men knew how it was done, they was all ears at hearin' these details. They sat quiet, waitin' for him to go on.

'When this was done, I dipped a long steel needle into the bowl, winding a small amount of the paste around its end. I warmed it over a flame until the small pearl of opium began to bubble. I then placed the smouldering opium into the bowl of my pipe and began to pull the smoke into my lungs, dragging it in until the bowl was empty.'

Tellin' his story, he looked away inta the night like he were there that first time in the opium den. I were peekin' through the tent flap, all ears and eyes by this time, as curious as all the others. When he talked about it I could almost feel what it were like meself. He were a good story teller, I'll say that for him. After a bit of a pause, he went on.

'It took about one hour for the entire procedure, and I drifted into the deep sleep of the opium smoker, the sleep that kills pain. Well, gentlemen, I have to admit that my life changed for the worse after that. I became addicted and could not give it up.'

At this, one of Patrick's mates piped up, 'Well, why didn't yer stop takin' it then?'

'It is not so easy once you are addicted. I made innumerable attempts to reduce the quantity. However, it can only be reduced to a certain point. Further reduction causes intense suffering and feelings so extreme I cannot even attempt to describe them.'

He went on then for over an hour, the men around the campfire hangin' on every word. They was spellbound. I never seen any of them so quiet before.

'I recount this story to you as a moral narrative. If any of you listening is taught to fear and tremble the dread opium, enough has been effected. And there, sirs, is my story. Make of it what you will.'

And then he walked away into the dark and none of us ever saw him again. He must've gone over to the Chinamen's tents to spend the night takin' opium. Patrick always wondered what become of him but we never did find out. It were a real mystery.

That's what it's like on the goldfields. Yer never know who yer goin' to meet.

We'd been in Eagle Hawk Gully for well past a year, almost two. People was flockin' to Australia from everywhere by then. One of the men got his hands on a copy of *The Emigrant's Guide to Australia*, tellin' of the great oppertunities in Australia for anyone prepared ter work hard. It warned about the dangers of snakes and spiders and the discomfort of mosquitos, flies and white ants, as well as the barren soil, but it didn't stop 'em from comin'. The *Guide* talked about the goldfields and what to expect. It warned folk they'd have to travel for up to three hundred miles to reach any of the goldfields and they should travel light, '*avoiding fancy waistcoats, dandy boots, or costly cravats and ties*'. Patrick laughed out loud at this, lookin' around at the worn-out dirty clothes of everyone in sight and imaginin' someone in a waistcoat and cravat out here. He thought that was a great joke and went to tell all his mates.

When he were gone, I sat there rememberin' what life were like off the diggin's and back in the old country. I hadn't thought about that for a long, long time. If they could see us now, whatever'd they think? I looked around at everyone and the conditions we was all workin' under and tried to see it all in me imagination like I were someone back in England. Nobody'd believe it, I thought!

A Frenchman, Antoine were his name (he had a funny way of sayin' it) what had just arrived at Eagle Hawk Gully, told us that Melbourne were now caterin' for the increasin' number of French people arrivin'. Why, there were even a French bar in Melbourne, where a lot of the customers spoke French! As well, he said, there was people from other places as far away as Canada, Switzerland, and Italy, and other places I never even heard of, all lookin' to make their fortunes over here. We had a mix of people at Eagle Hawk Gully as well. They brought their own music and songs with 'em. The Germans sang their songs with gusto and a beer in their hand, but they was drowned out by the Scottish Highlanders with their bagpipes! Patrick and me loved to hear all them different songs. He even sang a few Irish ones to add to the mix.

Antoine said that in Melbourne now, there was thoroughbred horses, luxury carriages, and eatin' places with different kinds of food. Strange food from all over the world. There was more churches, and public platforms in the streets and parks for meetin's. Oh, and even more pubs. Some grand houses was bein' built and people what had struck it lucky at the goldfields was buyin' houses they'd never imagined ownin' in their wildest dreams!

There was so much money around. But only for the lucky ones. The unlucky ones was in dire straits, even worse off than before, and with all that money floatin' around the cost of everythin' went sky-high. It were all right for the slumocracy, but others had to live as best they could. They was as bad off as we was in England before I left. Maybe worse. Some folk was worried about all the whores in the town. Much more than before. But what could poor people do? There was only that, or stealin', or both.

Antoine were real curious about the Blacks in this country. (As soon as he mentioned the Aborigines I remembered that time in the river — the two of us starin' at each other, as naked as the day we was born — another secret I kept to meself that I never forgot.) He said he read in the newspapers that a lot of 'em had died from illnesses like measles, influenza and syphilis caught from us colonials. Their health were so bad the whole race could die out, he said. He seemed to know a lot about it.

There was none too many policemen on the goldfields. Them that was around was mostly checkin' miners' licences and huntin' down sly grog operators. So diggers took matters inta their own hands.

Most problems was from thievin'. Diggers'd shoot offenders or force 'em out into the bush, tellin' 'em not to come back.

Some post got through to us all the way out here. I got a letter from Sarah. We still wrote to each other but the letters was few and far between. I couldn't wait to open her letter. I were in such a hurry I just tore open the envelope.

*5th May, 1854*

*Dear Maggie,*

*I do hope you are well. Thank you for your last letter telling me of your life on the goldfields, and how the children are doing. Our family is growing, and all doing well. William is pleased with how the business is going, and the children are all happy. They know nothing of hardship and play contentedly in the freedom and fresh air of this country.*

*We go on family picnics whenever we have spare time and sometimes we take a couple of children from the orphanage out with us for the day. My work there continues, and I am trusted with the care of these poor children and that they will be returned safe and sound to the orphanage. The look on their faces when I have to deposit them back there again after such lovely trips breaks my heart. But at least I have been able to offer them something. I so look forward to the day you return to us and our two families can all be together again.*

*Hobart Town is busier than ever, with more and more newcomers arriving. Small numbers of Quakers are emigrating here, not for the gold as it is our belief that wealth detracts from spiritual concerns. But that is just how we like to live Maggie dear. I know most people don't think like that. Some of our people continue to work towards better conditions for those in need but it is a slow road. I have never heard any more of the baby 'farms' and hope against hope that that is all finished and done with.*

*A lot of free women are coming over. It seems that the main reason is to look for a husband, as word has spread in England that there are many single men to choose from. We know that is true, but whether they will find the kind of rich gentleman they would like is another matter!*

*One of our Quaker friends, Mr. Howitt, visited some of the goldfields. I asked him if he had visited Eagle Hawk goldfields, hoping that he might have some news of you and Patrick. But he had not. We were eager to hear what life might be like for you all there. I do miss you both, and the children. We all send our love.*

*Affectionately,*

*Sarah*

This Sunday mornin' was abuzz with gossip about a woman being murdered!

Her dead body were found at the edge of the river by a woman who'd gone to fetch water to boil in the billy. The dead woman were covered in blood and she were badly bashed. She had deep gashes on her arms and her head had been smashed in by some heavy blunt tool, like the back of an axe. All of us women was sickened by this news and we was all wonderin' who the dead woman were and who would do such a thing. There weren't too much drinkin' durin' the week, but Saturday nights was a different matter. Not bein' allowed to work on Sundays, the men relax and drink more than usual. More fights happen on a Saturday night too — but apart from some punch-ups, forgotten about the next day, the men sleep it off, nursin' their heads and a few bruises on the Sunday. The stayers keep drinkin' until the early hours of the mornin', passin' out wherever they happen ter be.

But for whatever reason, someone must've got drunk and very angry last night. There were this dead woman. But who was she? Who would want to kill her? And why? Nobody heard any screams or even someone angry enough ter bash someone to death. It were real strange. Everyone were talkin' about it, and tryin' to guess who might've done it, but no-one could think why.

We found out who the woman was — one of the visitin' whores from outa town. But we never did find out who might've murdered her. The police didn't look too far. One constable just shrugged his shoulders and said, 'What does it matter, she was only an old slag.' Nobody never found out who done it. That's what it's like on the goldfields if you don't have nobody to look out for you.

More months went by and our lives at Eagle Hawk Gully didn't change much. The men dug, cradled and panned, from daybreak to nightfall. At the end of the day, they'd 'ave their dinner of mutton chops, damper and tea, and after a quiet smoke and yarn around the fire they'd stroll off and fall asleep in their tents. We was findin' gold — small lots, and Patrick were careful to store them away somewhere safe. I'd saved up a tidy sum from the lodgin's tent I rented out. So durin' our time at the diggin's we'd done well but we wasn't rich, not like some of the other success stories.

Then, on the tenth of this month of December 1854, we had the most excitin' find in the last hole! Our hole'd been fairly bottomed when we discovered a nice little nest of gold nuggets. Before that, most of what we found were good, but not worth much. This time it were different, and we finally had enough to make our lives back in Hobart Town very comfortable. Very comfortable indeed. We was careful to keep our success a secret. So we planted our gold, that is, buried it in the ground. Not a footstep passed by our tent without our imaginin' ourselves robbed of our precious treasure. We both stayed awake that whole night, scared someone would find out. As it was a Saturday night, we was even more anxious. So true it is that riches can bring trouble and anxiety.

At the crack o' dawn we started packin' up ready to leave the goldfields. We hardly slept a wink that night anyway. Patrick went into Bendigo to purchase a new horse and dray so we could take to the road again, return to Melbourne then back to Van Diemen's Land.

We was among the lucky ones what'd made their fortune. And we knew when it were time to stop. Many lost everythin', even their lives.

Chapter 19

# *Agnes*

*29th December, 1854*

After that lassie got murdered and nobody charged for the crime, I started tae get a mite nervous, especially after Maggie and her family left. Och, I thought tae maself, that could happen tae me. Better skedaddle while I still can.

I'd gathered taegither a tidy sum from ma sly grog trade and been lucky so far, but wi' the murder, and the clamp-down on the sly grog traders, it was startin' tae look as if things could get a lot worse. So I packed up ma tent, sold the rest of ma merchandise at a bargain price, and made ma way back tae Melbourne, plannin' tae get a ship tae take me back tae Hobart Town.

I found the same room tae rent in Melbourne as I'd had afore. I didnae want tae bide ma time too long there and spend all ma hard-earned cash. None o' that splashin' around like a lot o' the diggers did. By this time I knew a lot about drinks, but I'd been sellin' them out of a tent. Ma plan, ye ken, was tae get real good at the hotel business. So I visited a few o' the taverns and pubs — tae hae a couple o' drinks, aye, but tae see how they were run and what kind o' drinks they had for their customers and what-not. I watched and listened, tae know how it was all managed in a place that was all above board. Ma plan was to be owner o' ma own pub. Ma dream come true. Aye, I had enough cash for that now. Agnes MacDonald wi' her own pub.

I booked a passage on a ship, and while waitin' for the day tae come that I'd be on ma way back tae Hobart Town, I thought I'd look around agin for Kathleen — tae see what life had been like for her over the past couple o' years. On lookin' and askin', I found out that the lass was still in Melbourne and doin' very well for herself in vaudeville. Vaudeville eh? Never been tae one o' those theatre shows. I might go and see what she does. But first I'd deck maself out in some fancy new clothes.

And that's what I did. I had a good look in all the windows sellin' ladies apparel, and when I saw a dress I thought might be good for me, I walked in, bold as brass and asked tae try it on. I nae hae done that before. Never in ma life, all ma clothes bein' hand-me-downs or convict garb. I bought a bright red satin dress wi' all them flounces, and stays so tight I could barely breathe. The saleswoman in the shop talked me intae the stays, I wouldnae hae thought o' them. It were the first time I ever put them on. And that painful! All them ties that push and pull 'til your insides feel like they all be misplaced. I dinnae ken how the ladies can stand it. But I was set on lookin' ma best. I even bought a pair o' new boots. I could hardly get them on ma big feet, and the laces were tricky. A hat as well — a big yellow one with plenty o' feathers that stuck out past the brim in all different colours — and finished it all with green gloves up tae ma elbows. Lookin' at maself in the glass, I thought I didnae look too bad at all. I kept lookin' in the glass for a long time. You've come a long way Agnes MacDonald, I said tae maself, and watched the big grin spread over ma ugly face.

I took maself off tae where Kathleen was performin'. There was a colour poster out the front with a picture of her on it wearin' a low-cut, tight-laced gown. I was a bit nervous wi' all this. Never been in a proper theatre before, but I thought tae maself, ye be rich now ma girl and ye better get used tae it. The theatre was packed. More men than women in the audience, all excited waitin' for the curtain tae go up. There were a couple of acts before her but she was the main attraction! After a bit, there she was — lookin' the real professional. I couldnae take ma eyes off her. I looked around at the men in the audience oglin' her and at the shocked faces on the lasses sittin' next tae them, especially when she lifted her skirts tae show her legs! What a show! She be as good as any o' them, maybe better, I thought when it was ended. Ye had tae admit she was a beauty and her act was the best that night. I never enjoyed maself so much, not even in Crime Class with the Flash Mob. I might take maself tae the theatre more often.

After the show, I went tae the stage door at the back o' the theatre. There was a crowd waitin' for Kathleen, the star o' the show, tae come out. But when I saw her, her arms full o' flowers, and in the company o' two rich gentlemen, I changed ma mind about goin' over and sayin' hello. I melted intae the back o' the throng o' people eager tae meet this now-famous entertainer.

To ma surprise, the next time I saw her was on the ship bound for Sullivan's Cove. I'd just been thinkin' of her and that night in the theatre when blow me down I spotted her on the ship. Speak o' the Devil! As it weighed anchor from the port o' Melbourne we both sighted each other among the crowd on deck tae watch our departure. She recognised me and come straight over tae me.

'Agnes! We meet again. What have you been up to since we last saw each other?' she said, takin' me by ma arm and steerin' me tae a spot on the ship where we could talk taegither away from the noise. I told her what I'd been doin' at the goldfields and that I was on ma way back tae buy a small pub in Hobart Town with the money I'd made.

'Oh Agnes, I'm so pleased for you. I've done very well also, and am on my way back to...

She stopped all o' a sudden, and looked down. I wondered why she'd be wantin' tae leave Melbourne Town where she was doin' so well and had a good life. She must hae seen the puzzled look on ma face.

'You are probably wondering why I'd go back to Hobart Town...'

She fell silent, with a perculiar look on her face as if she was holdin' on tae a secret and wonderin' if she could trust me with it. Lookin' intae ma eyes, she said, 'Can I confide in you Agnes?'

'Aye, o' course ye can lass. What is it? Ye look as if there be somethin' on your mind.'

'Remember I told you when I was on assignment at the Crawfords I'd met a lad, Jeremy?'

'Aye, I remember.'

'And do you remember I said he'd urged me to try my luck in Sydney, where he was from? He said for someone with my talents there were lots more opportunities there than in Hobart Town.'

'Aye, I do.'

'Well we were a bit more than friends Agnes. We got real close.' She glanced around, like she was makin' sure nobody was listenin', then moved in a bit closer tae me so she could lower her voice even more. 'But one day he suddenly left. Just like that! Up and left and went back to Sydney. Alone. I thought it was because he didn't want to be burdened looking after a wife.'

I kept lookin' at her, tryin' tae take in what she was tellin' me, and wonderin' what I could say. Before I could think o' anythin', she took up the story.

'He left before I told him I was pregnant.' Rememberin' it all, the tears welled in her eyes. I thought, well, this is a bit more than I expected. And I waited for more tae come.

'I stayed on at the Crawfords' place after he left. I can tell you I was heartbroken as I'd had very deep feelings for him and I thought he felt the same. But when he up and left like that — without a word — what was I to do? You know what it's like for a single mother.'

'Aye lass, I do.' I thought back tae Scotland as soon as she said that, tae ma friend Peggy who had that bairn but no money and no-one tae look after the two o' them. I thought o' all the women in Scotland and Hobart Town who were in the same trouble and what had become o' them; poverty-stricken, with nae money and nae place tae live. Even the married ones oft ended up on the streets when their husbands left them or died, nought tae do but turn back tae whorin' or end their own lives. And stories of wee bairns found dead in the river. I wondered if Kathleen were tryin' tae tell me that. I could see there was more tae come in this story, especially as the lass was lookin' back down, not wantin' tae look me in the eye. Instead she was playin' with the ribbons on her bonnet and fidgetin' with her skirt. I sensed there was nae goin' tae be a happy endin' tae all o' this.

'I was determined to make a good life for the child and me, but for that to happen I had to find work. I kept mulling over what I could do. By this time, I had my ticket of leave so I was free to leave the Crawfords. I decided to stay on with them until people might see the tell-tale signs. Then I left for Hobart Town, and went to a friend's place — another ex-convict. She allowed me to stay until after the baby was born.'

The ship was well underway with a fair breeze blowin' and she was in full sail, slicin' through the water at a good speed — none o' the pitchin' and rockin' we had on that torture of a transport ship. Aye, it were one o' those rare times tae be at sea, with the full sun twinklin' on the water. Both of us were silent, me waitin' for her tae go on with her story.

'When the babe was just one month old, I — I knew what I had to do.' She paused again. I could see her face screw up with worry and the lines between her eyebrows furrow. I wondered what she were about tae say, thinkin' it must be the moment when she had tae make a choice that would change her bairn's life forever.

'I wrote a note saying the bairn's name was Katie, *She is well loved*, I wrote, *and the mother will be back to get her one day with full repayment for the care taken.* I bundled her up real warm, took her to the Queen's Orphanage in a basket and left her on the steps there before anyone was up, watching from afar to make sure that someone found her and took her inside.'

At this, she broke down and wept, her shoulders heavin', her body bent over as if she were in terrible pain. I felt so sorry for the lass and ma eyes filled with tears, imaginin' her heartache but knowin' full well that she didnae hae any other choice.

'Did ye ever sight Katie's father agin lass?'

'I did not. He doesn't even know about my Katie, so she just has me. All these years I've been waiting for the time I could come back and get her.'

We both sat in silence for a long while, lookin' out tae sea, I didnae ken what tae do or say. Ma mind went back tae the lass comin' out o' the theatre on the arms o' the rich gentlemen and I thought, she must hae made some money, and then, that's probably why she be goin' back tae Hobart Town tae see if she could get her bairn out tae look after it now and start a new life taegither. Then I thought o' the money I'd made maself, and how I might be able tae help them both. The bairn must be grown into a lass by now. I wondered if she looked like Kathleen. All this be goin' through ma mind.

'I got work in that bar in Hobart Town where you saw me that time Agnes, and that was the start of my journey into vaudeville. I moved to Melbourne to make more money and stayed there until I'd made enough to get my Katie out of the Orphanage and not have to worry about money until she's grown up. And now I can. As soon as I get settled.'

Och, I thought, that be a good endin' then.

# PART V

Chapter 20

# *Maggie*

*10th May, 1875*

I'm an old lady of fifty-seven now. Thirty-nine years since I arrived here on the transport ship. Why, my Patrick is sixty-two years old and my first livin' child, William, is a grown man of twenty-seven years with children of his own. After William and Lydia, then Louise joinin' us, and our boy Finian, we had another two children, Emma and Henry. Sarah's brood numbers nine children all together. Our very own currency lads and lasses, growin' up free as the wind.

I often think back about what happened to us all and how we all got to this point in our lives. After comin' back from the goldfields at the end of 1854 Patrick and me stayed in Hobart for a year or so before we come to live here on this property a few miles outa town. I met up again with Sarah, and Amy Richardson as well, once we'd settled. Agnes were still at the goldfields as far as I knew. I was thinkin' about startin' another flower shop. But Patrick had another idea.

'Do you still love lavender Maggie?' he asked me with a look on his face I knew well — sort of boyish and cheeky, like he knew the answer and wanted to tell me somethin', but I never could work out what it were when he were like this. My Patrick what had been by me side all these years. We was a good team, us two.

'It's me favourite of all the flowers.' I closed me eyes, imaginin' waves of lavender fields spread out before me. I lifted me nose in the air to savour their special sweetness. Not like any other scent. 'I can still smell Amy Richardson's gardens of lavender. I just have to think about it all waftin' under me nose like it were right in front of me.'

'You know, Maggie, you could have your own lavender fields. We've plenty of money now. We could buy some land a few miles out of Hobart and have our own purple fields, and the children could have horses.'

Me eyes lit up at this and I become so excited. I looked at him to see if he were just havin' me on. But I could see he meant it. I couldn't take it all in when he first put it to me. He had to keep tellin' me over and over again. It took weeks for him to convince me that we could do it. I knew we had the money, but me, with me own lavender fields — a girl from Cheapside — an ex-convict!

So we bought the land, and got started on plantin' straight away. When the plantin' were finished we built our house, overlookin' the lavender fields. With the help of some of Patrick's mates — there was plenty of them because everybody liked Patrick — it didn't take as long as we expected. We added a shed for the harvested flowers, and next to the shed we set up a small shop where we sold all sorts of items for the ladies: *pot-pourris*, sachets, soap, and small containers of lavender oil. We discovered that lavender is comfortin' when dabbed with a handkerchief on the forehead of a lady with a headache, and it's good for keepin' them mozzies at bay as well.

Visitors come from far and wide to our lavender farm, so we had to employ other people to help us — mostly seasonal workers what come for the pickin' season. We decided to set up some tables and chairs so we could offer tea and coffee to our visitors in a small garden set back from the fields themselves but overlookin' them, and this become a extra small business. I remembered all them coffee tents along the way from Melbourne to the goldfields and how easy it were to set one up. Me thoughts drifted back to Agnes and her sly grog *coffee shop*. For a long time I'd wondered how she were gettin' on. She said she'd done well on the goldfields the last time I saw her there, before we left. I'd sought her out to let her know we was goin' and we talked a bit about the murder, but not for long. Patrick were keen on us leavin' as quick as we could after our big find. And look at Agnes now, with her own pub right here in Hobart!

So this is where we are and where we always will be. I never get tired of lookin' at the fields and the gardens around the house. Even now, I have to pinch meself to know I'm not dreamin' it. Sarah and her family come to visit us often. They still live in town in the same house, burstin' at the seams with children and grandchildren when they all visit. Sarah loves comin' for visits in the countryside. And the Richardsons come as well. We've all stayed good friends over the years. Even old Agnes comes sometimes, but she's gettin' on now and has aches and pains in her body from the hard life she's led and the roughin's-up she got when she were growin' up in Scotland and all the fights she's been in durin' her lifetime. She don't get about too much these days. She's still got her pub but now she can pay for someone else to do all the hard work.

Patrick and me have had our hands full all this time: buildin', carin' for our property, and raisin' our children. We've had workin' horses, two ridin' horses for the family, farm carts, and later on that favourite of the girls: the four-wheeled *chaise* cart. They loved ridin' in it, all dressed up in their best and sittin' up real proud pretendin' they was princesses. All of this thanks to our hard work and lucky strike at Eagle Hawk Gully goldfields.

What a life we've had. And we both count our blessin's. Still, there's always been some problem or other we've had to deal with: bad weather what ruined crops some years, sickness and accidents — plenty of that; bouts of influenza layin' most of us low. Sometimes there was broken bones, kicks from horses, carriages upturned, and horses boltin' after they'd thrown their riders. Several times we had to send out one of our workers to fetch the doctor and his carpet bag of tools and medicines. They'd often have to ride back at break-neck speed across swollen rivers and storms, their wide-brimmed hats pulled down tight to protect them from the sharp rain spikin' their faces like needles.

Colic and dysentry beset us all at different times, and the threat of scarlet fever one year. The time the children had whoopin' cough had us real worried. We spent many a distressin' night sittin' up with them and waitin' for the doctor. Them doctors had to know all the right treatments: blood-lettin', lancin' of boils, and bein' quick to heal someone with a snake bite or accidental gun-shot wound. Times when we didn't send for the doctor I remembered some of the healin' things Dr. James taught me on the ship all them years ago. And some of the other women here knew remedies their mothers learned them back in the old country.

No matter how good life is, there's still problems to keep yer on yer toes. Always was, always will be. That's life though.

Earlier on when we was still in Hobart Town, before we come to live here, we heard rumours of someone what had sighted Finian.

This upset Patrick no end because it reminded him that he'd been unable to provide a good life for his younger brother. No matter that Finian had a mind of his own that got him into trouble, in spite of the help he got from Patrick. My Patrick weren't anythin' like his brother Finian. No, he were different altogether. He were steady and reliable — always like that my Patrick.

The fellow I'd glimpsed outa the corner of me eye in Melbourne all those years ago probably was Finian, as it turned out. We heard rumours he was in Melbourne about that time. Hearin' about the goldfields as we all did, he'd decided to move to Victoria, where he kept up his old ways, drinkin' and gamblin'; and he'd met up with all sorts of people, includin' a couple of young bushrangers — currency lads what took to bushrangin' for the fun of it. It were a lot easier stealin' from the diggers instead of slavin' away on the goldfields. That's what they would have thought.

No, Finian and his bushranger mates decided to rob people travellin' back alone from the goldfields, as well as stagecoaches, thinkin' it a lark to steal the gold they was too lazy to dig for themselves. Profit without too much work, and excitin' as well. I bet they spent everythin' they stole in the bawdy houses and pubs in Melbourne. Thinkin' these thoughts I had a pang of conscience as memories of me earlier life with Benjamin come floodin' back to me. I ain't never told Patrick about that part of me life. Even when he were that interested in bushrangers before Finian come on the scene. No, I never said a word about it. It were like another lifetime. Sometimes I wonder whatever happened to Benjamin and if he were still alive. But best not to think of it now.

Most of the bushrangers died young, around thirty. They was either speared by Blacks, got inta fights, or was killed in shoot-outs with police. Some of them was dobbed in to police by local settlers fed up with them and their antics and ended up in prison. Some died by receivin' a bullet in the head, themselves the ones lookin' down the muzzle of someone else's musket.

Two people what had managed to get away from Finian and his bushranger mates one time give the police detailed descriptions of them, and the police put up a Wanted Poster with drawin's of their faces. This were how we found out Finian had become a bushranger; by accident really. When we saw the Wanted Poster, Patrick got a awful shock. His face drooped and his eyes looked real sad. But he wouldn't have turned him in even if we knew where he were.

'Blood is thicker than water,' he said to me.

Along with the description of the stagecoach holdup, the newspaper give the names of them mixed up in it. Unfortunately for Finian and his mates, the police was tipped off about their planned attack by some local landowners they'd upset.

Sure enough, Finian and his mates was seen on their horses. Patrick read out the piece in the newspaper:

> *'Well-armed with rifles and muskets, their faces were covered with neckerchiefs, they held up the coach by surrounding it then ordered it to stop and shouted for everyone to get out and empty their belongings. They had empty saddlebags ready to be filled up with the stolen goods of honest people.*

Patrick looked up at me, then kept readin':

> *'This was what the police were waiting for, and they came out of hiding to quickly surround the bushrangers. There was a shoot-out, with people shouting, women screaming, and shots fired everywhere. One policeman was shot, the driver of the stagecoach was wounded, and two passengers were dead. The women were hysterical and one had fainted. Two of the bushrangers were shot dead, and the others were arrested and taken into custody.'*

The bushrangers arrested in this perticklar incident was listed by name: Joe Black and Fred Riley. The two men shot dead by the constables was Frank Cox and *Finian Sullivan.*

There it was, his name: *Finian Sullivan*. In the newspaper!

Patrick's face went white as chalk when he saw his own brother's name in the newspaper. He couldn't believe it, but there it was, in black and white.

After it were all over, we requested that his body be buried in our family plot, but the police refused.

'He was a wanted and dangerous man,' they told us, 'and this is not going to happen.'

We heard that they often cut off the head of a dangerous murderer and sent it to the authorities for medical science purposes. A murderer's body might be buried upright, so's he couldn't be resurrected when all the other Christians was. At least, that's what we was told. Who knows if it's true? But it set us to thinkin' about it all, and Patrick were that upset about Finian.

Finian had died in 1855, at the age of twenty-eight years. A wild son of Ireland.

But that weren't the end of Finian's story. As it turned out, we discovered that he'd left a seventeen-year old girl in the family way when he was hidin' out in the Huon Valley. (Yes, that were still the place for scarpers and bushranger camps.)

She had give birth to a little baby girl; Louise were her name. The baby survived but her mother died in childbirth. By the time of Finian's death his little daughter was almost five years old, bein' looked after by a woman in the hide-away Huon Valley camp. Turned out she had two children of her own. By the end of 1855, she moved in to Hobart with her own children and Louise, and looked up the brother that Finian had talked about. When Patrick met up with her and found out about Finian's little girl he got excited. Especially when he knew the woman no longer wanted the burden of lookin' after a child that weren't her own. We was only too pleased to take her in ourselves, to be one of us. From that time on, Finian's little fair-haired, brown-eyed child become a much-loved part of our family.

A few months after Finian died, we had another baby boy, and we named him Finian. It were strange, but these two — Louise and Finian; one who was Finian's daughter, and our own boy who bears his name — have always been much closer to each other than to any of their other brothers and sisters, even though there are a few years between them.

Our Finian is a dare-devil without any thought of consequences and he gets into all sorts of trouble. One time he challenged another young man to a race down the main street of town, gallopin' at full-speed. Wild young devils the two of them. The police constable shouted out to both of them to stop but they ignored him and kept up at break-neck speed. In the end, they both went before the magistrate and was give a hefty fine for the danger they put other people in, and for disobeyin' a police order. They was lucky they wasn't sent to prison. Patrick and me was angry at Finian and we made him pay the fine himself. But after a couple of weeks it were all forgotten. Louise is like that too. A bit wild.

Sarah and me sometimes talked about the different women from our past when we was alone together and no-one else within earshot. Bits o' gossip we heard, or a woman we'd bump into at the market, or on the streets, or sometimes we'd see a unfortunate one, drunk in a side alley. But there were good stories as well. None of us was convicts any more by this time. Those of us what was still alive was married, not always a good match though, and some were still gettin' into trouble for bawdiness and drunkenness.

Agnes bought the pub she'd dreamed of when she come back from the goldfields in 1855, and she were doin' well, pullin' in lots of customers. She told me once that she made sure she didn't do nothin' illegal; no cock-fights on her premises, and no waterin' down of drinks. Not like her sly grog trade on the goldfields.

But that were a sad year, 1855. In November a awful tragedy took place.

I first got wind of it through Sarah. Agnes had sent a young lad with a note to Sarah bein' as how they was both livin' not far from each other in Hobart Town, and Sarah got word to me about it. That's how I found out that Irish Kathleen had been raped and stabbed to death as she were leavin' the theatre the night previous. One of Agnes' customers was tellin' everyone in the pub about what'd happened. What a terrible thing to happen to the poor girl. And poor Agnes. How she'd loved Kathleen. Sarah and me, with our growin' families, never got to the theatre so we didn't have that much to do with Kathleen but Agnes saw her often, bein' as how Agnes liked to go to the vaudeville shows what had become popular in Hobart; the ones where Kathleen were the darlin' of the theatre-goers. The two of them would often have a drink together after a show. But on that perticklar night, Agnes were not at the theatre.

The constables caught the man what did it — someone saw him runnin' away from the scene, his clothes covered in blood. We was all that shocked. No-one knew why he did it, but there was a lot of men hankerin' after Kathleen and this man mighta done it in a fit of jealousy. That's what everyone were sayin', but we don't know. Agnes were beside herself with grief and anger. She never really got over it.

The three of us, Agnes, Sarah and meself, made sure that Kathleen had a proper burial, not like that poor soul from the transport ship what died on the day we arrived in 1837. We all remembered how we was told she'd be buried somewhere but who knows where and that there'd be no mark to say who she were or anythin' about her. We'd all looked at each other then, thinkin' we wouldn't want that to happen to us. We made sure Kathleen had a proper funeral and a headstone as well. So we was all at Kathleen's funeral together, three women in black, when the coffin were lowered into the ground and the Catholic priest said the last rites. It were a real sad day when we buried Kathleen, especially for Agnes. That were the only time I ever saw Agnes weep. She were real fond of Kathleen.

When Kathleen's body had been laid to rest, Agnes filled us in on Kathleen's secret about her child bein' left at the Queen's Orphanage and how, after years of wantin' to get her little Katie out of there, she were told that Katie had been adopted out. They weren't allowed to tell her where she was, or who adopted her. Kathleen were never the same after hearin' that distressin' news, Agnes said.

After the funeral the three of us was all much closer, and stayed in touch. My grown-up lads still go to Agnes' pub sometimes and she gives them free drinks and asks after the family. Agnes found it hard to get over Kathleen's death. I'd drop in on her sometimes to see how she were doin' and to have a chat any time I were walkin' past her hotel, and our conversation always went back to Kathleen.

We talked about how we might be able to find out what had happened to little Katie, just to put an end to Kathleen's sad story. I told her I'd talk to Sarah to see if she could find out anythin'. Agnes said that because of Sarah's connection with folk at the Orphanage — what with her helpin' out so often and knowin' the right people to ask, and with her own two adopted children from the same orphanage, she could probably find out.

After a time Sarah did manage to get hold of the orphanage records, for by this time we knew the date that Kathleen had left Katie on the orphanage doorsteps, and about the note, and that she'd written the baby's name was Katie. I were stayin' in Hobart Town at the time and she come to see me, all excited.

'We must meet up with Agnes straight away,' she said.

'What is it Sarah?' I said gatherin' my things together to leave quickly as it seemed to be so urgent.

'I'll tell you when we are all together. I want the two of you to hear it at the same time.'

Well, I thought, this is a mystery. I were that curious, but she wouldn't say no more about it. We almost ran to Agnes' hotel. On the way there Sarah didn't say a word, determined to say whatever it was, with Agnes present. Sarah waited outside the pub, bein' as how she is a respectable Quaker now, and I went in to fetch Agnes. When Agnes come out, the three of us walked to the nearest tea-house, sat ourselves down, then lookin' at us with her face flushed, she pulled a piece of paper out of her purse. It were the official paper that Sarah had managed to get from the orphanage, the very same piece of paper that Kathleen had not been allowed to see.

'Listen to this,' she said, her hand tremblin', and read it out aloud to the two of us:

*Girl baby of about four weeks of age. Left on doorstep of Queen's Orphanage on 4 February 1844. Note attached, apparently from mother, stating that the child was much loved, her name was Katie, and that the writer of the note would be back one day to collect her.*

'That'd be the note Kathleen told me about,' said Agnes, 'the one she put in the basket when she left her baby at the orphanage all those years ago.' The three of us nodded, then Sarah went on readin':

*Mother did not come back. Baby's name changed and adoption carried out. Adopted 15 February 1846 by Mr. and Mrs. Sarah and Joseph Cotton.*

Well, you could have knocked me down with a feather! We was as shocked as Sarah had been when she first saw it. Our eyes was wide in amazement, all of us lookin' around at one another. Imagine that! Eva, the little girl Sarah and Joseph had adopted nearly two years after she were born, were Kathleen's daughter! We was all speechless.

Later, when we looked at little Eva knowin' this bit of information we could tell then — she had the same green eyes and beautiful auburn hair, and even at a young age she was a sprightly little thing. Looked like she were goin' to take after her mother in the beauty department. The more she grew up, the more she looked like Kathleen and she become special to all of us. Agnes took young Eva under her wing, not havin' any children of her own, and she spoiled the little one. Every time she saw her she'd have a little present for her, and yer could see they loved each other.

All three of us women have loved Kathleen's child, and we saw more of Agnes because of Eva. Agnes took a special interest in Eva for the rest of her life. She softens up no end every time Eva's around her. Yes, it were Kathleen's funeral what really brought us all together for life. That were a dark day when we buried Kathleen. We was determined that whatever happened, none of us would be buried without a funeral and a headstone.

Many women in Hobart was still destitute, with no place to live. Kathleen could have ended up like that if she'd had to look after her babe alone. We all agreed she were right to place her baby in the orphanage. So sad though.

Funny how life has its twists and turns.

Birthdays come and went and the years went by. One year we went to the seaside for one of our picnics, quite a long way from where we lived, but everyone agreed it'd be nice to be at the seaside and the young people could enjoy a bit of sailin'.

It started out to be a lovely day and after a mornin' of laughter and a good feed at mid-day, some of the younger ones had a rest under the shade of a tree, others went off for a walk, and a few went swimmin'. Sarah's lad, James, one of the twins, had come by himself this time, as the rest of the family had somethin' else to go to. But James never missed any of these outin's, and he didn't want to give up the chance of sailin' his own sailboat with all of us.

James decided to go out on a lone sail. It were quite squally weather when he set out but he were a good sailor and he'd done this many times before. A couple of the men thought it might be a bit too dangerous to go out, what with them dark clouds on the horizon. But he said he'd be all right, and as he was a skilled sailor no-one thought any more of it. When he didn't return by late afternoon, we all started to get worried. Patrick rode his horse over to Sarah's place to tell her and William that James had gone out sailin' and hadn't come back at the time he said he would. William and Sarah was frantic, and followed Patrick to the beach where James had set out that afternoon.

When the three of them got there, still no James, and it were gettin' dark. My Patrick, Sarah's William, and two of the other men decided to go out in a boat to look for James. The squall had settled and the sea were calmer by this time. But there were no moon that night, and it were gettin' darker so they had trouble searchin' out at sea.

After a couple of hours they spied his upturned boat with nobody on board. They called out, 'James, James,' into the dark night, but there was nothin'. They stayed out for hours, then come back and everyone went home. Everyone, that is, except William and Sarah. Patrick went to the police to report James as missin' and then come home. At early light Patrick went back, met up with William and Sarah what had stayed there all night, hopin' against hope that their son might have swum to shore, maybe somewhere further along the coast. They was cold and shiverin' and their faces was ashen.

Later that mornin', the police reported his lifeless body had been washed up on shore further down the coast. They said it looked as if he'd been hit over the head, probably when changin' directions in the sailboat, and knocked unconscious before fallin' overboard. It cast a terrible pall over us all, and we was grievin' for a long time afterwards.

The minister attendin' his funeral read out that 'death was an ever-present anguish' and that James were 'exchanging time for eternity'. This didn't help us though — just them empty words — and along with Sarah, I mourned for years at the loss of this beautiful lad; a lad I'd known and loved as much as me own. Sarah never got over the loss of James.

People talk about England as 'home' even though most of them have never stepped foot on English soil. In 1868, Patrick took William and Lydia to England. I never wanted to go back meself, but we thought they might like to see what it were like. First they was thrilled about being there, but soon William was achin' to get back. We thought p'raps Lydia might want to stay as there are many excitin' things to do in London. But no, it weren't for her neither. 'It's too crowded in London,' she said, 'I miss my friends and the freedom, fresh air, and the wide open spaces.'

Some of the convict women was never able to get on, illness, drunkenness, in and out of prison, and madness from tryin' to cope with it all. We was all so sad to hear about three of the women on board our transportation ship what had ended up in the insane asylum. There was one or two charity societies what took some of the destitute women in. A lot of convict men died young, from alcohol or the hard life they'd led, and the floggin's. For whatever reason, it were mostly the women was left to fend for themselves and their children.

There's been changes over the years. Ships carryin' convicts stopped comin' out and they decided to change the name 'Van Diemen's Land' to 'Tasmania'. There was gas lightin' put in Hobart and we all went to see it turned on the first time, lightin' the streets up like it were daytime. There was horse-drawn buses, and steam trains in some places. Ladies' fashions changed and there was pictures of ladies ridin' bikes wearin' bloomers! Patrick had a good laugh when ladies started wearin' bloomers. He thought that were real funny and showed the newspaper pictures to all his mates.

But some things never change — there's still them what feels they are better than others. Folks are careful not to talk about convicts in the family. Secrets and lies, eh! Plenty of them. Ladies what is sure they don't have a convict past whisper behind their fans about them what might. Yer can't stop others wantin' to keep their privileges I s'pose. But most of us was happy livin' our own lives, gettin' on with our own affairs, not botherin' or wantin' to keep up with others. We was glad to be free, contented with our lot, and surrounded by family and friends what loved us. What more could yer want?

As we sit on the verandah of our home now, in 1875, lookin' out on our property, the rows of lavender fields reachin' out forever, the sun goin' down and the birds settlin' in for the night, Patrick and me both look at each other, thinkin' the same thought.

'It's a good life, isn't it Maggie?' he says to me. 'Who would have thought?'

And I says to him, 'Yes. Who would have thought?'

I never did tell me children I'd come to Australia as a convict. We didn't need to bring all that up. Most of the people off the transport ship I come over on was either dead or had changed their names and moved to other parts of Australia. Those, like me, what stayed on here, thought it better for everyone to forget the whole sorry past. Better for future generations as well.

Anyway, who would want to know all about that?

## *Recommended Reading*


Alexander, Alison. *The Ambitions of Jane Franklin.*

Bateson, Charles. *The Convict Ships 1787–1868.*

Boyce, James. *Van Diemen's Land.*

Cotton, Frances. *Kettle on the Hob: A Family in Van Diemen's Land 1828–1885.*

Courtenay, Bryce. *The Potato Factory.*

Damousi, Joy. *Depraved and Disorderly.*

Daniels, Kay. *Convict Women.*

Female Convicts Research Centre. *Convict Lives.*

Frost, Lucy. *Abandoned Women: Scottish Convicts Exiled Beyond the Seas.*

Frost, Lucy and Colette McAlpine (eds). *From the Edges of the Empire.*

Hill, David. *The Gold Rush.*

Hughes, Robert. *The Fatal Shore.*

Keneally, Thomas. *Australians: Origins to Eureka.*

King, Damian and Liz Schroeder. *Catherine McMahon: A Remarkable Convict Woman.*

Oxley, Deborah. *Convict Maids: The Forced Migration of Women to Australia.*

Smith, Babette. *A Cargo of Women.*

Stone, Gerald. *Beautiful Bodies.*

Summers, Anne. *Damned Whores and God's Police.*

Swiss, Deborah. *The Tin Ticket.*

Tardif, Phillip. *Notorious Strumpets and Dangerous Girls.*

## *About the author*

Lynne Hume is an Associate Professor and Honorary Research Consultant at The University of Queensland, Australia, with a PhD in Anthropology.

Her non-fiction books include:
*Witchcraft and Paganism in Australia;*
*The Religious Life of Dress;*
*Portals: Opening Doorways to Other Realities through the Senses;*
*Ancestral Power;*
*The Varieties of Magical Experience* (with Neville Drury).

She has also compiled and edited:
*Anthropologists in the Field* (with Jane Mulcock);
*Popular Spiritualities* (with Kathleen McPhillips).

*Strumpets of the Worst Kind* is her first adventure into writing fiction.

Lynne lives in Maleny, Queensland.